From Idea to Story

Each of these activities is equally important. Don't just sit down at the word processor and expect to write! Build up to it, and follow through on it by editing, polishing, and submitting your work to be published.

➤ **Daydream.** Let your ideas percolate. Jot down the good ones.

➤ **Throw sparks.** Throw seemingly unrelated or contradictory ideas together, and see what sticks. Use a notebook if you need to

➤ **Outline.** Find a beginning, middle, and end for y flesh out the bits in between on a sheet of p

➤ **Draft.** Write straight through from beginnin revise until you've finished a complete draft.

➤ **Take a mental holiday.** You'll probably assum Take a break from it, and come back fresh and well it's really working.

➤ **Revise.** Take your first draft as a rough skeleton of the story that's going to be. Rework it as thoroughly as you need to get it working.

➤ **Evaluate.** Is it a story? Ask yourself, or ask some sympathetic (but not indulgent) reader: Does this story have a beginning, middle, and end, and does the main character change? If not, keep revising.

➤ **Locate your market.** As a general rule, start with the best and work your way down.

➤ **Submit.** While the story is out, prepare a new envelope for your next market. If it comes back rejected, just pop it in the new envelope before you have time to get depressed. Continue until you make the sale!

The Three Rules for Getting Published

These are the three most important steps to establishing your career as a writer:

1. Write.

2. Finish what you write.

3. Send your work to an editor

(Repeat as necessary.)

alpha books

The Seven-Point Plot

This is a common means of plotting a story—though not the only means! If this suits your style, use it.

1. A person

2. In a place

3. Has a problem

For tension to occur, you have to be worried about someone. You only worry about people you identify with. Starting with character, setting, and a source of tension is a sure-fire way to keep the readers going.

4. The person intelligently tries to solve the problem and fails.

5. Things get worse.

Tension is escalated when things get worse, but no one likes to see fools blunder through life: Your character needs to take a genuinely good shot at solving his or her problem, but fail.

6. The climax

The climax is the final challenge, the ultimate "things get worse." If the character fails, you've got a tragedy; success means a happy ending.

7. Dénoument

This is what happens after the ending—the tying up of loose ends and a chance for everyone to catch their breath.

Cover Sheet Checklist

Here are some rules to remember for your cover sheet when submitting your manuscript to a publisher:

❏ Be sure to include all of your contact info, including phone, e-mail, and fax if you have it.

❏ Double-check the spelling of the editor's name.

❏ Keep your note short and to the point.

❏ Don't try to summarize your story.

❏ Include two or three recent publishing credits (don't forget to include forthcoming stories!).

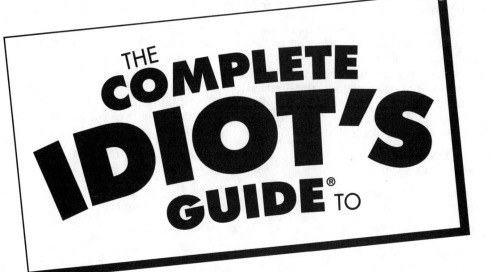

Publishing Science Fiction

by Cory Doctorow and Karl Schroeder

alpha books

Macmillan USA, Inc.
201 West 103rd Street
Indianapolis, IN 46290

A Pearson Education Company

International Standard Book Number: 0-02-863918-9
Library of Congress Catalog Card Number: Available upon request.

02   01   00   8   7   6   5   4   3   2   1

Interpretation of the printing code: The rightmost number of the first series of numbers is the year of the book's printing; the rightmost number of the second series of numbers is the number of the book's printing. For example, a printing code of 00-1 shows that the first printing occurred in 2000.

Printed in the United States of America

Publisher
Marie Butler-Knight

Product Manager
Phil Kitchel

Managing Editor
Cari Luna

Senior Acquisitions Editor
Renee Wilmeth

Development/Copy Editor
Lynn Northrup

Production Editor
Christy Wagner

Cartoonist
Jody Schaeffer

Cover Designers
Mike Freeland
Kevin Spear

Book Designers
Scott Cook and Amy Adams of DesignLab

Indexer
Aamir Burki

Layout/Proofreading
Angela Calvert
Svetlana Dominguez
Gloria Schurick
Julie Swenson

Contents at a Glance

Appendixes

Contents

7 The Writing Project 65

8 The Short Story 77

9 The SF Novel 87

23 E-Rights, E-Books, and the Future of SF Publishing   257

24 Contracts   269

Appendixes

Foreword

This is a book about several things, and it's sensible about all of them.

First, of course, it's a book about science fiction, the secret engine of our modern world. Mary Shelley invented it; Jules Verne and H. G. Wells refined it; and an American entrepreneur named Hugo Gernsback made it into a form of mass entertainment by founding *Amazing Stories,* the first science fiction magazine, in 1926. Since then, science fiction has been an essential part of our world—part dream, part nightmare, part engine of delight. Science fiction inspired the space program and the Internet; warned us away from nuclear war and environmental suicide; inspired us with visions of the infinite; and terrified us with reflections of our own cruelty. It has become part of how we think about ourselves.

Second, this is a book about the modern science fiction subculture, that complicated universe of writers, publishers, conventions, awards, artists, filmmakers, workshops, and fans. And in this book you'll find solid advice about dealing with that world— how to enjoy it, how to do business inside it, and even how to be part of it without being endlessly distracted by it.

And finally, this is a book about writing SF. Not, crucially, about "how to be a SF writer," but rather, "how to do SF writing." The distinction is crucial. Reams of airy nonsense are published daily about "how to be a writer." Cory and Karl tell you the truth: that there's really no such thing as "being a writer"; there is merely writing. In *The Complete Idiot's Guide to Publishing Science Fiction,* you'll learn, in concrete terms, how to turn your enthusiasm for science fiction into enthusiasm for doing the individual and particular things that go into writing it. You'll find practical, useable advice about how to take your science fictional ideas and bring them to dramatic life; about the individual steps by which you can grow an idea from an evanescent notion into a full-fledged story. You'll learn a wide diversity of approaches, from the old pulp writers' durable rules of thumb to the sophisticated methods taught at modern workshops like Clarion—and you'll be given the tools for selecting among them.

Science fiction is one of the most vigorous kinds of storytelling happening today. Too often, that vigor leads to confusing and contradictory advice to newcomers, advice marred by any number of well-meaning agendas. As the manager of the largest line of science fiction books in the world, I see any number of would-be writers, and even published writers, wasting their lives' energy on misconceptions, both about the commercial business of SF and about the work of composing science fiction stories. In *The Complete Idiot's Guide to Publishing Science Fiction,* Cory and Karl collect between covers some advice I've handed out myself, and a lot more advice I wish I'd thought of. Nothing can replace your own good sense and your own science fictional vision. But *The Complete Idiot's Guide to Publishing Science Fiction* offers a very straightforward and—there's that word again—*sensible* map.

Patrick Nielsen Hayden
Senior editor, Tor Books

Introduction

We're living in a science fictional world where humans have left footprints on the moon, where Internet piracy threatens the financial empires of the world, where parents worry about their children developing motion sickness from overuse of their virtual reality systems. We have satellite dishes on our roofs, cellular phones on our hips, and Global Positioning Systems in our cars.

Writing science fiction is an exercise in dreaming vigorously, disciplining your imagination, and playing with the world we live in and the worlds we fantasize about. George Orwell sugared his political ideas with science fiction; Mary Shelley did the same for her misgivings about technology run wild. Ray Bradbury uses the genre to recapture the wonder of his childhood, and William Gibson uses it to explore his personal universe of pop culture at light speed.

It's no wonder that you're thinking of writing science fiction. When you live in the future, it's only natural to want to write futuristically. You've seen the future arrive, watched it become mundane, and still you're dreaming about the future, a place that we all move closer to at the rate of one day every 24 hours.

We're like you. We dream about the future and, for a few hours every day, we live there, hammering it out on our keyboards. We've met with setbacks, frustrations, and rewards on the road to writing science fiction, and we're glad to have the opportunity to show you some of the steps along the way.

How to Use This Book

You've got a tickle in the back of your mind, an itch to write a story, an exhibitionist streak that moves you to see it in print. You want to quit the day job and commune with your laptop and your Muse every day instead of stealing precious moments on the weekends and in the evenings to get those ideas out. You've got the bug.

Turning the bug into a publication is a long and tricky process. Lots of people don't make it, and still more realize on the way that they're not really as interested as they thought they were. We can't make it easy for you, and we can't make it predictable, but we can draw you a rough map that'll take you from tickle to publication with a little luck and a lot of work.

We've divided *The Complete Idiot's Guide to Publishing Science Fiction* into five parts that logically explore the process of becoming a published writer:

Part 1, "Becoming a SF Writer," takes you on a tour that starts with a real work of science fiction: the day you accept your Hugo Award for best novel. We then work backward to show how you got there, taking you on a guided tour of the market, the community, the genre, and your peers.

Part 2, "Secrets of the Sci-Fi Masters," covers the craft of writing science fiction. We science fiction writers don't have the convenience of an agreed-upon reality like our lucky mainstream counterparts do: It falls to us to invent worlds from the whole cloth. We must then populate those worlds with characters who can be of any race and in any circumstance, and who act in plots that science fiction readers can recognize as science fictional. The chapters in this part take you through the process of building and populating your worlds, and then setting them in motion.

Part 3, "Publishing Your Work," is about the mechanics and niceties of publishing. We'll teach you how to look like a pro on paper, tell you who's buying what, and how to sell it to them.

Part 4, "Marketing and Self-Promotion," is the part devoted to your inner exhibitionist. We'll teach you what to do after you make your sale to ensure that you'll make another one, walking through the world of the Internet and real-world promotions, awards, and electronic publishing.

Part 5, "The Professional Writer," gives you some options for managing your writing career. We'll take you through contract negotiations, walk you through the tax benefits of becoming a writer, and tell you about the professional associations that'd be glad to take some of your savings and provide you with a world of services.

We've also provided appendixes with some model contracts, listings of publishers and agents, and a directory of Internet resources.

Sci-Fi Short Takes

As you read this book, you'll notice that it is liberally peppered with cartoon sidebars that provide definitions, depth, and detail on the subject at hand.

Infodump

These boxes contain tips and tidbits, helpful hints that you can employ while you strive for success. The term comes from writer's workshops and describes the classic mistake of overwhelming your reader with too much information.

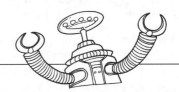

Danger, Danger!

When you see one of these boxes, you know that there's a pitfall ahead. Our objective for this book is to help you avoid all the classic beginner's mistakes: When you see one of these, take heed!

Factoid

Check these boxes for handy definitions of terms and jargon that are unique to science fiction, publishing, or our own idiosyncratic worlds.

"As You Know Bob ..."

In these boxes you'll find interesting anecdotes about the field. Science fiction has plenty of characters, both inside and outside of books, and there's no shortage of outrageous stories out there. The term is another workshopping idiom, describing a scene in which two characters tell one another something they already know, speaking strictly for the reader's benefit, as in, "As you know, Bob, we are marooned on a cold and distant world, stuck here these 25 years, ever since our exploration ship crashed when the giant star beast got sucked into our ramjet. Food is running out, and it's only a matter of time until we fall to eating one another."

Acknowledgements

Cory would like to thank all the people who made this book possible: Renee Wilmeth, the acquisitions editor; the research staff at the Merril Collection of Science Fiction, Speculation and Fantasy; the Cecil Street and Gypsicon workshops for all their support over the years; the gang at Steelbridge (and especially his business partners, Grad Conn and John Henson), for their understanding; his girlfriend Amanda Foubister; his mystified family; the writers, editors, and booksellers who helped him become the writer he is today: Martha Soukup, Jim Kelly, Scott Edelman, Gardner Dozois, Patrick and Teresa Nielsen Hayden, George Scithers, Mark Askwith, John Rose, Michelle West, and countless others. He'd also like to thank Karl Schroeder, his collaborator, for taking on this project with him—I couldn't/wouldn't have done it without you!

Karl would like to thank Renee Wilmeth and Lynn Northrup at Macmillan for guiding the project forward; Cory Doctorow for his faith and patience during this project; the unruly mob at Cecil for their patience over the many years it's taken for him to learn to craft a decent character; his agent, Donald Maass, for his support and hard work; David Hartwell at Tor Books for believing in Karl's vision; the Quick Beginnings team for keeping his life interesting over the past two years; his friends and his family, for implanting the writing virus in him at an early age; and, of course, Janice Beitel, for her love and support (and yer little dog, too!).

We would both like to extend our thanks to Patrick Nielsen Hayden, who wrote the foreword for this book—Patrick is one of the sharpest editors working in the field today.

Finally, we need to mention Keith Scott, a wonderful writer who workshopped with us for a decade before his death in 1999: Keith had much to do with our own development as writers, and he is sorely missed.

Special Thanks to the Technical Editor

The Complete Idiot's Guide to Publishing Science Fiction was reviewed by an expert who not only checked the accuracy of what you'll learn about in this book, but also provided invaluable insight to help ensure that this book tells you everything you need to know about publishing science fiction. Our special thanks are extended to Allan Weiss.

Allan Weiss is a freelance writer and editor and part-time instructor at York University in Toronto. He has published over a dozen short stories—both mainstream and SF—in various magazines and anthologies; his story "Ants" was nominated for an Aurora Award for best Canadian SF short story of the year in 1992. He has also published a comprehensive bibliography of Canadian short stories and scholarly articles on Canadian literature, including studies of Canadian SF.

In 1995 he was co-curator of the National Library of Canada's exhibit on Canadian SF, "Out of This World."

Trademarks

All terms mentioned in this book that are known to be or are suspected of being trademarks or service marks have been appropriately capitalized. Alpha Books and Macmillan USA, Inc., cannot attest to the accuracy of this information. Use of a term in this book should not be regarded as affecting the validity of any trademark or service mark.

Part 1

Becoming a SF Writer

You'd like to write science fiction. Maybe you already write the stuff but haven't had any sales yet. This part can help you start out on the road to success.

There are two things you must accomplish to become a successful SF writer: Become a writer of entertaining and thought-provoking stories, and market those stories successfully to a large audience.

We'll look at how you can take steps toward both of these goals by easing you into the process of writing and showing you how to plug into the SF writing and reading communities.

Chapter 1

Success at Last!

> ## In This Chapter
>
> ➤ An evening at the Hugo Awards
>
> ➤ How we thought it would be—and how it really is
>
> ➤ A look back at the golden age of science fiction
>
> ➤ How more science fiction titles are being published now than ever before

Scratch a science fiction reader and you'll find a science fiction writer.

Science fiction is the original home of the talented amateur. Since the mid 1920s, scientists and science enthusiasts have aspired to publication. Bradbury, Pohl, Ellison, and many of the rest of the Founding Fathers started out as fans, eagerly trading cheaply copied fanzines (small-press publications, usually produced for love, not money, on a subject dear to the publisher's heart) with other bespectacled proto-nerds.

Today more than ever, future-thinking individuals are taking up pen and paper (or computer) to write science fiction. That's a lot of competition, but you've got an edge: *You're* going to look like a pro from day one!

This book can help you do just that. We can't make you a writer, but we can help you avoid some of the pitfalls along the way to success. And we can help you ensure that you know where you are at every stage of your journey to success—and know what to do next.

But before we dive into the details, let's take a peek at the end of the road and dream a little bit about *the big time* …

The Winnah!

The scene opens with you, some years down the line, sitting uncomfortably in a crowded auditorium, waiting to discover if you've actually won a *Hugo Award*.

Accepting Your Hugo Award

"The tuxedo might not have been such a good idea after all," you think to yourself as you rise from the audience amid deafening applause and run a gauntlet of congratulatory pats and handshakes. The tuxedo looks good, does a better-than-average job of disguising the extra roll of fat that's pooled up when you weren't looking. The only problem: You think you may've missed one or two of the hooks, and your every movement inspires a chorus of ominous groans from your cummerbund region.

Factoid

The **Hugo Award** is the best-known award in science fiction, awarded annually by the fans and writers who attend the World Science Fiction Convention.

You take the stage stiffly, the spotlight blinds you, and the applause dies off. Your tongue thickens in your mouth, which has suddenly filled with dust. You clear your throat, and your patented postnasal symphony bounces off the amphitheater walls. The sound galvanizes you.

"Wow," you say, and smile the most charming smile of your life. A cameraman crouched at your feet captures that grin for redisplay on the jumbotrons over each of your shoulders. "Wow," you say again, and this time, there's a chuckling ripple through the crowd.

"When I wrote my first story, oh, back when the dinosaurs walked the earth, I dreamed about this moment." You pick up the rocket-shaped trophy from the podium and heft it. "All I can say is, it's about time!" You hold the Hugo Award over your head like a prizefighter.

"There's about 10,000 people I need to thank: my wife, all my ex-wives, my agent, my parents, my workshop group, my readers—hell, you're the ones who voted for this, thanks!—my editor, the Science Fiction and Fantasy Writers of America, all the writers who took me under their wings, all the bosses who unwittingly financed my early career … I don't know who else.

"Okay, I'm going to keep this short. I want to talk to the new writers in this audience, published and un-, and tell you a thing or two. The formula for a successful career is very simple: First of all, *write*. Second, *finish* what you write. Last, *send your writing to editors*. The rest of it—critics, Web sites, conventions, all of that—it's window dressing. In your careers the publishing industry will spit on you, grind you underfoot, ignore you, rip you off, hate you, and plot against you. Ignore it. Write, finish, and send, and you'll be bringing home a rocket ship of your own some day."

You ponder the rocket ship for a moment, and get ready to return to your seat. You can't—there's something else you need to do. You grab the microphone, throw back your head, and let out an ear-splitting "Yee-*haw!*" The applause swells, and you skip lively down the steps and back to your seat. Just as the cameraman turns away, your cummerbund explodes out from under your jacket, nearly blinding the exquisitely antique Grand Dame of Science Fiction in the next row. She just winks at you and passes it back.

You're at your second party of the evening before you get your tux reintegrated. It takes you that long to let go of your Hugo. The first party was the Hugo Winners' party, backstage after the ceremony. It was all of 20 minutes before you organized a rally of winners to run to the far more raucous Hugo Losers' party in the main convention hotel.

Danger, Danger!

Science fiction is full of gasbags who will seize on any opportunity to pontificate at length on whatever hobbyhorse they're riding at the moment. Whether you're at a party, a panel, or a podium, keep your remarks brief and to the point. You'll stand out.

Your agent corners you before you can struggle to the bathtub of beer in the corner. "I knew you could do it," he says, slapping you on the back. He rubs his hands together in undisguised glee. "The timing couldn't be better: I'm taking The Big Book to the *Frankfurt Book Fair* next month. I think we can get a few bidding wars going: The French love you, and the Germans really came around for the last title. This could be it!"

"As You Know, Bob ..."

Winning the Hugo Award for Best Novel is just about the finest thing that can happen to a science fiction writer. This award, named for Hugo Gernsback—who started the first science fiction magazine—and selected in advance by a vote of the registered members of the annual World Science Fiction Convention held over the Labor Day weekend, is the most widely respected award in the field. While some writers win the Hugo for their first novel (William Gibson won the "triple crown" of science fiction awards in 1984 for his novel *Neuromancer:* the Hugo, the Nebula, and the Philip K. Dick), it's more common for Hugo winners to be drawn from a pool of writers who've paid their dues. See Chapter 21, "Awards," for more.

Factoid

The **Frankfurt Book Fair,** held each October in Germany, is *the* event for foreign–rights sales. European and Asian translation markets are a lucrative addition to any writer's income. With so many editors present, it's not un-usual for bidding wars to take place, driving the sum paid for translations through the roof.

You gulp and smile a frozen smile. The Big Book has been sitting on your word processor for the last 18 months, and you've written 15 different last chapters for it, and discarded each one. You spent the last of the advance money on the tux rental, and your editor and agent have been tag-team *nudzhing* you for the last six weeks. In a memorable moment of exercised rhetoric, your editor (normally a sweet-tempered soul) had barked, "I don't need it *good*, I need it *Thursday!*" Your word processor and attempt number 16 are sit-ting in your hotel room, a block and a half away.

Your agent throws a chummy arm across your shoul-der. "Just get me the last chapter, damn it," he growls in your ear.

Paying Your Debts Forward

You're well into your third beer (or is it your fourth?) when you catch sight of a small commotion at the door. A pudgy kid in an ill-fitting suit is arguing in-tensely with the gofer. Nominally, this is a private party, open only to people on the Hugo ballot and their guests, but in practice, anyone with any pull tries to weasel their way in.

The pudgy kid—kid, hell, he must be at least 22, that's how old you were when you sold your first story, and when did you get so *old*, anyway?—tickles your memory. Right, you were introduced to him earlier that day, at the *Asimov's Science Fiction Magazine* signing. He edits a small-press fanzine called *Metadata,* and got an Hon-orable Mention in the Asimov's Undergraduate Science Fiction Award this year. Nice kid. He's got potential.

"Tom, right?" you say, smoothly interrupting the argument.

"Right!" he says.

"He's with me," you say to the gofer, and welcome him to the party.

You experience a moment of panic as you realize that you've lost your cummerbund, but you quickly locate it, worn around the head of your editor, who is launching into his trademark rendition of "Teen Angel," accompanied by a motley chorus of besot-ted, extra-large bestselling authors. Tom the magazine editor is hovering at your elbow with eyes like saucers.

"Having fun?" you ask.

"Tons!" he says, quivering with excitement. "Hey, can I ask you something?"

"Shoot," you say, and settle back in one of the few chairs in the suite.

"How can I get those guys to send me a story?" he asks. "*Metadata* really needs some big names, but I'm only paying a penny a word. I can't afford any real pros."

Ah, the short fiction market. When Hugo Gernsback founded *Amazing Stories* in 1926, he paid a penny a word for amateur fiction in a new genre he called "Scientifiction." Three quarters of a century later, science fiction magazines hadn't, allowing for inflation, substantially improved on the rate. It's been years since you've finished a short story, though you're continually tickled by ideas.

"How about a story by a Hugo Award winner?" you ask, thinking of the manuscripts languishing on your hard drive, ready for a rewrite.

Tom's pupils dilate further. "Really?"

"Sure," you reply magnanimously. "It might be a while before I can get you something. Is that all right?"

"Yeah!" Tom says. "Sure!"

Back in your hotel room, you get ready to dump your tux on the floor and climb into bed—you've got a 10 A.M. panel on Mars Exploration, after all—but your laptop catches your eye.

Ending number 16 isn't going to work out at all, you know that now. But it might make a great little stand-alone short story, a kind of alternate universe for your characters. It wouldn't take any work at all, really.

And before you know it, the maid is knocking at the door, the sun is streaming through the window, and you've just put the finishing touches on the last chapter *and* the short story. It's been years since you pulled an all-nighter, and the room has a surreal, sleep-deprived tinge. You fire up your fax software and fax the work down to the hotel desk, one story for Tom, one chapter for your agent.

Infodump

"In science fiction you pay your debts forward" is a truism in the field. Every success in science fiction owes a debt to the kindness of the science fiction community: the writers, the fans, and the editors. More than any other genre, science fiction is rife with mentorships, bursaries, and just plain niceness.

"As You Know, Bob ..."

Science Fiction and Fantasy Writers of America Grand Master Damon Knight's novel *The Rithian Terror* (1965) was originally titled *Double Meaning*. To this day, Damon makes a point of crossing out the publisher's title and replacing it with his own when someone asks him to sign a copy of the book.

You've got just enough time to get showered before your panel, and boy, do you need it. The all-nighter will have you dragging for the next couple of days, but you'll be in okay shape for the office on Tuesday.

Some day, you'll quit that day job.

The Golden Age of Science Fiction

We grew up on used books, moldering sci-fi paperbacks with lurid "commercial" covers and horrible titles that had been plastered on over howls of protest from their poor authors.

Best of all were the introductions to the short-story collections. They captured the heyday of the golden age of science fiction perfectly.

A typical anecdote went something like this: A gang of writers would meet for an enormous potluck spaghetti dinner. Over cheap wine and swing records, they'd bat around crazy story ideas, until one was so inspired that he rushed back to his typewriter.

After thumping away at the secondhand manual for a few hours, the writer would be in possession of a brand-new story, with a carbon copy for backup. He'd hike over to the offices of one of the dozens of science fiction magazines of the day and hurl the story *over the transom,* so the editor would see it as soon as he got to work.

Our hopeful writer then adjourned to a nice old diner, where Pop, the line cook, would serve her a nickel cup of joe and a 20¢ blue-plate special. After dining, it was back to the editor's office.

The editor, of course, eagerly devoured the manuscript as soon as he got in. If said editor was one of the legendary greats—say John W. Campbell—he'd have a nice long chat with the writer, suggesting revisions that would improve the story.

So the writer would take the marked-up manuscript back to his miniscule apartment and hammer away at the typewriter for a couple more hours, then slip it into an envelope and drop it into the mail in time for same-day cross-town delivery.

The next morning, he'd be back in the editor's office, signing a contract and collecting a check for enough money to cover a month's rent.

As for the novelists of the day, well, life was sweet. Any decent novel could be sold twice: once in paperback, and once in serial format to a magazine like *Galaxy* or *Analog*. The pool of science fiction readers was small but eager, and the idea of an obscure novel was ridiculous: Few enough titles were published every year that everyone who had an interest in the genre would be familiar with every title.

Factoid

Most book deals work on a **royalty** basis: You get paid a small sum for every copy sold. Traditionally, a publisher will pay you an advance against your royalties when you turn in your manuscript, based on the expected sales of the book. A **backlist** is the collection of older titles in a publisher's catalog. Science fiction writers have traditionally relied on long backlists as a steady source of income.

And even though there were fewer booksellers willing to stock science fiction, the stores kept the books on the shelves for a good long while. The publishers helped this along by keeping a healthy supply of their books in the warehouse for speedy delivery. An author with a large bibliography could eke out a living on the small but regular *royalty* checks her *backlist* generated. (For a more complete discussion of advances and royalties, see Chapter 24, "Contracts.")

As if that weren't enough, there were the wackos in Hollywood, who were like fairy godmothers. Every so often, a writer would get a call from a fast-talking Californian with a sizable bankroll, looking to *option* his work for film. No one was really clear on this mysterious option business, except that once you'd sold an option on a work, you couldn't sell it again until it expired.

Best of all were the fans, who held conventions around the country. A decent writer could garner all-expense-paid trips to exotic locales in exchange for appearing as guest of honor at a convention. The fans and writers vociferously debated the merits of every writer with near-religious fervor, and while they could be harsh, being criticized beat being ignored by a country mile.

Truly, it was a golden age.

Factoid

As the name implies, an **option** is an agreement giving a film producer the exclusive right to produce a movie based on a story—be it a novel, screenplay, short story, or nonfiction book. Option deals vary wildly, but are usually more than the advance paid on a novel. Options are time-based and must be renewed periodically.

The Modern Publishing World

The modern publishing world is a scary place. Editors are overloaded, and manuscripts are rejected lickety-split. It's a rare author who has the good fortune to receive personal feedback on a rejected manuscript, and even published authors are finding themselves in trouble.

Times Are Tough

Today the typical magazine editor receives up to 1,000 manuscripts a month, from both established pros and rank amateurs. The typical science fiction magazine publishes 8 to 12 stories per month. The typical rate for a beginning writer is 4¢ to 6¢ per word. The typical response time is around nine weeks.

Magazines jostle for shelf space in an increasingly competitive marketplace, and news vendors are reluctant to order any titles that fail to sell several copies.

The typical science fiction book editor is only slightly less swamped: 600 manuscripts per month for about 50 slots per year. Response times of two years are not unheard of. First novelists often see an advance of $4,000 to $6,000.

Many talented editors work in the field, but as their duties have expanded to fill every available moment, they find themselves unable to spare time to really develop all but the most promising writers. Instead, they look for ready-to-publish works in their *slushpiles*. Writers who are almost there still find themselves facing uninformative and anonymous rejection slips.

"As You Know, Bob ..."

In the 1970s, *Omni* magazine made science fiction history by becoming the first regular periodical publisher of science fiction with a circulation of over one million. Their pay rates were commensurate with their circulation, paying anywhere from $1,200 to $2,000 for short stories. In 1996, *Omni* unsuccessfully migrated from print format to an all-electronic edition on the Web. By 1998, the experiment was declared a failure, and *Omni* ceased publication altogether.

Booksellers can tear off the cover of a paperback book that hasn't sold after a certain period and return it for a refund. Inventory procedures in the megachains often have stores stripping books and reordering the same titles simultaneously. Smaller, specialized imprints like Women's Press Science Fiction have a difficult time surviving in this marketplace, and have folded in droves. On airport newsstands and in other high-traffic locations, unsold books can be stripped within days of appearing on the shelves.

The Hollywood option—formerly a common enough occurrence that writers realistically hoped to sell sufficient options to support themselves through lean times—has all but vanished. Studio accountants grew anxious at the number of unexercised options in inventory. Now, it's a rarity for anyone but a bestselling writer to be offered an option deal.

It's hard out there. A mania for mergers and acquisitions has gripped New York publishing over the last three decades. New multinational parent companies demand a different level of profitability—making it difficult for editors to seek out and mentor writers. Publishers, due to changes in the market, have cut backlists and editorial staff. Many modestly selling established writers, formerly able to survive on their backlist sales, are finding themselves out of print.

Factoid

The **slushpile** is the technical term for the pile of unsolicited manuscripts that every publisher faces. This pile can be huge, so it often gets put on the back burner. An editor would rather read something by a writer she knows than a complete unknown.

National chain bookstores often rely on a single distribution center, the economics of which dictate that only books that sell in volume are worth keeping on the shelves. More and more, chain-store buyers are effecting what publishers publish, so that established writers whose latest books sell poorly find it difficult or impossible to sell another novel, since their publishers know that the buyers won't take the risk on any more titles by that writer.

While this situation may seem bleak, this is also the age of the Internet, and entirely new publishing models are appearing on the horizon. Since the price of warehousing and shipping all that paper is one of the major factors in the current publishing crunch, new strategies such as on-demand publishing may reverse shrinking lists. (On-demand printing will theoretically let a publisher print only as many books as he sells. Right now, a publisher typically prints two or three copies of a book for every one sold.)

Online publishing has certainly become a new and energetic venue for emerging authors. We'll talk more about on-demand and online publishing in Chapter 23, "E-Rights, E-Books, and the Future of SF Publishing."

But Wait, There's Hope Yet!

But there are glimmers of hope. Despite everything, more science fiction titles are being published now than ever before. Hardcover publications—which are far more lucrative for writers—are on the rise. On-demand publishing, a technology that makes it possible for publishers to print and bind books to order, promises to revive the backlist.

"As You Know, Bob ..."

Tor Books, one of the world's leading science fiction publishers, has led the pack in innovative publishing techniques. They publish nearly 100 original SF, fantasy, and horror hardcovers per year. They also sell electronic versions of their titles for for reading on a variety of platforms, including the 3Com Palm, the Rocket eBook, the SoftBook reader, and Microsoft Cleartext. Their aggressive campaign to resurrect the backlist includes an on-demand scheme for a line of paperbacks, which are profitable in much smaller runs. Tor also throws the *best* parties at conventions.

Science fiction, once perceived as a genre for adolescents and nerds, has gained widespread acceptance in the mainstream. There's more science fiction on TV and in movie theaters than ever before, and the demographics of media science fiction (or SF, as we'll be referring to it throughout the book) include both the monied, older set and the young, who will grow up to be the next generation of science fiction consumers.

The world of electronic publishing, while still in its infancy, looms on the horizon. Already, Internet booksellers such as Amazon.com are challenging the iron fist of the chain stores. Further down the road, "publication" to handheld electronic books will open a multitude of possibilities for specialty presses, author-driven publications, and instant, accurate royalty reporting.

The Least You Need to Know

➤ Science fiction is full of people looking to help out new writers.

➤ Even "successful" writers often have to hold down day jobs.

➤ Short-fiction pay scales haven't budged much since the 1930s.

➤ Times are tough for science fiction writers, but there's hope as new developments promise more writer-friendly publishing arrangements.

Chapter 2

First Steps on the Road

In This Chapter

➤ So, you want to be a science fiction writer?

➤ Science fiction's early roots

➤ Myths and pitfalls for the beginning writer

➤ Dreamer or draft horse: What's your writing style?

➤ Flexing your writing muscles to keep them strong

➤ The business of writing

Let's get down to brass tacks. How do you become a successful SF writer?

The only way to become a better writer is by writing, day in and day out, whether you're feeling inspired, discouraged, pressured, or brain-dead. Very simply, you learn to write SF by writing SF.

And, just as you wouldn't consider a career in brain surgery without at least learning a little about the gray stuff, you shouldn't consider writing SF without first familiarizing yourself with what others have done.

This chapter introduces you to the pragmatic, results-oriented approach we'll be using in this book. It will also explain some key things to know—that you can't run before you walk. We all have to start somewhere, and you may feel discouraged if your early stories don't work to your satisfaction, or worse yet, don't sell. We all go through this. It's a necessary part of learning to be a writer.

With this chapter, we'll tell you what you need to know to start writing SF.

Reading—the Classics

There are almost as many varieties of SF as there are SF writers (or readers). We're unlikely to find a better sign of the *genre's* health than the sheer sprawling chaos that faces anyone trying to summarize what it's all about. At all its edges SF blends seamlessly into other genres, and strange hybrids abound: SF westerns, erotic cyberpunk novels, Edwardian-technology space travel stories, even the occasional incomprehensible text written by a mainstream literary author getting his or her feet wet in SF.

Factoid

A **genre** is a category of artistic works sharing similar style or content. Science fiction is a genre of literature. We commonly speak of subgenres as being finer divisions within this first category.

Who Cares About That Written Stuff? I've Watched TV

If your sole exposure to SF is through the movies or TV, you're in for a shock. Literary SF bears little resemblance to its media counterpart. Written SF is a fully developed field, an intellectual and creative free-for-all of global proportions. The SF of film and television can barely hint at the variety and depth of stories in the literary canon. Bear in mind that almost none of the greatest works of literary SF have ever been put on the screen. If you want to write SF, you *must* read it, or you'll simply have no idea what you're getting yourself into.

Infodump

A very important reason to familiarize yourself with the field is so you don't repeat something that's already been done to death. For instance: "Here's my new story. The idea is, what if all those little nanotech robots they want to put in our bloodstreams ran amok and became a new kind of *disease?* Clever, huh?"

Any self-respecting SF editor can rattle off 10 stories that come across his desk at least once a week in one form or another. If you send editors such a story, they're likely to send it right back.

There's no excuse for not knowing when a story idea's been done to death.

Finding Your Niche

So, what kind of SF are you going to write? You might try your hand at all of them. The greater your range, the more marketable you'll be. The greater the variety of stories you tell, the better you'll become at telling stories.

Still, you may have a favorite kind of SF, a type of story you've devoured since you were a kid. If that's the case, dive into writing in that vein. But beware: Reading and writing only in one area is a formula for quickly running out of ideas. Writers who read every available kind of fiction—including fiction outside of SF—have the richest palette of colors to choose from when they go to paint a new world.

Writing—the Well-Told Yarn

You may have gone through a series of university English courses that convinced you that …

➤ Writing is hard.

➤ It's a serious artistic activity that demands knowledge of literary theory and history.

Well, we're here to tell you that science fiction is intended to be fun! Fun to read, and fun to write. We're not ashamed to admit that SF is popular fiction. In SF, literary pretensions are far less important than a good solid plot.

Don't worry about whether your work qualifies as postmodern or impressionist, or whether your characters aren't completely well-rounded. Just get the story down. Later, as you progress in your career, you'll be able to develop the extra writing muscles and fine control that will allow you to turn your craft into an art. Just as nobody starts out bench-pressing 300 pounds, you shouldn't expect to start out writing classics.

Have fun with your writing. If you're not having fun, neither will your readers.

Infodump

There's nothing wrong with studying literature—quite the contrary. The more you know, the more tools you'll be able to muster as a writer. Ultimately, though, reading and analyzing literature use a different skill set than writing literature. Courses can take you only so far. You have to do the rest.

SF's Modern Roots

The acknowledged "father of science fiction" is, of course, French novelist Jules Verne (1828–1905). He is the author of such classics as *20,000 Leagues Under the Sea* (1870), *From the Earth to the Moon* (1865), and *Around the World in Eighty Days* (1872). Classics though they are, his books probably wouldn't get published if he were writing today.

Verne's audience was keenly interested in the science of the day, including such topics as taxonomy. Verne was all too willing to stop the story and expound at length on subjects such as the classification of midwater fishes in the Pacific ocean. His readers ate this stuff up; modern readers, raised on MTV and *Quake,* tend to yawn and move on to something with a higher body count.

English SF's greatest founding father was British novelist Herbert George Wells (1866–1946), who single-handedly fixed in the public's imagination some of the most archetypal SF ideas. In books like *War of the Worlds* (1898), *The Invisible Man* (1897), and *The Island of Doctor Moreau* (1896), Wells anticipated many, if not most, of the anxieties that plague us today. His books unflinchingly examine alienation, class struggle, and the perils of scientific meddling in nature. For instance, in *The War in the Air* (1908), Wells predicted aerial warfare and declared that it would lead to a global military apocalypse. In his preface to the 1941 edition of the book, he railed against society for ignoring his warnings.

Alive and Well in America

After Wells, the history of SF takes up in America. During the Depression and well into the 1940s, there was a thriving short-fiction industry in the United States. Dozens of magazines published monthly issues almost as thick as phone books that were crammed with stories. These were the famous *pulps,* and this was the period often referred to as the golden age of science fiction, as we mentioned in the previous chapter.

Since the magazine market was huge and insatiable, writers strove to top one another's ideas. Thousands of lurid, ridiculous, impossible stories flowed out of the pens of America's golden-age writers. Inevitably, some absolute classics appeared as well—works like Asimov's robot stories, and A. E. van Vogt's *Slan,* which was so popular that it spawned a catch-phrase, "Fans are slans." In the middle years of the twentieth century, SF fans could recite this phrase to one another and wink; *they* knew what it meant, even if nobody else did.

Factoid

The **pulps** were mass-market fiction magazines printed on very low-quality newsprint ("pulp paper"). It's hard to believe today, but there were once hundreds of these magazines available, and an average issue could be an inch thick, containing dozens of stories. One issue of a pulp could provide many evenings of good reading—and valuable service in the outhouse afterward.

Cold-War Visions

Consolidation of magazine distribution, the rise of the paperback, and television effectively killed the pulp market. In the 1950s and 1960s, the number of magazines declined sharply, and so the SF readership became more dedicated. This dedicated readership was more willing to accept experimental works, and in the 1960s experiment flourished. This was a period of great anxiety in Western society, and bleak dystopian visions were easily accepted by the reading public. B-movies about alien invasions flourished, fed by Cold War paranoia.

During this era the next great SF movement was born: the New Wave. New Wave authors such as Brian Aldiss crossed the line between respectable mainstream literature and the SF ghetto with impunity. There was greater emphasis on character, as well as the broader political consciousness we associate with the late 1960s. Feminist SF was born during this period, as was ecological SF.

SF in the Age of the Internet

Just as punk rock was born out of the ashes of 1960s' idealism, cyberpunk was born out of the pessimism of the 1970s. The oil crisis, pollution, and growing ecological awareness led many people to rethink their attitudes toward technology. While SF had always maintained an ambivalent attitude toward science, often warning of its dark side, cyberpunk took that ambivalence to new heights.

Since the writing is the important task, we'll turn to it now. The next thing you need to know is what is and isn't true about writing. With that in mind, we turn to the mythology of writing—what writing is not.

Myths and Legends

There may be no art form more shrouded in myth than writing: A writer is a solitary intellectual, laboring alone in a small room, splendidly isolated, and genuinely inspired because of this isolation. He sends a manuscript to an editor, who, blown away by the talent and depth of the work, buys it on the spot. Hefty advances, book tours, and interviews follow. Very little of this picture reflects reality. There is no one way to write or become successful as a writer. Each of us has to find our own way as artists, and whatever method works for you is the right method. Maybe the worst myth about writing is just the idea that you can learn The Way to do it.

The Myth of Talent

If you believe that some people are just naturally talented at something, then you close the door to understanding how they do what they do. Worse, you judge yourself according to their standard. They are talented, you are not. *Ergo*, you can never do what they do.

Factoid

We've separated the following discussion into **myths** and **legends.** A myth is a romantic notion with no foundation in reality. A legend is something that's been true, here and there, for a few writers, so people assume that it will also be true for them. (An example of a legend is the six-figure advance for a first novel; sure it's happened, but like winning the lottery, it's not likely to happen to you or me.)

This is rubbish, pure and simple. The truth is, *talent is enthusiasm.* People are perceived to have a talent in an area because that area has captured their imagination. They think about it all the time; they fantasize, they practice ... in short, they work in that area.

You will become talented at whatever captures your imagination. In order to be a talented SF writer, you need to develop enthusiasm for the activities that go into writing SF.

The Myth of Splendid Isolation

Doubtless there are a few unfortunate writers who don't know anyone else in the field, and labor alone. Such people are the exception. Writing—and SF writing in particular—is highly social. Few SF writers hide in their basements. Most of us are curious about each other's work and eager to help fellow writers. There is an extensive and robust network in the SF community; there always has been. New writers appear on the edges of this network, and slowly move inward as they become better known. Nowadays, e-mail is the medium of choice for maintaining the network, but personal contact, usually at SF conventions, is traditional and treasured.

Many of us are naturally gregarious, but even the shy writers get out and party. Why? Simple professionalism. After all, how are you going to learn about the pitfalls and opportunities of any profession without regular contact with your peers? Writers trade horror stories about this or that publisher. We trade advice. We trade ideas. And we trade market news.

The fact is, the more contact you have with your peers, the more you tend to be energized and enthusiastic about what you're doing. Building and maintaining a good network of friends and contacts should be a top priority for you if you want to break into SF writing.

Infodump

SF fans are notorious for telling writers exactly what they think of their work. It can be humbling, but talking to your readers is one of the best ways you can keep your creative compass pointed in the right direction.

The Legend That Writing Is the Road to Fame and Fortune

There was a time, about 70 years ago, when you could eke out a living just writing short stories. That was in the golden age of pulp fiction magazines. A lot has changed in 70 years ... except, of course, the pay rate per word in the short-fiction market. In other words, 70 years ago you might make $200 for a short story, which would be enough to live on for several months. Today, you'll probably make ... $200, if you're lucky.

The number of SF writers who are rich is minuscule. The number who make their living writing fiction is larger, but it's still not a big number. The only thing

SF has going for it is that it's probably easier to make a living writing SF than any other genre fiction, with the possible exception of romance novels.

If all of this sounds depressing, remember that those of us who are working SF writers love what we do. Writing is terrific fun. Seeing your name in print is a rush, and we guarantee that, no matter how small the check for the sale of your first story is, you'll want to dance down the street with it.

The Legend of Inspiration

We don't deny that inspiration exists. There will be times when the Muses swat you over the head and you simply must run to your word processor and write. Such moments are all very well, but don't rely on them. Inspiration is overrated. More important, it's not central to most people's writing process.

"As You Know, Bob ..."

It's generally accepted that if you want to make a career writing SF, you need to crank out about one novel every 9 to 12 months. Even at this steady rate, most writers won't be able to live off the avails of fiction until they've published their fifth book. It's at about this point that they'll have a regular inflow of royalties and receive good advances for new works.

Writing mostly consists of planning, then following that plan as you draft the scenes of your story. When things are really rolling and you're in what we call a "state of flow," writing can be an exhilarating, intoxicating experience. One of the biggest mistakes beginning writers make is to equate this sense of creative intoxication with creativity itself. Don't confuse that exalted state where the words flow without any effort to your best work. Just because you drag yourself to the computer, snarl at the cat, and proceed to write three pages at a rate of two cups of coffee per page doesn't necessarily mean you're producing bad work either.

While inspiration may exist, it's not something working writers usually fit into their schedules. We rely on our own resources rather than the unreliable Muses.

Myth: Writing Is Not One Activity, but Many

The myth is that writing is some mysterious, creative, single activity that you do while sitting in front of the computer. Other writers, particularly those writers you admire, appear miraculous to you; their work is given to them by the Muses, and that's the end of it.

To build a house, you need zoning permits, architectural designs, engineering specs, construction permits, and a work gang whose members have many different talents and who use different talents at different stages of the job. But when it comes to writing, we tend to think there's only one activity involved. Ask a writer what she's doing, and she'll probably respond, "I'm writing." To be a writer is to be many different things, and not all at the same time. Once you understand this, you'll also understand some important things, like how to avoid writer's block and how to improve your writing in areas where you're weak.

Infodump

It's to the advantage of writers to make the audience think they're brilliant. It's part of the showmanship of the profession. Nobody wants to admit that they edited a particular paragraph 20 times, or that the most brilliant piece of prose in the book is actually an adaptation of a speech you read in some Roman senator's memoirs. Writers hide the details of their labor. But that labor is multifarious, and tough.

Your Cast of Characters

Chances are there are aspects of your writing that you like, and others you think need improvement. In fact, you might be quite frustrated at your deficiencies in some area, and think about yourself in terms such as, "I'm bad at plot" or "I can't create believable characters." An activity like plotting is different from the activity of creating characters. When you're sitting at the word processor you may think you're doing one thing—writing—but your activity changes depending on the demands of the story and your own interests. At one point you may be plotting; at another, characterizing. These are different skills and different activities. If your characters aren't very well-defined, it's probably not because you're a bad writer, but because your interests lie in another area and most of your practice has been in that area. You can always get better at characterizing (or plotting, or whatever). You just need to balance your activities a bit better.

For instance, let's imagine a room full of writers. Each (like characters in a story) has strengths and a flaw. These are our characters:

➤ **The dreamer** has a whole universe in his head, but can't get that first scene written.

➤ **The draft horse** has nine different versions of Chapter One.

➤ **The academic** has lots of file folders crammed with notes, but hasn't started the story yet.

➤ **The editor** never gets to Chapter Two because Chapter One "just isn't quite right yet."

➤ **The biographer** has 200 pages of dialog and character development, but nothing has actually happened yet.

➤ **The plotter** has a lot of action going on, but there are no people in this story.

➤ **The essayist** uses the story to make a point, and woe to any character or drama that gets in the way.

Every writer is every one of these characters, to some degree. Our strengths and flaws complement each other. When we follow our strengths and begin to improve our writing, we can easily overbalance the writing process; the strength turns into a weakness. For instance, let's assume you have a good imagination. Maybe you can sit down and run movies in your head, and to the extent that you do this before writing, you can picture, then execute, vivid scenes. But if you developed this talent too much to the exclusion of all else, you would be a great daydreamer but would neither be inclined nor know how to turn those daydreams into stories. Your own strength would have overpowered you.

Infodump

Are you a draft horse or more of an editor? An academic or a plotter? Rate yourself in each area. Allow yourself 35 points and allocate them among the different types. The more proficient you feel you are in a certain area, the higher the score should be (for example, 5 for dreamer, 10 for draft horse, and so on). Then, commit to spending a little more time on the low-numbered areas for the next month. That time could be spent reading, contemplating, practicing, or editing existing drafts. The point is to achieve some balance, not in a New-Agey sense, but in an architectural or structural sense: You want to balance your skills at the various tasks that make up writing.

Writing as a Daily Activity

If you want to develop a particular muscle, you have to use it. The only way to build up muscle mass, strength, and tone is through regular exercise. We all know that, and we're used to applying such a philosophy when it comes to our health. Surprisingly, though, few beginning writers apply this sensible attitude to their own work.

Nobody starts off as a brilliant writer. We get better by working at it. The best way to do this is to write every day, rain or shine. As with any other set of muscles, your writing muscles will atrophy if they're not used. If they're underused, they may not atrophy, but they won't get any stronger, either. Bingeing on writing once or twice a month will not benefit you as much as working steadily at it, day in and day out.

This is particularly true of novelists. Although it's possible to write a novel in a week, we don't advise it.

Off and Running

Your next step is to write. We'll be talking about the mechanics of writing in upcoming chapters, as well as the secrets to creativity and how to develop marketing savvy. All of these things are important, but the most important thing is that you *write*. Each of your writing personalities is itching to get started; each needs its exercise in order to become stronger. Put aside worries about success, talent, isolation, and the sheer size of projects like novels.

Just sit down, take a deep breath, and let the daydreams begin.

The Least You Need to Know

➤ Science fiction has a long and rich history.

➤ There are many myths and legends about writing.

➤ You do not possess one skill or talent called "writing," but many different skills, all of which contribute to your ability as a writer.

➤ You improve as a writer by improving in many different areas. Problems with writing can be easily isolated in one or another area that you need to strengthen.

➤ Weaknesses in your writing probably lie in activities you don't enjoy, such as editing or revision. The key to improving in such areas is to find ways to enjoy doing them.

➤ There's no way to write SF without reading it. You should at least be familiar with the classics of the genre.

Chapter 3

The Varieties of Science Fiction

In This Chapter

➤ From space opera to cyberpunk: the many varieties of science fiction

➤ The infinite possibilities in science fiction

➤ Readings for the writer

Now that we've established that reading SF is right up there with brushing your teeth and eating your vegetables in terms of importance, let's move on to the feast itself.

In the following sections, we give you a summary of some of the main categories of SF, fantasy, and horror. It's impossible for us to cover all the bases here, because there are so many works of SF that are impossible to classify, and so much variety within the categories. Hopefully what follows will serve as enough of a guide to let you explore further on your own.

Speculative Fiction

"SF" is usually taken to stand for science fiction, but some critics insist that it means speculative fiction. After all, a lot of what gets published under the heading of SF really has nothing to do with current science. It's speculation, pure and simple. We could hardly call the universe of Lovecraft's horror stories scientific, nor, these days, could we believe that Edgar Rice Burroughs's Barsoom is an accurate picture of Mars. Who cares? The stories are good, and for most of SF, that's all that matters.

Hard SF: The Radical Core

No, that's not "hard" as in difficult, but hard as in the hard sciences: physics, chemistry, etc. Hard SF is the subgenre that puts the "science" in SF. At its simplest, it's just fiction in which nothing occurs that is impossible, either by our current understanding of science, or within the carefully worked out framework of the story.

Infodump

Many hard SF writers relax the scientific rigor of their stories "around the edges." For instance, you might set a story on an alien planet and ensure that all the critical plot elements come from real scientific possibilities. At the same time, your characters may have arrived at this world in some faster-than-light starship—an impossibility according to current science. Because it's peripheral to the main premise, how your characters got to the planet doesn't affect the "hardness" of the story.

In other words, the hard SF writer is constrained to writing about events that could happen. Much of the wonder in hard SF comes from discovering just how wild and fantastic the natural world is. It's also fun to explore what's possible for the future of humanity, and this is what hard SF excels at. Some of the possibilities are mind-boggling, but hard SF requires that we consider them as real possibilities—things like nanotechnology, genetically engineered immortality, interstellar travel, and artificial intelligences that surpass our own.

Hard SF can be a lot of fun to write. It's challenging, because you must remain true to the known world (or the rigorous rules of your made-up world), while spinning as engaging a tale as you can. If your characters get into trouble, you can't bail them out with some easy solution such as a teleporter, warp drive, or force field! They've got to work with what's really there.

Small wonder, then, that hard SF is the home of the rugged individualist, the character who can strip down his crashed life pod and build a beacon out of the parts. Hard SF tends to be optimistic about the benefits of technology, and most hard SF displays an inspiring faith in the value of the enlightened, scientific world view. These things—the faith in and adherence to reason, the optimism, the sense of wonder at the natural world—are what make hard SF the core of science fiction.

Many hard SF writers come from a scientific background. Some, like Robert Forward, are working scientists. Others, like Poul Anderson, are professional writers. One thing they share, however, is a desire to make scientific ideas accessible to nonspecialists. Hard SF writers are amazed and dazzled at the discoveries and theories of science, and want to make this sense of excitement accessible to the rest of us.

Places to start in reading hard SF:

➤ *Mission of Gravity,* by Hal Clement

➤ *I, Robot,* by Isaac Asimov

➤ *Timescape,* by Gregory Benford

➤ *Rendezvous with Rama,* by Arthur C. Clarke

➤ *The Flight of the Dragonfly,* by Robert Forward

"Soft" or Sociological SF

Science fiction is a grand playground for ideas. The only rule for the genre, really, is that anything goes. This freedom has paradoxically made it possible for some writers to say very pointed things about the human condition and the world in general that they could not have expressed so well in mainstream fiction. There is a tradition in SF of authors creating worlds that bring some social issue or moral problem into sharp relief.

The obvious examples, of course, are the twentieth-century *dystopias: Brave New World* and *1984.* These works are far from unique, and, despite their age, are quite relevant today. *The Island of Doctor Moreau,* originally about vivisection, remains a chilling commentary on the dark possibilities of genetic engineering.

University English courses often cover such dystopias, and alternative *utopias.* Utopian/ dystopian stories form a tiny part of the grand tradition of speculative fiction, however. SF authors often take one problem and use the lens of SF to examine it thoroughly. Frank Herbert's classic *Dune* is a good example; it's really a thorough exploration of the pitfalls of what's often called "the leader principle"—the belief in a Messiah or *Führer.*

"As You Know, Bob ..."

If there's hard SF, surely there must also be "soft" SF? As a matter of fact, yes. Sociological or psychological stories, such as *Fahrenheit 451* and *The Left Hand of Darkness,* are sometimes referred to as "soft SF." We've preferred to lump them under speculative fiction here, but it's equally valid to call them soft SF (see the "'Soft' or Sociological SF" section for more).

Factoid

A **utopia** (from the book of the same name by Sir Thomas More) is a perfect society. Conversely, a **dystopia** is a perfectly awful society. George Orwell's *1984* is a dystopian novel. (Oddly enough, few novels have been written in the third category, subtopia, which refers to that sprawling area of strip malls and warehouses on the edge of any city.)

In soft SF, the writer creates a world that best shows off the issues in question. By creating a planet whose people change sex at regular intervals, Ursula K. Le Guin was able to discuss many issues of gender and politics in *The Left Hand of Darkness*. Similarly, H. G. Wells's *The Time Machine* is not a classic simply because with it he invented the modern time-travel story; the society that the time traveler visits also lets Wells comment effectively on Victorian society.

This kind of SF is concerned with the scientific accuracy of its devices. What counts as real is what serves the theme.

Places to start in reading idea fiction:

➤ *Dune,* by Frank Herbert

➤ *The Dispossessed,* by Ursula K. Le Guin

➤ *The Foundation Trilogy,* by Isaac Asimov

➤ *Fahrenheit 451,* by Ray Bradbury

➤ *Stand on Zanzibar,* by John Brunner

➤ *A Canticle for Leibowitz,* by Walter M. Miller Jr.

Space Opera

… And then we have *Star Wars.*

Space opera is the mode of SF most familiar to the public. That's because it's what translates best to the movie screen … and let's face it, it's fun!

The universe of space opera is engaged in a tug of war between good and evil. Its denizens are saints, sinners, and ravenous aliens. Characters zip across the galaxy in hyperdrive starships, save planets and occasionally the universe, smuggle, steal, fight, and, time and time again, escape death by the skin of their teeth. This is adventure fiction, pure and simple.

Some people seem to think that George Lucas invented this kind of story. In fact, everything in *Star Wars* is, at the very least, an homage to earlier works, or—at worst—outright stolen from its literary predecessors. The wonderful atmosphere of the *Star Wars* movies comes straight out of the golden age pulps of the 1930s and 1940s. Conventions such as blasters and laser pistols, hyperdrive, interstellar empires, and space smugglers were all established then.

One of the finest craftsmen in this field was actually a woman, Andre Norton. Between about 1950 and 1970 she wrote dozens of novels with titles like *Sargasso of Space* and *Uncharted Stars.* Here we find brave members of the Space Patrol, plucky Free Traders, and the daring Scouts who survey new planets. Most of Norton's novels take place in a sprawling, ancient galaxy full of the archeological remains of extinct alien empires, as well as live aliens who may be either enemies or allies.

The market for space opera is as strong as it ever was. It's usually considered a juvenile market—aimed toward kids—but the fact is that many adult SF readers grew up on this stuff, and they love to return to it. You can't go wrong writing a strong, original space opera epic.

Places to start in reading space opera:

➤ *The Zero Stone,* by Andre Norton

➤ *A Fire Upon the Deep,* by Vernor Vinge

➤ *A Princess of Mars,* by Edgar Rice Burroughs

➤ *The Skylark of Space,* by E. E. "Doc" Smith

➤ *The Uplift War,* by David Brin

➤ *Ginger Star,* by Leigh Brackett

The SF Mainstream

SF has a whole spectrum of styles, ranging from rigorous hard SF to space opera and *science fantasy*. Most SF falls somewhere in the middle of the spectrum: not measuring itself solely by how well it reflects current science, but not completely fantastic either.

Some of the best SF ever written falls into the SF mainstream. You could say it's an area of maximum possibility; you can play with scientific ideas and introduce fantastical elements as needed to round out the story. For instance, most space-based SF stories use the idea of hyperdrive (or warp drive in *Star Trek* terminology). While impossible by hard SF standards, hyperdrive is just so darned useful that almost nothing gets written without it.

Places to start in reading mainstream SF:

➤ *The Mote in God's Eye,* by Larry Niven and Jerry Pournelle

➤ *Stranger in a Strange Land,* by Robert A. Heinlein

➤ *The Stars My Destination,* by Alfred Bester

➤ *Ender's Game,* by Orson Scott Card

➤ *Bios,* by Robert Charles Wilson

➤ *Eon,* by Greg Bear

➤ *Deception Well,* by Linda Nagata

Factoid

Science fantasy straddles SF and fantasy: You may find wizards, magic, and spaceships in the same story. No attempt is made at realism in this kind of storytelling; the tale is more important than any scientific accuracy or even believability. While SF writers usually strive to be technically accurate, getting the tale working is generally higher on their list of priorities. In science fantasy, all bets are off and anything can happen.

Cyberpunk

Cyberpunk is the *film noir* of literary SF. It's stylish, sexy, and dark. The optimism and faith in science that so characterize hard SF are often missing here. Science is a doorway into the future enslavement of humanity by its own technology, and salvation lies in co-opting that technology, according to the cyberpunk authors. Technology is not to be trusted, but we can't live without it. It is this uneasy relationship with technology—like sleeping with a cobra—that makes cyberpunk so compelling.

The writer most often credited with the "invention" of this movement is William Gibson, but as with all other modes of SF writing, you can find examples of it going back decades. Both John Brunner and J. G. Ballard can take credit for first highlighting the "stickier" side of technology—the side that includes contact lenses, pacemakers, genetic surgery, and facial recognition programs. The cyberpunk authors took this mode of writing, labeled it, and took it as their own. It's thrived now for a good 20 years.

Infodump

Style is everything in cyberpunk. It's a world of black leather, mirror-shade sunglasses, and street-talking hackers. The most successful cyberpunk stories, both on screen (like *The Matrix*) and on paper (William Gibson's *Neuromancer*), have shared a masterful sense of style.

Now *this* is SF that does well on the big screen! Two classic SF films are utterly cyberpunk in style: *Blade Runner* and *The Matrix*. Numerous other, less successful films have adopted this style, to the point where the dressed-in-rags but cybernetically plugged-in hero is fast becoming a cliché (*Road Warrior* chic).

Most cyberpunk is concerned with the near future. For this reason, it's often topical, dealing with subjects like cloning, ecological collapse, nanotechnology, artificial intelligence, genetic engineering, and, of course, the Net. Unfortunately, the world is catching up to many of cyberpunk's predictions at an alarming rate.

Places to start in reading cyberpunk:

➤ *The Shockwave Rider,* by John Brunner

➤ *Neuromancer,* by William Gibson

➤ *Islands in the Net,* by Bruce Sterling

➤ *Snow Crash,* by Neal Stephenson

➤ *City Come A-Walkin',* by John Shirley

Time Travel and Alternate History

"Time is a kind of space," said H. G. Wells's time traveler, thus launching a new kind of SF story. Time travel gives us the chance to visit ancient Rome, or go on dinosaur hunts, or change the past. These are some of the most fun SF stories, because we would all like to know what it was like to live in other ages; perhaps to be a nobleman or a queen in Byzantium, or to watch the building of the Pyramids. Time travel also gives the traveler god-like powers. The ability to change history, and the moral and logical problems this raises, fuels many time-travel stories.

Closely related to time travel is the idea of alternate worlds; you need to look no further than the *Sliders* TV series for a good example of alternate universes.

Time travel and alternate worlds merge in the alternate history. In alternate history stories, we start by speculating what would have happened if some historical event had not occurred, or had happened differently. What if Napoleon had won the battle of Waterloo? What if Rome had not fallen? The possibilities are endless.

"As You Know, Bob ..."

In Einstein's theory of relativity, anything that goes faster than light is automatically also going backward in time. This is a little detail about faster-than-light (FTL) travel that is carefully swept under the rug in most interstellar epics.

"As You Know, Bob ..."

The "grandfather paradox" is the most famous conundrum in time travel. What if you went back in time and killed your grandfather before he could have children? Would you then not have come into existence either, and therefore, would you not be able to go back in time to murder your grandfather? As far as we know, the only time travelers who have ever adequately solved this paradox were Bill and Ted, in the movie *Bill and Ted's Excellent Adventure*.

Places to start in reading time travel and alternate history stories:

➤ *The Time Machine*, by H. G. Wells
➤ *The Man in the High Castle*, by Philip K. Dick
➤ *The Guns of the South*, by Harry Turtledove
➤ *The Condition of Muzak*, by Michael Moorcock
➤ *The Anubis Gates*, by Tim Powers

The Varieties of Fantasy

Fantasy is not just SF with elves and magic. Most science fiction is fundamentally materialistic; it's founded on the belief in the objectivity of the world. Fantasy, on the other hand, is usually idealistic: In fantasy, the inner world of the psyche is often more real than the physical world. Indeed, the physical world is little more than a cloudy mirror reflecting the soul.

You'll find many kinds of fantasy on the bookshelves these days. Let's look at a few of them.

High Fantasy

High fantasy represents an ongoing market for those readers who were dazzled by J.R.R. Tolkien's *The Lord of the Rings* and want to read more stories like it. High fantasy seeks to deliver what Tolkien delivered: richly developed worlds peopled by believable characters, with an overall atmosphere of magic and wonder. Such worlds are a refuge from the drab, technocratic world of everyday life. They are places where traditional values hold sway, but both men and women can be equally heroic; and where nature is an ally and friend, to be wooed with magic rather than pillaged with machinery.

Danger, Danger!

People can grow passionately fond of their favorite high fantasy characters—we know one writer who received death threats from a disgruntled fan, because the fan's favorite character died in Book III of his trilogy!

High fantasy has at its basis a kind of idealized society, and most high fantasy plots revolve around a threat to that society. One or more of its members, often the lowliest, must face up to the threat and return the world to its natural state. (You'll note that this is a good capsule summary of *The Lord of the Rings*.) The threat is usually personified evil in the form of a sorcerer, warlord, or unchained demon. High fantasy allows a lot of scope to explore character and relationships.

High fantasy is thriving, with dozens of books being published each year, many by new authors. A recent phenomenon in the market is the fantasy series or decalogy (10-volume story), as exemplified by Robert Jordan's epic *Wheel of Time* books.

Places to start in reading high fantasy:

➤ *The Lord of the Rings,* by J.R.R. Tolkien

➤ *The Wheel of Time* series, by Robert Jordan

➤ *Tigana,* by Guy Gavriel Kay

➤ *Chronicles of Thomas Covenant the Unbeliever,* by Stephen R. Donaldson

➤ *The Mists of Avalon,* by Marion Zimmer Bradley

Traditional Fantasy

Some critics, such as author John Clute, don't consider many high fantasy stories to be fantasy at all, and point to a different literary form as the true bearer of the title. Why?

In traditional fantasy, unlike in SF, there is no objective "outside" world. The world is a reflection of the psyches of the characters; the characters may also be symbolic reflections of the world. What occurs in the mind can just as easily occur physically, because there is no real distinction between the two.

"As You Know, Bob ..."

The Western tradition of magic, which goes back centuries, is founded on the notion that the whole world exists within the soul of each one of us. A magician is simply someone who has the force of will to change the part of his or her consciousness that corresponds to an outside part of the world. Changing that internal object automatically means changing the external, "real" one, with real, physical results. Or, as the sorcerers say, "As above, so below."

This being the case, traditional fantasy is more dreamlike, less dependent on logic—and certainly is not scientific!

Much of what passes for fantasy these days is just SF in disguise: Adventures told in worlds where the physical laws are different, allowing "magic" in one form or another. But there is still a physical world in these stories, and it is still more "real" than what goes on in the minds of the characters. So these tales, which are often written in high fantasy mode, are still rationalist, materialist fiction—science fiction.

Well, that certainly sounds like an academic argument! It is, until you look at some of the traditional fantasy of the pre-Tolkien era. It's remarkable, and obviously different from high fantasy. In traditional fantasy, illogical and impossible things happen all the time, but we don't question them. They fit the psychology of the situation, after all. The dreamy sense of being transported to another kind of existence is the hallmark of traditional fantasy—and explains why stories such as the Arthurian legend have remained popular, not just for years, but for centuries.

Infodump

We've developed a quick way to identify such pseudo-SF fantasies. A lot of fantasy stories use what we call the "utility theory of magic." In the utility theory, magic is a kind of natural force, like magnetic fields, and magicians perform magic by tapping into this force. It's like plugging into a wall socket. Because this is a purely materialist conception (even if the magician shapes the result with his mind), we tend to think of these stories as a form of SF, rather than as truly fantastic.

Traditional fantasy and high fantasy blur together. If you want to write about a fantasy world peopled with complex and socially diverse characters, and with stable "laws" of magic, you're squarely on the SF side of high fantasy. If your worlds are quirky, unpredictable, and operate not according to laws but according to the logic of dreams, then you're writing in traditional fantasy mode.

Places to start in reading traditional fantasy:

➤ *The Worm Ouroboros*, by E. R. Eddison

➤ *Gormenghast*, by Mervyn Peake

➤ *The Book of Knights*, by Yves Meynard

➤ *The Chronicles of Narnia*, by C. S. Lewis

➤ *A Wizard of Earthsea*, by Ursula K. Le Guin

Dark Fantasy

Dark fantasy takes the internalization of the outside world one step further: In dark fantasy and horror, the physical world is a reflection of the subconscious, dark, and animalistic side of our psyches.

Dark fantasy appeals to lovers of the Gothic. Vampires abound in such tales, as do demons and seductive magic that lure people away from civilization and morality. Dark fantasy plays with the uncomfortable attractiveness of evil.

Places to start in reading dark fantasy:

➤ *Interview with the Vampire*, by Anne Rice

➤ *Blood Roses: A Novel of Saint-Germain*, by Chelsea Quinn Yarbro

➤ *The Dark Tower* series, by Stephen King

➤ *Dark Ladies,* by Fritz Leiber

➤ *The Thief of Always,* by Clive Barker

Modern Urban Fantasy

Modern urban fantasy is a comparatively recent trend. These are stories set in the present day, with all its technology, industry, worries, and distractions. Into this mundane world, however, a little magic appears ... and so the characters in a modern urban fantasy take a journey away from their ordinary lives. Modern urban fantasy brings a sense of wonder back into the details of everyday life.

In modern urban fantasy, the city's still full of trucks, garbage, and workers laying asphalt. In the bushes, though, there are wood elves and other fabulous creatures, who sometimes maintain the lives of the trees and hedges, without our knowledge.

Places to start in reading modern urban fantasy:

➤ *Jack, the Giant Killer,* by Charles de Lint

➤ *Little, Big,* by John Crowley

➤ *Arc of the Dream,* by A. A. Attanasio

➤ *The Fionavar Tapestry,* by Guy Gavriel Kay

"As You Know, Bob ..."

Horror stories are an exploration of the dark side of ourselves, even if the monsters seem physically real. By confronting this objectified evil, the hero of a horror story faces that part of himself. Horror stories are satisfying to us not because we like to watch people suffer, but because the horror story is a journey of discovery in just this sense.

The Least You Need to Know

➤ There are many varieties of SF, each of which has its classics. You should be familiar with the major works in any area you choose to write in.

➤ You can spend a lifetime exploring SF. Don't expect you'll ever know it all.

➤ If you read the core works, you'll soon be familiar enough with the territory to begin to write SF yourself.

Chapter 4

Fans and Conventions

In This Chapter

➤ SF's unique fans

➤ Fans and authors

➤ Science fiction conventions

➤ Connecting to fandom

➤ Get involved—volunteer!

Fandom is almost as old as science fiction itself, and many writers started out as fans. Fans can be a source of great publicity and support throughout your career. While often portrayed in the media as obese men in Starfleet uniforms and Spock ears arguing violently about *Battlestar Galactica* trivia, fans influence books sales and awards, even though they represent only a tiny fraction of the overall audience of science fiction.

Slide Rules and Spock Ears: The Fans

If you've never been to a science fiction convention, you've probably gotten your ideas about science fiction fans from movies, *Saturday Night Live* sketches, and the occasional TV coverage on slow news days. The fandom story is a lot more complicated than that. Fandom can be a lot of fun—but it can also be a trap.

The "average" fan doesn't exist. *Fandom* is a tapestry of varied humanity, ranging from devoted volunteers whose lives are consumed by the genre to mildly interested "weekend warriors" who occasionally dip their toes in the fannish waters.

Still, there is some truth in the media cliché of the typical fan: rotund, peevish, out-landishly attired, and belligerent. Any convention will have a few people who match this profile. Lots of theories seek to explain this, but one thing that everyone agrees on is that science fiction is a literary genre that appeals to outcasts, especially in their teen years. Kids who are too smart, too fat, too thin, covered in zits, cursed with speech impediments, or stuck in wheelchairs have, for decades, turned to science fiction for escape into a fantastic realm where virtue triumphs, toads are revealed as princes, and intellect saves the day. Generally speaking, fans mature into balanced, healthy adults, but these adults remember what it was like to be a social pariah and are fabulously accepting of people's foibles.

Factoid

Fandom is a catch-all term for everything in science fiction fan subculture. Fans are notoriously playful with language, and fan-nish lingo is rife with puns and word play. **Fanac** refers to fan-nish activity, including wearing costumes, playing games, and re-creating historical events.

There is a wonderful camaraderie among fans, who often travel the world to hang out with close friends whom they know principally through the Internet or letters and only see once or twice a year. In many ways, fandom presaged the geography-independent communities spawned by the Internet, and indeed, fans were online before any other social group. Many fans have outgrown, overcome, or accepted whatever awkwardness they may have felt in their teen years, and have blossomed into erudite professionals with broad interests.

Fannish activity (*fanac*) runs a broad gamut:

➤ Costuming, both competitive and hobbyist

➤ Writing and performing music, often humorous or historical

➤ Amateur publishing

➤ Gaming, especially strategy and role-playing

➤ Amateur science and technology projects, including support for private space ventures

➤ Visual arts, especially painting and sculpture

➤ Historical re-creation

There are many more. A big convention (or "con") will have examples of all of these and more. Some fans actually earn their living through fanac, and others are professionals in related fields. There's a temptation to dismiss fans as obsessive hobbyists, but nothing could be farther from the truth.

I'm Your Biggest Fan!

Unlike other forms of literature, SF fans and writers are typically in pretty close contact with one another. Fans feel comfortable approaching writers in person and through correspondence, and are notoriously blunt with their opinions.

Scratch a Fan, Find a Writer

One of the most prominent forms of fanac is writing: convention reports ("conreports"), *slash* fiction, fan fiction, letters, shaggy-dog stories, humorous songs, slogans, and buttons, It seems like every fan considers himself something of a scribbler. There are fans who are more prolific than any professional writer, filling up photocopied 'zines, con-reports, and Web pages with alarming speed. Some fannish writing is of professional quality, and there are fan reviewers who are taken every bit as seriously within the field as the professionals writing for *The New York Times Review of Books*.

But fan writing and professional writing are very different animals, and must be approached differently. Professional writers write for professional markets: They produce material that meets the needs of editors who are running for-profit concerns and whose employers expect them to make decisions that will generate revenue.

By contrast, fan writers write for the sheer joy of writing. When they submit material to an editor, that editor is a hobbyist, who seeks to publish material that takes his or her fancy, regardless of the commercial potential.

Fan writers sometimes make the jump into pro writing. Indeed, William Gibson's first contributions to the field were comics drawn for photocopied fanzines. And some professional writers still consider themselves fans and contribute to fanzines when the mood strikes them.

Fan writing is a fine and worthy undertaking, then, with a few caveats:

Factoid

Slash is a subset of fanfic, with homoerotic themes; the name comes from the slash in the story descriptions, as in "Kirk/Spock" or "Riker/Picard."

➤ Fan writing doesn't pay. If you're a writer who is attempting to build a professional career, you should know that fan writing is not the best way of accomplishing that.

➤ Fan writing is a timesink: Every minute spent pursuing fannish interests is a minute you don't spend on your professional objectives.

➤ Fan writing is potentially dangerous; since it *feels* like professional writing, it has the potential for giving you the illusion that you're being productive, when really, you're just amusing yourself.

Keep these points in mind when you pursue fannish activities, and you'll be in good shape.

Smile and Nod

Having fans kicks ass. There's nothing better than publishing a story or novel and getting a rush (or even a trickle) of mail and e-mail from fans who enjoyed your work. One of the best things about SF is that writers aren't put up on pedestals—they wander the halls of conventions, chatting with old friends and making new ones. Fans feel free to approach writers, shake their hands, and tell them what's on their minds.

This can be great. Fans are often well-read, thoughtful individuals who have terrific feedback for your work. Some fans may even be students, writing papers on your work for English class (or science class, if you're a hard SF writer). Just think, your material could be *curriculum!*

However, there's a line every writer has to draw between fan appreciation and obsession. That line is different for every writer, and it's one that you'll have to trust your gut on. Some writers are endlessly entertained to learn that a fan has taken on the persona of one of their characters in a role-playing game or costuming contest. Some think it's cute that a fan has written a short story set in their universe. Some are flattered that a fan has undertaken a painting or sculpture project based on their work.

But some writers are not amused by any of this. Writing is a solitary occupation, after all. You don't really *owe* your fans anything except the best writing you can produce. Having a fan quiz you in minute detail about a story of yours—especially one that was inspired by some personal emotion—can be torture.

"As You Know, Bob ..."

Some fan writing, like fan fiction and slash fiction, is virtually impossible to publish commercially. These works are set in other writers' copyrighted universes and involve copyrighted characters, and commercial publication would violate those copyrights. Fannish small-press publications are often tolerated by writers (though less often by their litigious publishers) but money-making publication is another matter altogether.

When you feel the need to draw a line—that is, to let a fan know that you're not interested in continuing a conversation, either electronic or face-to-face—you should. Be polite, be gentle, be friendly, but be firm. Don't allow yourself to get drawn into arguments, and *don't* lose your cool. Bad behavior is remembered by fans and writers alike, and the last thing you want is a reputation as a crank.

Pros and Con(ventions)

The science fiction convention dates back to the mid 1930s, when fans in Philadelphia and in Leeds, U.K., first held scheduled gatherings of fans from out of town. Conventions began as a gathering of literary enthusiasts and writers (often the same people) who came together to discuss fiction, science, and art. Since then, conventions have sprung up around the world and have become increasingly specialized, evolving into regional cons, media cons, relaxacons, costume cons, national cons, and commercial cons.

Danger, Danger!

A cool head is doubly important with fans who have a bone to pick. It can be excruciating to hold your tongue when a fan comes up to you to let you know that he thinks your writing stinks, or worse, that he likes your old stuff, but your new stuff is crap. Writerly egos are notoriously fragile, and it can be rough to endure the amateur critiques of self-appointed arbitrators of genre literature. But unless you feel like the erstwhile critic and you have something to teach each other, arguing with that person is a waste of your time and will only raise your blood pressure.

Writers and Cons

Attending a convention can be very good for a writer. It presents an opportunity to meet other writers and editors, to attend panels on the craft of science fiction and the state of various areas of scientific endeavor, and to drink cheap—or free!—beer.

The cost of attending a convention is generally reasonable, in the $20 to $50 range for three days, and conventions generally secure a discounted rate on hotel rooms for people who travel long distances to attend.

If you've sold a story or two, you can often arrange to attend a convention for free, in exchange for your participation in the programming. Just write or e-mail the convention's organizing committee a few months in advance and offer your services. Remember, though, that they may already have filled their program; if a convention looks interesting, don't skip it just because they don't put you on the dais on your first visit. Showing up and being an interesting person is an excellent strategy for long-term future good relations. (A directory of convention Web sites appears in Appendix D, "Online Resources.")

When you volunteer to be a program participant at a convention, it's important to remember that you are the guest of a group of dedicated volunteers who put their labor and money into running the convention, and recoup the costs by charging admission. It's your responsibility to justify their hospitality by actively participating in lots of programming activities and making yourself available to the public. Writers who spend the whole weekend hiding out in the *Green Room* or ditch their panels are viewed as poor sports, and are really not living up to their responsibilities.

While every convention is different, there are a few activities that you can expect to find at nearly every con:

➤ A costuming competition at which amateur and professional costumers compete with elaborate outfits inspired by genre literature

➤ A video room where rare and classic genre movies are shown from early in the morning to late at night

➤ A gaming room for role-playing and strategy games

➤ An art show/silent auction where fan and professional art is displayed for purchase

➤ A dealer's room where new and used books and memorabilia are on sale

➤ Panels on a variety of subjects ranging from the craft of writing to science research to fanac

➤ Signings and readings by professional writers

➤ A guest of honor speech, followed by a Q&A session

➤ A poorly attended dance with a disk jockey

➤ Organized "filksings" where fans gather to sing historical and humorous folk songs

The variety of activities is stunning. It's a good idea to try to attend as many different programs as possible to get a good sense of what appeals to you. At the same time, it's important to remember the basic necessities while at a convention. Make sure you get six hours of sleep every night and eat at least two nutritious meals per day: It's easy to run yourself ragged and live on beer and potato chips all weekend, but this can leave you a quivering wreck come Monday morning.

Meals represent some of your best networking opportunities. You may find yourself on a panel with an author or editor with whom you want to chat. Ask the person if he has any plans for lunch, and suggest that you meet at the hotel restaurant. Likewise, drop by the hotel bar in the evening and join one of the inevitable tables full of writers and/or editors for a drink.

The Convention Continuum

While every convention has its own character, it's possible to characterize conventions by their style.

Convention Type	Description	Examples
National	These conventions are the cornerstones of the fan calendar, drawing attendees and guests from around the world. They are often the home of major award ceremonies.	WorldCon, World Fantasy Convention, NASFIC, CanCon
Academic/ Professional	Conventions centered around written science fiction. Attendees are usually writers, editors, theoreticians, and serious readers. Few or no traditional fannish activities are undertaken.	Readercon, Fourth Street Fantasy Convention, WisCon, MythCon
Regional	Your basic volunteer-run convention. Attendees are usually local to the convention. A social, fannish atmosphere prevails.	Philcon, Ad Astra, Boskone, Capricon, Minicon
Media	Devoted to nonwritten science fiction (i.e., *Star Trek, Babylon 5*).	Toronto Trek, United Fan Con
Commercial "Creation"	Conventions run by commercial concerns, usually media-oriented. Few or no panels, lots of big-name stars charging money for autographs.	*Star Trek* conventions

To locate the convention nearest to your home, check the listing of convention Web sites in Appendix D. Every science fiction writer should attend a convention or two, just to see what traditions they've become involved with. If your first convention experience isn't as good as you'd hoped, try another kind of con—conventions can vary widely in character and level of organization.

The Least You Need to Know

➤ There is no such thing as an "average" SF fan. Fans run the gamut from devoted volunteers to weekend warriors.

➤ Getting involved in fandom is a useful way for a writer to promote himself and meet interesting people.

➤ Fandom can steal your time. Remember that no matter how much fanac feels like writing, it isn't.

➤ Every professional SF writer should attend a convention or two, just to get a sense of what they're like.

Writer's Workshops

"Writer's workshop" is a catch-all phrase that describes anything from a group of peers who gather once a month to review each other's work to high-priced classes given by big-name pros and editors.

In today's publishing world, editorial feedback is a scarce commodity indeed. For many writers, workshops fill the void that was once occupied by professional editors with the time and resources to nurture the writers' careers.

A good workshop will offer you many things: a sounding board for working on new ideas; proofreading and copyediting services; training in thinking critically about your own work; news about new markets; and a spirit of friendly competition.

Filling the Void Between Your Mom and Your Editor

The first thing you write—and possibly the second, third, or even tenth thing—probably won't be publishable. It's not uncommon for writers to work at their craft for years or even decades before they're ready for prime time.

If the only thing you do with your work is submit it to editors, it might be years before you get any feedback—other than form rejections. You may be blessed with patient, supportive friends and family who are willing to read your work, but unless they're writers themselves, their advice will be of limited value when it comes to improving your craft.

A workshop fills the void between your mom and your editor. Good workshops involve critical feedback from your peers, and are reciprocal; that is, you are expected to think critically about your peers' writing.

Danger, Danger!

Some writers give up on workshopping because they assume that they're just not "workshop writers," when the problem lies in the workshop, not in their temperament. A bad workshop can be worse than no workshop at all, but you should try a couple of different ones before you decide that workshopping isn't for you.

While your original reason for joining a workshop may be to hear what people have to say about your work, the real benefit comes from trying to improve the stories written by your workshop-mates. The ability to see the problems with a story and find solutions to them is one of the hardest skills for a writer to acquire and refine.

This skill is very different from the kind of literary criticism you may have dabbled with in English class. Analyzing and critiquing published fiction is an academic exercise in every sense of the word, not occupied with the improvement of the works under the microscope. Your comments will never be integrated into a revised edition of *To Kill a Mockingbird*. You will never have the opportunity to see Jack Kerouac's work evolve based on your ideas.

Long-running workshops provide exactly this opportunity. You and your workshop-mates form a symbiotic relationship, and as you watch the effect that your ideas about writing have on their work, you can fine-tune those ideas and apply them to your own.

And that's the heart of the matter: learning to think critically about your own work. While writing a story is a creative process, revising it is analytical, and requires the ability to distance yourself from your intimate knowledge of your intentions for the story. Regularly critiquing the works of others is the best training for this.

That's not the only benefit, of course. Workshops also provide:

➤ A venue for experimenting with new styles and ideas

➤ A source of information about new markets

➤ Deadlines to keep you writing regularly, even before your fiction starts selling

➤ Camaraderie and support during dry spells

➤ A pool of potential partners for collaborative projects

Workshopping for Complete Idiots

While there's no perfect way to improve your writing through a group of peers, we've found some ways that have worked for us (and others we know). We've also tried some things that definitely *don't* work for us. Here are some of our do's and don'ts; you can find out for yourself which ones are true for you, too.

A Jury of Your Peers

We belong to the Cecil Street Irregulars, a science fiction writer's workshop started in 1987 by legendary author/editor Judith Merril. Judy had been doing time as writer-in-residence for The Spaced Out Library, the science fiction reference library she founded in 1970.

"As You Know, Bob..."

Writer-in-residence programs are run at libraries, colleges, Web sites, and community centers around the world. A writer-in-residence is usually a well-known local novelist or non-fiction author who receives a stipend for working with new writers on developing their craft. Finding a writer-in-residence is a matter of phoning your local schools and libraries, or consulting a directory of writing Web sites (see Appendix D, "Online Resources"). A writer-in-residence can be a wonderful resource for locating other writers in your area, as well as getting good, professional feedback on your work.

If any one factor has contributed to the longevity and success of the Cecil Street Irregulars over the years, it was that we started off as peers. There were no superstars in the group, nor were there writers who were holding the rest back. Why was this important? Because it meant that when you submitted a story to the workshop, you knew that the feedback that you'd get would come from writers who were at least as good as you.

The flip side of that is critiquing others' works. Critiquing the work of writers who are significantly junior to you is a dull, mechanical exercise, focused on things like grammar, spelling, and the basics of story structure. At the same time, trying to dissect the work of someone far more senior can be nearly impossible, since their talent may mask the problems with their stories.

When you critique a peer's work, you engage critical faculties that have direct applications in your own work. You stretch your analytic abilities to see the problems and solutions in the work, and develop skills that will come into play the next time you plan or revise a story of your own.

Constructive Criticism

Constructive criticism is the next most important aspect of successful workshopping. The critiques that you give and receive should identify the problems with the story. No matter how important it is to hear about the things that worked in your story, your real improvement will come when you hear about the problems. While as a writer you may already have a good idea what the problem is with your story, a good critiquer will offer a solution. And as you critique others work, try to find not just problems, but how to fix them.

Infodump

It's only courteous to consider all the advice offered by your workshop-mates. However, nowhere is it written that you have to *take* all that advice. Remember, it's your story, and you have the final say.

For example, a constructive critiquer might …

➤ Point out that there are more characters in the story than the plot can support, and go on to suggest which characters can be cut without sacrificing the storyline.

➤ Tell you that the story lags in the middle third, and go on to suggest a scene that can be cut or shortened to pick up the pace.

➤ Express dissatisfaction with the way the story ends, and suggest a way of bringing things to a more satisfying resolution.

There's a fine line between offering suggestions and rewriting someone else's story. Different workshops have different policies on how far suggestions can go.

How a Workshop Works

Here are some guidelines for healthy workshopping:

➤ In advance of the workshop, one or more of the writers distribute a manuscript in submission format (see Chapter 12, "Mechanics").

➤ Distribution of manuscripts is done in an agreed-upon fashion: Manuscripts may be mailed, e-mailed, physically handed out, or left at a library or similar location.

➤ Writers who are passing out manuscripts may discuss what sort of criticism they're looking for.

➤ Writers who are passing out manuscripts *don't* talk about what they were attempting to accomplish with the story—that's the story's job.

➤ The group agrees on a date to critique each story. Some workshops will do more than one story per session, others will restrict critiques to one per session.

➤ Group members read the piece at least twice, annotating the manuscript and adding written notes, along with their names.

➤ At the next session, each writer delivers his or her critique within an agreed-upon time limit.

➤ Critiques should focus on structure and story, not on grammar and spelling (but mark grammar and spelling fixes in the manuscript).

➤ The writer may not speak during the critiquing, unless a critiquer asks him or her a direct question.

➤ Direct questions to the writers should be for clarification regarding typos and such, not about the story itself. This portion of the workshop is about hearing critiques, not debating them. The debate comes later.

➤ Each critiquer speaks in turn, without interruption.

➤ After the critiques, the writer has the opportunity to deliver an uninterrupted rebuttal.

Infodump

The most successful workshops meet on a regular, scheduled basis. The schedule might be once per year or once per week, but everyone in the group knows when and how often they can expect to get together. This gives the group's writers deadlines to work toward.

➤ After the rebuttal, there is a free-for-all discussion of the story.

➤ When the session is done, all copies of the manuscript are returned to the writer.

➤ Workshops should have at least 4 members, and not many more than 15. Larger groups take too long to work through a critiquing session, while smaller groups lack the people to really deliver a variety of opinions.

These rules are mostly simple courtesy, but it's important that everyone in the workshop agrees to them in advance and abides by them while at the workshop.

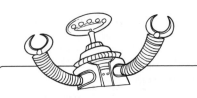

Danger, Danger!

Beware of workshops that allow writers to submit unfinished stories. Critiques of unfinished stories can't really address problems with structure or characterization—the two most important areas of a critique— because you can't know which people and plot elements are crucial to the story until you know how it ends.

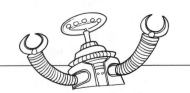

Danger, Danger!

Peer workshops are not-for-profit concerns. At most, the costs associated with peer workshopping should amount to taking up a collection to cover the subsidized rental of a room at a library or community center. Each writer covers his or her own transport and photocopying costs. Peer workshops that charge "fees" are almost certainly scams.

It's crucial to remember that the writer doesn't speak until the critiquing is done. A workshop's responses are supposed to simulate the responses of an editor who is reading the story without the benefit of auctorial commentary.

Workshops need to agree on a method for reviewing longer works, like novels. Generally, it's useful to distribute novels in chunks, along with an outline.

All workshops go through dry spells when their members are too busy or uninspired to produce work. One way to keep a workshop going during these periods is to issue a mutually agreeable challenge. Often, these challenges are inspired by a new theme anthology or theme issue of a magazine, and ask the writers to produce a story for that market by the next session. In the Cecil Street Irregulars, challenges have resulted in several sales.

It's Your Workshop

All right, you're sold. You want to join a workshop. Now what?

Finding a local workshop is pretty straightforward: Just check all the places where writers congregate (libraries, community centers, colleges or universities, bookshops) for notices advertising workshop vacancies. Ask the other writers you know as well as English teachers and writers-in-residence for recommendations.

Generally, a workshop will expect you to "audition"— that is, to send them a story for critical evaluation. The workshop will privately meet to discuss your story, then either invite you to attend a session or drop you a polite note thanking you for your interest but letting you know that you're not a good fit for them.

Once you're sitting in on a workshop, it's time for you to audition *them:* Do they have anything to offer you? Over your entire participation with a workshop, you should be on guard for the classic pitfalls of workshopping.

Pitfall	Explanation
Writing Avoidance	This is the most dangerous of all workshop pitfalls. Going to a workshop and hanging out with other writers can *feel* like writing, even when no writing is being done. Workshops whose members aren't writing should be, well, avoided.
Never-Ending Critiques	A sign of an immature workshop is never-ending critiques. Solid, well-established workshops have critiquers who know how to stick to the point and deliver their critiques in a few minutes. Workshops that haven't progressed to this point should have time limits for critiques.
Personality Cults	This is a by-product of the notoriously fragile writerly ego. When a workshop forms around a single individual who calls all the shots and sets the whole tone for the workshop, alarm bells should go off. A workshop is about diversity of opinion, not receiving wisdom from on-high.
One-Sided Takers	Workshops are about give-and-take. A workshop that allows participation from writers who don't submit their own work is best avoided—members have to earn the right to critique your stories by allowing their stuff to be critiqued.
Uneven Levels	A workshop where the writers are all at different levels is not the place you want to be. The advanced writers are bored by the less-advanced work, while the neophytes are daunted by the pros. Workshops are for peers.
Peanut Galleries	Every word of every critique is potentially precious. Workshops that allow "cross-talk" during critiques, especially humorous remarks, risk interrupting a suggestion that makes the difference between a good story and an award-winner.
Been There, Done That	Sometimes, it's useful to put a story through a workshop again, after it's been rewritten. But stay away from workshops that are willing to look at the same manuscripts again and again: This is really a subtle form of writing avoidance, one that allows writers to concentrate on old business rather than develop their skills with new stories.
Workshopping to Win	"Revenge critiques" that focus on rewarding authors who've said nice things about your work and punishing those who had harsh criticism. Needless to say, this defeats the whole purpose of workshopping.

Infodump

If you can't find a workshop, start one! If you have friends who are writing at the same level as you, you're halfway there: Just find a place to meet (libraries are a good bet) and pick a schedule. Attracting and auditioning members is as easy as putting up notices on campus, at libraries, and online. Make sure the whole group knows the rules of workshopping, and get going!

If there are no workshops in your locale, you might consider joining an Internet-based workshop. These are very similar to traditional workshops, but without oral critiques. Appendix D gives you pointers to some Internet-based workshops. You might also have good luck by posting a message to the Usenet newsgroup rec.arts.sf.written.

Other Kinds of Workshops

Peer workshopping is one way of improving your writing. Another is to attend classroom-style workshops. No workshop has been more influential in SF than Clarion.

Founded in 1968 by Robin Scott Wilson, Clarion is a six-week workshop held annually at Michigan State University. Its alumni include such genre greats as Dan Simmons, Bruce Sterling, James Patrick Kelly, Octavia Butler, Martha Soukup, and Kim Stanley Robinson.

The faculty are equally impressive: For 27 years, Kate Wilhelm and Damon Knight anchored the faculty team, teaching alongside of the likes of Nancy Kress, Fritz Leiber, Harlan Ellison, Judith Merril, Joe Haldeman, Tim Powers, and Thomas Disch.

Class sizes are between 17 and 20. Students range from precocious teenagers to senior citizens, and are all promising to begin with. Over the six-week writers' boot camp, each student is expected to write around six stories and critique hundreds more. Intensive one-on-one sessions with instructors are mixed with marathon group sessions and long nights of pounding the keyboard.

Even with the many scholarship programs available, Clarion is expensive—nearly $2,000 including dormitory fees—and a six-week leave of absence from your job may be a tough trick to manage. As a result, writers who attend Clarion are committed and motivated. Attendees often undergo major changes in their lifestyles on return from Clarion: quitting their jobs, divorcing their spouses, changing cities. It's common for people to find lifelong friends among their Clarion classmates.

Cory attended Clarion in 1992, with classmates like Becky Maines, Dale Bailey, Felicity Savage, and Jeff Vandermeer. He is still in close contact with many of his classmates. Every summer, a group of Clarion alumni stage a mini-Clarion in a different city, a week-long intensive writing and critiquing session.

A sister program, Clarion West, is run on nearly identical principles in Seattle every summer. While there is some friendly rivalry between the two programs, no one seriously argues that there are any real differences in quality. Students usually choose which Clarion they attend based on their geo-graphical proximity and their interest in a given year's lineup of instructors.

More information about Clarion and Clarion West can be found online:

➤ Clarion: www.msu.edu/clarion

➤ Clarion West: www.sff.net/clarionwest/

Clarion may be the oldest science fiction work-shop of its kind, but it is by no means the only one. Viable Paradise, in Martha's Vineyard, Massachusetts, is a one-week intensive teaching workshop, with a very high teacher-to-student ratio. While Clarion is an intense and exhausting experience, Viable Paradise's stated goal is to "teach students to think like writers." Find more information on Viable Paradise at www.sff.net/paradise/.

In a similar vein is the Milford Workshop in Torquay, England. Milford differs from Clarion and Viable Paradise in two respects: It is a peer workshop (there are no instructors); and it is a critiquing-only workshop (writers aren't expected to write while there). For more info on Milford, check out www.jeapes.ndirect.co.uk/milford/.

Infodump

While Clarion has an impressive track record, the majority of suc-cessful writers have never—and will never—attend. Obviously, Clarion is not the only way to learn to write and publish. There are people who are not tem-peramentally suited to work-shopping in general and Clarion in particular. You may be one of them, and that's fine.

The Least You Need to Know

➤ Workshops fill the gap between feedback from your mom and selling to an editor.

➤ Workshops are juries of your peers and involve both critical feedback to and from other workshop members.

➤ Workshops must follow an agreed-upon protocol to work effectively.

➤ A bad workshop is worse than no workshop, and some people just aren't suited for workshopping at all.

➤ You can find a workshop in your area by checking libraries, community cen-ters, colleges or universities, and bookshops; or start your own.

➤ Clarion-style workshops are grueling but effective; however, they're not for everybody.

Part 2

Secrets of the Sci-Fi Masters

You think your writing is great, until you pick up a novel by a classic SF master and read it. How did he come up with all that stuff? You despair that you'll never be able to do that.

Despair not! In this part we'll reveal a number of tools and tricks you can use to spark your own creativity, find innovative story ideas, and build unique and engaging worlds and characters.

You can learn to write original and engaging SF. Here's how.

Chapter 6

Where Do You Get Your Ideas?

In This Chapter

➤ Origins of a story

➤ Creative exercises that work

➤ Building your own idea factory

➤ Books to write with

Every SF writer wants the reader to finish reading his or her story and say, "Wow!" This "sense of wonder" is a central part of the genre, and any story that evokes it will be successful.

Some writers are so adept at pulling new wonders from their hats that it's downright intimidating. Could you ever do that? Or do they just naturally have an imagination way beyond yours?

Writers, like athletes, have to train. Writers train their imaginations. Nobody assumes that bodybuilders were born with big muscles; they worked to create them.

Story Sparks

The average SF writer walks around with a head full of half-finished (and often half-baked) ideas. Anything might generate a story idea—the news, a chance conversation, something he read. Such ideas take the form of little snippets, like "What if you could use nanotechnology to reshape someone's face at will, thus making him into a real-life doppelganger?" Or, "Maybe we could build giant balloon habitats in the upper

Infodump

Having an idea for a story is all fine and good, but by definition, a spark doesn't yet go anywhere. It's not a complete idea. But sparks are valuable, and you should encourage yourself to come up with them.

Infodump

Daydreaming is one of the best ways to generate sparks. Most of us had this talent quashed in school, which is a tragedy, because it's the basic tool you'll use as a SF writer. Cherish your daydreaming time; even the most random notion or imagined place can become the basis of a story.

atmosphere of Uranus." We refer to such half-finished ideas as "sparks." They aren't complete enough to become the basis of a story. If we're interested in a particular area (say, nanotechnology), then we tend to accumulate sparks in that area. Sparks can be anything: ideas for gadgets, visions of alien places, bits of dialog that don't lead anywhere. Some writers jot them down in an idea notebook. Most just let them ferment in memory.

The writer with a lot of sparks and no story usually thinks of himself as "blocked"—feeling the urge to write, but having no subject to write about. The sense of frustration this engenders is extremely valuable; it sets the subconscious mind in motion to try to come up with a storyline.

Stories happen when these sparks come together in new combinations. Suddenly everything—character, setting, plot, and idea—just fits into place. It's a frustratingly random occurrence for most authors, but there's a lot you can do to encourage the process, as we'll see.

The Spark Supercollider

Most working fiction writers can recount an experience in which they had several seemingly unrelated ideas suddenly combine into a single, perfectly complete story. It happens like magic, and most authors would like it to happen more often.

It's very simple, though, when you think about it. Just as you can't have a dramatic conflict without two or more entities clashing (even if it's "you" vs. "yourself"), you can't make a SF story with just one idea.

Karl had two completely unrelated ideas floating around his brain for years. The first concerned an alien "strongbox" that has been placed in close orbit around a "burster" neutron star. The story would be about people going in to retrieve the strongbox. Very dramatic; it seemed like a no-brainer to write this story.

Try as he might, he was unable to get the story off the ground. At the same time, however, he'd been daydreaming about the idea of temporarily downloading one's personality into a robot that goes out and has experiences, then comes back and uploads them again. One day these two seemingly unrelated ideas combined unexpectedly, and the novella "The Engine of Recall" was born. (It was subsequently published in the winter 1997 issue of *Aboriginal SF*.)

Now here's why SF is an art and not a science. Story ideas don't combine in a predictable fashion. The very nature of innovative thinking is that ideas complete one another in an unexpected way. This would seem to be discouraging; maybe the good writers out there have some talent or genius that lets them recognize these good combinations. Maybe you don't.

Well, look at it this way. If you throw a die once, your odds of coming up with a six are one in six. If you throw it 10 times, you'll probably get a six at least once. If you throw it a hundred times, you'll almost surely get a bunch of sixes.

A working SF writer spends more time generating sparks, combining them, trying to write stories, and discarding their failures and trying again. It's that simple.

Playing with Ideas

SF writers love to play "what if." We do it all the time. "What if the earth really was hollow?" Or "What if part of future marriage ceremonies was for the bride and groom to exchange a *sense,* so that she could feel what he felt with his right hand, and vice versa?" This is all idle speculation, of course, but idle speculation is valuable in generating stories.

The "supercollider" that sparks the story is usually the subconscious. Our subconscious minds are always working, and often if we just let something percolate there long enough, a story will pop up on its own.

It's quite possible to throw ideas together consciously, however. One creative exercise that can help bring story ideas out is called mapping. This exercise involves a pen and a sheet of blank, unlined paper. In mapping, you jot down a short description of an idea in the middle of the paper, and circle it. Then you start writing down variations on the idea, or questions about it, and join these descriptions to the central idea with lines or arrows. You end up with something that looks a bit like a spiderweb made of circled sentences. Do this quickly; it's important not to think too much about what you're doing. If you really get into it, you may end up with a page covered in crazy doodles, scratched-out lines, arrows crossing arrows, and question marks.

Danger, Danger!

Mapping is just one example of a creativity exercise. There are many books on creativity on the market, notably Edward de Bono's *Lateral Thinking: Creativity Step by Step.* The key to using such books is to use their techniques sparingly. It's possible to overregiment your creative exercises, and that's bad for creativity.

If it works, you'll also end up with one little sentence or paragraph somewhere on the page that you've circled five times and under which you've written *that's it!*

Mapping is a great way to rid yourself of stale preconceptions. For instance, by looking at alternative ways a story could begin or end, you can often solve plot problems.

Infodump

Another way to play with plotting ideas is to take a favorite book or movie and write down in point form the events of the opening chapter/scenes. Then write another version that does the same as the original. For instance, write in point form an alternate opening to *Star Wars* that still gets Luke, Obi-wan, Han, and the droids together.

There are many other exercises you can use to jog your creativity. Many writers engage in this sort of creative thinking without knowing it. For working SF writers, tossing ideas around is habitual; they will rarely resort to using pen-and-paper tricks like mapping, but that's because they do the same thing in their heads.

If you don't habitually play with ideas, do it deliberately for a while. Eventually, the habit will sink into your subconscious, and coming up with ideas will seem easier and easier.

The Truth About Inspiration

There's no doubt that inspiration does strike. We've written and published stories from the most unlikely sources, including one tale that sprang forth full-blown in a dream. It's wonderful to feel inspired, and your most productive periods will almost certainly be those times when the Muse whispers in your ear.

But as we pointed out in Chapter 2, "First Steps on the Road," there's a problem with inspiration: It's not predictable. Worse, inspiration does not automatically equal quality. As with any complicated problem that you gnaw on half-consciously, storytelling issues may suddenly snap into sharp relief. It's that essential "A ha!" moment that we all love. But that moment can't happen until your mind, both conscious and subconscious, has worked the problem over thoroughly. Ninety percent of what comes out of that "A ha!" moment is stuff that you've done consciously or semiconsciously over a period of days, weeks, or months. The mysterious other 10 percent gets all the press, but "A ha!" really only means that the long process of working through something has been finished. Your inspiration didn't come from nowhere. You worked to attain it.

The other thing to remember about inspiration is that it isn't necessarily good. Writing from inspiration is not the same as writing well. In order to write well, you need to go back and scrutinize your work dispassionately, both the mundane stuff and the stuff you did while inspired. Beginning writers tend to enshrine their inspired passages, refusing to edit them. Then, when the story isn't working right, they try to fix it around the inspired bits. These sacred passages may be the very heart of the problem; at the very least, they may be in the way of a sound global edit.

Beware of your inspired work. Embrace it when it comes, but afterward treat these pieces as you do any other. Be prepared to change them or cut them.

From Idea to Outline

An idea is not a story. It's the *interaction* of idea and character that generates a SF story. In other words, your ideas have to have an effect on the characters. You have no other way of getting the reader to care, no matter how earth-shattering your insights might be.

As an extreme example, say you've had the tremendous insight that subatomic particles don't actually move—it's the space in between them that expands and contracts, like rubber bands. Well, so what? How will knowing that change your down-and-out hero's fortunes or outlook?

The key things a good SF idea can do are …

➤ Threaten your characters, possibly through the actions of a villain

➤ Be a means of solving your characters' problems

➤ Provide the catalyst for a change in your character that resolves the story

➤ Provide a setting or situation that throws new light on the character or on society

> **"As You Know, Bob …"**
>
> In *really* bad SF, the characters are only there to talk about the ideas that are the real heroes of the story. When you have two enthusiastic engineers discussing relativity as they spiral to certain doom in the heart of a black hole, you've got the kind of story that gives SF a bad name.

In every case, the idea has to directly affect the characters' lives. If it has no such effect, it should not be in the story.

Writers often create stories that they think are SF, but which are really just Westerns, romances, mysteries, or some other genre with SF set-dressing. In the 1981 Sean Connery movie *Outland,* Connery plays a frontier-town sheriff who dispenses his own brand of justice. It just so happens that the frontier town is set on a distant moon. Big deal. It's still just a Western.

The sci-fi setting of *Outland* has no effect on the characters or situation. Take the setting away and the story would be exactly the same. So, why pretend it's SF at all, except as a gimmick to try to boost sales? Readers of SF can always see through cheap tricks like this. Beware of taking the ordinary and putting it in costume. It'll still be ordinary.

Does *Star Wars* fall into this category? No, because its characters are fully engaged with the politics and mysticism of their universe. The story itself is classic good vs. evil and could have been set anywhere. But the characters are very much a part of the universe they inhabit.

If your ideas directly affect the characters, and either threaten them, support them, or decide the way they develop as humans (or nonhumans), then you've got the makings of a story.

Innovation in SF

Make no mistake: The most important part of a SF story is the story itself, not whatever innovative ideas you may have put into it. If the story is uninteresting, it won't matter if your ideas are dazzling. On the other hand, you can make hackneyed ideas sing if they engage your characters in an exciting way.

That said, SF relies more on conceptual innovation than any other branch of literature. New SF ideas usually come from science or technology, but they can also come from philosophy, history, theology, or indeed any intellectual endeavor.

"As You Know, Bob ..."

Science fiction is not stylistically innovative. In fact, it's downright conservative. This isn't necessarily a failing; it's because you can only change so many aspects of a story before you lose the reader. If the reader already has to deal with strange alien practices and environments, burdening him with new stylistic tropes will just add to the confusion. Hence, most SF relies on "transparent prose" to convey its new ideas.

SF writers pay a bit more attention to scientific advances than most people. By the time a new theory or discovery makes it to the papers or evening news, the SF crowd has probably been chewing on it for six months. If a SF writer wants to be topical, it pays to stay about a year ahead of the popular press in one's thinking.

SF writers are frequently so far ahead of the curve that you wouldn't find their ideas in any scientific journal. Or they take an old idea and put a new spin on it, so you think, "Why didn't I think of that?" It can be a mysterious ability, viewed from outside.

The truth is, SF writers are skeptics. They don't believe anything they're told, and it is this skepticism that leads to innovative thinking. A key talent for this business is the ability to immerse oneself completely in an area of thinking—whether it be physics, paleontology, or the history of the Romanov dynasty—*while thinking about how things could be otherwise.*

More exactly, a SF writer reading up on any given subject is constantly looking for dramatic possibilities. The writer may plow through the entire Principia Mathematica and strive to comprehend it all ... or not. The hunt is for anything that will generate story sparks. The SF writer neither believes nor disbelieves any of those new ideas; they're all just grist for the mill.

Know Thy Subject

The more you know about a topic, the more ideas you'll be able to come up with. You can certainly do some *hand-waving* when you go to create the planet on which your characters live, for instance. You could say, "The planet Valvorus had two moons, both large and close. The nights were serene on Valvorus, the oceans calm."

Not only is this description of Valvorus fairly bland, it's also impossible. If the planet Valvorus has two large, close moons, the following description would be more accurate:

> The jagged volcanic peaks of Valvorus reared out of an ocean beset with kilometer-high tides. A few human settlements huddled on the edges of the hundred-kilometer-wide, rubble-strewn tidal flats. Every 12 hours, tidal waves accompanied by howling winds tore off the ocean, hurling debris inland, including the much-feared land sharks, which would grab anyone foolish enough to be outside, then retreat at a gallop into the churning foam. Overhead, the planet's two giant, close moons watched over the spectacle like Olympian gods.

Well, okay, the prose here is a bit purple. The point is that the more the writer knows about planetology, the more he'll know about the effect that moons have on a planet. A simple decision to give the planet two large moons would be cosmetic for a writer who didn't know much about tidal forces. For the writer who does, the simple addition of those moons sparks numerous new ideas based on how the planet reacts to their tides.

Factoid

Hand-waving is when you or your characters spout some plausible-sounding explanation for something, then quickly move on to another topic before the reader has time to think about it. This happens in *Star Trek* all the time; for instance, whenever the writers want the crew to become trapped on a planet's surface. "Ach, Captain! We can't get a transporter lock on them because of the Zondervan Rays from the Barglefurst deposits at the pole!"

An Idea Library

You can't create in a vacuum. Most writers are voracious readers. As a SF writer, you've probably got fairly idiosyncratic reading habits. We know SF writers who love to read trade magazines of the arms industry; others enjoy flipping through the daunting pages of *Physics Review Letters*.

It pays to build up a library of interesting and unusual books. The more perspectives you have available to you the better; if you're writing fantasy, it would be useful to have access to copies of *How to Make and Use Talismans,* by Israel Regardie, and *The Night Battles,* by Carlo Ginzburg, for instance. Like a magician's bag of tricks, your library of unusual and mind-expanding books can help you come up with wonderful ideas for your fiction.

A Mind-Expanding Reading List

This is a random selection of books we've found very effective at sparking new ideas. It is far from a definitive list, and we include it more as an example of an "idea library." You may want to compile your own idea library, or you might discover that you've had one all along. Your own library can be expected to be just as diverse. (As an exercise, you might try to figure out which five of the following were picked by Cory, and which were picked by Karl.)

➤ *Giordano Bruno and the Hermetic Tradition,* by Frances Yates (University of Chicago Press, 1991). If you're even considering writing fantasy in which magic plays a part, you should read this book.

➤ *The Acme Novelty Library* (Fantagraphics Press, 1993–1999). Gadgets, gadgets, gadgets!

➤ *The Amok Fifth Dispatch,* by Stuart Swezey, ed. (Amok Press, 1999). An essential guide to the weird, this tome contains reviews and listings of every wildly non-mainstream idea, cult, or publication going.

➤ *101 Unuseless Japanese Inventions,* by Kenji Kawakami, ed. (HarperCollins, 1995). A trip down the back alleys and dead ends of human invention.

➤ *The Garden of Ediacara,* by Mark A. S. McMenamin (Columbia University Press, 1998). Flawed, but still fascinating look at the strange multicellular life forms that preceded plants and animals on Earth.

➤ *Learned Pigs and Fireproof Women,* by Ricky Jay (Farrar, Straus & Giroux, 1998). A study of the weird and wonderful world of sideshows and circuses. About as alien a human culture as you can get.

➤ *Computers as Theatre,* by Brenda Laurel (Addison Wesley, 1991). A glimpse, perhaps, at the future of human-computer interaction.

➤ *A Story as Sharp as a Knife,* by Robert Bringhurst (Douglas and McIntyre, 1999). The complete collected literary works of a forgotten people: the Haida. This book is an insight into the deep history of storytelling.

➤ *Faster: The Acceleration of Just About Everything,* by James Gleick (Pantheon, 1999). A good grounding in the world view of cyberpunk-speed, technology, and disposability in the twenty-first century.

➤ *The Starflight Handbook,* by Eugene F. Mallove and Gregory L. Matloff (John Wiley & Sons, 1989).

The Least You Need to Know

➤ Creativity isn't something mysterious that you either have or don't. It can be learned.

➤ The dazzling ideas of the SF masters are the result of hard work. You can learn how to work the way they do.

➤ Inspiration isn't all it's cracked up to be. Your own mind and the tools of your craft will provide you with results as good as those the Muses may throw your way.

➤ There are tried-and-true ways of jogging the creative side of the brain. Professional SF writers use these techniques habitually.

➤ Much of the innovation in SF comes from people exploring alternatives to the accepted wisdom of the times. Explore alternative sciences, philosophies, and art forms.

➤ The more you write, the more you'll exercise your creative muscles. Don't wait for inspiration: Make it!

Chapter 7

The Writing Project

In This Chapter

➤ The impossible task of finding time to write

➤ Your valued daydreaming time

➤ Choosing your form: short story or novel?

➤ Outlining and draft work

➤ Revision (with training wheels)

➤ The shape of a writing project

Writing involves daydreaming, outlining, draft work, editing and revision, polishing, and strategic thinking about markets. While it's important that you master each of these activities, they do represent different ways of thinking. You should organize your writing time so that each activity has its own period.

For instance, rather than re-reading what you've just written as you draft a story, consider ignoring typos and logical errors while you draft. Later, print the story, and give it a read over in bed. By separating the activities of drafting and editing, you give each a chance to develop its own pace and method.

Finding Time to Write Is Impossible

The most common complaint we hear from beginning writers is, "I'm too busy these days to write." This is a crock. We're *all* busy, working writers no less than anyone else. The fact is, the title of this section says it all. You can't *find* time to write. It's impossible. You have to *make* time.

Of course, making time to write is a lot harder if you think of writing as being a single activity. If you try to carve time out of your busy week to sit down at the word processor and do draft work, you'll find it very hard going. Most beginning writers believe that this one activity—sitting at the word processor—is all there is to writing. In fact, as we discussed in Chapter 2, "First Steps on the Road," writing consists of a number of different kinds of activities. Part of the problem we find with making time to write is that we try to cram all those different activities into that one block we've set aside for sitting at the word processor. Naturally, it doesn't work.

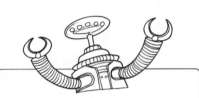

Danger, Danger!

Procrastination is the worst obstacle facing most writers. One of the best writers we know has had it so bad that he once resorted to cleaning the oven rather than sitting down to write!

What happens when you finally get that spare three or four hours on the weekend to write? You go to the word processor, sit down … and find that your mind's a blank.

Of course it is. You've committed yourself to a period of draft work without having first done the daydreaming, brainstorming, outlining, and perhaps editing of prior work that makes draft work possible.

You end up doing that work now, so at the end of the four hours, you haven't written a single word. You may have edited, outlined, and daydreamed, but you don't associate those activities with writing. So you think you've accomplished nothing.

And now here's the secret of making time to write: Each different writing activity demands a different kind of time.

You can write in the shower. You can write on the bus. You can write at the office, or in front of the TV. All you have to do is perform the appropriate kind of task in each of these time slots. If, when the weekend comes, you find four hours in which to do draft work, you could write half a chapter in that time, provided all the other preliminary work has been done in other time slots.

Daydreaming

We all daydream. Unfortunately, after having had our knuckles rapped for it in class, many of us feel guilty when we do it. Get over it! Daydreaming is one of your most important activities as a writer. Learn to be proud of those times when you sit slack-jawed, staring at a wall. If anyone asks you what you're doing, you can truthfully answer, "I'm working."

Your daydreaming time can happen anywhere. The trick is to be aware that you're doing it. Most of our daily fantasies go by half-consciously, and we forget them immediately. Learn to know that you're doing it, and commit to paper or file the products of your daydreaming.

Infodump

Keep an idea diary. If you work at a computer all day, leave a small text-editor file or mail message open, and when ideas come to you, jot them in this. Then save the file or mail the message to yourself at the end of the day. The important thing is to recognize when your daydreams spark interesting ideas. Then find some way of ensuring that you remember those ideas. Don't try to schedule this creativity. Just be ready to catch the moment when it happens on its own.

Outlining

In Chapter 6, "Where Do You Get Your Ideas?" we looked at a number of ways to smash ideas together and look through the debris for new stories. Once the story idea is there, you should probably write it out for yourself as an outline.

If you're writing a novel, you're going to need an outline when you go to sell it. Editors appreciate having a detailed (but not lengthy) summary of the book's storyline to refer to as they read the work. (This should typically be only a few pages in length—short and to the point.) The best way to produce this outline is to progressively modify your working version. Flesh out the outline as you go, and when you've finished the novel you'll also be ready to format it for an editor.

Not all writers work from outlines. We advocate it because writing is, in part, a dialog between you and the paper. The act of writing down your ideas may force you to clarify them. Seeing the sequence of scenes for your story in black and white often inspires a useful re-evaluation of the story. (Of course, if you're totally inspired and know exactly what you're going to write, then go for it. Outlining will probably just slow you down in this case.)

Infodump

Outlining is a nice activity for after supper, when you've got your feet up and maybe the TV on. Sit down with a sheet of paper and start writing a point-form list of the major events in your story. Trying to think of what happens next when you're in the middle of writing a scene is a lot harder. If you've got a sheet of paper tacked on the wall over the computer showing the flow of events, writing the draft will be that much easier.

There's nothing complex or mysterious about an outline. It's just a list. You can fill in the points in greater detail as you go, but the important thing is to start with the skeleton of the story. You can flesh it out later if it helps you during draft work.

Different in Kind: Short Story and Novel Projects

A lot of writers try their first novel after a few years of success at selling short stories. Some of the very best, top-rated short story artists find themselves unable to make the transition to the long form. Often it's a matter of temperament: Some of us are just happier in the short form. Sometimes, though, a writer will take her daily schedule for crafting short work, developed and perfected over many years, and try to write the novel using it. This won't work.

Short stories lend themselves to brief, frenzied bursts of intense writing. Writing a short story usually involves a lot of caffeine. In terms of time, you can write a short story in a single weekend—sometimes in a single sitting. The fuel for a short story can be pure enthusiasm.

It would be suicidal to try to apply this high-energy, time-intensive approach to writing a novel. (This is not to say it can't be done: the first draft of Karl's first novel, *The Claus Effect,* was co-authored with David Nickle in three days.) Novels typically take a year or more to evolve. Enthusiasm alone won't cut it for work like this. Neither, unfortunately, will caffeine.

If writing a short story is like riding a roller coaster, writing a novel is more like doing the dishes: something you do day in, day out, without much thought to whether the whole process will ever end. For this reason, managing your time is much more important for novel writing than short stories.

"As You Know, Bob ..."

One way to write a novel is to commit to producing one page a day, every day. Karl did this with his first (unpublished) work. That being in the days before word processors, he did it on a typewriter. He would type one page, and leave off at the bottom even if he was in the middle of a sentence. The next day, he would insert a new sheet, finish the sentence, and continue. This is an extreme case of a good general point: Break big projects down into small manageable chunks. Oh, and that first novel? It took two years to complete two drafts, and oddly enough, when it was done it was exactly 365 manuscript pages long. Coincidence, of course.

Harnessing the Draft Horse

We hope that by this point you're beginning to think of writing time as more than just the time you spend at the word processor. That time is important too, of course. If you've been doing your daydreaming and outlining in other available time, you'll find a great load off your mind when you sit down to do draft work. In mid-project, you'll find that having done editing during other periods also gives you a tremendous boost at draft time. This is because there's nothing worse than the "blank page" phenomenon when you sit down to write. Facing that blank page (or screen) utterly clueless as to what you're going to do next is the quickest way to writer's block and depression. If you sat up in bed last night going through a printout of your last scene, then the blank page is not going to be a problem. If you're uninspired, you can start by entering the edits you made last night. As you work, ideas will almost surely start to flow.

This is a general principle: Anything else you do (editing, outlining, polishing, etc.) serves as great prep work for a draft session. These other activities keep you in touch with the story and help get your juices flowing.

Limit Interruptions

Once you're working on the draft, you are in "un-interruptible" time. Unplug the phone. Close the door. If it helps, put on music to tune out household distractions. And don't look at the clock.

When Karl's mother was working on her second romance novel, she found the only place she could work was the bathroom. It was the only room in the house where the kids knew they couldn't interrupt her.

Infodump

Keep a writing journal. This is a record of when you write (including when you've edited, daydreamed, outlined, etc.) including notes about what prevented you or interrupted you, what helped, and so on. Don't use the journal to try to plan ahead. It's a tool for finding patterns in your natural schedule. If after a while you find that you always have a productive day after an evening spent editing the manuscript in front of the TV, then you can start planning. The important thing initially is to gather the information.

No Editing

As you've probably guessed, draft time is also not the time to edit. Editing while writing new material opens you to the "Lot's wife" phenomenon: Looking back can turn you to stone. (Or a pillar of salt, in her case.) You should have other time periods available for things like editing and planning. Rely on that time, and forget everything except the scene at hand when you're doing the draft.

Am I Finished Yet?

Write until you have a feeling of accomplishment, but not until you feel you are finished with what you're working on (unless you've actually typed "THE END"). Why? Well, simply because if you end the draft session completely satisfied, it'll be harder to get yourself started next time. If you end the session itching to continue, you'll have momentum that will carry forward. You'll be busting to finish that scene for the next few days, so you're going to be more likely to make time for another draft session. Then, when you sit down again, you'll just dive right into the work.

It sounds like trickery. Maybe it is, but it works.

Working until you actually finish also means you're more inclined to keep working after you get tired. You may finish the scene, but the end will probably be uninspired. You're likely to come back later and throw out the end and do it again, so it's pointless to push to finish it the first time.

Setting the Goals

Most importantly, set realistic goals for yourself. Writing a page a day every day is easier than writing seven pages every Saturday morning. In time you'll learn what your natural energy is, and how much you can expect from yourself. Until you know, set your expectations low.

"As You Know, Bob ..."

When to do draft work? Saturday mornings, Sunday afternoons, early weekday mornings, and lunch hours are the most common for working writers. You need time when you're fresh, unpressured, and haven't had your head filled with a thousand other details and chores. Regularity is better than amount when it comes to this time. Writing for half an hour every morning before leaving for your job works better than piling the whole week's writing into your Saturday. If you miss a morning you don't lose much work, but if that Saturday gets filled by some other activity, then you've lost the whole week's work.

On Second Thoughts: Revision

Finishing a story is a euphoric experience. After typing "the end," we have a tendency to run around the house waving our hands in the air. This self-reward is richly deserved, and you should revel in it.

Finishing a draft of a story or novel is just the beginning, unfortunately. There's an old truism in writing that says, "Writing is rewriting." Depressing, but accurate. Once you've got the basic story down, you'll probably need to go back and tweak it, at least a little.

Luckily, revision is a discrete process that you can plan and execute more easily than draft work. You can read the completed manuscript anywhere, and better still, you can get other people to read it and render their opinions. Copyediting can be done anytime—over lunch, while watching the news, and so on.

See if you can summarize what your story is about in one sentence. If you can do this, then read your manuscript critically, and cross out everything that doesn't pertain to that summary.

How Do I Know If I'm Done?

The euphoria of finishing a draft easily blinds us to its flaws. Luckily, there are solid techniques you can use to clear away the clouds and see what you've really done. We'll look at three of them here. Basically, here's how you can tell if you've produced a complete and polished story:

1. Through reading (your own and others' stories):

   ➤ Make sure you're familiar with the kind of literature you're trying to write. How does your story compare?

   ➤ Make sure you read outside your area. Broad familiarity gives you something to compare your work to.

   ➤ Keep up with what's current.

2. Through distance:

   ➤ Take a holiday. Work on something else for a while before coming back to revise your draft.

   ➤ Read the story aloud (or get someone else to).

   ➤ Read the story in printout form, not just on the screen.

3. Through others' reactions:

   ➤ Let people read the story and comment on it. Don't argue or be defensive; solicit suggestions.

   ➤ Submit the story to a writing workshop (see Chapter 5, "Writer's Workshops").

   ➤ Submit the story to an editor who you know will provide some feedback.

Know Your Weaknesses

In Chapter 2 you may have done the short exercise provided, in which you rated your skills in the various areas (draft work, characterization, editing, and so on). Now is the time to return to that exercise.

In what area of writing are you weakest? Let's say it's characterization. If you know this about yourself, you can return to your newly minted story knowing that you should be suspicious of the characters.

Here are some more simple techniques you can use to make revisions go more smoothly:

➤ As with every stage of the project, expect to spend more time getting started than doing the real work. This is normal.

➤ Check for "throat-clearing." This happens when your story really starts five or six pages in; the first few pages turn out to be unnecessary, and can be cut. (This is also known as a "fish-head.")

➤ If you can't bear to delete some wonderful but unnecessary prose, cut it and save it in a separate file. Maybe you'll be able to use it somewhere else some time.

The Phases of a Writing Project

Just as each kind of writing activity needs its own kind of time, each phase of the project needs a different kind of time. Beginnings are different from endings. One invaluable skill for the working writer is the ability to tell how to shift gears with each phase of the project.

Beginnings

While the beginnings of stories may happen fast, longer projects, such as novels, begin slower. In the first couple of chapters, you'll be getting acquainted with the characters and world, and finding your style. Hence, it will probably take you more time to write the beginning of a novel than later sections.

You may find you are stalling out in bigger projects. This can be a sign that you actually don't have enough material for the form you've chosen. Maybe it should have been a *novella* instead of a novel. If you stall, skip ahead. If things start to flow again, then it was just a glitch; you can go back and flesh out the problem spot later. After all, you're working from an outline, aren't you? You know what's supposed to happen next.

Take it slow, and enjoy this part of the story. Don't hurry to get into the meaty parts. If you rush, your beginning won't stand on its own, and it has to in order to pull the reader in.

Danger, Danger!

One rule of thumb about potential problems in the story: If you suspect there's a problem with something, there probably *is* one. Never assume readers will miss something; if there's a flaw, they'll find it. Far better for you to nip it in the bud. This means you need to be hypercritical about your own work. That's not fun, but the result will be that you'll be genuinely satisfied with your story when you're done revising it.

Factoid

A **novella** is a short novel; a fictional prose narrative that's longer and more complex than a short story.

The Scary Middles

Somewhere around the middle of the project, the whole thing will start to look unmanageable. This is particularly true of novels. Don't panic! This is normal.

If you find yourself panicking in the middle of a project, focus on anything that jogs you out of the ruts you're in. Write something else. Change your main character's name. Rethink the outline. Or, best of all, just go away and do something totally unrelated to writing for a while. Your subconscious needs to work during the middle of a story, so the best thing you can do is distract your conscious mind and let your subconscious get on with its work.

The most important conscious activity you can do in the middle of the project is to break it down into smaller chunks. Because of the tendency to try to keep everything in mind, you'll give less attention to each story element than it probably deserves. If you find you're hurrying through scenes in order to nail down the storyline, you're probably not paying attention to things like scene-setting, description, and those minutiae of character that make reading enjoyable.

This is the time to begin fleshing out your outline. Take it from its point-form origins to a 10-page storyline if you need to. Or you can try the tested and valuable technique of writing down scenes and scene fragments on 3 × 5 index cards, then taping them above your word processor. You can shift them around at will, looking for creative new plot patterns.

All these techniques amount to mastering *focus*. By focus we mean the ability to zoom out and look at the grand plan you're trying to execute; and then forget that, zoom in, and focus on describing a character's tunic properly in the particular scene you're doing. Focus becomes harder and harder to maintain in the middle of the project; but if you're aware of this and take it into account, you can sail right through the story without a problem.

The Finale

Never delay the end. This is the time when momentum is critical. Chances are, you'll be enthusiastic enough to want to finish as soon as you can anyway.

"As You Know, Bob ..."

Not everybody writes in sequence. Writers often skip ahead, or even leave writing the opening of a story or book until everything else is done. You'll have to experiment to find out what works for you, and under what circumstances.

Danger, Danger!

Exhaustion is the danger in the middle of a project. You've got so many plates spinning that the tendency is to try to pay attention to everything at once. The more complicated the story you're telling, the harder this is going to be. For this reason it's important for you to take mental (and physical) holidays in the middle of the project. Obsessing about it will kill your creativity.

It's a good idea, though, to make an extra effort to clear up time for writing the finale.

Sometimes the end you had in mind at the beginning turns out not to work when you reach it. If this is the case, you need to step back and ask yourself what the story is really about. It may have turned into something you didn't intend. If you're happy with it, this isn't a problem; but your outline may now be pointing in the wrong direction, and your mental image of the tale may not fit the reality. At times like this, it's perfectly possible to get stuck on the last page.

For instance, it may have happened that you have completed the action of the story without the main character having changed the way you intended. If this is the case, your problem probably lies earlier than the end itself—likely in the crucial turn of events of the climax. This is where the fate of your protagonist is decided, after all. If he takes a turn at this point that you didn't intend, your planned ending may no longer be appropriate.

Infodump

This is the time to throw out any rules you've been following. If the story doesn't have its own shape by now, it never will. If any part of a story is going to "write itself," it will be the ending—provided you've known all along where you're going.

It's also possible that your outline or plan for the story is wrong. When you come to the end, you may find that it's impossible for the characters to make the decisions or undergo the changes you'd planned for them. In this case you have two choices: Change the characters (which will probably require a complete rewrite) or let them do what's right for them and see where they lead you at the end. The second approach is better; often the characters will surprise you, and their ending will be superior to the one you originally had in mind.

The Least You Need to Know

➤ You can't find time to write; you have to make it.

➤ Each part of your writing project needs its own kind of time. Don't try to cram them all into "draft time."

➤ Daydreaming, outlining, and editing are activities you can do anywhere, anytime. It's a good idea to do one or all of them just before you do draft work, to get your creative juices flowing.

➤ The beginning, middle, and end of a writing project need different kinds of time. Be prepared to shift gears as you go, so that you keep your writing machine running smoothly.

Chapter 8

The Short Story

> ### In This Chapter
>
> ➤ How genre stories are different from "regular" ones
>
> ➤ The three parts of a short story
>
> ➤ The Seven-Point Plot and other writing techniques
>
> ➤ Rewriting as a necessary evil

The short story was once the most common form of narrative in America. In the heyday of the pulps, thousands of magazines published millions of stories of every variety. Today, the short story has fallen into disrepair. A handful of "slick" mainstream magazines publish a story a month; one or two prominent literary journals like *Granta* and a profusion of 'zine-level literary mags publish a little more, but that's it for the mainstream. Most major awards have at least one short-fiction category, and some have as many as three!

Short stories are the ideal venue for experimentation and growth. Writing a novel is an investment measured in weeks, months, or years; a short story can be written and polished in a few days. It's far less heartbreaking to give up on a short story than to stick a novel in a drawer.

We're Not in *The New Yorker* Anymore, Toto

While science fiction can be perceived as outside the mainstream literature or fiction market, it tends to follow certain traditional plotting conventions that are the descendants of adventure stories. SF strives to be exciting and fast-paced. Even though these stories may deliver a deeper message, that message is sugared with easy-to-grasp action sequences.

Infodump

Science fiction authors such as Kurt Vonnegut, Margaret Atwood, Lewis Carroll, and even Ray Bradbury successfully bridged the boundary between science fiction and mainstream fiction and literature. They would argue that many of these generalization might not be true.

Factoid

"Murdering your babies" is a workshopping term that is most often applied to short stories. Writers who give in to temptation and include fascinating but secondary elements in their stories risk detracting from the main action, and are told to "murder their babies" or "kill their darlings"—to cut those elements no matter how much they love them.

Mainstream stories usually put more emphasis on character growth and personal revelation. It's not unusual to read a mainstream story where the "action" consists of, say, a dinner party at which the narrator realizes that he's not happy, but neither is anyone else. Incautious readers might miss the point entirely and be left wondering why they just read 7,000 words about canapés.

There is another critical difference between genre stories and mainstream ones: Genre stories are *speculative*. Genre writers invent *worlds*—technologies, magic systems, alien races—that sit in the foreground of the story. Sometimes, especially in hard SF, the technologies *are* the story: The plot is constructed around revealing a really cool technology that the author has dreamed up.

Genre stories are built around a single idea, a single theme. They are one-trick ponies, written to be read in one or two sittings. Novels are three-ring circuses, with the space to meander down side roads and explore subplots. The hardest part of short-story writing is picking a single subject and sticking to it— *"murdering your babies"* where necessary—no matter how tempting it may be to explore ancillary ideas that occur to you while you're writing.

Beginnings, Middles, and Endings

In a genre short story—and in most other kinds of literature—there are three parts to the narrative, each with its own purpose: the beginning, the middle, and the end. These all work together to create a sense of rising tension in the reader that pulls them along through the story. These plot elements are like a locomotive, pulling a train that contains all the things the writer is trying to accomplish with his story: capturing an emotion, exploring a political idea, demonstrating a new technology.

The beginning of a story has to have a "hook"—that is, it has to capture the reader's interest. Good hooks are tricky to accomplish. They need to pique interest without confusing the reader. They need to create a sense of action, but that action can't be so hot that there's nowhere to go from there.

Here's a great hook from Bruce Sterling's "Taklamakan," originally published in the October/November 1998 issue of *Asimov's Science Fiction* magazine:

> A bone-dry frozen wind tore at the earth outside, its lethal howling cut to a muffled moan. Katrinko and Spider Pete were camped deep in a crevice in the rock, wrapped in furry darkness. Pete could hear Katrinko breathing, with a light rattle of chattering teeth. The neuter's yeasty armpits smelled like nutmeg.

In one short paragraph, Sterling establishes a cast of characters, a setting, danger, and enough weirdness to keep the reader going.

As we've seen, a hook should also work to set the scene for the story and introduce some of the key players. It should hint at the "theme" of the story—the reason that you've decided to write *this* story. Nailing the hook is one of the trickiest parts of a story.

The middle of the story serves to create a sense of escalating tension. Every page of your story needs to have a reason to turn to the next: some sense of danger, some risk, some mystery that grows closer to resolution.

There are many ways of creating rising tension, some of which are outlined in the next section, but there is no definitive technique. If you're working on a story and you find yourself stuck, try asking yourself where the tension in the scene comes from, and whether the stakes have been raised since the last scene. If the tension isn't rising from scene to scene, it's hard to keep up the action.

Finally, the ending is the payoff for all that tension. The stakes are as high as they can get, and the writer gives readers what they've been craving since page one: release. The bad guy is vanquished (or the hero dies), the quest is completed (or it fails), the new technology saves the day (or it fizzles miserably).

The climax doesn't have to tie up all the loose ends in a story. Usually, there's a short scene or two that follows the climax in which everyone catches their breath and the writer takes a moment to wrap up all the threads she's created in the story.

"As You Know, Bob ..."

You may think you've got your hook nailed, but sometimes what you think is your hook isn't. Cory is forever writing stories that have a great hook on page three, but that isn't apparent until the whole thing is finished. Often, Cory's rewrites consist of nothing more than cutting the first two pages. For him, the hook only comes once he's finished the rest of the story.

A Short-Story Cookbook

Lots of writers have favorite techniques for thinking about a story. These techniques are here to get you thinking about how *you* think about your own stories—they're not to be viewed as the final word in the creative process.

Why You Should(n't) Use a Recipe

Stories have structures: character development, risk, rising tension, climax. These structures go deep in our culture, informing the plotlines of everything from classic myths to great works of literature to the most banal of sitcoms. From birth, we're taught to recognize and understand the conventions of narrative.

The rule? If you abide by the conventions of Western narrative, your audience will instantly recognize what you're telling as a story. They won't waste their time trying to figure out who they're supposed to care about or where the action is taking place.

But the rules don't always apply. Everyone has their own ideas about what constitutes a story and how you should write them, and *they're all correct*. Stories are about problem-solving, character transformation, accomplishing an emotional effect, and lots of other things besides. There is no one true formula.

A given technique is only *one* way of writing a story, and when that technique works, you should use it. When it doesn't, you should abandon it without a backward glance.

The Seven-Point Plot

One of the most common and most controversial recipes is writer, critic, and editor Algis Budrys's Seven-Point Plot. For supporters of this methodology, the Seven-Point Plot is almost scripture—every story can be judged by how well it adheres to the recipe. For the detractors, Seven-Point Plot stories are predictable, manipulative, and mechanical. Cory actually uses the Seven-Point Plot to sketch out all his stories, and finds it an invaluable tool. The best thing about a Seven-Point Plot story is that it guarantees that there is a degree of rising tension throughout the story, so that every time your readers finish a page, they have a reason to flip to the next.

Here are the seven points:

1. A person
2. In a place
3. Has a problem

These first three points are usually hit in the first paragraph, or even the first sentence. The idea is that for tension to occur, you have to be worried about someone. For you to be worried about someone, you have to identify with that person. By immediately identifying a character, a setting, and a source of tension, you provide your readers with a reason to go on reading.

Note that the "problem" in this case can be something as simple as being late for a train or walking into a job interview. You don't want to make the problem too dire, since the story won't have anywhere to go from there.

4. The person intelligently tries to solve the problem and fails

5. Things get worse

Points four and five are called a *try/fail sequence.* Your character's attempt at resolving his or her problem has to be intelligent, otherwise your readers will stop identifying with the character. Despite this, the character has to fail, otherwise the story is over. Note that failure in this case needn't be a total rout: Your character may accomplish his nominal goal (defusing a bomb), only to discover that this doesn't meet his long-term objective (there's another, bigger bomb underneath the first one).

"Things get worse" is another way of saying that the stakes are being raised for your character: She

> **Factoid**
>
> A **try/fail sequence** is a scene or collection of scenes in which a character tries intelligently to solve his or her problem and fails. The failure worsens the problem. This is the core of rising tension.

misses the train and so now has to run across town to deliver an important message to someone who is about to make a terrible mistake. This is the "rising" part of "rising tension." At every turn, your character's personal danger increases, until her entire future rests on overcoming the final challenge.

6. The climax

We call this final challenge the "climax." A climax is just another try/fail sequence, but one in which everything is at stake. Either your character succeeds at this, in which case you've got a happy ending; or he fails, which yields a tragic ending.

7. Dénoument

Dénoument is a French word meaning "outcome." In a Seven-Point Plot story, the dénoument is what comes after the climax. It's an opportunity for your audience to catch their breath, think about what they've just read, and have any loose ends tied up for them. A good example of dénoument is at the end of *Star Wars,* when after blowing up the Death Star, Luke, Han, and the gang are presented with medals by Princess Leia.

The Emotional Effects Approach

The emotional effects approach is radically different from the cold logic of a Seven-Point Plot. In this approach, a writer begins with an emotional effect that he wants to achieve. Usually, this is a strong emotion that the writer himself has recently undergone; say, the birth of a child, the death of a loved one, or a particularly horrible betrayal. The writer then works backward, dreaming up a set of characters and a sequence of action that leads up to that effect.

This approach is very unstructured, but when it works, it produces stories that are deeply moving and memorable. As the Pulitzer Prize–winning sportswriter Red Smith once said, "There's nothing to writing. All you do is sit down at a typewriter and open a vein."

There are some pretty significant downsides to this approach. First of all, you need to have a moving emotional experience to draw on. All of us have these, but not all of us want to share them, and even for those of us who don't mind sharing, the supply is limited. Writers who run out of material for this sort of story end up repeating themselves, producing work where every story ends on the same note.

The other risk is this technique's lack of structure. Figuring out *how* to achieve your emotional effect is a nontrivial task, and it's quite possible to work your guts out on the story without achieving your emotional effect.

The Transformation Machine

The Transformation Machine is a term that Cory learned from Hugo Award–winning author James Patrick Kelly.

"As You Know, Bob ..."

James Patrick Kelly is a fabulous writer and teacher. On Cory's first day of Clarion, Jim gave him the single most important piece of advice he's ever gotten. Cory's manuscript "The Adventures of Ma n Pa Frigidaire" was up for critique. The other students all praised it highly, but when it came to Jim, the tide turned. Jim held up the manuscript and said, "Cory Doctorow, you are an asshole. You've managed to convince 17 talented writers that this story is worth reading, despite the fact that it is utterly devoid of any emotional content." For Cory, that was the kick in the head he needed to think about communicating with his writing, as opposed to being merely clever.

In the Transformation Machine, the story is a black box that is used to change a character. The protagonist steps into the box on the first page and steps out on the last, utterly transformed.

When approaching a story with this technique, the question you need to ask yourself is, "Whose story is this?" That's easier asked than answered. But consider Orson Scott Card's *Ender's Game*. The idea is that a race of insect-like aliens have fought and lost a war with humanity. The earth is arming a force to fend off the next wave of invasion, which, due to lightspeed restrictions, is 80 to 100 years in the future. Young children are drilled in an ROTC-like training facility whose objective is to teach strategy and leadership. Who is best suited to being transformed in this story?

Card decided that this should be the story of one bright child, a child so bright that his instructors have identified him as the best hope for the earth's future. If this child were to start off confident, likeable, and skilled, there wouldn't be much opportunity for his development. Instead, Card invented Andrew "Ender" Wiggin, a shy, sensitive, and physically small character, who has to struggle through the book to learn to inspire leadership, face bullies, fight battles, and persevere in the face of great hardship. *Ender's Game* is Ender Wiggin's story—he is utterly transformed by it.

The Fork

Another technique is Damon Knight's "Fork." Knight pioneered a storytelling style in science fiction that formed the basis for much of the classic SF we know today, especially Rod Serling's *Twilight Zone*.

In the Fork, the writer's objective is to present two clear possible endings to the story:

➤ Victory or defeat

➤ Life or death

➤ Success or failure

However, these two possibilities are actually misdirection. While the author is establishing these two possibilities, he is simultaneously and subtly foreshadowing a third, entirely different ending. Just when the reader thinks he has it all figured out, the writer springs the third ending on him, and it is suddenly, blindingly obvious that the third ending was the author's intent all along.

A great example of this is the *Twilight Zone* episode "Will the Real Martian Please Stand Up?" in which a busload of people are stuck at a roadside diner, waiting for the snow to clear. A quick headcount reveals that there's one extra person in the diner, and paranoia sets in, convincing the passengers that the extra person is a Martian masquerading as human. The action proceeds as each character explains why they couldn't be the imposter, and we are led to believe that the least credible of these is the true alien. When the road finally clears and the passengers depart, two men are left in the diner: a dapper old gent and the soda jerk. The soda jerk looks on in alarm as two extra pairs of arms emerge from the old gent's overcoat, but the alarm changes to smugness as the jerk pushes up his paper hat to reveal a third eye—there were *two* aliens in the diner all along, each unaware of the other.

This story sets up a couple of possibilities: Either there is indeed an alien, or the passengers are engaging in mass hysteria. The payoff—that there are two aliens—is gently hinted at throughout the story, but the other two possibilities overshadow it, until the truth is revealed and the audience slaps its collective forehead and says, "Of course!"

The crucial element of a Fork story is that the third ending *must* be foreshadowed, but that the foreshadowing has to be subtle enough that no one notices it until the last moment. Simply springing a third ending on the audience at the last moment won't do. That's just cheating.

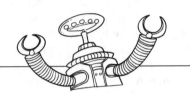

Danger, Danger!

The Fork is similar to a horrible writing mistake called a "Deus Ex Machina." In a Deus Ex Machina, the story is ended by divine (or authorial) intervention. A classic Deus Ex Machina ending is "... and then he woke up. Thank heavens, it was all a dream." What distinguishes a Fork story from a Deus Ex Machina is that the Fork's ending is subtly hinted at all through the story.

A Final Word

These are just a few of the techniques that writers use to make their stories work. None of them is the last word, nor do they have to be used one at a time: You can use the Seven-Point Plot to map out your Transformation Machine, and twist the ending with the Fork. Over time, you'll invent your own combinations as you find your own style.

The Dreaded Rewrite

There are two kinds of writers in this world: those who loathe rewriting and avoid it at all costs, and those who just can't stop tinkering with their stories, even though they've long since reached the point where the thing is as good as it's gonna get.

To some authors, rewriting is a necessary evil. It's a rare story indeed that is ready to go out to market the moment the last word is written, and so rewriting must be undertaken.

The best tool for this, by far, is a good writer's workshop. However, if you don't have a workshop of your own, you'll need to find a substitute. The key to a successful rewrite is perspective. A writer who's just nailed down the last scene of his story is in a rotten position to judge how well the whole thing holds together.

If you've got access to a reader you trust—someone who understands the mechanics of writing as well as your general schtick—you can get that person to read your story and give you a detailed critique. This is basically a two-person workshop, and it works fine, except when it produces a *folie à deux*, with both writers reinforcing each other's bad habits.

Another strategy is to try to separate yourself from the work through a mechanical analysis. Try this:

1. On a fresh sheet of paper (or word processor document), write out a short description of each scene in your story, i.e.: *Craphound and Jerry are driving through the countryside when they happen upon a kick-ass rummage sale. Craphound spots a nice bit of detritus, and Jerry violates the Code of the Craphound by attempting to buy the piece out from under his buddy. Craphound produces a wad of bills, buys the stuff, and storms off in a huff.*

2. Beneath the description, write out what you think that scene lends to the story, i.e.: *This sets up the main conflict in the story: Jerry has violated his own code of ethics, and in doing so has alienated his best pal. This sets the scene for a description of how Jerry developed his code, and what his friendship with Craphound means to him.*

3. Now, rate the importance of that scene, on a scale of one to 10, i.e.: *9.*

4. Count the words in the scene your summary refers to, and make a note of the length, i.e.: *2,000.*

5. Repeat for each of the scenes in your story.

Now, analyze the results. Are you devoting too much verbiage to unimportant scenes? Are you skimping on the length of key scenes?

Once you've identified the scenes that are too long or too short, you can start thinking about *why* those scenes are the length they are. Is that long bit in the middle the result of a character who doesn't do anything for the story? Is the setup too short because you've left out key details that you didn't think of until halfway through the story?

Some people don't need this at all. They finish a story and immediately know what parts they didn't give their all to, or that were made obsolete by later developments. Those are very, very lucky people, but they have their own cross to bear: They tend to keep on rewriting, long after they've fixed all the real problems in their stories. This is

Infodump

The easiest—and slowest—means of gaining perspective on your stuff is to let it mellow. Stick your new story in a drawer (or a directory of your hard drive) and leave it there for a while, until you've forgotten exactly what you had in mind with each scene and word. Take it out of the drawer and *voilà*, you're looking at it with fresh eyes.

Danger, Danger!

Beware of falling into the trap of overpolishing your story. This is a subtle form of writing avoidance—really, it's a strategy for avoiding putting a manuscript in the mail to a publisher and so risking rejection.

85

a trap. Multiple rewrites produce diminishing returns; that is, your second rewrite will probably only improve the story half as much as your first, and twice as much as your third.

A final note on rewriting: You're either writing or you're rewriting. A fatal trap for both novice and established writers is second-guessing yourself while you write. It's vital that you put on your writing hat when you're writing, and keep the rewriting hat in a drawer until you're done.

The Least You Need to Know

➤ Where novels are complex, short stories are one-trick ponies, written to be read in one or two sittings.

➤ The hardest part of short-story writing is picking a single subject and sticking to it.

➤ The beginning, middle, and ending of a short story all work together to create a sense of rising tension that pulls the reader along through the story.

➤ No story-writing technique is definitive, but techniques such as the Seven-Point Plot and the Fork make great starting points and are useful when you're stuck.

➤ Almost all stories need rewriting; but don't tackle it until you're done writing.

Chapter 9

The SF Novel

In This Chapter

➤ Just a long novel, not a short story

➤ Building a world

➤ Structuring your novel

➤ Some tips to try when you're running dry

In this chapter, we'll look at the biggest project you're likely to ever attempt as a SF writer: writing a novel. Here we'll look at things from the novelist's point of view. We'll also look at worldbuilding: how to create dramatic SF settings that are believable, without overloading yourself or writing an essay for the reader.

Finally, we'll provide some tips on how to get past the rough spots in creating large works, and how to know that you're on track.

Not What-If but How-Then: How Novels Differ from Short Stories

A novel is not just a long short story. The way a novel is put together is radically different from the short form. We'll return to that topic in a moment; more important to note first is that novels have a different purpose from short stories. The difference is particularly sharp in SF, which has always had strong traditions in both forms. SF writers have often used the short story to introduce a single new idea or premise, but have used novels to explore whole societies. If SF short stories are about the what-if of new gadgets and discoveries, SF novels are about the how-then of worldwide change.

In the classic Arthur C. Clarke story "The Nine Billion Names of God," a group of monks use a computer to randomly combine all the possible letter combinations for the name of God. When this process is complete, they believe, the world will end. The technocrats who sell them the computer are laughing about the idea as they walk away from the monastery; as they walk, overhead, "without any fanfare, the stars were going out."

This is a classic what-if story: What if the monks were right about God? Now contrast it to Ursula K. Le Guin's novel *The Left Hand of Darkness,* in which a visitor from earth gets caught up in the political machinations of a kingdom on a distant planet. The people on this planet are physiologically bisexual, and consider the single-sexed visitor to be a freak. The novel confronts the issue of gender difference squarely and in great detail, through incident, dialog, and character development. Like "The Nine Billion Names of God," the novel hinges on a single central premise. Unlike the short story, *The Left Hand of Darkness* holds a mirror up to society itself, and provides a detailed and complete critique of present sexual mores.

Both of these stories are considered classics. However, what the authors set out to accomplish is different in kind, as well as in detail. Clarke (who is also an accomplished novelist) set out to puncture the balloon of Western scientific rationalism. He did so in one deft stroke. Le Guin wanted to present the feminist analysis of gender in a readable and engaging way. She succeeded admirably in making difficult and controversial ideas about identity digestible for the American audience of the 1960s and 1970s.

Infodump

You can write a short story on enthusiasm, adrenaline, or caffeine. Not so with a novel. A novel is a major investment of time and emotional energy. You may have a single aspect of a short story that you're enthusiastic about, and that's enough to get you through the whole thing. But a novel requires that you be enthusiastic about a whole bunch of things. This is why novels are more suited to expressing an entire side of yourself, rather than a single idea.

Maybe you're not feeling quite that ambitious as you approach writing your first novel. Well, a novel doesn't have to have that kind of political ambition. Clarke's own *Rendezvous with Rama* is more a Boy's-Own adventure in space than a commentary, but it does systematically illustrate the "shock of the new" that would accompany humanity's first contact with an alien intelligence. Rather than having a political agenda at the core of this novel, Clarke presents a sentiment, but does so in breathtaking detail. Rama exemplifies Clarke's vision of the alien as such. In a sense, it presents his entire perspective on a particular subject.

Because writing a novel requires a large commitment of your time and energy, it's fair that the novel should contain more of your ideas and attitudes than a mere short story. So, you write a short story to present an idea; you write a novel to present your whole *perspective* on an idea.

In the novel you present a broader vision of your imaginative universe. At the same time, you do so in a carefully constrained manner. The remainder of this chapter presents our ideas of novel writing (which may or may not work for you). Basically, we'll abide by these principles:

➤ You don't write a novel the way you write a short story.

➤ A novel lets you explore character and ideas in complete detail.

➤ Exploration requires a map; that map should be neither too spare nor too detailed.

➤ Writing a novel is like building a house; there's a time to hammer nails and a time to stand back and look at how the whole thing's leaning.

A Total Immersion Experience

A short story focuses on a single outcome, theme, or moral. In a novel, on the other hand, you have room to expand. You can include subplots and digressions galore. Your heroes can go astray, show their silly or dark sides, and even decide to temporarily quit the action. You can describe the landscape in detail, even if what you describe won't affect the story. In other words, every rule about focus and concision in short-story writing can be broken in a novel. (We hope this doesn't encourage you to be boring. That remains a cardinal sin, whether you're writing novels, short stories, poems, or economics papers!)

The thing about novels is that as a reader you can immerse yourself in them. You can spend days, even weeks, exploring and imagining the world

Infodump

You'll probably write a whole lot more about your novel's world and characters than you wind up keeping. That's normal. Put it in, and in later drafts you can take a more critical eye to the detail. Who, what, and how much actually adds to the feel of completeness? What detracts? You'd be surprised how much can be taken out.

the writer evokes. You will never be criticized for crafting a novel in such a way that the reader believes they know the people, places, and history of the story's world. As with anything else, of course, doing this well requires a light touch. Including the Never-Never Land Census of 3650 probably won't contribute much to the reader's experience, however fascinating you as a writer might find it.

Multiple Characters, Multiple Plotlines

There's more than one way to say something. In short stories, you typically have to make a single, clear statement of theme. You have one plot, one or two key characters, and a single arc of action. In a novel, you can explore the same theme in a hundred different ways. You can use multiple characters and plotlines to do this.

You shouldn't have to plan subplots too much. They will suggest themselves as you write, because your characters will constantly be trying to go off in their own directions. The main thing is to ensure that the subplots (and lesser characters) serve the purpose of the book. Often they won't, and then you cut.

As a rule of thumb, you can keep any character or subplot that is entertaining, as long as it does not start to become its own story. Minor characters, for instance, have a tendency to run away with things. This is because minor characters can be more colorful than leads. Because your minor characters' stories may not serve the same theme as the main plot, you should beware of letting them take center stage.

Worldbuilding

One of the most magical aspects of SF is the feeling of being transported to a different world—a world that may seem fantastical, wondrous, but always real. Whether you're reading about Arrakis, Tatooine, Ringworld, or Chiba City, the best SF writers endow their settings with a feeling of gritty realism. These places live, and it's easy to suspend your disbelief and dive into the story. Often we find ourselves turning the pages just to find out what fascinating new place we'll find around the corner.

This kind of showmanship can be intimidating. It's easy to put a book down and say, "Wow, I could never come up with something like that!" Of course, it's in the writer's interest to make it look like the world he's created is complete. You're supposed to be wowed. But now that you're looking at SF as a writer instead of as a reader, it's time to look behind the mesmerizing facade. You've been Dorothy, in awe of the majesty of the Wizard; it's time to be Toto, and look behind the curtain.

What a World Is

The most important thing you should realize is that fictional worlds do not exist on paper. They exist in the mind of the reader, as a result of cues and guidelines provided by the writer. After all, no matter how exhaustive your description of a world might be on paper, it will not come to life until the reader takes it as his own, and visits it in his imagination. It is the reader who will ultimately see the color of the sky and smell the scent of a new earth. Your task as the writer is not to do this for him (except in a preliminary manner) but to provide the means for him to do it himself.

Your experience of the world will not be the same as your reader's. It is the reader's task to visit the world. It is your task to point to it. In order to point to a new world, you will have visited it yourself. But most of the SF writers I know don't experience this in quite the same way as their readers.

"As You Know, Bob …"

Many writers use a single word to create an aspect of their story's world. They may not even know themselves what that word "really" means. For instance, the first sentence of William Gibson's novel *Count Zero* is, "They set a slamhound on Turner's trail in New Delhi, slotted it to his pheromones and the color of his hair." Great! But what's a slamhound? It's never actually explained, but since the word fits with the style of the rest of the story, readers accept it, and can freely make up their own meaning for it.

The "Backless Maiden"

There is a story in the Arthurian cycle of a knight who was tempted by a beautiful maiden who would never turn her back on him. When she brought him to her house she cooked him a fine meal. But as she stood before the fireplace, he saw the light of the fire behind her eyes, and realized she would not turn her back to him because she *had* no back: She was the animated mask of a woman, and he was in great danger.

A science-fictional text is a "backless maiden," and one of our chief dangers as writers lies in not realizing it. There is no more to any fictional world than the words on the page. The world comes to life because of the inferences and associations readers make based on those words. So, the task of the SF writer is not to exhaustively describe: It is to find that set of images, metaphors, and scenarios that will inspire the reader to see more than the words themselves describe.

If you think about it, this kind of lets us off the hook. The reader is our active collaborator. Provided we give the right hints, the reader will create the world in all its stunning detail. So, it is not necessary for us to imagine everything that the reader might want to experience. The reader will fill in the blanks. It is the writer's responsibility to make sure that those dots are lined up properly, so that the reader doesn't end up imagining a world that doesn't go with the story the writer wanted to tell.

Backstory Is Not Story

A lot of writers spend years developing a universe for their stories. The game is great fun, after all. These writers have written encyclopedias about their imaginary worlds, and the process of thinking the place through produces countless story ideas. This is good. All too often, though, the writer finds all this *backstory* detail crippling when it comes down to actually writing a story or novel. Either all their creative energy has gone into the worldbuilding, leaving none for the story; or all the facts about the place have been decided, and everything the writer produces has to conform to them. Halfway into a story, the writer finds that some crucial event can't happen because that would violate the history, physical structure, or social mores of the invented world.

When this happens with novels, the writer often ends up creating highly convoluted (and unsatisfying) plot structures because he wants to explain everything to his own satisfaction.

There is such a thing as satisfying yourself. There is also such a thing as satisfying the reader. The only way to satisfy the reader is to ensure the internal consistency of your story. By requiring that the story conform to your world plan, you require that it be consistent with a plan to which your reader doesn't have direct access. How is the reader to know what's up and what's down?

The reader does have access to that plan in the case of realistic novels set within historical time frames. Indeed, in such novels the reader will feel internal consistency is violated if you violate an external consistency (historical fact) that the reader is familiar with. SF, however, supports itself entirely on its internal logic; there are very few SF paradigms so familiar that the reader will be guaranteed to know them (hyperdrive being one such exception).

Factoid

Backstory is the name we use for information about the world that you as a writer need to know, but the reader may not. Novels usually have room to include a good deal of backstory, but be judicious with it. Try not to burden your early chapters with history lessons. If the reader becomes sufficiently interested in the plot, he'll want to know your backstory. It doesn't work the other way around.

The reader doesn't know the full background for your world, and is unlikely to care until you have engaged his emotions with the strength of your story. *The Lord of the Rings* has a very intricate and detailed background, but the background is interesting because the story itself is solid. For this reason many SF writers use their imagined worlds only to inspire story ideas. When it comes to writing, they demand that the world change to suit the needs of the story. No matter how much effort they may have put into imagining the world, it can all be discarded if it doesn't serve the needs of the plot, characters, and theme.

The Value of Inconsistency

If you'd like to study internal vs. external consistency further, take two examples: the first being Larry Niven's *Known Space* series, the second the universe of John Varley's *Invasion* stories. Niven required that each of his *Known Space* stories be consistent with previous ones; the final result was that he ran out of options for new stories in this universe.

In contrast, Varley's novel *Steel Beach* belongs partially to the same universe as some of his other stories, but diverges wherever it needs to for internal consistency. As Varley says in the introduction to the novel, "*Steel Beach* is not really part of the Eight Worlds future history. Or the Eight Worlds is not really a future history, since that implies an orderly progression of events. Take your pick."

For Niven, half the fun was inventing wild new stories that didn't contradict what he'd already done. In a sense, everything that happened in known space was part of one big story, and he wanted to be internally consistent within that tale. For Varley, each story or novel is an atomic unit, indivisible and ultimately unconnected to the others. The *Known Space* cycle is one of the most successful and popular series in SF history. On the other hand, Varley has no limits on the stories he can tell in the Invasion universe. Take your pick; but we advocate Varley's strategy, particularly for beginning writers. It'll be better discipline for you to invent a new universe for every story.

Creating Dramatic Milieus

For us, the best imaginary worlds are those that are dramatic in their very foundation. When the world itself is designed to produce dramatic situations, you can mine it creatively for years.

The original *Star Trek* is an example of a milieu designed on dramatic principles. The transporter, for instance, exists because you can't waste screen time with your characters flying everywhere. It allows smooth scene transitions. The holodeck permits adventure outside the normal environment of the ship. The very fact that the series was set on an exploratory vessel meant stories would arise naturally.

Not all interesting ideas are dramatic, and not all imaginary worlds naturally generate conflict. We could imagine a parallel earth where Nicola Tesla's wilder scientific ideas bore fruit; this world has broadcast power, and wars are fought by remote-controlled robots. The doomsday weapon is not

"As You Know, Bob ..."

A dramatic setting is one with lots of possibilities for conflict. Worlds balanced on the edge of disaster, or travelers who are far from home, are naturally dramatic. Technologies with great capacity for misuse are more dramatic than those with no downside.

nuclear power (which doesn't work in this universe), but a giant harmonic oscillator that will cause the earth to shake to pieces if switched on. Unfortunately, the ideas, while interesting, don't of themselves generate conflicts. We could set a story in this world, but the motivating force behind the story would probably have to come from something other than Tesla's science. So why use this imagined universe? Why not just write a mainstream story in the first place? If the ideas are decoupled from the story, they will just get in its way.

Danger, Danger!

You can't get away with suggesting something really interesting and then not follow through on it. Any time you imply something fascinating about the history, geography, or technology of your world, your readers will prick up their ears. They'll file this item away and expect to have it explained before the end of the book. Beware of raising expectations and then not fulfilling them.

In contrast, there's no need to hunt around for conflict if your universe is one in which humanity has been enslaved by aliens. Just writing about day-to-day life in this world will draw the reader into conflict. More subtly, new science can have story-generating qualities. What if faster-than-light travel turned out to be so easy and cheap that any garage tinkerer could build a starship if he had the plans? Imagine millions of curious or disaffected people fanning out across the galaxy in home-built starships. Surely there's a story or two in that!

The Story Makes the World

Full-fledged worldbuilding is a fun but not necessarily useful activity for a writer. Most of us imagine the worlds we write about in detail, but it's usually after we've begun a story, and the story constrains the possibilities of the world. As writers, our creative energies are best directed at the story itself, because if we tell that well enough, the readers will create their own world, more completely and intensely realized than we could tell it to them.

Ultimately, the only place your literary world will thrive is in the imagination of your reader.

Novel Structure 101

You can get a Ph.D. studying nothing but novel structure. The artistic tradition of the novel goes back centuries—so what are you possibly going to learn in an *Idiot's Guide* that can set you on the road to writing one? Wouldn't a few university courses be necessary to even think about such a grand project?

In a word, no. Remember, studying the completed thing is not the same as studying how to create it. Even studying how another novelist works isn't as valuable as figuring out how *you* work. You could take a thousand courses on novel structure and still not be able to write one. On the other hand, you may be able to write one but not explain how you do it.

Rather than looking at novels from the point of view of the critic or the academic, then, we'll look at them from the point of view of the construction gang that's going to put one together: namely you, in the form of your various alter egos, the dreamer, the draft horse, the editor, etc. (see Chapter 2, "First Steps on the Road").

You'll start with the daydreaming stage. Novels take a long time to gestate, and you can expect to accumulate ideas, notes, even half-finished short stories whose characters you want to use somewhere. If you've written and abandoned three or four short stories all set in the same universe, chances are you should write a novel set in this universe.

The Arc of Dramatic Action

We've talked about the arc of drama in the context of short stories. In the novel the arc is extended and, as we'll see in a moment, contains arcs within arcs. There can even be several different actions happening simultaneously (plots and subplots).

The key difference between short stories and novels in this sense is that in a novel your characters will not undergo single, simple changes that drive the end of the story. In a novel, character change is gradual and involves much more struggle. You can be content to spend 100 pages with a character not changing in any way—provided that character is entertaining.

As you think about the novel, but before you begin to work on it, you should develop a clear notion of the full sweep of the story. You can get away with just throwing characters into the action in a short story, but not here. This is the time to let the schemer take over from the daydreamer. Plotting a novel differs from plotting a short story in several clear ways:

➤ You'll spend as much time introducing your hero, and getting us interested in him or her, as you would on an entire short story. Plan an opening for the novel, of short-story length, that will bring us into the world of your story.

➤ You establish setting and situation slowly, revealing only a little at a time. This material is usually spread out over a number of chapters.

➤ The plot isn't revealed all at once. Don't have someone appear on page one and tell us what's coming. Present a fairly minor situation, and let it snowball over the first few chapters. Doing this allows you to start numerous subplots; they differ in that they don't snowball quite as far.

➤ Novels have what's known as a cyclothymic rhythm: The tension builds to a mini-climax, then is relieved (the characters win, and relax), then tension builds again, to a higher level this time, and the corresponding climax is greater. This process continues until the ultimate climax of the novel. Look at the overall shape of your novel to make sure the action will follow such a rhythm.

When you're satisfied that you have an extensive enough story that you can make a novel out of it, you can proceed to the outlining stage. When outlining, bear in mind that novels have a *fractal structure*. A fractal looks the same on any scale. As we'll see in this section, novels have some fractal qualities.

Factoid

A **fractal** is basically any mathematical structure that is the same on any scale. For example, think of coastlines. From orbit, an ocean coast looks like a jaggedy, bumpy, irregular line. But any part of that coastline, viewed from an airplane, also looks like a jaggedy, bumpy, irregular line. Viewed from the roof of a boathouse, any nearby stretch of shore also looks this way. Even if you kneel on the beach and look at the space encompassed by your outstretched hands, the line between water and sand will still be jaggedy, bumpy, and irregular.

Literary criticism provides many terms useful for categorizing story structure: prolog, epilog, dénoument, scene, act, climax … the list goes on. We use some of these terms in this book. You already know from previous discussions how stories have a hook or dénoument, establishing scenes, buildups, reversals, climaxes, and finales. From all these terms, you'd think that writing a novel means learning a bunch of different ways to write. In some ways that's true, but if it's true that every part of a novel is a different kind of story, it's also true that all parts are stories, and all share a common basic structure.

Many artistic constructs have fractal qualities. Music is famously fractal. So are large works of literature, at least in the sense that they are dramas within dramas.

If you look at the novel as a whole, it's a story that has a beginning, a middle, and an end. There's a dramatic arc to this story, beginning with relative calm, moving to struggle and jeopardy, and ending with climax and resolution. The key point is that if you look at each of these parts in isolation, it has the same structure. Novels, films, and plays are often split into acts and scenes. An act has a complete story arc of its own—a beginning, middle, and end. So does each scene. Wheels within wheels, drama inside drama, a novel is the same at every scale.

The difference between these scales is that each level of drama serves a different purpose. For instance, your opening chapter will introduce your world, your characters, and the situation. It probably won't have a disastrous reversal, threat to your hero's life, and a climactic battle. That kind of drama happens in later chapters. Your opening chapter will, however, have its own hook, development, crisis, and resolution—though the crisis may be mild, as in Chapter One of *The Lord of the Rings*, which has Bilbo Baggins wondering who the strange visitor at his door is. For a novel, the climax of Chapter One is often merely whatever makes us curious enough to read Chapter Two.

We're not advocating that you learn some esoteric system of codifying your work. The idea is simply that novels are big projects; it's easy to get lost, particularly in the difficult middle where the story can seem directionless. If you write an outline for the book based on the idea that every part can be broken down into smaller parts that work essentially the same way, the project as a whole doesn't look so intimidating. You can do the work in easy, bite-size pieces.

Outlining, the Fractal Way

Take your existing outline, or start a new one, and in point form write the big picture: a line or two each describing the beginning, middle, and end of the story.

Now take your beginning, and in point form, write its structure: a line or two each describing its beginning, middle, and end. Take this mini-list and slice it into chapters. Don't agonize over how to split it up, just make an arbitrary choice.

Danger, Danger!

You don't want all the parts of your story to have the same *kind* of hook, conflict, or resolution. If every scene, chapter, and section ends with a fight, your readers will lose interest because it's all too predictable. The delight in reading comes from knowing that *something* is going to happen, but not knowing what. If you become predictable, the reader doesn't have any reason to finish the book; they already know how it will end.

Now take the first few chapters, and for each one, write a line or two describing its beginning, middle, and end. If you'd like to go further, you can divide these descriptions into scenes. You should probably leave them undefined, because things will change as you write.

If you want, you can outline the entire book in this way. You probably won't want to go into great detail for anything more than a chapter or two ahead of where you are now in the book. There's no point in outlining the ending in minute detail if you come up with new ideas on the way that change it. As you approach each scene, you bring it into sharper and sharper focus; keep your outline detailed for as far ahead as you need in order to feel comfortable with where the story is going. Then just write, confident that you are on track and that when you come to each part of the book, you'll know what you have to write, if not necessarily how you'll write it.

Tips to Keep You Going

Now all you have to do is write the book!

It's not that simple, of course. The important thing to realize is that writing a novel is like every other kind of large construction project. You don't try to do everything at once. This is why we've suggested you spend a lot of time on the outline: This is your blueprint. From the blueprint stage, you'll proceed to writing a first draft, and for this, you just let your Draft Horse side take over. Write, don't rewrite, at this stage.

Don't Look Back

Lot's wife is famous for looking back as she and the rest of the family were fleeing Sodom and Gomorrah. For this indiscretion, she was turned into a pillar of salt.

As you write, you'll discover you need to change events or characters or places earlier on in the novel. Some writers are able to revise backward as they go, but we don't advise it for those just starting out. Rather than going back and revising now, just note the change you'll have to make and keep going, if possible. Only if you can't envision how the change will affect your next chapters should you go back.

Infodump

You may stall out completely. Sometimes the beginning of a novel starts going in the wrong direction, and if you keep going that way nothing will work. In that case, going back before you finish the draft would be a good idea.

It's perfectly possible to go back and rewrite Chapter One 20 times without ever getting further. Just keep going. And whatever you do, don't turn around!

Take a Break

Somewhere between 100 and 300 pages into the novel, you will become confused and stagger to a halt. This is natural; there seems to be a point in novel writing where the slope steepens quickly, and you find yourself holding onto the reins of a dozen plots, subplots, unresolved conflicts, and inconsistencies. This is not actually a sign of failure, it's a sign that you're in the Perilous Middle of a normal writing project.

The best thing you can do at this stage is take a break from the writing. Far from being an admission of defeat, this time off lets you rally your troops. (To continue the military metaphor here, you could say that you, the general, have ridden far ahead of your army, and now you have to wait for it to catch up.) You need to go back to your original outline, and even further, to your original notion of what you wanted to do with the novel. Take the highest possible overview of what you want to do. After all, you're drowning in minutiae.

Rather than try to fix everything at once, it's time to break the job down again into bite-sized pieces. Solve one problem at a time until you feel the forward momentum starting again. Then resume the draft.

Finishing

The good news is that by the time you get near the end of the novel, you'll probably find that the slope has reversed itself, and you're now barreling downhill. Endings can be a lot of fun, and they deserve your complete attention. It's natural to write the last few chapters in a single burst of energy. And once you're done, you'll know such a giddy feeling of accomplishment that you'll almost certainly start thinking about writing a second book.

Let yourself revel in this experience for a while. You don't want to tackle the second draft of the novel too soon.

What? We're not done yet? Well, no: Writing is rewriting. Leave the book alone for a few months, then come back and crank up your editorial skills. Starting again with your original conception of what you wanted to do with the book, go through and ruthlessly cut, expand, or reshape. Only by doing this will you be worthy to pass into the final stage of being an author: submitting your novel to a publisher.

But that's a topic for Chapter 13, "Submit!"

The Least You Need to Know

➤ Short stories and novels are different literary forms. Writing short stories can help prepare you for writing a novel, but you can't write a novel the way you write shorter fiction.

➤ Novels have much more scope for subplots and minor characters than short stories. You can say more with a novel.

➤ It's easy to go overboard planning out the world of your novel and its history. Don't worry about details that aren't relevant to the characters.

➤ A novel is built out of stories inside stories inside stories. Look at each level of your outline and ensure that each level forms a story, with a beginning, middle, and end.

➤ Break novel projects down into small, manageable chunks. You can't think about all of it at once. Build your novel as you would build a large office tower: piece by piece.

Chapter 10

Science Friction: Struggles with the Subject

In This Chapter

➤ It's not as hard as it looks

➤ Writing believable SF

➤ Rules of consistency

➤ Make sure you're understood

➤ Fundamentals of storytelling

There's a little word attached to SF that scares a lot of people. That word is "science."

Just how much do you need to know to be a science fiction writer? Do you need a degree in something like nuclear physics? Or can you get by "winging it" with your science? Will a little hand-waving be enough to satisfy your readers?

There is a perennial debate about this in fans' and writers' circles. The truth is, published SF runs the gamut from just plain factually wrong to scientifically airtight. It has always been this way, despite the nostalgic longing some people have for a "golden age" of science-based SF. SF has always been about storytelling more than science. Some of the worst literature in the field is the scientifically accurate stuff. At the same time, science has always been the springboard for new ideas in the genre, and the more you know about it, the more options your imagination has.

Do I Have to Be a Rocket Scientist?

Science fiction and fantasy blur together imperceptibly. The question you have to ask yourself as a writer is, what kind of fiction do you want to write? Chances are, it's the kind of fiction that you like to read. Your task is not to become an expert in science so that you can write some generic kind of "scientific" fiction. Your task is to become comfortable with the concepts in the kind of fiction you want to write.

This idea will be pretty heretical to those *hard SF* fans who are sold on the notion that SF can only start from a scientific premise. Sure, it can start there. But it can also start from any other conceptual premise—it can start from anywhere in the imagination. This is what gives SF its power.

What kind of SF do you want to write? Do you want to write *Star Trek* novels? If that's the case, you do need to know a little about physics and astronomy. It's probably more important that you know *Star Trek* science, which is not like twentieth-century science. Most of what goes on in *Star Trek* is flat-out impossible by today's standards. The show's science is little more than sleight of hand—a made-up jargon that bears no resemblance to reality.

It's a consistent jargon, however, and the show's developers know what it means. So it behooves you to know it too, if you want to play in their sandbox.

It may not be real science, but it's the consistent set of rules for the universe in which you're writing. So, if you want to write for *Star Trek,* you need to know the rocket science of the *Star Trek* universe, if not necessarily the science of ours.

The Writer's Universe vs. the Scientist's

Science and fiction serve different purposes. Science fiction often serves an educational function, introducing difficult technical ideas to a popular audience. Educational as it might be, however, SF is *not* science. Science is a largely undramatic, meticulous process in which measurement and categorization are usually more important than visionary insight. Indeed, vision and drama can be dangerous to the cause of science, because they can lead the practitioner down blind alleys.

A scientist does not concern herself with what she would like to be true. She is concerned only with what she can prove to be true. As a SF writer, you're not subject to the same restriction. Nor should you be; as storytellers our purpose is not to describe the workings of the natural world, but to dramatize our changing relationship to that world. Scientific discoveries can help us do that. So can purely imaginative inventions of our own.

You might be surprised at how passionate some fans are about scientific accuracy in SF. This is because many people view SF as a kind of champion of Western rationalism—a tool to be used in the war against ignorance and superstition. Fans (and writers and editors) who take this attitude view hard SF as the only "true" SF; everything else is corrupted by romanticism, fantasy worst of all. In their opinion, fantasy is useless because it is pure escapism, whereas hard SF serves as a potential blueprint for the actual future we are building.

Danger, Danger!

It's possible to know too much. If you swallow current scientific orthodoxy on some subject, you could deliberately avoid using certain ideas, only to find out later that they're possible after all. Look at high temperature superconductivity. It was widely held to be impossible until the 1980s, when the first high Tc substances were created. What does that say about, say, faster-than-light travel? As a SF writer, you should be willing to go out on a limb for new ideas.

"The Core of Mars Is Made of Ice": B-Movie Science

The requirement that you be consistent only within the story doesn't mean that you can get away with being sloppy. People who read SF tend to be well-educated, and in some cases they'll be more widely read than you are. When, in the movie *Total Recall*, Arnold Schwarzenegger announces that "the core of Mars is made of ice," a certain segment of the audience winces. What had been shaping up as a nice hard-SF premise—that melting the Martian permafrost could create an atmosphere for the Red Planet—is utterly spoiled by this preposterous declaration. (The core of Mars is made of molten iron, as is any other self-respecting planet.)

One of the pleasures of reading SF is anticipating where the story can go, based on our own knowledge of science. As in mystery novels, where figuring out who killed Mr. Body is half the fun, so figuring out how the heroes will escape the tidal forces of a giant planet or survive a night of –100° temperatures is a game many SF readers love to play.

It's common for readers of mystery novels to throw the book at a wall if the writer hides the crucial clues to who the murderer is. This makes the reader's attempts to figure out the puzzle futile—because there was no puzzle! In the same way, refusing to follow the consistent rules of your own story's universe infuriates SF readers.

You'll cause your readers to throw your book at the wall if you violate one of your own premises, whether you do it because you're trying to be clever, or because you haven't researched the subject well enough. Your readers will also pitch the book if you demonstrate less knowledge of the subject than they have. For instance, you might try to be clever by inventing some new physics—say, a faster-than-light drive—that results from crushing photons into a tightly packed ball. Your readers can't pick apart the details of your faster-than-light drive per se; once you've said it's possible, you can have it work any way you want. The only problem is, photons can't be packed to begin with; they can all happily occupy the same space. Your failure to understand ordinary physics makes your faster-than-light physics unbelievable; your physics-literate readers will know that it's a case of B-movie science.

Danger, Danger!

The best research tool you can have is enthusiasm. If you treat research like a chore, you'll never learn anything. Beware of thinking that you have to read about subjects that bore you. First, there's an interesting side to everything, if you can find it. Secondly, you should follow your heart: If you really don't enjoy science, you'll probably enjoy writing fantasy more.

Sources

The best and most obvious research tool for writers today is the Internet. There are numerous Web sites that provide daily updates of the latest scientific developments. Two that provide a raw feed of press releases are www.artigen.com and www.eurekalert.org. For more popularized science, you can visit www.sciam.com (the Web site for *Scientific American*) or www.discovery.com. Just browsing these sources for a while should bring you up to speed on current research in many different disciplines.

Your local bookstore or library will usually have a science section. If a subject sparks your interest, you should head there to read up on it, rather than relying on Web sources. Why? Because there is no editorial function on the Web. Surfing at random, you're as likely to end up reading pseudo-science or downright wrong material as peer-reviewed findings.

Of course, your job as a SF writer is not to believe any of this stuff anyway, but rather to use it as grist for the mill. Reading about established science remains the best way to develop good critical thinking. Understanding of how real scientists work will stand you in good stead when you roll up your sleeves to research something like perpetual motion or UFOs.

Another invaluable source is magazines like *Wired* that engage in shameless boosterism of the latest gadgets. Technology is changing even faster than science. A good number of the products that will be available a year from now would be considered science fiction right now, such as air cars and voice-activated pocket computers.

Finally, read science fiction. Your peers are your best research assistants.

A Vampire's Little Rulebook

Storytellers have always known that the fantastical must obey rules. This is why there are important limitations on what vampires can do, for instance. Imagine a vampire who can walk in the sunlight, is not afraid of garlic or the cross, and cannot be killed by a stake through the heart. We have something that's harder to believe in. After all, if there are vampires like this, why haven't they ravaged the whole world by now?

Infodump

Constraints and limitations are a good thing in art. For instance, let's say you're writing a space opera-type novel, with competing galactic empires fighting a war. You've got your average *Star Wars* or *Star Trek* space battle if you use conventional notions of star travel. But now, add the constraint that faster-than-light travel has to start out and end near a massive object; say, nothing smaller than a star will do. Now the invading force has to literally dive out of the sun; battles are fought in a blazing environment where the smallest scratch on your mirrored hull will let killing heat in. Instead of reducing your storytelling options, this constraint actually generates new ones.

Vampires that are limited in key ways are more believable. They are necessarily furtive because of their limitations. In fact, most vampire stories revolve around the consequences of these limitations. This is true for nearly all fantasy. The plot of *The Lord of the Rings* hinges on a limitation of Sauron: He has put a large part of his life-essence into the One Ring. If that ring is destroyed, so is he, and he cannot attain his full power without it.

This aspect of storytelling applies to SF as well. Scientific limits play the same role in SF as garlic or the cross do in vampire stories. They give the storyteller something to hang the tale on.

Any new technical invention could be used to place constraints on what your characters can do. Creative constraints will generate plot as your heroes try to get around them.

Suspension of Disbelief

It really doesn't matter how preposterous your science is, as long as it's believable. Once again, look at *Star Trek*. There are about a hundred more elements and elementary particles mentioned in that show than we know exist. Starships move like naval vessels, and of course there's the problem of sound in space. People travel by having their bodies torn apart and beamed across space. And almost all aliens are bipedal, breathe the same air as us, are capable of interbreeding, and in fact differ only in the shape of their respective foreheads.

It doesn't matter that all of this is ridiculous from a scientific standpoint. We suspend our disbelief because these elements of the *Star Trek* universe always work the same way. They are internally consistent, and they follow rules that make sense within the framework of the stories told.

Internal and External Consistency

Consistency is the demand that things make logical sense. If you give the hero an invincible weapon in Chapter One, you need to explain why he can't use it to defeat the villain in Chapter Ten. If a character acts one way all the time, you'll need to explain why she changes and suddenly acts another way. The demands of consistency in SF extend to the scientific and physical ideas you're using in your story:

➤ **Internal consistency** is simply getting the facts of the story itself straight. It applies to the characters, situations, timing, and setting of the story. These things are internal because they don't rely on history, physics, or geography that exists independently of the story.

➤ **External consistency** is the demand that you fit the facts of the world we know. Thus, if you say you are setting a story in the earth we know, you can't place the island of Sumatra between Greenland and Iceland. You can't have faster-than-light travel in 1960s America and still say it's the America we know. That's a violation of external consistency.

➤ **Narrative consistency** is most familiar to us from watching bad movies. When the hero runs out of a room wearing one shirt, and we cut away to outside the room only to see him emerge wearing a different shirt, that's a consistency problem. Or, in movie-speak, a continuity problem.

Sleight of Mind

It never pays to draw the attention of the reader to the shakier ideas in your story. Better to use sleight of hand: Distract the reader so he doesn't think too much about what you've just done. This applies to matters of character and plot as well as ideas. For instance, in the movie *Jurassic Park,* the tyrannosaurus is introduced standing behind a fence. Later, when it crosses the fence and chases our heroes back across it, suddenly there's a hundred foot drop right where it was standing. We're not inclined to think too much about that little problem, because, well, there's a tyrannosaur rampaging across the screen!

Similarly, SF writers rarely mention the fact that in an Einsteinian universe, starships traveling faster than light will also be going backward in time. Better to just not mention it. The alternative is to invent some elaborate scheme for getting around the problem, and that's likely to raise more questions than it answers.

Fiction is always selective in what it says. You never talk about the hero's bowel problems in a romance; you don't talk about tragic death in a comedy. You're always aiming at a particular effect, exclusive to other possibilities. In SF, this requires a certain sleight of mind to allow us to believe in the universe you present.

"As You Know, Bob ..."

Continuity is a big problem in novel writing. It gets tedious to flip back and forth reminding yourself of stuff you set up three chapters ago. Was your hero carrying that backpack with the flashlight in it when he set out? If not, he won't have the flashlight now. To solve such problems, some writers keep a consistency bible: a notebook where they jot down who's wearing what in which scene, and so on, so that they can keep it all straight.

Conventions: The Story's Framework

In order to move the story along, SF authors typically use conventions. Here's a short list of common conventions, any one of which could stop a story dead if the author had to explain it:

➤ Starships that travel at faster-than-light speed

➤ Artificial gravity in space

➤ Inhabited planets with earth-like environments

➤ Hand-held energy weapons (lasers, blasters) with tremendous power

➤ No advancement in political science in the future; future politics always resembles our own

Most SF stories are 90 percent conventional elements, with 10 percent innovation. It has to be this way, otherwise the reader is left at sea, unable to decide what to focus on. You can think of the conventions as the conceptual skeleton or framework of the story. The key ideas that make this story unique are added on top of that framework, like the unique facade of a building.

"As You Know, Bob ..."

SF is often criticized for the conventional nature of SF characters. But if SF is not about character, then it's as logical for them to be conventional as it is for the setting of a parlor drama to be. No one criticizes Joyce for not describing unique and striking rooms in *Ulysses*. He's writing about people, not places. In SF it's often the other way around, and no one should criticize SF writers for placing the emphasis in the proper place here as well.

Making Your Ideas Accessible

Early writers such as Jules Verne saw no problem here. His audience was used to reading extended prose, and there was no hard line between essay and fiction. When Verne wants to make a technical point, he simply stops the action and lectures ... sometimes for many pages.

That kind of lecturing doesn't cut it these days. In fact, the bar keeps getting raised higher and higher. Readers don't want to spend any time figuring out the world anymore, they just want to get on with the action.

If your story is set in an exotic environment that the reader's not going to understand without explanation, you have a problem. You have to get the readers interested in the story, but you also have to get them up to speed with your premise.

Time-Honored Expositional Tricks

Luckily, there are other, better ways of introducing ideas. Here's a short list of common (and not-so-common) techniques:

> ➤ **The "infodump."** As you may have gathered from the sidebar of the same name in this book, an infodump is where, like Verne, you stop the action and lecture. It's generally frowned upon, as the following snippet should make clear:
>
> "Blastula, you villain, I have you now!"
>
> "Ha ha, Dirk, what you fail to realize is that you are not standing on an ordinary throw-rug, but rather a particularly ravenous member of the species Mixumplitl!"

The Mixumplitl's tendrils whipped around Dirk's torso, and he screamed as it dragged him down.

The Mixumplitl was first discovered in the year 2145 by an explorer named Markaby, during his travels on the planet Armstrong. During the planet's unusually strong spring rains, an odd celestial phenomenon occurs, which Markaby called the ...

Well, you get the idea.

➤ **The "Rod and Don" conversation.** Another of our sidebars is named for this trick. This technique involves two characters telling one another something both already know. They are speaking strictly for the reader's benefit. Check out the following example:

"There it is," said Rod. "Mars!"

"Yes," agreed Don, "and as you know, Rod, the Red Planet was aptly named after the Roman god of war. Aptly, because you and I are even now leading the invasion force that will bring wrack and ruin to the inhabitants of this warlike planet!"

Rod: "Ha ha!"

Don: "Ha ha ha!"

And so on.

➤ **The walkthrough.** This is a thinly disguised lecture. In it, a character from outside the action is given a guided tour by another character. It's Rod and Don with one character who is ignorant. Actually, walkthroughs can be very effective: *Brave New World* is one big walkthrough. They can also be cleverly disguised; many SF novels open with characters waking or arriving in strange circumstances, and having to learn where they are. As they learn, we learn.

➤ **Acclimatization.** This technique is one of the most subtle ways of introducing ideas. You let the reader get comfortable with character and situation, while dropping hints that there is more to know. William Gibson does this sort of thing extremely well. The first time you introduce the technology or idea that will be central, you do so casually, almost as an afterthought. Perhaps the thing is only named, not explained. Later, you see a character using the technology or catch the edge of a conversation involving the idea. But it's still not central to the scene. Finally, after a few repetitions like this, you have the main characters engage the technology or idea fully. By this time the reader is comfortable with it. Done right, this technique can be used to educate the reader without the reader even knowing that it's happening. For an example, read the opening chapters of William Gibson's novel *Neuromancer,* and trace the explanation of cyberspace, cyberdecks, and "jacking in."

109

➤ **Redefinition and example.** This is the most ambitious and difficult way of presenting new information. Quite simply, you invent a new language for your ideas, or remap existing words, and just start using them. Readers have to puzzle it out for themselves. In *Stars in My Pocket Like Grains of Sand,* Samuel Delany remaps our words for gender, so that "she" refers to any person, asexually, while "he" refers to the object of desire, of either gender. It takes a while to figure out what's going on, as the world is full of she's who sometimes become he's for a while. It's up to us to figure out what it means.

Infodump

Acclimatization and redefinition are very difficult techniques to master. They're also novelistic methods, because their effect needs time to accumulate in the reader's mind. If your Rod and Don conversations work and aren't too intrusive, you might as well keep them. Better to use what's guaranteed to work than try to be too clever.

Dramatic Rhythm and Exposition

Let's get down to brass tacks. Exposition and drama are intertwined in SF. Knowing when to introduce a piece of information is as vital as knowing when to threaten your hero.

As a simple rule of thumb, *you should not explain more than your reader needs to know to understand the conflict at the current point in the story. If you can explain more seamlessly, and it will contribute to the drama or depth, then do so.*

You may be proud of your ideas, and hopefully by the time readers finish your story they will be delighted with them, too. It's unlikely that you can get them excited about these ideas on page one, however.

Your reams of research are only valuable if they serve the story. Even if you need to explain a great deal, it's unlikely that you need explain it all at once. Chances are that no matter where you are in the story, you are in the midst of some sort of conflict. (If not, you may have a plotting problem.) What do your characters know about the world that pertains to this present conflict? And what does the reader need to know in order to understand the conflict?

Provide the reader with enough information to get him through the scene or chapter. It doesn't matter if it's only partial, or even if it's oversimplified. Just make sure you don't give the impression that this is all there is to know.

As an example, take Chapter One of Tolkien's *The Lord of the Rings.* Gandalf tells Frodo (and us) enough to get him started on his quest. He doesn't tell Frodo about ents, elves, Moria, or the Nazgul. That would be too much information; more importantly, it would disappoint and perhaps confuse the reader to know too much too soon. Rivendell would not be so exciting if we'd known about it from page one.

Danger, Danger!

There's a workshopping term that we use to describe writers who subject the reader to too much information: "I've suffered for my art, and now it's your turn!" Many writers think that because they spent a great deal of time and effort researching something, they should include it in the story. This is a bad idea. Include what's necessary to move the story along and make your point. Everything else is just grist for the mill.

As the story progresses, the background unfolds; in the case of *The Lord of the Rings*, this "backstory" includes mythology and history, geography, and day-to-day practicalities. We learn through a variety of devices, including campfire stories, poems, council discussions, and by visiting places. There was a great deal that Tolkien could not find a place for, and this he put into appendixes. The remainder later became *The Silmarillion*.

While Tolkien is famous for his worldbuilding, it's good to remember he knew when enough was enough. While we have access to most of his notes and side stories, he kept the bulk of them out of his epic.

Science Is the Variable, Storytelling the Constant

Is H. G. Wells' *The War of the Worlds* obsolete? Should we stop reprinting and reading this novel? After all, its premise is that hostile aliens live on Mars, and they fire an invasion force at Earth from giant cannon.

Of course, a story can't become obsolete. Scientific theories can, when they are supplanted by more explanatory ideas. If the science was really the most important part of SF, then *The War of the Worlds* would no longer be read, would it?

Aether, N-Rays, and Cold Fusion

The details of scientific theory are constantly being rewritten. The number of obsolete scientific theories vastly outnumbers the number still used. This is only a problem for those SF writers who think they are presenting big-T Truth to the reader in the form of scientifically based stories. A flurry of cold-fusion stories were written immediately after Fleischmann and Pons announced that they had created fusion in palladium. Most of those stories never saw the light of day. Those that did look quaint now, 10 years on.

"As You Know, Bob ..."

Beginning writers sometimes knock themselves out trying to come up with totally new ideas. They act as if they were researchers trying to top some current theory. But a SF story isn't "better" just because it uses new ideas. If your story is good, it doesn't matter that it uses old or conventional ideas. It'll still be good SF.

On the other hand, if you let the reader know that you're deliberately using an outdated theory, you can have a lot of fun. Speculating about what things would be like if some theory had proven to be true is little different from speculating about as-yet undiscovered science.

A good example of this kind of SF is the novel *Celestial Matters,* by Richard Garfinkle (Tor Books, 1996). The premise of this novel is that Aristotelian science is true, including pre-Newtonian physics, spontaneous generation of organisms, and the caloric theory of heat. It's great fun taking these ideas to their logical conclusions.

Timeless Values

If the science isn't the most important part of SF, then we're left with more traditional literary values like theme, character, plot ... in short, storytelling. SF is storytelling using a uniquely broad repertoire of ideas, but it is storytelling nonetheless.

The best research you can do toward writing SF is therefore to read literature—any literature, and as much of it as possible. SF is a literary art form, and no amount of education in the sciences can make up for a lack of reading in the arts.

Yes, ideas are important. They are what distinguishes SF from other genres. But if ideas are all you're interested in, you should be writing essays.

Read the classics. Read Dante, Milton, Faulkner, Joyce, Chinese poetry, and Hindu Vedas. Read children's books, philosophy, biography, and history. These will give you the most valuable tools for writing SF, and indeed any fiction.

There is no substitute for good storytelling. You may use science as a jumping-off point to telling your tales, but you shouldn't be intimidated by it, and you shouldn't let it bog you down. Science in fiction is part of the craft, something to learn to use and perfect just as you learn to use character, and plot, and style.

The Least You Need to Know

➤ Science fiction is not science. You don't need to be a rocket scientist to write it.

➤ SF requires a suspension of disbelief on the part of the reader. Even if your science is flat-out wrong, your story may succeed if the reader buys into it.

➤ Your science should be internally consistent with the rest of your story. This is more important than making it consistent with objective, real science.

➤ Your science needs to support the story, not overwhelm it. Be sparing with your exposition.

➤ Most SF readers are scientifically literate. If you make a real mistake, they will notice, and you'll never hear the end of it.

➤ Your science may go out of date, but good storytelling never does.

Chapter 11

Character in SF

In This Chapter

➤ SF: Land of the cliché?

➤ The high hurdles of SF prose

➤ Crafting a character

➤ Integrating character and idea

Let's face it: Science fiction is constantly getting hammered from literary corners for its characters—or lack of same. This stems directly from the perception that, because many SF characters are hackneyed, partial, flat, and even ridiculous, SF must be some attempt at "real" literature that failed.

This is entirely untrue. There are many examples of SF with complex, resonant characters. However, it *is* harder to create well-rounded, complete characters in SF than in other forms of literature. We can hardly cover the whole subject of crafting characters in one chapter. There are hundreds of books and articles out there on characterization; what could we say here that they haven't said? Instead of re-inventing the wheel, we'll guide you through some of the special problems and opportunities that arise when you create characters in SF and fantasy.

Barbarians and Women in Brass Bikinis

As SF writers, we must admit there are a lot of awful characters in our beloved genre. After all, you don't get mainstream literary novels with covers that feature semi-nude women in harem outfits being threatened by giant bugs. That sense of style is uniquely ours.

There are so many character clichés in SF, in fact, that we could hardly list them all here. How could a genre be built so thoroughly on clichés and stock characters and still have any literary value?

Beyond the Clichés

There's another possibility. Maybe the paucity of good characters in SF is not a sign that the genre is trash. Maybe it's not entirely a sign of incompetence on the part of SF writers. Maybe there's something about science fiction itself that works against character. Indeed, this is the case. Unlike mainstream literature, SF does not tend to embody its themes in characters. More often, it communicates its meanings through setting or idea—by showing the reader a new technology or society.

"It's Turtles All the Way Down"

Everything that happens in a mainstream story pertains in one way or another to character. This relationship to character goes all the way down to the level of how we read the sentences that make up the narrative. By contrast, SF doesn't just focus on ideas as another element, like plot or theme.

Reading SF is an exercise in exploring the objective part of the text. Just as mainstream literature is about character on every level, so SF is often about the object on all levels. (Or, as early physicists said about the structure of the universe, "It's turtles all the way down.")

There are many strong and memorable characters in SF, but they serve the ideas of the story, and not the other way around.

"As You Know, Bob ..."

A famous astronomer was lecturing on the solar system. When he finished, an elderly lady approached him and said "You're wrong, you know. The earth actually sits on the back of a giant turtle." Thinking quickly, the astronomer said "Ah, but what does the turtle sit on?" Unfazed, the lady laughed. "You can't fool me," she said. "It's turtles all the way down!"

What We Take for Granted in Ordinary Fiction

There's another reason why character is under-represented in SF. Consider what happens when you read a mainstream novel set in, say, upstate New York. When the main character charges out of his house into a snowstorm and slams the door of his car, you find it easy to empathize with him. After all, houses, snowstorms, freezing weather, and cars are all familiar to us, at least by reputation. As we read, we register each of these details quickly and subliminally, while our main focus remains on the character. The writer has a similar experience: She can throw cars, gas stations, planes, and bistros into the story without having to think deeply about them. Her focus can remain on the character as she works.

We Take Nothing for Granted in SF

Science fiction, sadly, cannot work this way. When the character angrily dons his re-breather, cycles through the airlock of his arcology, and stalks into the frozen Martian wastes, our focus *has* to waver away from him and on to the objects and actions of the narrative. In order to be able to make sense of the text at all, we as readers have to actively conjure in our minds the meaning of "rebreather," "airlock," "arcology," etc. Conceptualizing these things takes mental resources that, in a mainstream book, we would be using to contemplate the state of the character.

For the writer, the parallel experience occurs. Having created an alien or futuristic milieu, the writer has the obligation to be true to it. This means that, instead of thinking about the character's state of mind while easily dropping in well-understood details like "car" and "snowstorm," he must focus his attention on the mechanics of exiting a Martian colony. It's difficult to do this while giving character its due.

"As You Know, Bob ..."

Mainstream literature has as many conventions as SF does. If SF is rife with stock characters, mainstream literature is rife with stock ideas. Just as a space pirate may be an unexamined cliché in SF, so gender identity, political allegiances, and relationships to the environment, to name a few, are routinely used tropes of mainstream stories. The categories of the ordinary world are taken as givens in mainstream literature; we could just as easily say *they* are clichéd.

So here we have an explanation—but not an excuse—for the lack of good characters in SF. The kind of work that goes into creating SF and the kind of work we do when reading it make focusing on character difficult.

What Makes a "Good" SF Character?

If SF uses ideas rather than character to communicate its meanings, then a good SF character is one that supports or exemplifies those ideas. This isn't the same as saying that SF characters should be simple mouthpieces for the author. The function of character may be a bit different in SF than the mainstream, but it is no less important that your characters be credible.

Your characters are the gateway into the worlds of your stories. The reader enters the story by identifying with the characters. The stronger the identification, the more vivid the experience. For this reason, it doesn't matter how detailed and wonderful the futuristic world you've created is by itself. Without an inviting and open gateway, that world will be forever closed to the reader.

The best SF characters are those who are accessible to us, but also very much a part of the worlds they inhabit. The vivid characters of the *Star Wars* movies, for instance, are successful even though they are relatively two-dimensional. Han Solo doesn't just inhabit his world, he helps define it for us.

In science fiction, you have all the normal responsibilities that a writer faces for creating strong characters. You also have the responsibility to make the character fit your invented world.

Infodump

Having characters serve your ideas does not mean they should be slavish salespeople for your imagined world. In George Orwell's classic novel *1984*, Winston Smith is completely ground down by the world he lives in. It is precisely his "unfitness" for and hatred of the world he lives in that makes him the ideal protagonist.

Creating Vivid Characters in Science Fiction and Fantasy

You can be happy about the characters you create if they are engaging, believable, and sympathetic. This is true of any literary creation, naturally.

No matter how engaging your characters are, in a SF story they'll be fighting with your setting and ideas for the reader's attention. The results of this battle of priorities have traditionally been …

➤ Flat, stock characters (for instance, crusty space captains) who need no real introduction. Such characters let you get on with the plot and ideas without worrying about character.

➤ Flat, stock settings (for instance, the standard Dungeons-and-Dragons–type fantasy world) that also need no introduction. In this case, the hackneyed setting lets you concentrate on character because you don't have to worry about the world.

➤ Rigid separation of character and setting, resulting in the author having to stop the action every now and then to lecture about the setting or ideas.

➤ "Rod and Don" conversations where the characters tell each other stuff they already know so the reader can catch up.

➤ Characters who act for no apparent reason, because the writer can't find anywhere in the narrative to stop and explain their motivations.

➤ Idiotic plot devices necessary to get the characters to do something they otherwise wouldn't do, just so we can get them to Neat Planet B or fulfill some other agenda.

Note that some of these techniques will actually work to strengthen a story in certain circumstances. Taken together, however, they pretty much catalog all the worst habits of SF writers.

Infodump

Stock (or "flat") characters can be useful. When you need to use a walk-on character (say, a pizza delivery boy) in a scene, making that character as typical as possible lets you keep the reader focused on the characters that the scene is really about. If your delivery boy turns out to be wacky, unique, and eloquent, he'll distract the reader. So stock characters can be good—just not as your heroes.

Strategies for Success

It should be clear by now that every SF story presents its own challenge to characterization.

Whose Story Is It, Anyway?

The first thing you have to decide on is your story's point of view. Whose story is it? It's often said that the real heroes of science fiction are its ideas. In the early years of SF, a lot of writers took this literally, and wrote stories in which the characters were mere mouthpieces for a lecture by the author. (The interchapters in Verne's *20,000 Leagues Under the Sea* are a great example of this kind of verbal diarrhea.) Readers today are a bit more discriminating and demand well-rounded characters as well as good ideas.

So whose story is it? One thing to remember is that readers tend to root for the underdog. If you craft a lantern-jawed hero with no flaws, people are not going to identify with him. Some authors, such as Orson Scott Card, go so far as to say that the best protagonist in any story is the person *who has the most to lose*.

Even intrinsically powerful heroes must be sympathetic. Take Superman, for instance. People admire Superman for his power, but they like him because of his essential loneliness. Imagine if his home world of Krypton had not been destroyed, and if instead Kal El were here on earth as a tourist. In that case, the whole Superman myth would start to look a little sinister. Even Superman has his human side, otherwise we wouldn't be able to see him as a hero.

Heroes we like are people who have both strengths and flaws. The strengths are what will get them through 90 percent of the story. The flaws are what keep them from achieving the last 10 percent. Much of the delight in reading fiction comes from seeing the inner struggles that people go through in life. You can't go wrong if your story's ending hinges on your hero having to undergo an inner change at the climax of the story in order to be able to win.

Would *Star Wars* have been so satisfying if Luke had simply kept his targeting computer on and ignored Obi Wan's ghostly voice? Maybe he could have blown up the Death Star using only the targeting computer. But the satisfying payoff of Luke's ultimate step on the path toward becoming a Jedi would have been missing from the story.

Competing Needs on Page One

You're faced with competing needs at the beginning of a SF or fantasy story. You need to establish the setting and overall shape of the story; you also need to establish your protagonist. Setting is usually easy for mainstream stories—you can start with a simple sentence like "It was a hot evening in L.A." This one sentence gives us the setting, and now we can move directly into the characters and conflict.

Now consider the first sentence of Michael Skeet's short story *Breaking Ball:* "They still play baseball on Mars." Does it tell us enough about where we are that we can move straight into the characters and conflict? Obviously not. This one sentence raises more questions than it answers, and Skeet knows this—he deliberately chose this opening to pull readers into the story through their natural curiosity. More to the point, this single sentence says something about both Mars and the narrator: that Mars has been settled for some time, and that the narrator has an interest in baseball and is apparently nostalgic about the Martian form.

Since you have to establish both the setting and the main character at the beginning of a SF story, consider ways in which your protagonist can *interact* with that world on the first page. You could start in the middle of a laser-pistol battle, or—as Samuel Delany does in his novel *Triton*—with the main character walking home from work through a bizarre and alien cityscape.

Danger, Danger!

When writers resort to a "Rod and Don" conversation or Great Horking Chunk of Exposition on page three to explain where the characters are and what's going on, it's usually because they haven't shown the characters interacting with their world on page one. Difficult as it is to do, showing the relationship of your world and hero at the start saves you a lot of painful rewriting later on.

A Lesson from James

"Bond, James Bond," that is. Ever notice how every Bond movie opens with an action sequence? This action sequence pulls us into the film, of course, but it's also a mini-resumé of James's skills. We often see him wearing a tuxedo and charming the ladies, then scaling a wall, slitting throats, hacking into a computer, setting off bombs, machine-gunning people, and escaping, all in the space of five minutes.

After that little sequence, we have absolutely no questions about what sort of person James Bond is. The rest of the story can get underway without any time-consuming backstory or dialog establishing his character.

We're not advocating starting every story you write as if it were a Bond movie. However, you can cram an amazing amount of information into the opening of a story, by *showing* all of it and *telling* us nothing. William Gibson is a master of this kind of narrative. Just as an exercise, read the first page of his novel *Count Zero*. Take a pen and paper, and write down every fact that you know about Turner and his world by the end of that one page. It'll be a *long* list.

Character-Building as Worldbuilding

Your characters are open windows to the world you've built. At its crudest, this means each character represents some concept or faction in the story. Darth Vader does this effectively in the first *Star Wars* movie, but, of course, his character needed fleshing out in the other *Star Wars* movies. In fleshing it out, George Lucas gave us important backstory about Darth Vader's universe and its history.

The history of your character is a minihistory of your story's world. Take the opportunity to flesh out the background of your characters in such a way that we learn more about both them and their world. The following example is a snippet of narrative that describes both character and his world at once:

> David Ndali's right eye hurt; one of the magsails at the port must be taking off. Every time a ship lifted off the pad, its magnetic wake played havoc with the cheap cybernetic eye David had gotten after he lost his original in a street fight. It was impossible for him not to notice the yachts of the wealthy arriving and leaving with plundered goods, and every liftoff was a reminder of where he had come from, and how limited was his own future.

Take care to unite character and world within the narrative, and you can avoid the "Rod and Don" dialog and massive expositional chunks so common in pulp SF.

Opportunities in Narrative Style

A lot of SF gets into trouble because writers thoughtlessly use a realistic mode of writing. *Realism* is great in Hemingway's stories, but in SF it opens you to the temptation to lecture.

> ### Factoid
>
> The three main modern narrative modes are **realism, impressionism,** and **expressionism.** Realism is basically straight reporting of facts: "Character A did this, and B resulted." Most hard SF is written in realistic mode. An expressionistic narrative tries to show the consciousness of the narrator, not the objective world; Harlan Ellison's *A Boy and His Dog* is expressionistic. And impressionists try to show the flow of experience itself, before it is organized by the analytical mind. H. G. Wells's *The Time Machine* is impressionistic SF.

You can use the flow of your characters' consciousness to present their background as well as important story ideas. William Gibson uses an impressionistic style in *Neuromancer* to seamlessly introduce ideas like cyberspace. He doesn't lecture us on the idea, nor does he drop us right into it. The novel's hero, Case, goes about his life, with cyberspace mentioned and cyberdecks occasionally shown, until we're familiar with their presence. We don't yet know what they do, but by the time Case uses one we're ready for it. Interestingly, the hero of this prototypical cyberpunk novel does not enter cyberspace himself until page 52. Since we see things through his eyes, we don't really "get it" until then either. Since Case is essentially addicted to his cybernetic connections, however, we care a lot about cyberspace by the time we see it.

Note that Gibson is not above stopping the narrative to lecture; he does so, in fact, on the page prior to Case's first entry into cyberspace. He uses the device of a television voice-over—but we still know it's the author talking. Because he does this sort of thing sparingly, he can get away with it.

The Denizens of SF: A Survey

Let's take a quick look at what makes a "good character" in different kinds of SF and fantasy. The subgenres of SF are diverse, as we saw in Chapter 3, "The Varieties of Science Fiction." What works in one kind of SF may not work in another. We'll take just three examples here: hard SF, space opera, and fantasy.

Hard SF: Engineers' Dreams

It sometimes seems that if hard SF writers could, they would dispense with having characters altogether. (There's a joke that the director's cut of the movie *Twister* has everything in it except the actors.) For some hard SF authors, the characters are literally nothing more than mouthpieces for ideas. Some hard SF novels are nothing more than 300-page "Rod and Don" dialogs. But they sell.

Human nature is not the only source of the sublime. Hard SF writers realize this, and they try to communicate the wonder of the natural world; therein lies the appeal of this subgenre. To some extent, it's valid to say that focusing too much on issues of character in such a work muddies the point.

At the same time, readers like to identify with someone in stories they read. In hard SF, we want to experience natural and technological wonders through a character in the story. SF writers who fail to provide characters with whom the reader can share the sense of wonder will largely fail to communicate it at all.

If you are writing hard SF, you still need to create sympathetic characters who have strong emotional reactions to the places and events of the story. The readers take their cues from these characters. The need for such characters explains why so much hard SF takes the form of a "tour," where a knowledgeable character shows a newcomer a wondrous world. Captain Nemo and his captives in *20,000 Leagues Under the Sea* are the prototype. We also have these examples:

➤ People who awake after a lengthy sleep or hibernation

➤ Veterans teaching recruits

➤ Primitives kidnapped by villains who must figure out their surroundings to survive

➤ A professor or inventor of a traveling device and his (often stowaway) passengers

In all these cases, one character serves as the voice of the author, and the other is a stand-in for the reader.

"As You Know, Bob ..."

Hard SF is not always this rigorous, of course. At its simplest, it is SF based on known science. Many SF writers find that the constraints of known physical laws give them greater, not fewer, opportunities for drama. If the characters don't have an easy out—using some magical technology such as hyperdrive—they are forced to be more creative, and the result can be very interesting. So, when not purely about ideas, hard SF has plenty of space for rich characterization.

The previous narrative strategies work. The alternative to them, if you want more richly textured characters, or just want to avoid the "travelogue" SF story, is to show your readers enough of your main characters that they understand where the charcaters' own sense of wonder is coming from. This is more difficult and may involve forays into backstory and even religious issues that a hard SF writer struggling with some detail of quantum mechanics may feel he has no time for. If you take the time, though, the reward will be a connection between yourself and the reader through the very sense of wonder that motivates us to read SF.

Space Opera

Space opera is the home of dashing and romantic characters. Han Solo in the *Star Wars* movies is the perfect space opera rogue; you'll find his like in hundreds, if not thousands, of paperback adventure novels published in the last century. Space opera is the domain of the "type" character—strong vivid characters who are easily categorized. The space-pirate or rogue is one such type; another is the apprentice or squire character, such as Luke Skywalker in *Star Wars, Episode IV.*

Infodump

One of the most prolific writers of engaging space opera is Andre Norton. She published dozens of rollicking adventure novels, primarily between 1950 and 1970. Her books are full of crumbling interstellar empires; free trader starships packed with cagey, streetwise crew members; and mysterious aliens offering knowledge at a dangerous price.

In archetypal space-opera stories, the main character is usually a youth who is blocked by tragedy or poverty from realizing his or her great potential. This young person gets swept up in conflicts beyond his control, and ends up coming out on top after developing his original potential while trying just to survive. Readers of space opera love the underdog. Luke Skywalker is far from unique in the genre.

A danger of using such stock characters is that if you deviate from the conventions where they originated, they begin to be visibly flat, and may easily become unbelievable or inappropriate. Stock characters limit you to stock situations. Space pirates limit you to spaceships that can heave-to and board one another, so the crusty space-pirate character is not going to work so well if your universe uses correct astrophysics, with ships following ballistics, Hohmann transfer, and minimal-energy trajectories.

Fantasy: Where Character Rules Reality

The case of fantasy is different. Fantasy is "about" character, but not in the same way as mainstream fiction. The mainstream is generally founded on realism—the notion that literature describes reality, and that good literature describes the reality of the human psyche. Key to this ideology is the notion that the human psyche is an actor in a real, physical, and stable world. This physical world can be taken for granted when writing fiction.

Fantasy turns this notion on its head. In fantasy, the physical world doesn't really exist; the world is a reflection of the characters' psyches. In fantasy, *character makes the world.*

If you are writing fantasy, you are entering a world where character and physical world overlap. Each one reflects the other. There is nothing in a fantasy world that does not have psychological or symbolic meaning, because there is nothing that is completely external to the characters.

The best way to get a sense of how character works in fantasy is to read the classics. Here we are not referring to *The Lord of the Rings,* because it is the direct source of most of the pseudo-fantasy that is written today. (This is not to say it isn't a great work; it just has too many poor imitators.) The stories that most richly show how character works in fantasy are works like *Gormenghast,* by Mervyn Peake; *The Worm Ouroboros,* by E. R. Eddison; or new works such as *The Book of Knights,* by Yves Meynard.

"As You Know, Bob ..."

Most modern "high fantasy" novels are actually science fiction, though the author may not know it. One indicator of such pseudo-fantasy is when the author uses what we call the *utility theory* of magic, in which magic is a kind of energy, often called *manna,* that certain people can tap into. Magicians cast spells by literally "plugging into" this energy. This notion of magic is purely physical and materialistic. It is a scientific notion, not a fantasy notion at all.

Danger, Danger!

J.R.R. Tolkien wrote *The Lord of the Rings* in a realistic, if pastoral, style. This is one of the sources of its appeal; it was the first great fantasy epic to adopt the trappings of realism. At the same time, Tolkien knew the mythological and fantastic very well, and grounded his realistic narrative in a very nonrealistic world. Recent imitators have tended to adopt both a realistic style and realistic metaphysics, resulting in fantasy in which most of the literary "magic" is missing.

In short, regardless of what fantasy characters may think about their world, they are actually its source, not its product. In fantasy, world and character are one.

The Least You Need to Know

➤ Characterization is harder to do in SF than in other literary forms.

➤ Different kinds of SF each have their conventional ways of handling character. These ways have evolved out of the particular difficulties each kind of SF raises.

➤ You can create vivid, believable, and memorable characters in SF if you are aware of the pitfalls of convention.

➤ SF writers have developed a set of strategies to get around the problems of exposition vs. character common to SF. Using these strategies, you can craft stories that are both good SF and good drama.

Part 3

Publishing Your Work

This is the scary part: sending your precious story to an editor. The publishing world can seem mysterious and threatening, but in this part you'll learn how to make your way through the maze of queries, SASEs, contracts, and revisions—to the ultimate goal of having a published story on the newsstands.

Submitting and, equally important, resubmitting short stories and novels require knowledge of the markets and a plan. We'll show you how to have both.

Mechanics

The modern editor wears many hats: publicist, designer, sales rep, circulation department gofer, advertising shill, and classifieds clerk, just to name a few. Editors often complain that the only time they have to actually *read* a manuscript is after work, or during their commutes. (Many editors are clustered around major cities, especially New York, but editorial salaries are more geared to cheaper locales, such as rural Mexico. As a result, long commutes feature heavily in the daily round of the modern editor.)

In other words, your work will likely either be read by a grumpy person before she's had her first cup of coffee; or by a grumpy, tired person stuck on a busy train in the final stages of caffeine withdrawal after a hard day at the office.

It's incumbent on you to make as good an impression as possible. In this chapter, you'll learn about making that prose stand out as work by an aspiring professional who will be a pleasure to deal with.

Looking Like a Pro

Proper manuscript formatting isn't a mystery, nor is it overly complex. Beginning writers often obsess about format, as though there were some magical configuration of words and pages that will punch through an editor's ennui and seize her attention with the tenacity of a terrier. In fact, it's the writing that carries the story: The aim of formatting is to be invisible.

"As You Know, Bob ..."

There are many reasons for the plain format of story manuscripts. The more invisible the formatting, the more an editor can judge each work on its own (literary) merits. Double-spacing provides room for an editor to mark up a manuscript if necessary, and by insisting on left-justified Courier, the editor can guess word lengths simply by counting the pages. Twelve-point type is easier to read than ten point.

If you were sending a resumé around to a bank, you'd probably opt for thick, creamy paper, elegant typefaces, and hyped-up marketing prose enumerating your well-rounded accomplishments. After all, every other resumé on the manager's desk would be similarly tarted-up. Failure to match their level of enthusiastic hyperbole would doom you to the wastebin. Right?

This is exactly opposite to the *modus operandi* in science fiction publishing. The standard manuscript evolved in the era of the Underwood Noiseless Type-Writing Machine, and even though you're using a 16-page-per-minute, 600-dots-per-inch laser printer, your manuscript needs to look like it came off a clunky old manual. You want your manuscript's format to disappear from the editor's consciousness, leaving only the story behind.

Each page in the body of a manuscript adheres to the same format, whether it's part of a novel or a short story. This format is engineered for maximum readability and ease of reconstruction in the event some careless soul knocks a pile of manuscripts to the ground, mixing up thousands of pages.

Some general guidelines, then, for manuscript preparation are ...

➤ Use a nonproportional typeface, such as Courier or Monaco. (A nonproportional typeface is one in which every character is the same width, so that an "i" and an "m" occupy the same amount of space.)

➤ Leave a ragged-right margin (also called "rag-right" or "left justify"). Your right margin should not be even ("justified").

➤ Double-line space your manuscript. This means leaving a full, blank line between every line of type, which leaves room for editorial annotations.

➤ Leave a 1-inch margin all the way around your manuscript pages.

➤ Use a ½-inch or five-space indent for new paragraphs; don't leave a blank line between paragraphs.

Proper manuscript format.

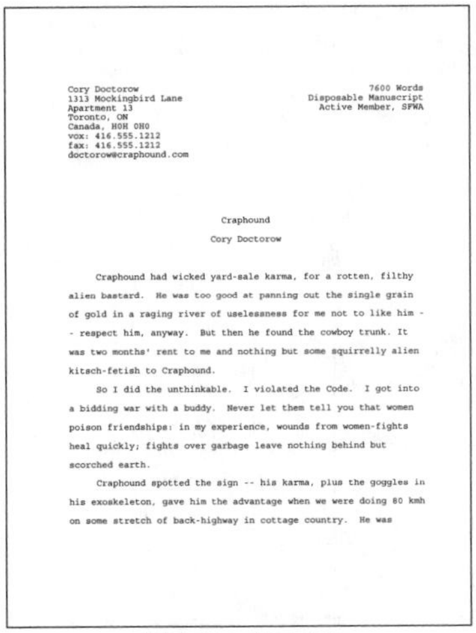

First page, short story

First page, novel

First page, chapter

Body page

➤ Don't use hyphens to fit long words on the end of a line. The sole exception is when a word is already hyphenated, like "form-factor"; it's permissible to put "form-" at the end of one line and "factor" at the start of the next.

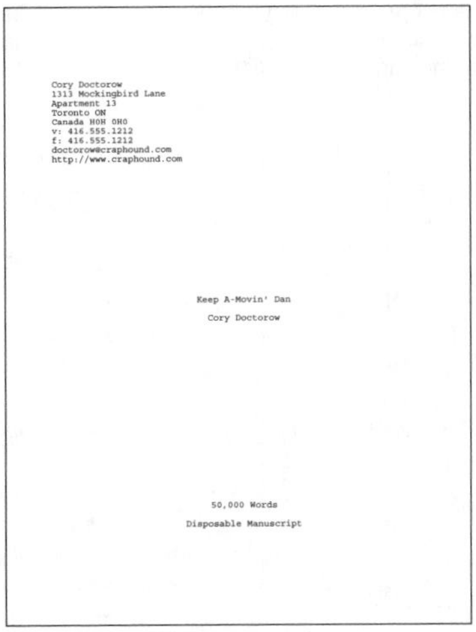

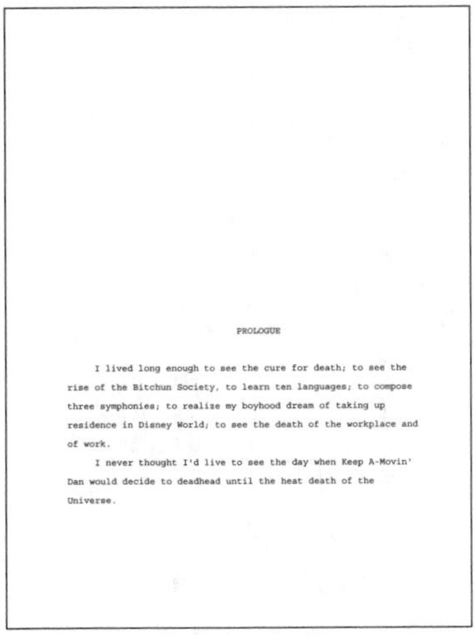

➤ Ensure that "Widow/Orphan" protection is turned off in your word processor. This is a feature that automatically prevents paragraphs from spanning pages, and you *want* your paragraphs to do this, if necessary, otherwise the word count will be thrown off.

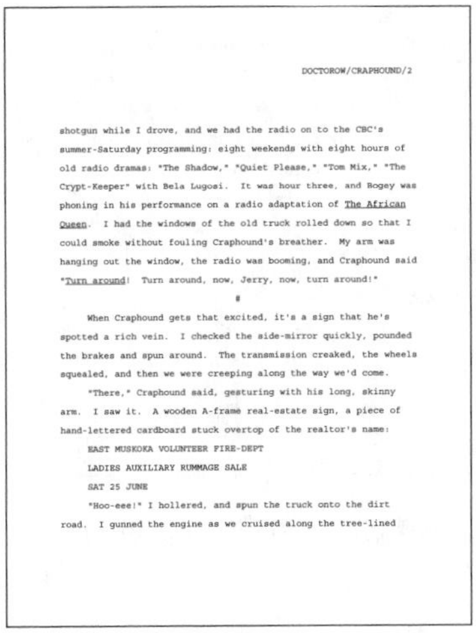

➤ Indicate scene breaks with a centered pound symbol (#). If you just use a blank line, it's possible the typesetter will miss the break if it appears at the top or bottom of a page.

131

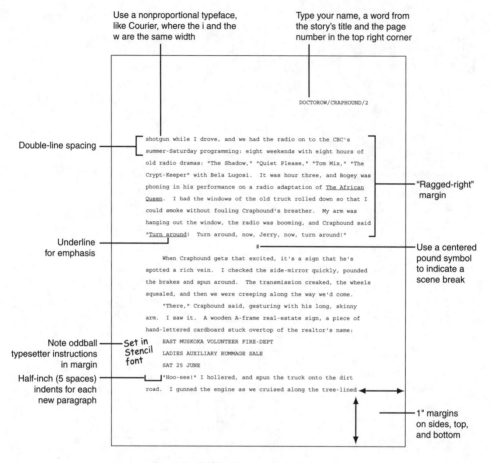

Use a nonproportional typeface, like Courier, where the i and the w are the same width

Type your name, a word from the story's title and the page number in the top right corner

DOCTOROW/CRAPHOUND/2

Double-line spacing

shotgun while I drove, and we had the radio on to the CBC's summer-Saturday programming: eight weekends with eight hours of old radio dramas: "The Shadow," "Quiet Please," "Tom Mix," "The Crypt-Keeper" with Bela Lugosi. It was hour three, and Bogey was phoning in his performance on a radio adaptation of The African Queen. I had the windows of the old truck rolled down so that I could smoke without fouling Craphound's breather. My arm was hanging out the window, the radio was booming, and Craphound said "Turn around! Turn around, now, Jerry, now, turn around!"

"Ragged-right" margin

Underline for emphasis

#

Use a centered pound symbol to indicate a scene break

When Craphound gets that excited, it's a sign that he's spotted a rich vein. I checked the side-mirror quickly, pounded the brakes and spun around. The transmission creaked, the wheels squealed, and then we were creeping along the way we'd come.

"There," Craphound said, gesturing with his long, skinny arm. I saw it. A wooden A-frame real-estate sign, a piece of hand-lettered cardboard stuck overtop of the realtor's name:

Note oddball typesetter instructions in margin

Set in Stencil font

EAST MUSKOKA VOLUNTEER FIRE-DEPT
LADIES AUXILIARY RUMMAGE SALE
SAT 25 JUNE

Half-inch (5 spaces) indents for each new paragraph

"Hoo-eee!" I hollered, and spun the truck onto the dirt road. I gunned the engine as we cruised along the tree-lined

1" margins on sides, top, and bottom

A page from the body of a manuscript.

➤ Use 20 to 25 lb. nonerasable paper. With thinner paper, the words on the next page "bleed through"; thicker paper produces overweight, unwieldy manuscripts.

➤ Use black ink on white paper. This is hands-down the most readable combination, and readability is your key concern here.

➤ Use fresh ribbons or toner cartridges in your printer or typewriter: No faded gray type, please!

➤ Indicate emphasis with <u>underlines,</u> not *italics*. The italic versions of nonproportional typefaces look too much like the normal ("Roman") versions and won't stand out.

➤ If your manuscript calls for nonstandard type (block-indents, boldfacing, weird typefaces), note this in the margin beside the type affected; don't try to typeset it yourself. Never reduce character or line spacing; this disrupts word counts.

➤ In the top-right corner of every page except the first, put your surname, a word from the title, and the page number (for example, DOCTOROW/CIGSF/3). That way, if a pile of manuscripts is dropped and mixed together, it will be easy to put yours back in order.

➤ Keep your manuscript in one piece with a paper clip or rubber band. Don't staple your manuscript, in case someone has to make a copy.

It may seem like an awful lot of rules to remember, but if you focus on keeping the finished product looking like it came off a typewriter, your format will be invisible and only the story will enter the editor's consciousness.

You should also make sure that you follow some common-sense rules for manuscript punctuation. For more details on punctuation, refer to a style book like *The Chicago Manual of Style* or Strunk and White's *Elements of Style*.

Danger, Danger!

You should not place a copyright notice anywhere on your manuscript. Under the terms of various international Intellectual Property treaties, you automatically retain copyright to any works you create until such time as you explicitly sell or give those rights away. Copyright notices are the mark of the rankest amateur, and they imply that editors are looking to steal ideas from writers.

Infodump

"British" or "Commonwealth" spelling and punctuation can be a real problem for Brits, Canadians, Caribbeans, Aussies, and Kiwis when submitting to U.S. markets (and vice versa). In general, Commonwealth markets are a lot more comfortable receiving work with American punctuation and spelling than the other way around, so your safest route is to stick to American standards.

Mark	Name	Notes and Usage
;	Semicolon	Used to set off two complete, related sentences; a semicolon is less forceful than a period.
...	Ellipsis	Used to set off sentence fragments or excerpts. An ellipsis has *three* dots. Be sure that your word processor doesn't substitute a typesetter's ellipsis for the three dots.
....	Ellipsis and period	When a sentence fragment falls at the end of a sentence, it is followed by a period.
"	Quote mark, double quote, inch mark	Used to indicate a quotation. Periods, commas, exclamation marks, and question marks should fall within the closing quote (e.g., "Hello there," he said). Colons and semicolons go outside the closing quote. Be sure that your word processor doesn't substitute curly quotes (" ") for these.
'	Apostrophe, single quote, foot mark	As an apostrophe, it is used to indicate contractions in words like "can't" and "won't." As a single quote, used to indicate quotes-within-quotes, such as "Then he said, 'Don't you dare,' and you know me, I can't resist a dare," Tom said. Be sure your word processor doesn't substitute curly quotes (' ') for these.
—	Em dash	Used to set off parenthetical comments in sentences—this is a subordinate clause—and not surrounded by spaces. Be sure that your word processor doesn't substitute a typesetter's dash (-) for the em dash.
#	Pound, hash, octothorpe	Used to indicate a scene break. Place centered on its own line.
-	Hyphen	Used to join compound words like "form-factor" and "best-of-class."

A Word About Word Counts

Word counts are more complicated than you may suspect. Editors aren't really concerned with the number of words in a manuscript; they're concerned with how many pages your book or story will occupy. Consider the following passage from "Craphound," by Cory Doctorow:

"Maybe fifty bucks," I said.

"Fifty, huh?" he asked.

"About that," I said.

"Once it sold," he said.

"There is that," I said.

"Might take a month, might take a year," he said.

"Might take a day," I said.

Now consider this one:

> The fates were with me again, and no two ways about it. I took home a ratty old oriental rug that on closer inspection was a nineteenth-century hand-knotted Persian; an upholstered Turkish footstool; a collection of hand-painted silk Hawaiiana pillows and a carved Meerschaum pipe. Scott/Billy found the last for me, and it cost me two dollars. I knew a collector who would pay thirty in an eye-blink, and from then on, as far as I was concerned, Scott/Billy was a fellow craphound.

Both passages will occupy roughly the same amount of space in a magazine, but the first one is 39 words long, while the second is 84 words long. If magazines used actual word counts as the basis for payment, only independently wealthy writers could afford to put dialog in their stories.

Luckily, this isn't the case. When editorial guidelines ask for a word count, the number they want is roughly 250 × (the number of complete pages in a manuscript), rounded to the nearest hundred.

In other words, if your story is 27.5 pages long, the word count would be:

$$250 \times 27.5 = 6,875$$

rounded to the nearest hundred, it is 6,900

Word count is one of the biggest reasons for standard manuscript formatting. If writers submit work with randomly chosen typefaces, letter sizes, spacing, and margins, it becomes impossible to make accurate word counts, and that means that it's impossible to figure out whether the publisher has room for the story in a magazine.

Infodump

The rule of thumb for word counting is 250 words per page. For a more accurate measure, you can use the following procedure: Count the number of lines on a manuscript page, multiply that by the number of characters you can fit on a line, and divide by six. This is the true number of words per page in your manuscript.

Short Stories

The first page of a short story serves many purposes: It is a reminder of your return address, the story's word count, and your credentials. It also provides a space for your editor to send notes to the typesetter.

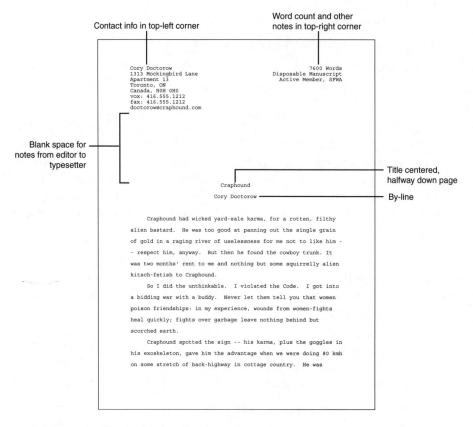

Contact info in top-left corner

Word count and other notes in top-right corner

Cory Doctorow
1313 Mockingbird Lane
Apartment 13
Toronto, ON
Canada, H0H 0H0
vox: 416.555.1212
fax: 416.555.1212
doctorow@craphound.com

7600 Words
Disposable Manuscript
Active Member, SFWA

Blank space for notes from editor to typesetter

Title centered, halfway down page

Craphound

Cory Doctorow

By-line

Craphound had wicked yard-sale karma, for a rotten, filthy alien bastard. He was too good at panning out the single grain of gold in a raging river of uselessness for me not to like him -- respect him, anyway. But then he found the cowboy trunk. It was two months' rent to me and nothing but some squirrelly alien kitsch-fetish to Craphound.

So I did the unthinkable. I violated the Code. I got into a bidding war with a buddy. Never let them tell you that women poison friendships: in my experience, wounds from women-fights heal quickly; fights over garbage leave nothing behind but scorched earth.

Craphound spotted the sign -- his karma, plus the goggles in his exoskeleton, gave him the advantage when we were doing 80 kmh on some stretch of back-highway in cottage country. He was

The first page of a short story.

The first page of a short story is slightly different from all the other pages:

➤ In the top-left corner, your name, address, phone/fax numbers, e-mail address, URL, and other contact information should appear.

➤ In the top-right corner, the word count and any notes on the manuscript or your professional affiliations should appear (e.g., "Disposable Manuscript").

➤ Leave half the page below this information blank. This gives the editor room to make notes to the typesetter.

➤ Halfway down the page, centered, should be your title (don't underline or uppercase the title).

➤ Beneath the title, place your *by-line.*

➤ On the next line, begin your story.

Factoid

Your **by-line** is the name that your work is published under. This should usually be your real name. There are exceptions: You may want to include professional honorifics (Dr. or Ph.D.), middle initials (when your name is similar to that of another writer), or familiar versions of your given name ("Billy" instead of "William"). Some writers choose to write under an alias (or pseudonym) for personal or professional reasons.

Novels

The first page of a novel serves many of the same purposes as the first page of a short story: It is an administrative page with contact, by-line, and word count information, and leaves room for editorial notes.

Like short stories, novels have a different first page:

➤ In the top-left corner, your name, address, phone/fax numbers, e-mail address, URL, and other contact information should appear.

➤ Halfway down the page, centered, the novel's title should appear.

➤ On the next line, also centered, your by-line should appear.

➤ On the last line of the page, centered, your word count should appear.

The next page is formatted like a regular manuscript page, except that the top half should be left blank. Halfway down, center your chapter title and/or number. The first page of the first chapter should be numbered "1"; the title page doesn't count.

Start each chapter with a fresh, half-blank page.

Proof and Research

It's not enough to run your manuscript through your word processor's spell-checker (although that's a good start). You should thoroughly proofread every word you send to an editor (that includes your cover letter!).

Proofreading is the process of examining every word in the manuscript, looking for typos, punctuation errors, incorrect grammar, and other errors. You should also keep an eye open for continuity problems, such as a torn shirt on page 4 that's miraculously fixed on page 12, as well as consistency in character and place names.

The first page of a novel.

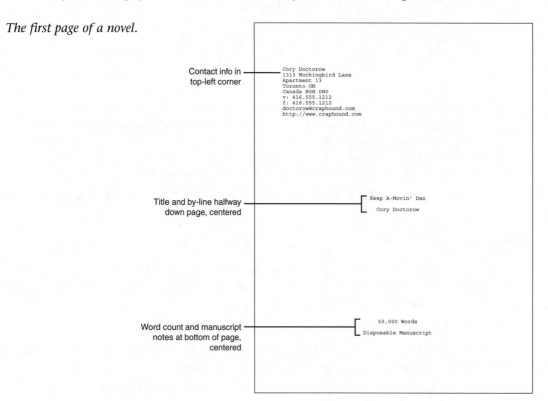

Contact info in top-left corner

```
Cory Doctorow
1313 Mockingbird Lane
Apartment 13
Toronto ON
Canada H0H 0H0
v: 416.555.1212
f: 416.555.1212
doctorow@craphound.com
http://www.craphound.com
```

Title and by-line halfway down page, centered

```
Keep A-Movin' Dan

   Cory Doctorow
```

Word count and manuscript notes at bottom of page, centered

```
50,000 Words

Disposable Manuscript
```

Danger, Danger!

It may seem like an efficient move on your part to simultaneously submit your story to multiple markets. Don't! Few editors are willing to consider a manuscript while another editor has it on her desk. You may think that you can get away with simultaneous submission, but editors know and talk to one other—some are even married to each other! If you get caught simultaneously submitting to a market that requires exclusive submission, you can kiss your credibility good-bye. It just isn't worth it.

There are as many styles of proofing as there are proofreaders. The biggest challenge is to force yourself to examine each and every word: By this point, you're probably so sick of your manuscript that this is the last thing you want to do.

Sometimes, it helps to get a literate, compassionate friend to do a first pass over your manuscript. If you have such a friend, *treasure that person.* It's still important that you personally do a final pass.

Choosing Your Market

The next step is to find a market for your polished gem. For short stories, this means magazines, contests, and anthologies. We've included an appendix of short-story markets at the back of this book, as well as the addresses of various Web sites that carry up-to-the-minute listings of new and defunct markets.

Your two prime considerations in choosing a market are payscale and appropriateness. In other words, you want to send your work to the highest-paying market out there that publishes work like yours.

Infodump

Refer to the market listings in Appendix B, "Publisher Listing," and ensure that the market looks for standard formatting. Rarely, markets will have some important variation on the standard format. Most often, variants come from contests that require that your name appear only on the cover sheet and not within the manuscript itself.

The Least You Need to Know

➤ Manuscript format is based on a tradition that grew out of typewriter-era technology.

➤ Word counts reflect pages filled, not actual words.

➤ Start with the highest-paying markets and work your way down.

➤ Simultaneous submissions aren't allowed!

Submit!

The previous chapter covered the mechanics of formatting your manuscript professionally. In this chapter, we tackle the actual business of submission: cover letters, postal matters, rejection letters, and, of course, publication.

As with manuscript format, the key concept to remember here is *simplicity*. Keep cover letters short, keep queries polite, and keep yourself busy at your keyboard during the interminable waits.

Writers are forever attempting to uncover hidden messages enciphered in their rejection letters, but again, *keep it simple*. When an editor expresses regret at not buying your story, chances are she means it. When an editor asks to see something else, she's not just being polite. Take rejections at face value and enjoy a sane career.

Cover It!

The biggest mistake you can make with a cover letter is to include too much. A cover letter should be, at most, a single page, and it can often be just a single, short paragraph. You should *never* use a cover letter to explain or summarize your story: If reading the manuscript doesn't tell the reader everything he needs to know, you need to rewrite it.

There are four objectives you want to meet with your cover letter:

➤ Provide your contact information.

➤ Specify the details of your submission.

➤ Recount your relevant credentials.

➤ Introduce yourself.

In the top-right corner of your cover letter, enter your name, address, phone number, and as many of the following as you have: fax number, e-mail address, and Web address (URL). This takes care of contact information.

Below this, flush left, enter the name of the editor you're writing to and then the address of the magazine. Leave a blank line and enter the date.

Below the date, begin with a salutation, such as "Dear Ms. [Editor's Surname]." Unless you know the editor personally, don't address him by his first name. Never start a cover letter with "To Whom It May Concern"; if you don't know the editor's name, look it up on the magazine's masthead, the publisher's Web site, or get it by calling the publisher. Don't presume to use familiar versions of the editor's name (Isaac Asimov was legendarily prickly about being addressed as "Ike").

Infodump

In science fiction, a short-short story has fewer than 2,500 words; a short story has fewer than 7,500 words; a novelette has fewer than 17,500 words; and a novella has fewer than 40,000 words.

Now, begin your first paragraph. Cory likes to say something like, "Please find enclosed my novelette manuscript, 'Craphound.'" The important thing is to introduce the title and length category of your manuscript.

Continuing, insert any special remarks about the manuscript: "The manuscript is *disposable,* and I've included a SASE for your response."

Now we come to credentials. What's a credential? It's something that suggests that the editor should pay attention to your manuscript; something that indicates a level of professional acclaim. Usually, this means prior publications in magazines the editor is likely to have heard of. Note that this doesn't preclude small presses or Web 'zines, but if the market is small to the point of utter obscurity, don't bother listing it. Other possible credentials include professional certifications, graduation from major genre workshops, creative writing degrees, other degrees that relate to your story, awards, and prizes.

Note that rejections from other editors are *not* credentials. Neither are nice things that your friends say about the story, self-publication in print or online, or qualifications in fields unrelated to writing or the subject matter of your story.

A good credentials section might look like this:

I am a recent creative writing graduate from the University of Kalamazoo, where I published several short stories in the *Kalamazoo Review,* a literary journal. My recent publications include:

"Duran Duran Duran: A Garage Band Story," *TransMeta,* Fall 2000

"The Last Words of Brad Disney," *InterSkiffy* (www.interskiffy.com), Summer 2000

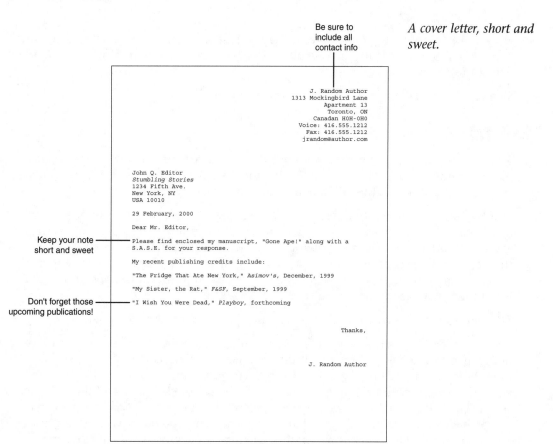

Be sure to include all contact info

A cover letter, short and sweet.

Keep your note short and sweet

Don't forget those upcoming publications!

```
                                        J. Random Author
                                   1313 Mockingbird Lane
                                          Apartment 13
                                           Toronto, ON
                                        Canadan H0H-0H0
                                    Voice: 416.555.1212
                                      Fax: 416.555.1212
                                     jrandom@author.com


        John Q. Editor
        Stumbling Stories
        1234 Fifth Ave.
        New York, NY
        USA 10010

        29 February, 2000

        Dear Mr. Editor,

        Please find enclosed my manuscript, "Gone Ape!" along with a
        S.A.S.E. for your response.

        My recent publishing credits include:

        "The Fridge That Ate New York," Asimov's, December, 1999

        "My Sister, the Rat," F&SF, September, 1999

        "I Wish You Were Dead," Playboy, forthcoming


                                              Thanks,


                                              J. Random Author
```

Factoid

A **disposable manuscript** is a manuscript that the editor doesn't need to return to you. In the old days of carbon copies, only writers with personal typists would dream of this, but with the advent of laser printers, it's often cheaper to print a new copy of the manuscript at your end than it is to pay for return postage from the publisher's. Publishers don't really care if your manuscript is disposable or not, except to make sure that they don't throw away your only copy.

List four or five of your publications at the most, giving preference to recent sales and major markets. Keep mentions of small-press sales to an absolute minimum—one or two at the most.

Sign off with a "Thank you" or "Sincerely," and you're done!

Mail It!

The manuscript is clean, the cover letter is done, you've researched the *perfect* market, so now you want to get it into an editor's hands as quickly as possible. Maybe you are even thinking about registered mail, or FedEx, or Priority Courier.

Think again. Magazines often rely on P.O. boxes for submissions (priority mail services often won't deliver to a P.O. box), while publishing houses have mailrooms that efficiently sort and deliver mail internally. If you send your manuscript via a service that requires a personal signature from an editor, it will often mean interrupting work to sign at the front desk, or worse, a lunch hour wasted in line at the post office. This is not the way to get off to a good start with an editor.

The *only* acceptable way to send your manuscript is by regular postal mail.

But the envelope! Surely, a regular envelope isn't nearly enough protection for a Work of Art such as your story! Sure it is. Padded envelopes—especially envelopes with horrible shredded paper filling—are total overkill (your manuscript is made out of *paper*, why does it need padding?). Besides, padded envelopes stack poorly and slide off the shelves onto the floor. While we're on the subject, licking an envelope is a perfectly acceptable way of sealing it. You certainly don't need to tape the envelope shut, nor do you need to staple, glue, or wax-seal it. Opening an overly sealed envelope is an amazing pain in the butt, and not the way to get yourself remembered favorably by an editor.

If you're mailing an entire novel manuscript, you can package it in a cardboard box—the kind that copy shops give you your papers in—or bind it with a couple of rubber bands.

You're almost done now. All that remains is the SASE (pronounced to rhyme with "mace"), short for "self-addressed stamped envelope." This is the envelope that the editor will send your contract or rejection back in. If you've opted for a disposable manuscript, you can use a regular, business-size envelope, also called a #10. Otherwise, you'll have to fold up an envelope big enough to mail the whole package back to you. Write your address in the center, affix sufficient postage to get a letter (or the whole manuscript, if you've opted not to use a disposable manuscript) from the publisher to your place, and slide the whole thing into a big envelope.

Be sure that the big envelope is big enough that you don't need to fold your manuscript—reading a manuscript that won't lie flat because it's been folded in thirds is a pain.

Infodump

In addition to a SASE, you might want to include a stamped post-card, so that the publisher can drop you a line when the manuscript arrives to let you know that it made it all right. Note the postcard's presence and purpose in your cover letter.

When you're submitting to a foreign market, be sure to include postage that's valid in the publisher's home country. In the U.K., U.S. stamps are only good for collectors! You can buy stamps from most countries' postal services' Web sites, or you can purchase International Reply Postage Coupons (I.R.P.C.) from your post office. You'll need one I.R.P.C. if you're an American mailing a disposable manuscript to Canada (or vice versa), and two I.R.P.C.s for overseas transactions.

Visit your post office for sufficient postage to mail the now-completed package, stick it in a mailbox, and go home and start to work on your next piece.

Electronic Submission

It may seem to you that all this business with paper manuscripts and postal mail is archaic. After all, it's the twenty-first century—the future!—and this is *science fiction*, the place that's always lived in the future. Why not just *e-mail* your manuscript?

You're right. Now forget about it. Editors have enough to do without printing out your manuscript. And if you think that they're going to read your piece off the screen, you've got another think coming. Most editors already have glasses thick enough to distort space and time—the last thing they want to do is read a single extra word off the screen.

The same thing goes for faxes. If every one of the 1,000+ manuscripts that a major publishing house receives in a given month arrived by fax, they'd need to install a bank of 10 or 15 machines just to handle the load.

Of course, there are some markets that encourage electronic submission. If you've followed the instructions for manuscript formatting, it should be pretty easy to convert your manuscript to a format that lends itself to an easy e-mail. Don't worry about centering, but you'll have to make sure that the underlines come through in the manuscript. Surround underlined text with <u>underscores</u> or *asterisks*. Next, insert an extra line break after every paragraph. You're ready to e-mail!

Infodump

Just about the only constructive thing you can do with your frustrations at response times is to keep track of them. *The Black Hole* at www.critters.org/users/critters/blackholes/ is a project that tracks response times from various genre markets. Start submitting your own data points, and help out other writers.

Danger, Danger!

Whether you're sending in a query or a withdrawal letter, remember the importance of professionalism. No matter how miffed you are that the editor has sat on your manuscript for 18 months, resist the temptation to express this anger. Editors all talk to each other, and your poison pen will only garner you a reputation as a jerk.

God, I Hate Waiting!

This chapter would've been written a lot faster, but for the constant interruptions engendered by Cory's regular trips to the mailbox. Which is to say, editors take their sweet time in responding to unsolicited manuscripts. After all, they didn't *ask* you to send them your story—why should they drop everything to get back to you? (Actually, even when they ask for a story, they still take their own sweet time in getting back to you.) At the time of this writing, Cory has 10 stories out at market. Three of them were sent more than a year ago. Two have been with a single editor through three magazines for over *eight years*. The others were mailed anywhere between a month and three months ago.

There are a number of factors that influence the speed of response, all of them out of your control. Some editors like to hang on to good stories that don't make the cut until they have a moment to write a personal note explaining how much they regret rejecting it. Some have assistants who quickly reject sub-par stories, but pass on anything that looks professional to the editor for (eventual) personal attention. Some only read sporadically—monthly, or even seasonally. Anthology editors notoriously hold on to everything they think they might want until the submission deadline for the anthology has passed, and then make their decisions (for this reason, sometimes it's a good idea to wait until the last minute to send stories to anthologies). Some have family or health problems that keep them away from slush-reading for months at a time.

Patience, then, is the watchword of the happy science fiction writer. Once you've put your manuscript in the mail, forget about it. Oh, not literally—you should keep track of your submissions—but don't obsess over your manuscripts.

The single most important activity you can undertake while waiting to hear back from an editor is to *write your next story*.

You don't need to wait forever, though. If you haven't heard back from an editor within about 12 weeks (24 weeks for novels), send a query letter. Don't call with queries—chances are, an editor will have to look in several places in order to figure out if your manuscript is indeed on-site. A good query looks like this:

Dear Editor So-and-So:

My records show that I sent you my manuscript "Garbagesucker" on December 11, 1999. I am writing to ensure that it arrived safely. I've enclosed a SASE for your response.

Thanks,

J. Random Author

Chances are you'll get a letter within a few weeks that says that they've got your manuscript in custody and you shouldn't bug them.

After a while, if you haven't heard back from an editor, you may want to withdraw the manuscript—that is, to take it away from them so that you can send it elsewhere (remember, submitting work to multiple editors is a no-no!). A good withdrawal letter reads like this:

Dear Editor So-and-So:

My records show that I sent you my manuscript "Garbagesucker" on December 11, 1999. As I have not received a response to date, I am withdrawing the story from your consideration.

Thanks,

J. Random Author

You don't need to wait until the editor writes back acknowledging the withdrawal—most never will. Just print another copy and send it elsewhere. This is another good reason to use disposable manuscripts!

You Hate Me! You Really, Really Hate Me!

Rejection hurts. Kate Wilhelm, one of the founders of the Clarion Workshop, is famous for having her students hold their manuscripts aloft and recite, "This is me, this is my story." You are not your story! When a story gets rejected, it's the *story* that's being rejected, not the writer. Often, it's not even the ideas that drive the story that are being rejected, it's the execution. So when an editor scrawls, "Sorry, too clichéd" across the bottom of the rejection for your heartrending story about your personal experiences with the lingering death of your parents, they're not criticizing your parents' death, they're criticizing the way you wrote about it.

Small comfort, but there it is.

Rejection is a fact of life for any writer. It's not uncommon for a writer to spend years being rejected by anonymous forms before she receives her first personal rejection from an editor. The ability to face interminable, faceless, infinite rejection is the most important criterion in a writer's long-term success.

"As You Know, Bob ..."

Kate Wilhelm served as assistant editor on *Galaxy* magazine for years under chief editor Frederik Pohl. Every week, they would receive an execrable manuscript from a young man who was every bit as rotten as he was prolific. Every week, they would send him a form letter rejecting the story.

The day came when Pohl was ready to retire, and he wrote to the would-be writer. "Dear Author, for years you've sent me a new manuscript every week, and while I've never done this before, I feel I must tell you: You are not a writer. You may feel compelled to write, and if this is the case, I suggest that you show your work to your friends and family. It is my opinion that your writing will never be publishable, and that you are wasting your money on postage." He sugarcoated it some, but that was the gist.

The next week, Wilhelm, now chief editor, opened her first batch of mail and found a manuscript by the same writer.

The cover letter read, "Dear Mr. Pohl, thanks for your kind note. For years I've sent you manuscripts without receiving a single personal comment back. To be frank, I was ready to quit. But then your letter arrived and inspired me—rest assured that you'll continue to receive my stories!"

Not All Rejections Are Created Equal

Some rejections are just photocopied pages (*Playboy* uses quarter-pages!). This doesn't mean that your story is rotten, but it does mean that the editor in question was too busy to take the time to respond personally. Some editors *never* respond personally except to buy the story or request a rewrite. (You'll find more information on coping with rejection in Chapter 17, "Anatomy of a Sale.")

Sometimes, an editor—or an editorial assistant—will write a few lines at the bottom of a form rejection, or will take a moment to check off a few boxes on a checklist.

Some editors keep multiple versions of their form rejections, running the gamut from polite and generic to enthusiastic and encouraging.

If you're on friendly terms with the editor—or if she has a lot of time on her hands—you may get a handwritten or typed note explaining how much she liked the story, and how much she regrets not buying it.

While moving up through the various tiers of rejections is a useful way to measure your progress, there's one thing to keep in mind: *Unless an editor specifically asks to buy the story, or to see the story again after a rewrite, the editor doesn't want to see the story again.* Sending an editor the same story twice is borderline harassment.

There's an exception—if you significantly rewrite a story, you may want to send it to an editor who's previously rejected it, but if you've been diligently writing while your work is out at market, chances are you've got a new story to wow that editor with.

Danger, Danger!

While saving your rejections (or wallpapering with them) is fun in a self-destructive kind of way, it's a private kind of fun. Inexplicably, writers sometimes feel the need to staple *other editors' rejections* to their cover sheets. While every editor knows that they're not every writer's first choice, it doesn't make sense to rub their noses in it. Even if an editor suggests another market for your story, you probably shouldn't mention that fact when you submit it there. It's just sabotaging yourself.

Rejection Is the Best Medicine

So what do you do when you get rejected? Try, try again. Print a new copy of the manuscript, address an envelope to the next-best market, write a new cover letter, and put the package in the mail.

Most editors are way too overworked to casually spend the time to write a personal note unless they see promise in your story or in you (it's a truism that rejections apply to your manuscript, but acceptances are endorsements of you, personally). When an editor has taken the time to comment personally, it's worth a note of thanks in your next submission to that editor. You might actually want to start with that editor for your next piece, even if she's not the best-paying editor in the business.

As you continue to trade manuscripts and rejection letters with the editors in the field, chances are that you'll build some sort of relationship with them. Some editors like to get very chatty and friendly with their writers, while others prefer to maintain their distance. Take their lead: If an editor signs a rejection with her first name, address her by her first name with your next cover letter.

Getting rejected is an integral part of the process of breaking out in the field. Sending editors stories on a regular basis, stories that improve as you get more practice, is how you'll eventually convince an editor that you've got enough promise to take a chance on. This is especially true of short-fiction markets, whose best writers are forever being poached by novel editors or commissions to write *Complete Idiot's Guides*.

To Rewrite or Not To Rewrite

Editors of big-ticket science-fiction markets usually get more publishable material than they know what to do with. Consequently, it's not uncommon for editors to simply buy the best works that cross their desks. But rarely, an editor will see enough promise in a manuscript and its author to request a rewrite.

Factoid

On spec stories are written "on speculation" that an editor will want to buy them. The opposite is a commissioned piece, like this book—an editor contacted us and asked us to write it.

If you're lucky, the editor's rewrite suggestions will be good ones, ones that you'd be delighted to implement. Chances are, they'll make the piece a better fit for the market: After all, editors know better than anyone what their readers are looking for. If the suggestions are good ones, by all means, undertake the changes and fire the manuscript back to the editor as soon as possible.

But remember: An editor's suggestions are just *suggestions*. The editor didn't commission the piece, you wrote it *on spec*. You've got the final say. If an editor's suggestions will change the story in such a way as to ruin it, then, by all means, reply with a short, polite note thanking the editor for his feedback but declining to do the rewrite. If you're lucky, you may be able to sway him into seeing it your way—but don't count on it.

The Least You Need to Know

➤ Cover letters should be short and to the point.

➤ Keep your queries and withdrawals short and polite.

➤ Editors reject stories, not writers. Don't take rejections of your work personally.

➤ Making regular submissions to editors is the best way to demonstrate your promise and progress.

➤ Publication takes time—sometimes a looooong time.

➤ Don't wait around to hear back from an editor—return to the business of writing!

Chapter 14

Short-Story Markets

In This Chapter

➤ High-profile markets for short stories

➤ Starting with the slicks

➤ Specialty markets and the small press

➤ Selling stories outside the U.S.A.

➤ Seasonal markets, anthologies, and contests

The 1930s was the golden age of the pulps, with over 1,000 titles published during that decade, spanning many genres: war, romance, Western, historical, fantasy, adventure, mystery, and others. Hundreds, if not thousands, of short stories were published every month. The short story was an easy way for a new writer to break into the market.

This is hardly the case today. The market for mainstream short fiction has dwindled to a few prominent literary journals, a plethora of low-budget literary magazines, and a single short story per issue in slick markets like *The New Yorker*. In science fiction, half a dozen major markets—magazines with widespread newsstand distribution—persist.

Writing a short story is less time-consuming than writing a novel, so the volume of short stories in circulation is larger—though this doesn't necessarily imply more competition, since many of these stories are so horrible that they hardly qualify as rivals for a serious writer's work.

The Bigs

These are the biggest, most popular markets in the field, with the highest profile. Nevertheless, they are endangered—between the first and final draft of this book, *Science Fiction Age* vanished from the stands.

"As You Know, Bob ..."

Every market *says* it's open to new writers, but the truth is, most of the fiction that major markets publish is by writers with track records.

Steven Silver—an accomplished sci-fi fan and bibliographer—maintains a site at www.sfsite.com/~silverag/debut.html that tracks the first publications by various science fiction authors. By checking to see how many times each market appears in this list, it's possible to create a rough index of how open each one actually is to new writers. In doing this, we've only considered writers whose first stories were published in the last 20 years. Keep in mind, though, that Silver's survey is hardly exhaustive, and that editorial tastes do change from time to time.

There are five major genre magazines and two original anthology series in the United States. Some notes on each follow, but these are no substitute for actually familiarizing yourself with these publications by reading them and gauging their styles.

Market: *Amazing Stories*

Editor: Kim Mohan
Debut Stories Since 1980: 11
Address: P.O. Box 707, Renton WA 98057-0707
URL: www.wizards.com/amazing
Publication Schedule: Quarterly
Subscriptions: $10.95/4 issues
Lengths: 1,000 to 10,000 words
Payment: 3¢/word and up, on acceptance
Average Response Time: 87 days
Anomalies: Standard manuscript plus Social Security Number with the address on first page.

Amazing is the world's oldest SF magazine, and it's been through several incarnations over the last 75 years. In 1982 *Amazing* was acquired by TSR, the publishers of *Dungeons and Dragons*. In 1995, *Amazing* ceased publication and TSR's financial situation went blooie. In 1997, Wizards of the Coast acquired TSR and its holdings, including *Amazing,* and relaunched the magazine in the summer of 1998 at the World Science Fiction Convention in Baltimore. The latest incarnation of *Amazing* is slick and smart, and it bolsters its sales with regular tie-in stories from the *Star Trek, Babylon 5,* and other universes. The artwork and design are arguably the best in the industry.

Danger, Danger!

If Mohan has an editorial failing, it's that he pays too much attention to the stories he rejects, writing long, detailed letters full of suggestions for improving them. It's hard to fault him for this, but his response time suffers as a result, averaging 87 days. Periodically, *Amazing* closes its doors to new writers, drowned in raw slush. Before submitting to *Amazing,* it's a good idea to check its Web site—or send a SASE (self-addressed stamped envelope) for guidelines—and confirm that it's currently reading work by new writers.

Market: *Analog*

Editor: Dr. Stanley Schmidt
Debut Stories Since 1980: 20
Address: 475 Park Avenue South, 11th Floor, New York, NY 10016
URL: www.analogsf.com
Publication Schedule: 11 issues/year
Subscriptions: $13.97/6 issues
Lengths: 2,000 to 20,000 words
Payment: Sliding scale depending on length, approximately 6¢ to 8¢/word, on acceptance
Average Response Time: 35 days

Published since 1930 (as *Astounding Stories of Super Science,* later *Astounding Science Fiction;* it was rechristened *Analog* in 1960), *Analog* is the home of hard short science fiction. *Analog* generally tops the circulation figures of all the genre magazines, though that is often attributed to the large number of institutional subscribers, like science and engineering faculties and firms. In addition to short fiction, *Analog* occasionally serializes novels, though rarely novels by first-timers. *Analog*'s stories are sometimes sneered at as "Engineer Fiction" by detractors who claim that *Analog*'s readers don't care about prose and character, preferring gadgetry and science. Examination of the magazine hardly bears this out, though, since the stories are generally well-written and expertly plotted, though perhaps less experimental than those in other magazines, particularly sister magazine *Asimov's*.

Though *Analog* is almost exclusively full of hard science fiction, Schmidt frequently implores audiences at SF conventions not to exclude him from their list of markets—he's happy to stretch the definition of hard science fiction to include well-written stories that he thinks his readers will enjoy. Schmidt's stable of writers exhibit a great deal of camaraderie, sporting "Analog Mafia" buttons and appearing as a musical combo at conventions.

Market: *Asimov's*

Editor: Gardner Dozois
Debut Stories Since 1980: 17
Address: 475 Park Avenue South, 11th Floor, New York, NY 10016
URL: www.asimovs.com
Publication Schedule: 11 issues/year
Subscriptions: $13.97/6 issues
Lengths: Up to 15,000 words
Payment: Sliding scale depending on length, approximately 6¢ to 8¢/word, on acceptance
Average Response Time: 54 days

Infodump

Dozois is one of the best-read editors in the business. He also edits an annual *Year's Best Science Fiction* anthology, and exhaustively reads professional, semiprofessional, electronic, and foreign markets for stories to include.

Asimov's is a relative newcomer to the scene, founded in 1977 as *Isaac Asimov's Science Fiction Magazine*—though Asimov himself never served as regular editor. *Asimov's* has a reputation for publishing edgy, experimental fiction, including some material that barely qualifies as science fiction. The sister publication to *Analog, Asimov's* definitely qualifies as the wild, out-of-control child that the family contemplates sending to military school.

But at its core, *Asimov's* publishes character-driven, human fiction, including some nontraditional fantasy (no sword-and-sorcery). It's a winning strategy, one that has netted Dozois ("Doze-wah") 11 Hugo Awards for Best Editor since he took over in 1986. Dozois is one of the best-read editors in the business; he also edits his annual *Year's Best Science Fiction* anthology, and exhaustively reads professional, semiprofessional, electronic, and foreign markets for stories to include.

Market: *Black Gate*

Editor: John O'Neill
Debut Stories Since 1980: N/A
URL: www.blackgate.com
E-Mail: john@blackgate.com
Publication Schedule: 4 issues/year
Subscriptions: No information available at this time
Lengths: Any length
Payment: 6¢/word
Average Response Time: N/A

We're proud to have been chosen to announce the creation of *Black Gate,* a new quarterly fantasy publication in trade-paperback format. Editor/founder John O'Neill founded the sfsite.com SF supersite, and had moved away from digital publication and into the world of paper editions. O'Neill is seeking "accessible, epic fantasy" suitable for all ages. We define "epic fantasy" as fiction that incorporates strong elements of heroic myth, adventure-oriented themes, and colorful settings. We are open to fantasy of all types—including urban fantasy, science fiction, comedy, horror, sword & sorcery, and romantic fantasy—if it is well written and original. We will also consider fiction with adult content, but are being very selective."

Market: *The Magazine of Fantasy and Science Fiction*

Editor: Gordon Van Gelder
Debut Stories Since 1980: 23
Address: P.O. Box 1806, New York, NY 10159-1806
URL: www.fsfmag.com
Publication Schedule: 11 issues/year
Subscriptions: $25.97/11 issues
Lengths: Up to 25,000 words
Payment: 5¢ to 8¢/word
Average Response Time: 12 days

Another grand old man of the genre, *F&SF* has been in business since 1949. *F&SF* is also known for its literary bent, especially since its editorship was assumed by Gordon Van Gelder, who also serves as a book editor for St. Martin's Press, and previously co-edited the high-brow *New York Review of Science Fiction.*

As the title implies, *F&SF* publishes both fantasy and science fiction. Van Gelder is also a special fan of literate humor. His speedy response time and the high volume of new writers in his stable makes *F&SF* an excellent market. As one of the two major markets for a broad range of fantasy, *F&SF* is overloaded with fantasy submissions, and is more interested in science fiction.

Market: *Realms of Fantasy*

Editor: Shawna McCarthy
Debut Stories Since 1994: 2

Address: P.O. Box 527, Rumson, NJ 07760
Publication Schedule: 6 issues/year
Subscriptions: $16.95/6 issues
Lengths: Up to 10,000 words
Payment: 5¢/word (varies with length)
Average Response Time: 46 days
Anomalies: Prefers to see only one story by a given writer at a time—don't send a
   second story until you hear about the first

Realms is an infant in the field—in business only since 1994—but McCarthy's no
newcomer, having served as Hugo-winning editor for *Asimov's,* as well as co-editor of
the influential *Full Spectrum* anthology series. *Realms* is the last professional fantasy-
only market left standing; however, McCarthy stretches the bounds of fantasy to include anything that isn't out-and-out SF.

Realms is part of Sovereign Media's lineup of magazines, and like all of Sovereign's
titles, it's big and glossy, looking almost like a gaming or media magazine. This is
deliberate, as the look of the magazine attracts a lot of readers who eschew the stuffy-
looking digest-size magazines like *Analog* and *F&SF.*

Market: *Starlight*

Editor: Patrick Nielsen Hayden
Address: c/o Tor Books, 175 Fifth Avenue, New York, NY 10010
Publication Schedule: Approximately every 24 months
Lengths: Any length to "longish novellas"
Payment: 7½¢/word
Average Response Time: 200 days

The third volume of this anthology series closed to submissions in June 2000, though
volume four will certainly be open sometime soon. *Starlight* is a wildly successful project that anthologizes original fiction—original in the sense of "not reprinted," and in
the sense of "startling and new." Nielsen Hayden is a Senior Editor at Tor Books, and
has undertaken *Starlight* in the tradition of the grand anthology series of SF's short-
fiction heyday, such as *Orbit* and *Full Spectrum,* which published regular collections of
ground-breaking, world-class work.

This is no easy task. The first two volumes of *Starlight* were quite late in closing to
submissions, as Nielsen Hayden kept reading new submissions past his stated deadlines until he had enough stories that met his criteria to fill a volume. He also tends
to wait until he's got every worthy submission in hand before he rejects any of them,
which leads to long—sometimes excruciating—response times. But people keep sending him stories, because of *Starlight's* deserved reputation for quality, award-winning
fiction (the first two volumes and the stories in them have so far won a Nebula
Award, a World Fantasy Award, a Sturgeon Award, and a Tiptree Award!).

Market: *Avon Anthology*

Editor: Jennifer Brehl
Address: 1350 Avenue of the Americas, New York, NY 10019
Lengths: Up to 40,000 words
Payment: 10¢/word
Average Response Time: 365+ days

Avon recently underwent a restructuring that gutted its science fiction department, leaving Brehl practically the last person standing. Despite this, she is soldiering on with this original anthology series, which has a nearly identical criteria list to *Starlight:* original, literary science fiction. Brehl has yet to publish a single volume of this series, or, indeed, to respond to some submissions that have languished in her slushpile for over a year. Nevertheless, the money is good and the world has room for more than one *Starlight*.

Bigger Than the Bigs

Mainstream magazines like *Playboy, Harper's, Atlantic,* and others—called "slicks"—all publish fiction, including science fiction and fantasy.

Why Slicks?

Why would you consider sending a story to one of these magazines? Well, for one thing, there's the money: While a short story in *Asimov's* might net you $700, *Playboy* might give you $2,000 for it. When you consider that first novels often draw advances as low as $6,000, the logic of submitting to the slicks gets even more compelling.

Since the slicks are less concerned with the abstruse definitions of science fiction and fantasy, they are a good place to send *slipstream stories* that are betwixt and between. Some slicks, *The New Yorker* in particular, have a reputation for being more amenable to experimental and stylized writing.

The most popular genre magazines have a circulation in the 60,000 range, while *Playboy* has a circulation in excess of 3.5 *million*. That's a lot of exposure—and you don't even have to take your clothes off. Reaching millions improves your name recognition, which gives other editors a good reason to include you in their magazines. It also increases your chances of being read by teachers and professors, who might include you on a class reading list, and also of being noticed by anthologists who might reprint your work.

Factoid

A **slipstream story** is one that is betwixt and between, such as a story that is plotted like SF but contains no actual speculative elements. Slipstream writers, like Kurt Vonnegut, are often claimed by both science fiction and the mainstream.

Why Not?

So why *wouldn't* you want to send a story to the slicks? Well, first of all, they aren't science fiction magazines, and tend not to have a lot of hardcore SF readers in their audiences. Those hardcore readers are the people who nominate writers for awards. It's almost unheard of for slick publication to lead to fan-voted awards like the Hugo.

Another reason is that the slicks are long shots. Most slicks publish only one story per month, and commission a significant number of those, so that they only buy as few as four or five stories per year from the slushpile. So you're competing with short-story writers from every genre and every corner of the earth for one of four annual slots. These are very long odds, even by science fiction publishing standards.

There are a lot of slicks, and while their response times tend to be pretty good, it could still take as long as a year to show a story to every single slick before you're ready to start showing it to the genre magazines where your real chances are. Cory usually sends his stories to one or two slicks before trying the usual suspects.

Infodump

Playboy has long been science fiction's home among the slicks. Fiction editor Alice Turner, at least, reads *Playboy* for the articles, and isn't any more interested in stories with explicit sexual content than any other editor in the business.

Slicks and Stones

Appendix B, "Publisher Listing," has an exhaustive list of slicks for you to try out on your own. As with the genre magazines, it's important for you to take a close look at their fiction before sending in your own—make sure your stories aren't wildly inappropriate.

Small (Press) but Powerful

The small-press magazine—a magazine without widespread distribution that subsists largely on subscriptions and sales at conventions and specialty stores—has an honorable place in the world of science fiction. While some of these magazines are strictly amateur efforts, others are small because they're specialized and are very good within that realm of specialty. Small-press markets often pay professional rates, as well.

Many writers get their start in the small-press world. Small-press editors are often inclined to mentor beginning writers, and provide much-needed advice for new writers who need to develop their craft.

The thing that really differentiates small-press magazines from the bigs is their readership, which is almost exclusively drawn from hardcore science fiction fandom. Some draw their readership exclusively from writers who hope to sell them a story—not that this is a bad thing, since it's a good way to familiarize yourself with your peers, the writers who will be moving up the ladder with you.

We've included specific notes on the best of the small-press markets below and a full listing in Appendix B. The world of small-press is very volatile, so for current info, your best bet is to consult a Web source, like The Market List at www.marketlist.com.

Staying Power

There are small-press markets that are decades old, with venerable traditions and loyal readers. These guys are doing something right!

Market: *Aboriginal Science Fiction*

Editor: Charles C. Ryan
Address: P.O. Box 2449, Woburn, MA 01888-0849
Subscriptions: $17/6 issues
Lengths: 2,500 to 4,500 words
Payment: $200.00
URL: www.aboriginalsf.com/

Ryan prefers hard SF or SF with an adventurous bent.

Market: *Weird Tales*

Editor: George Scithers
Address: 123 Crooked Lane, King of Prussia, PA
   19406-2570
URL: www.sfsite.com/dnaweb/wrdlib.htm
E-Mail: owlswick@netaxs.com
Lengths: Up to 10,000 words
Payment: 3¢/word and up
Subscriptions: $16/4 issues

This is the current incarnation of a magazine that's been around since 1923(!). Fantasy, horror, and sword-and-sorcery are preferred.

Infodump

Weird Tales has one of the best guidelines in the business, a lengthy polemic on writing and submitting SF. You can find the guidelines at their Web site, or by e-mailing owlswick@ netaxs.com. They're also notable for responding by letter to al-most all submissions.

Street Cred

Some small-press markets have credibility—as measured in awards, critical notice, and reprints—far beyond their circulation. Often, these are the homes of stories that are too wild for the more mainstream magazines.

Market: *Absolute Magnitude*

Editor: Warren Lapine
Address: DNA Publications, Inc., P.O. Box 2988, Radford, VA 24143-2988
URL: www.sfsite.com/dnaweb/abssum98.htm

Lengths: Up to 25,000 words
Payment: 1¢ to 5¢/word
Subscriptions: $16/4 issues

Lapine publishes action/adventure stories based on hard SF.

Market: *Century*

Editor: Robert K. J. Killheffer
Address: P.O. Box 150510, Brooklyn, NY 11215-0510
URL: www.centurymag.com/
Lengths: 1,000 to 20,000 words
Payment: 4¢ to 6¢/word
Subscriptions: $20/4 issues

Killheffer publishes extremely literary science fiction, with an equally extremely erratic schedule.

Market: *The Silver Web*

Editor: Ann Kennedy
Address: P.O. Box 38190, Tallahassee, FL 32315
Lengths: Up to 8,000 words
Payment: 2¢ to 3¢/word
Subscriptions: $10/2 issues

Kennedy publishes literary SF/horror. Submissions are read January through September.

Canadians and Other Aliens

Though SF is often considered an American genre—it probably has something to do with movies like *Independence Day*—there are thriving SF communities all around the world. And throughout the Commonwealth, there are science fiction magazines that publish short stories. We've listed a number of them in Appendix B, and you'll find our favorites coming up.

Submitting to a foreign market is pretty much the same deal as submitting to a U.S. one, but remember: Your SASE has to either have postage on it that's local to the magazine's homeland, or has to include I.R.P.C.s sufficient for return postage. For overseas markets, that means *two* I.R.P.C.s.

If you sell to a foreign market, you will get paid in foreign currency. Most banks will accept checks drawn on nearly any currency, but may hold them for 30 or even 120 days, so be forewarned. If you find yourself regularly selling to a foreign market, you might consider opening a bank account in that market's currency, especially if you do other business in that country—every time you change money, you lose a little in the deal.

For Canadians who are selling regularly, a U.S. bank account is indispensable. Every Canadian has the occasional need for U.S. dollars—you might even check if your bank will give you a U.S.-dollars credit card, so that you can conduct Internet purchases in U.S. dollars without getting stung in the exchange.

Market: *On Spec*

Editor: Jena Snyder
Address: P.O. Box 4727, Edmonton, Alberta, Canada T6E 5G6
URL: www.icomm.ca/onspec/
Lengths: Up to 6,000 words
Payment: CDN$100 to CDN$180
Subscriptions: US$18/4 issues (in the U.S.), CDN$18/4 issues (in Canada)

On Spec is Canada's best-established SF magazine, publishing anything in the genre. Strong preference is given to Canadian submissions.

Market: *TransVersions*

Editors: Marcel Gagne and Sally Tomasevic
Address: P.O. Box 52531, 1801 Lakeshore Road West, Mississauga, Ontario, Canada L5J 4S6
URL: www.salmar.com/transversions/
Lengths: Up to 6,000 words
Payment: CDN2¢/word
Subscriptions: US$24/4 issues (in the U.S.), CDN$24/4 issues (in Canada)

TransVersions is a relative newcomer in Canada with a track record for publishing strong, quirky genre fiction.

Market: *Eidolon*

Editors: Jonathan Strahan and Jeremy G. Byrne
Address: P.O. Box 355, North Perth, Western Australia 6006
URL: www.eidolon.net
Lengths: Up to 10,000 words
Payment: AUS$20
Subscriptions: AUS$45/4 issues (outside of Australia), AUS$27.80 (in Australia)

This is Australia's oldest science fiction magazine, publishing impressive fiction by Australia's finest writers.

Market: *Interzone*

Editor: David Pringle
Address: 217 Preston Drove, Brighton BN1 6FL, UK

Infodump

To convert currencies, try this free Web site: www.xe.net/ucc/.

URL: www.sfsite.com/interzone
Lengths: 2,000 to 6,000 words
Payment: £30 to £35/1,000 words
Subscriptions: US$32/6 issues, £18/6 issues (in U.K.)
Anomalies: Will only consider a single story by a given author at one time

Interzone is a well-established U.K. magazine that is respected around the world. Known for publishing nontraditional SF and fantasy, *Interzone* also publishes a fair bit of perfectly traditional SF.

Contests and Anthologies

The fashion of publishing original anthologies of science fiction and fantasy waxes and wanes with the times. During the 1990s, Mike Resnick edited nearly 20 theme anthologies, and Ellen Datlow and Terri Windling edited a series of alternate Fairy Tales anthologies. In the 1980s, there was a mania for "shared world" anthologies, with the *Darkover, Thieves' World,* and *Heroes in Hell* series publishing volume after volume of short stories written by different writers in the same universe.

Things have slowed considerably since then. Three or four anthology series—*Starlight,* the Avon anthology, the SFF.net anthology, and the Canadian *Tesseracts* series—are basically it in the professional market, though a few small-press projects are always on the go.

Submitting to a theme anthology (where all the stories are written around a single theme) or a shared-world anthology (where all the stories are written with a single set of characters in a single setting) can be a risky business. A story written for a narrowly themed anthology can be very hard to sell elsewhere if the anthology's editor rejects it. Datlow and Windling's fairy tale anthologies sparked a positive glut of unsaleable fairy tale manuscript making the rounds of fantasy magazines. Many of these stories ended up stuck in their authors' drawers, never to see the light of day again.

Anthology editors also buy differently than magazine editors. They have a tendency to only reject the very worst stuff outright, and hold onto everything marginal or better until they're ready to actually start assembling the book, just in case a marginal story fills a gap left by two better ones. This can lead to response times that border on fanciful—a year, sometimes two isn't unheard of. When it comes to theme anthologies, withdrawing a story is pointless, since there's nowhere else to send it.

A very few writers have had great success in "crashing" closed anthologies. Having read the announcement in *Locus* that an editor has sold an invitation-only theme anthology to a publisher, they write a story to the theme and mail it to the editor and cross their fingers. I think of this as the writerly equivalent of skydiving: exhilarating, difficult, and risky (because a rejected story written for the specific, narrow parameters of an anthology is basically impossible to sell elsewhere). Nevertheless, it's tremendously rewarding to sell a story to an "unsellable" market.

"As You Know, Bob ..."

Some anthologies are seminal and define turning points in science fiction. Bruce Sterling's *Mirrorshades* brought the cyberpunk revolution to light, defining a generation of writers who dominated the genre through much of the 1980s. Likewise, Harlan Ellison's *Dangerous Visions* and *Again, Dangerous Visions* were the definitive anthologies of new wave SF in the late 1960s and early 1970s. A third volume, *The Last Dangerous Visions,* is legendary for being nearly 30 years late—and still counting—in being published.

Contests have grown even sparser than anthologies. A few contests persist, mostly aimed at new writers, like the *Asimov's Undergraduate Award for Excellence in Short Science Fiction and Fantasy Writing* and the infamous *Writers of the Future* competition.

Writers of the Future is a high-stakes competition for writers with fewer than three professional sales, sponsored by Bridge Publications, the publishing arm of the Church of Scientology, a cult started by SF writer L. Ron Hubbard in the 1950s. The contest is judged by leading, non-Scientologist writers who are often legendary in the field, and awards an annual grand prize of $5,000. The winners and runners-up are published in a popular anthology series, and are invited to a weekend-long writer's workshop. In its early days, the contest and the Church were kept rigorously separate, but lately it has drawn a good deal of fire from writers who feel the workshop and its teaching methods have drawn uncomfortably close to the agenda of the Church.

The Least You Need to Know

➤ Know the market before you submit.

➤ Start with the highest-paying markets and work your way down.

➤ The slicks are long shots, but their rates and circulation make them worth trying.

➤ Some small-press markets have credibility far beyond their circulation.

➤ Writing for theme anthologies is risky because you might end up with a story that can't be sold elsewhere.

Chapter 15

Publishing Your Novel

In This Chapter

➤ The SF publishing world today

➤ What you should know about the industry

➤ Steps and missteps on the road to publication

➤ What works in today's markets

Science fiction is a novelist's genre. While there are many short-story gems out there, and more being written every day, it's generally conceded that the real sweep and power of SF can only be appreciated in longer works. The best SF evokes entire worlds, and this is only really possible in the novel. Here you as an author have the broadest possible canvas on which to paint your ideas.

The readership for SF novels is much larger than for short stories. At some point you'll probably want to make the leap from writing short fiction to novels, if you haven't already.

The State of the Industry

1999 was a pretty good year, overall. There was some shrinkage and consolidation in the industry during the 1990s, but the number and variety of SF and fantasy novels being published at the turn of the millennium is still 50 percent higher than it was in the 1980s. The only area that's being hammered is horror, a market that today is 50 percent *smaller* than it was in 1990.

Fantasy sales have been more consistent in the past decade than SF sales. In 1999, there were slightly more fantasy novels sold than SF novels. This is a good time to be writing either kind of fiction.

Infodump

Editors today are under great pressure to buy books that will make the publisher a profit. Luckily, most recognize that there is no formula for doing this; nobody really knows what's going to sell and what won't. Still, the editor who buys your book will probably have to justify his decision to his boss. This makes it even more important for you to project a professional image in your manuscript preparation and queries, because your editor may have to use your material to make his own (internal) sales pitch.

What the Numbers Mean

There were about 250 SF novels published in English in 1999, and about 275 fantasy novels. Of these, 57 percent were previously unpublished works, down from 64 percent in 1989, according to the *1999 Year in Review* issue of *Locus* (February 2000).

The drop in the percentage of new books sold may look bad from your point of view; after all, that 57 percent represents the market for your own work, right? It's true that it benefits beginning authors when publishers buy more new works, but how will you feel in 10 years when you've become established? Traditionally, SF authors have made a living from having a number of books in print, and the majority of those will be reprints.

For the long-term health of your writing career, it's good if the percentage of new books creeps down a bit. After all the hard work you've put into writing your novel, you'll want it to stay in print, after all!

Your Chances

If 57 percent of the SF and fantasy novels being published right now are new, that means the major book publishers are buying new works at the rate of about one every working day!

Publishers rely on new talent. The reading public loves to discover new authors, and editors know this. If you have a novel, you should submit it; you have nothing to lose and a whole career to gain.

Publishing Myths and Legends

In previous chapters we identified the myth of talent, the myth of inspiration, the myth of splendid isolation, and others. We suggested that the best way to grow as a writer was to abandon these myths in favor of a more realistic approach to writing.

There are a lot of myths about publishing, too, but there are also legends. A legend, unlike a myth, is something that has happened or could happen, but is so rare as to be practically mythological.

The Legend of "Being Discovered"

The problem with lotteries is that people win them, thus encouraging millions of people to buy tickets—and not win. Every now and then, a completely unknown first-time author sends an unsolicited manuscript to a publisher, it's bought, and becomes a runaway success. This does happen, but not nearly as often as you might think. Most manuscripts by unknowns that a publisher receives languish on the slushpile. It's not that they won't get read, but keep in mind these points:

➤ The slushpile at any major publishing house can contain hundreds of novel manuscripts on any given day.

➤ It'll take a long time for the editor to get around to any manuscripts on the slushpile.

➤ The first reader of slushpile submissions is usually not one of the senior editors, and may not even be a member of the editorial staff, but rather whoever in the office has nothing to do that day.

Publishing is a business, and as in any other business, the more a prospective employer or customer knows you, the better your chances of doing business with them.

Infodump

Why isn't the editor busy reading the slushpile? Well, put yourself in her place. You've got a stack of 100 novels by complete unknowns to read, plus a stack of 10 novels by established writers whom you know, or who have been represented to you by an agent whom you know. Which pile is a higher priority for you?

You certainly can simply mail your manuscript to a publisher who's never heard of you and then sit back and wait. After all, this "over the transom" technique works just fine with short stories. You increase your odds of selling the book, however, if you know before you send it that your manuscript will end up on the desk of the editor, and not in the slushpile.

There are two ways to ensure that your novel gets the attention it deserves:

➤ Hire an agent to shop it around for you.

➤ Cultivate some sort of business relationship with the editor, even if it's only by sending a query letter giving your credentials and briefly describing the book.

The Legend of the Lifelong Marriage

It used to be that an author would publish with a particular house and work with a particular editor for his entire career. In the fabled "golden age," when it was common for people to work for one company for 35 years, an editor could develop a stable of authors and cultivate them over time.

In movies and TV shows about writers, we commonly see their editor visiting them at home, walking their dogs for them so they can get a book done, and generally tending to them like the hothouse flowers writers are.

In the past, it was an industry truism that in general, 85 percent of books published will lose money, 10 percent will break even, and 5 percent will make a profit. Publishers have traditionally paid for the 85 percent with the 5 percent. What this meant for the relationship between editor and author was that the editor would guide you as you grew in skill and popularity. Maybe your first three or four books wouldn't make money, but eventually you'd break into profitability and settle in for a long relationship with your editorial partner.

Things don't work that way today. In the past 20 years or so, most of the major publishing houses have been bought by multinational conglomerates for whom the bottom line is everything. Company reorganizations seem to happen almost weekly, and unprofitable book lines are ruthlessly jettisoned. There are few editors today who can confidently say they will be working at a particular house, and with a given stable of authors, for the next 10 or 20 years.

It's less likely today that your editor and you will get to know each other well. This is a shame. The upshot is that your editor has to rely more than ever before on your reputation, professionalism, and credentials when making a decision to buy your book.

How *Not* to Approach a Publisher

Professionalism is the key. This means there's a whole host of ways you can turn off a prospective publisher. Remember, publishing is a business, and when you go to sell a novel, you are presenting yourself as a prospective business partner for the publisher.

Some strategies are winners, and others are losers.

The Splashy Entrance

Some writers insist on throwing caution and manuscript format to the winds, and print their novel on 60-lb. bright orange card stock, so that it's guaranteed to stand out when stacked in the slushpile. These authors will also package the whole deal in a vivid box tied with a ribbon.

Such manuscripts stand out, all right. They practically scream "Avoid me!"

First of all, anything you do to muck with standard manuscript format may make your novel stand out, but it will also decrease its readability from the editor's standpoint. He'll have to get past that bright orange color. Some authors typeset their novel, so that it resembles a published book. Others go even further, and have the thing bound and printed. This makes it almost impossible for the editor to use his by-now habitual techniques for judging manuscript length, among other things. It also makes you look like a prima donna right from the get-go. Any editor who picks up your neatly typeset masterpiece will be afraid of altering a single word of it, for fear of how you'll respond.

The other kind of splashy entrance authors attempt is to waltz up to an editor at a SF convention and pitch their book. Some even bring the manuscript with them to wave under the nose of the editor.

This is the literary equivalent of cornering a doctor at a cocktail party and telling him all about your aches and pains. The best reaction you're likely to get is, "Damn, I thought I'd left all this at the office!"

But don't editors come to conventions to find new talent? Yes, they do, but a SF convention is to an editor what golf games are to high-powered executives: a chance to meet friends, clients, competitors, and prospective customers on a more personal basis. Business may happen on the golf course, but it's more of a place to get to know people. Many editors entered the field as booksellers, artists, or writers, and attending conventions lets them reconnect with former colleagues from their past lives. Trust and a good working relationship are important in business, after all. The same is true of SF.

Danger, Danger!

The worst thing about the splashy manuscript trick is that it gets done so often that slushpiles commonly have a few of these purple monstrosities stacked together. Far from being unique, the splashy manuscript is a tired old trick that editors develop a knee-jerk reaction against.

Self-Publishing

Don't self-publish. We couldn't be much clearer than that; but why the stigma against self-published authors?

There is a stigma, and it comes from the perception that self-published writers are not "real" writers. However true or untrue this may be, the fact is that most people in the publishing industry view self-publishing as the last resort of the failed author. People publish themselves because no one else will publish them. After all, any self-respecting writer should be able to get other people to pay him for his work. Having to pay others to read it (which is what self-publishing usually means) is a sign that your work can't stand on its own.

These days this particularly applies to Internet publication. Some authors post published stories on their Web sites as a form of advertising. It's becoming common practice for authors to provide a sample chapter of an upcoming book on their site, as a way of attracting potential readers. This is not the same as posting previously unpublished work.

It's implausible that any editor would buy a novel that you've previously posted to the Internet. They consider it already published, and self-published at that. There are rare exceptions, as when an Internet publication becomes a runaway hit. As usual, of course, the exception proves the rule: For every such success, there are a thousand failures.

Winning Strategies for Selling Your Novel

So what *does* work? What are some strategies that will put you in the game? None of them guarantee that you'll be published (the only way you can guarantee that would be to buy the publishing house yourself ... but that would be self-publishing again).

Trust the Slush

Despite the fact that the odds are stacked against you if you submit an unsolicited novel, you can still sell it in this simple and time-honored way. The secret here is to ensure that the manuscript radiates professionalism. It must follow manuscript format, have a comprehensive outline or synopsis attached to it, a cover letter detailing your credentials, and an SASE (self-addressed, stamped envelope).

The biggest problem with the slushpile is that it is slow. As with any other time when you're waiting to hear from a publisher, of course, you can use the waiting time to write some stories or start a new novel. Just make sure you do one thing: Set a time limit on how long you'll let the manuscript languish at any given publisher.

This time limit should be a minimum of three months, and a maximum of 12. If you haven't heard back by the end of this period, send the publisher a polite letter asking what's happening with the submission. If the publisher does not reply, or beats around the bush, it's probably time to write them another polite letter withdrawing the submission.

Submit a Query

Freelance writers often sell a story idea using a project proposal. You can do this with books, too, but it almost never works for first novels. Established writers can pitch a novel idea to the publisher, because their editor knows from prior experience that the writer can do the work. The same is not true for untried novelists.

Most publishing houses will ask to see the whole manuscript for your first novel. You can send the publisher a *partial*. Partials have the advantage that the established writer doesn't have to write the whole novel "on spec"; she can find out early on if her publisher is interested. The editor has the chance to get involved in the book early in its gestation, so the editorial process becomes much smoother. It's a good arrangement for both parties.

If you've queried a publisher and gotten a positive response, they'll be expecting your manuscript when it does show up. It might still end up on the slushpile, but at least it'll be on top. Certainly the editor will turn to your manuscript before he looks at one written by someone he's had no contact with.

Infodump

Be firm with your self-imposed time limits. Karl once had a novel manuscript languish at a top U.S. publisher for three years before he withdrew it. He tried not to pester them; when he did send a letter or (after a while) phoned to ask about its status, he was told they were "seriously considering it." After 36 months of this, they rejected the book, without offering an explanation or critique.

Factoid

Established writers often use **partials** to pitch new novel projects to their publisher. The partial consists of a synopsis and sample chapters (usually the first three). Sending a partial almost guarantees a response of, "Sounds interesting, why don't you send the whole thing?"

Use an Agent

Consider using an agent (see Chapter 22, "Agents") if you're not sure you know your way around the publishing industry. If you wouldn't know a good contract from a bad one, or a good publisher from a cutthroat subsidy house, then an agent can help you avoid a lot of pitfalls.

It's your literary agent's job to know the publishers, and know his way around a contract. He'll also provide you with an objective assessment of your work. If your agent says your novel needs work, he's probably not kidding around.

Many authors have hired an agent after they've sold a novel. Why? Because bringing in an agent at contract negotiation time will almost certainly result in your getting a better contract. It may result in a bigger advance or royalty—in which case, the agent's paid for himself by the end of negotiations.

Build Credibility and a Name

For the determined writer, the best way to guarantee you'll sell your first novel is to dive into the SF writing and publishing community with both feet. Meet the editors at conventions or other events; buttonhole other authors. Learn who's who in the industry, and what editor likes what kind of fiction. Most importantly, prove your abilities by writing and selling good science fiction and fantasy.

The moral of the "legend of being discovered" is that while it's possible to sell a novel as a complete unknown, it's a heck of a lot easier if you've got a name. This is nothing to moan about; it's just an admission that publishing works the same way as any other business.

Danger, Danger!

No amount of charm can substitute for having a good story to sell. You can charm every editor in the business, but if your work isn't up to snuff they won't buy your stories. So if you want to know which is more important to the development of your writing career, writing ability or self-promotional ability, the answer has to be writing ability.

We're not saying that you need to have a Nebula Award–winning story out there before the publishers will pay attention to you. In general, editors are inclined to think the best of new writers. People will give you breaks if you show promise and indicate that you're working hard. A couple of sales to semipro magazines, followed by a couple more to the pros, suggests you are improving, and that a novel by you might be worth looking at. For most editors, this impression will be further bolstered if they've met you in person and you've impressed them as someone they could work with.

Many successful SF writers have come out of fandom. The vast and energetic network that is the science fiction fan community has deep ties with the writing and publishing communities. A good reputation in fandom can do you no harm in publishing circles; although, once again, fandom is not writing. Credibility in the fan community is not a currency that can buy you a novel sale, or even a short-story sale in any major market. What fan reputation demonstrates is a genuine love for the subject, and possibly a commitment to promoting SF. By itself, this kind of reputation will not get you sales, but it can help.

Be Relentless

Determination and patience are essential traits in a writer. Don't be discouraged if a particular publisher decides not to buy your novel. There are others. Most importantly, at this level of the publishing industry, buying decisions are agonized over and take time.

Some major writers were rejected by all the big-name publishers before having their work picked up. The classic example is Stephen R. Donaldson's *Chronicles of Thomas Covenant the Unbeliever,* which was rejected by everybody before at last being picked up by Del Rey.

Where to Sell

We've included a list of reputable SF and fantasy book publishers in Appendix B, "Publisher Listing." Before submitting to a publisher, make sure you know how they prefer to be approached. It won't do any good to send a query if they explicitly say that what they want is the whole manuscript. You'll just slow yourself down with that kind of approach. Check their requirements, and make sure you're familiar with what kind of books they publish. It's easy to visit a local bookstore and review what's on the shelves.

If there's a line of books from a particular publisher that you enjoy, perhaps that's where you should start. If your writing style matches what their editors like to buy, you're ahead. But don't try to second-guess any publisher by saying to yourself, "I've got them figured out: If I write a novel using such-and-such ideas and with this kind of action and characters, then they're sure to buy it." After all, whatever you see on the shelves is what they were interested in buying one or two years ago. If you want to know what they're interested in today, you'd better ask them.

Infodump

Rejection means a lot less than you think. Legend has it that John Kennedy Toole committed suicide because of his failure to sell *A Confederacy of Dunces.* Too bad he didn't stick around, because the book did sell after his death and went on to win a Pulitzer Prize!

The Least You Need to Know

➤ The market for SF and fantasy novels is very good right now.

➤ Publishers are always looking for new talent. You have nothing to lose and everything to gain by trying to sell novel-length work.

➤ Avoid using cheap gimmicks to gain the attention of a prospective publisher. Go through the tried-and-true channels.

➤ Your reputation is your best salesman. Short-story sales, script sales, or some other reliable track record will impress the editors more than a ton of charm and self-promotional savvy on your part.

➤ Don't be discouraged by rejection. Some of the biggest names in SF were rejected by a dozen or more publishers before their first novels were published.

Chapter 16

The Work-for-Hire Novel

In This Chapter

➤ The nature of work-for-hire

➤ How to get your name in the pool

➤ The big franchises

➤ Gaming novels: try or avoid?

➤ Upsides and downsides to work-for-hire

➤ Doing the work

A lot of the books in the sci-fi section of your local bookstore are probably media tie-ins, gaming novels, or other packager-run work. In fact, there's likely as much shelf space given over to *Star Trek* and *Star Wars* novels as there is to regular SF. In this chapter we'll look at this burgeoning market, so that you can decide if it's right for you.

Writing work-for-hire fiction is a bit different than writing in your own universe. We'll examine these differences, as well as the advantages that playing in someone else's sandbox can provide. Armed with the facts and fallacies, you can then decide whether work-for-hire is for you.

Book Packagers and Media Tie-In Publishing

At one time or another while visiting your bookstore, you've probably randomly flipped through a Harlequin romance, *Deep Space Nine* novel, or Dungeons and Dragons adventure book. If you're like most writers, your first reaction was, "I could do better than this!" Eyeing the dozens of similar titles on the shelf, you begin to wonder if you've been missing out on a writing gold mine.

The answer is, it depends on you. Some writers thrive on *work-for-hire*. Others, even the best prose artists, just can't do it. Work-for-hire writing is demanding on both your time and your creativity. It only *looks* easy. If, however, you're one of those proud few who can do it, work-for-hire can be lucrative and fun.

Factoid

Work-for-hire typically means writing a novel or short story that is set in an already-established universe. For instance, you might land a contract to write a *Buffy the Vampire Slayer* novel, in which case you will be writing in the Sunnydale of the TV series, and using the already-established characters of the show. These are not your settings or characters; they are owned by someone else. The only way you can sell a *Buffy* novel is if that someone else hires you to write it; hence, "work-for-hire."

The rules of work-for-hire writing are very different from anything we've covered so far in this book. Your options and responsibilities are different. Your contracts and rights are also very different than they would be with a standard publishing house. Some of these differences can become traps for writers who don't know about them beforehand.

Before we look at how work-for-hire is different for you, the writer, let's define it properly.

Work-for-Hire: It's Their Sandbox

Most published books that trade on a particular brand name or copyright owned by someone are produced on a work-for-hire basis. *Star Trek, Star Wars,* the *X-Men,* and *Xena,* for instance, are trademarked or branded names. What this means is that the characters, settings, and worlds of these stories are owned by someone (usually a corporation). These license owners are the only people who can produce books about these characters.

If you are contracted to write a novel set in such a universe, you are working for the license owners. You do not have any rights to the world or characters beyond the project you are working on.

Actually, contracts in which the publisher retains the copyright for a work-for-hire novel are illegal under U.S. copyright law. The copyright for a work-for-hire novel is yours, regardless of what the contract says. (Note that we're talking about the copyright on your specific work, not the rights to the characters or storyline, which the publisher is explicitly lending you in contracting the novel.) Of course, no one has ever contested the practice of work-for-hire publishers, and you probably wouldn't want to be the first to do so. Just bear in mind that if you sign such a contract, you are being taken advantage of.

Danger, Danger!

Never, ever write a story set in somebody else's world or using their characters, and try to sell it without their permission. It's almost impossible to pull this off, and if you do, you will be sued, and you will lose the lawsuit. The characters and worlds of an author or media house are literally owned by them. You are exposing yourself to civil action which will probably result in substantial judgments against you.

Size of the Market

In 1999, 17 percent of all SF and fantasy titles published in North America were media-related—a whopping 191 original novels. This includes "young adult" *Sabrina, the Teenage Witch* books, *Star Trek* and *Star Wars,* and *The X Files.* There were 29 *Star Trek* novels published, compared to 10 set in the *Star Wars* universe.

For television-related titles, series that are currently in production obviously do well; there were 14 *Buffy the Vampire Slayer* novels published in 1999. However, even shows that are no longer being made may have strong followings. Despite no longer being in production, the *Babylon 5* universe saw four new novels published in 1999.

Comics-related novels are intermittently a good market, depending on the yo-yo business cycle of the comics industry. Marvel averages a dozen or so comics-related novels per year.

Gaming has proven to be a consistent source for new fiction. The biggest producer of gaming-related novels in recent years has been Wizards of the Coast/TSR, who in 1999 alone published 34 novels. The rest of the gaming community combined produced about half that number in the same time frame.

These numbers show work-for-hire writing to be thriving. Now is a good time to be setting your sights on this market.

The Cuts of the Pie

When a book packager approaches a publisher with a project—say, a *Star Trek* novel—both the packager and the publisher expect to see a return from the project. For the publisher, it doesn't make any sense to negotiate an advance for a project like this that's any higher than they would give any of their own authors. So advances for work-for-hire novels tend to be about the same as those for author-owned works.

In other words, as the author of a work-for-hire book published by a major publisher, you will be dividing your advance with the packager who brought you the project. Since it's not likely to be a bigger advance than you'd get for a project of your own, you'll be making half the money for the same amount of work.

Infodump

Gaming publishers work a bit differently. They often own both the rights to the game and their own publishing operation. You may receive both a full advance and a competitive royalty. Because you're selling into a niche market, however, don't expect you'll be able to get rich this way either.

Of course, if the story in question is set in a milieu and uses characters that are licensed from a third party (someone like, oh, say George Lucas), then the license owners will want a cut of the advance as well. Since this could itself be 25 percent, you as the author might receive as little as $1,500 for the novel you wrote.

Some packagers offer a flat fee for a work-for-hire project; you won't necessarily be receiving royalties for the book.

Getting a Foot in the Door

Don Bassingthwaite has published six work-for-hire novels for companies such as White Wolf and Wizards of the Coast. While he acknowledges that most work-for-hire publishers seek out the talent for projects they already have in mind, he points out that they can only choose from people they know about. There are several tried-and-true ways of getting on a publisher's short list of potential authors.

Don describes his own entry into the business this way: "A story for *White Wolf* magazine got used instead as a mood setting piece in one of their game products and after that, I just kept reminding them that I'd be interested if they ever decided to do regular fiction. When they did decide to do fiction, I was invited into the anthologies and then eventually asked to do the various novels I published with *White Wolf*. That got me publishing experience, so when I decided to go back to doing tie-in fiction, I could go to game companies and say, 'Are you planning to do fiction? Are you interested in looking at proposals? Here's a sample of my tie-in work.'"

You can try sending proposals to work-for-hire publishers, but as Don points out, they usually have their own ideas about what they want. They're not likely to run with your proposal as it stands. If they like your writing, however, they may consider you for a project they've developed in-house.

Writing credentials with other projects are your best asset in trying to land a work-for-hire contract. Because such projects are often done very quickly, with no maneuvering room if the author turns out to be incompetent, publishers want to know ahead of time what kind of work they can expect from you. While you're toiling away at the novel, after all, somebody in production may be designing the cover, and they may be slotting you into a fairly complicated printing schedule. If you don't come through with the goods, there's going to be more than just embarrassment going around.

The only real proof that you can deliver is evidence that you've delivered in the past. Luckily, it's possible to build up your credentials, as any writer does, from short-story sales and work-for-hire shorts, to journalistic work and nonfiction book-length work, or straight to work-for-hire novels.

There is no one path that works. But if you follow the general strategy of building credentials and keeping yourself in the eye of the publisher by sending them proposals or queries, you stand a good chance of landing a contract.

Star Wars and *Star Trek* Novels

The most visible work-for-hire novels on the stands are those set in the *Star Wars* and *Star Trek* universes. *Star Trek* novels have traditionally sold so well that there is usually at least one on *The New York Times* bestseller list.

"As You Know, Bob ..."

Many writers consider a top–10 standing on *The New York Times* bestseller list to be the ultimate sign of success. Of course, the *Times* has its own criteria for selecting books, and it's just one of many measures of success. Your book might reach the list, but if it was overprinted and only 20 percent of the print run sold, your publisher might still lose money on it.

This should be enough to set any self-respecting author salivating. The possibilities seem limitless, if you can just land a contract for one of these babies. Can you do it? Yes—but there's a catch.

Tightly Controlled Empires

The conglomerates that control TV and movie tie-in publishing are rather like the Empire in *Star Wars:* powerful, inaccessible, and always hatching plans of their own. They are the license owners of these stories, and they are very careful about what gets done with them. If they are publishing books set in a series-in-progress, then they already know what's happening next in their shows. This has a lot of implications for how they contract writers.

The license owners generally have a very good idea of what they want to see in print. In fact, they usually know exactly what story they want written next. Knowing this, they are able to hunt around for published writers whose work matches what they're after. Then they'll approach this author to do the work.

A lot of people write *Star Trek* novels, then try to sell them. This rarely works, for the above-stated reason: The license owners are looking for particular stories. Good stories that don't align with their vision are rarely accepted.

The number of *Star Trek* novels languishing in drawers, never to see the light of day, must number in the hundreds, if not the thousands. This illustrates a general principle, which we'll belabor in the next section: *Never do the work before you are contracted to do it.*

Speed Publishing

By the time a movie comes out, the novelization has almost certainly been contracted out, written, and published. The books are waiting in the warehouse, ready to go into the bookstore in time for—or as a teaser for—the opening of the film.

Once media license owners decide to do a novelization, they act quickly. Since this can happen while a show is still in production, you're not likely to hear about the possibility in advance. By the time you know about the film, the novelization is probably already underway.

In the Realm of the Gamers

Game-related stories have been big at least since *Dragon* magazine published its first *Dungeons and Dragons* story, way back in the 1970s.

Today there are a half-dozen game companies producing novels related to their products. Some of these are one-time experiments, such as the novelization of the computer game *Doom*. Some, like the *Forgotten Realms* role-playing books, run into the dozens, and even have subseries within the main series.

The gaming crowd is different from the SF publishers you'd deal with for your own projects. They tend to control their own products, sometimes to such an extent that you, as author, have little or no access to the gaming universe you're supposed to be writing about. Games are often the work of a small number of people who want to keep tight control of their intellectual material.

Indeed, a lot of gaming novels today are written by the developers themselves. This says nothing one way or the other about their quality; what it does suggest is that breaking into the gaming market can be more difficult than with other work-for-hire projects.

"As You Know, Bob ..."

The biggest gaming novel publisher today is Wizards of the Coast/TSR. Their products range from Pokémon card games to role-playing games and CD-ROM products. They produce a number of fiction series, including *Magic: The Gathering, D&D—Dragonlance, D&D—Forgotten Realms,* and *Star Drive.* An aggressive company, Wizards recently acquired TSR, the original maker of *Dungeons and Dragons,* as well as several successful card-game companies.

The Dilemma of Quick Publishing Credentials

Many writers think that writing a tie-in is a shortcut to recognition—a foot in the door of the publishing industry. It is and it isn't.

If you've been contracted to write the novelization of a movie like *The Phantom Menace,* then you've got it made. Unfortunately, the packagers don't hire unknowns to write books at that level.

If you've landed a contract to write one or more gaming novels, things might look good for you. Writing credentials are writing credentials, after all. If you've got one or more such books under your belt, publishers will treat you a bit more seriously when you approach them with your own project in hand.

Moving from Tie-Ins to Your Own Stories

Most people who write tie-ins eventually want to get some of their own stories published. This isn't a universal thing; a lot of writers really enjoy writing in a universe whose parameters have already been set for them. Writing a tie-in can be intensive, focused good fun, and these writers wouldn't trade it for the angst-filled years-long job of coming up with their own world and characters. Besides, the money can be good.

Assuming you have gone the tie-in route, however, and now want to publish your own work, can you do it? Definitely. Will you find yourself farther ahead than if you'd started out writing your own novels? Probably not.

Bringing Your Audience with You

If you move from writing tie-ins to writing your own books, you won't automatically bring your old audience with you. If your own books are substantially similar to what you've been doing for the packager, and if you can find some way to communicate with the fans of your tie-in books, you may be able to bring some over. More than likely, though, their interest was in the branded, licensed characters and worlds you were writing about, not in your own writing. Most will probably stay with what they know and like.

Building a fan base is therefore essential if you're writing tie-ins and want to move over to writing your own stuff. Communication with your readers, whether at conventions, by mail, or through the Internet, is your best bet for building your own brand loyalty.

Most authors who begin to publish their own original novels find that they are starting from scratch in building an audience. The publishers know this; they will not automatically assume, since your last tie-in sold 40,000 copies, that your first solo novel will do the same. In that sense, writing tie-ins puts you no further ahead.

Infodump

It's possible to use both work-for-hire and your own fiction to promote one another. If you are selling short stories set in your own universe, readers who like your work there may recognize your name on the bookstands and pick up one of your work-for-hire novels. If you sell a *Star Wars* novelization, for example, your name will be sufficiently widespread that a positive effect on sales of your other work is almost inevitable.

Making a Living?

How much of an advance might you expect for a work-for-hire book? It can range as high as you would get for your own fiction novels. If the work is done for a book packager, however, you'll be splitting the advance with them. If there is also a license owner in the equation, they will take some too. You could end up getting as little as $1,500 for writing a full novel.

Since you'll likely take anywhere from a few weeks to eight months to write the book, it should be obvious that work-for-hire SF and fantasy do not a living wage make.

Nor is it likely that work-for-hire writing will give you time to pursue your own work. The work-for-hire project will likely consume all your writing time, as well as use up your creative juices.

For instance, you might have negotiated a nice contract to write a gaming novel in three months. The advance is actually enough to live on for that amount of time.

You apply yourself full-time to the novel and finish it in a month and a half. Now you've got the rest of the time to write your own fiction!

Or do you? Just as you type "The End," the gaming company phones you up and says they've redesigned the game. They want you to take your novel in a different direction now. Suddenly you've not only lost your planned writing time, but by hurrying through the project you've actually wasted your time and energy.

This kind of scenario happens more than publishers would like to admit. It's easy for the schedule to slip because of rewrites or complete conceptual reworkings of the material. If your rent depends on the project, you may find things a bit thin on the table for the next few months.

Why do it at all, then? Well, if you're not dependent on this income for your daily wage, the money from a work-for-hire project can come in very handy. Buy that DVD player you had your eye on. Pay off the car. Fix the roof. Work-for-hire may not be a living wage, but it's good money if you don't let the project consume you.

> **Danger, Danger!**
>
> Planning is crucial in writing on a work-for-hire schedule. You can't afford surprises. For this reason, having clear rules in the contract about what you'll be delivering and when is important.

Writing a Work-for-Hire Novel

The biggest mistake writers make when they approach work-for-hire is thinking it will be easy. Somehow, they believe that they can slack off when it comes to writing in somebody else's milieu.

Don Bassingthwaite points out that the publisher's goals for a work-for-hire novel are exactly the same as they are for any other work: to produce a good book and have it do well in the marketplace. Just because you're working in an already established milieu does not mean you should take the work any less seriously.

Writing a work-for-hire novel is easier than writing your own only because the settings, characters, and often the situations have already been determined for you. You don't have to spend a great deal of time worldbuilding when you do work-for-hire.

The fact that the setting is predetermined is actually a two-edged sword, however. As Don points out, it creates new challenges that you wouldn't face with your own stories. "You can't kill characters off at random, you can't blow up important things, you can't continually hold out the threat of apocalypse only to have it averted at the last minute because someone else is going to have to deal with that after you. To a certain extent, working within those limits is actually a good thing—I think it can make you a better writer because you can't just go for a quick fix."

You may also have to deal with fans of the genre who know a lot more about the worlds you're writing in than you do. You may have read one or two of the books in the series, and browsed the series bible; they've read *all* the books, twice. If you slip up on some detail of their beloved world, they'll notice, and they won't forgive you for it.

The Contract

Work-for-hire contracts tend to be very different from the sort of contract you'd sign for your own work. They tend to take much more than a standard contract, and offer you less for it. You would do well to fight for as much as you can get on a work-for-hire contract, because at best you're still unlikely to get terms as good as those you'd get for your own work.

Following is a list of critical contractual clauses commonly lacking in work-for-hire contracts. These are things you should fight for if you don't see them in your contract:

➤ You should not have to begin work on the project until you've seen your first payment.

➤ Ensure that you've been approved to do the work by the licensor of the property; get written assurance that the publisher has the right to contract you for this project.

➤ You should be paid for your time, not for the product. If the project is cancelled, you should be paid a pro rata portion of the advance proportionate to the work completed, but never less than 50 percent of the agreed-upon advance.

➤ You should work from an approved outline and should not be required to revise beyond the scope of that outline. If such extra revisions are necessary, you should be paid extra to do them.

➤ Delivery payment must come within 30 days of delivery, whether or not you will be called upon to do revisions later.

➤ Your credit on the cover should be agreed upon in advance, and if another writer is brought in to "doctor" the book after you're done with it, you should have an escape clause in the contract allowing you to have your name removed from the cover.

➤ If you're going to get royalties, they should be sent along with statements and contract details to you or your agent. There should be a clause giving yourself customer audit rights.

➤ The licensor, publisher, and packager should cross-indemnify you over legal liability with respect to any material supplied to you or added to the manuscript by anyone other than you.

If any or all of these items are missing from your contract, you open yourself to all manner of abuses by the publisher or rights owner.

Danger, Danger!

Writers are often inspired by TV shows (the "Hey, I could write a better episode than that" syndrome). Novelizations are different from episodes, however. Experienced work-for-hire authors know that movie scripts need to be expanded by 100 percent or more in order to become novels. A good idea for an episode of *The X Files* may not be a good idea for an *X Files* novel, because the formats, lengths, and pacing of the two kinds of stories are very different. Beware of imagining an episode of your favorite TV show and then trying to make a novel out of it.

Punctuality Is a Virtue

Work-for-hire books are usually done on a schedule. Sometimes the schedule is very tight. It's important that you take this timeline seriously; writing a work-for-hire is not like cramming for exams.

Many writers do, in fact, write the bulk of their work-for-hire books at the last minute. Some rent hotel rooms for the weekend and hole up there with the word processor and several pounds of espresso coffee. It's not so much that this approach doesn't work, but it's supremely risky. If you put off working on the book then get the flu on the weekend that you had scheduled to write it, you're screwed.

Don't Get Too Involved

In technical and marketing writing, you quickly become used to projects being pulled out from under you. Companies and products change direction very quickly. Often weeks or months of painstaking work will have to be thrown out because the organization or product has taken a new direction.

The same can happen with work-for-hire fiction. For this reason, you shouldn't get too emotionally involved with your own work-for-hire prose. You may have written a masterpiece, but if it turns out not to meet the new marketing plan of the company you've done it for, you'll have to shelve it. For this kind of work, getting paid for doing the job is much more important than seeing any particular piece of prose in print.

The Least You Need to Know

➤ Work-for-hire novels are written under license to the people who own the rights; for instance, George Lucas owns the rights to *Star Wars*.

➤ The work-for-hire market is large and healthy.

➤ You're unlikely to make a living wage writing work-for-hire, but it can be a fast track to seeing your own name in print.

➤ Work-for-hire does not guarantee a market for books published under your own name.

➤ Work-for-hire projects won't help you clear up time for your own writing; they tend to eat that time.

➤ You can use work-for-hire projects to develop the discipline of your craft and to supplement your income.

Chapter 17

Anatomy of a Sale

In This Chapter

➤ How to cope with rejection

➤ You sold it!

➤ Getting published (finally!)

➤ Sell it again (and again)

Writing fiction is a waiting game. You wait for inspiration to strike. You drum your fingers impatiently until your workday is out so that you can write. You wait for your workshop to critique your manuscript. You wait some more while the revised piece is rejected, with glacial sloth, by a variety of editors. Finally, you are rewarded: An acceptance letter!

What comes next is a long, long, *long* wait. Or rather, a series of merely long, long waits. You wait to hear back about revisions. You wait for a contract. You wait for a check. You wait for the title to show up in stores, then you wait some more for your contributor copies. More waiting ensues: Do the reviewers like it? Are the sales figures good?

Cory is quite possibly the *least* patient man ever to walk the earth. Seriously. If the International Olympic Committee ever approves of Extreme Fidgeting for the Olympics, you can bet that Cory'll bring home the gold for Canada. If *he* can cope with all this waiting, so can you.

How do you cope? The answer is twofold: First, you need to understand the process at the other end, and get a sense for just why it takes so! damned! long!; next, you need to find something productive to do with your time while you wait—say, writing your next piece.

Coping with Rejection

You're going to get rejected a lot over the course of your writing career. Rejection, death, and taxes are the fledgling writer's only sure bets (and while cryotechnology may stave off death forever, no such hope looms for rejection). Successful writers understand that rejection is a fact of life, and they know how to deal with it.

Death, Taxes, and Rejection

When you pour your heart, soul, and guts out on the page, how can you *not* take it personally when an editor rejects a manuscript?

The first thing you need to understand is what a rejection really means: Your piece isn't right for the market. That doesn't mean it isn't good enough, it means it isn't a good enough *fit*. For whatever reason, your piece doesn't fit into the editor's plans for the magazine. Maybe they published a similar piece recently and the publisher or the readers complained; maybe they're full up for humorous/experimental/straight-ahead/ short/long pieces for the next year or two; maybe the editor just wasn't the right audience for the story. (Of course, the possibility exists that it just wasn't good enough, but every story you write should be as good as you can make it.)

Cory likes to assume that editors who reject his stories are worried about the unseemly appearance of a magazine that wins too many awards, and so have turned the story away to give another, less privileged editor a crack.

Infodump

One reason to send your work to small-press magazines like *Weird Tales* is that their editors often take the time to write detailed rejections, explaining exactly why they bounced your story.

Rejection is a fact of life, and doesn't mean that the story isn't any good. Cory's first professional publication was "Craphound," in *Science Fiction Age*. After buying the story, editor Scott Edelman rejected no fewer than 20 of Cory's stories, including "Visit the Sins," which, after publication in *Asimov's*, was reprinted in David Hartwell's *Year's Best SF Volume 6*. Does this mean that Edelman made a mistake in not taking "Visit the Sins"? Not at all—it just means that the story wasn't a good fit for *Age*.

Decoding Rejection

There's a trend in established writerdom to poke fun at the efforts of newbies to establish a hierarchy of rejection. The thinking goes that rejections should be taken at face value, that second-guessing an editor's intention is a waste of time. Just accept the rejection and move on to the next market.

We have a very different take on things. As has been noted, writing is a pretty thankless task, and doubly so before you've been published. Just about the only yardstick an unpublished writer has to judge her progress by is the quality of rejection she's getting.

And there *is* a definite hierarchy of editorial response. From bottom to top, it goes like this:

➤ Generic form rejection

➤ Personalized form rejection (i.e., "Dear Cory," scribbled on the top)

➤ Personalized form rejection, with a note (i.e., "Thanks for sending it—try me again, okay?")

➤ Personal note (i.e., "Hey, Cory, great seeing you at the WorldCon. Things are good here—how's by you?")

➤ Personal note with a reason for rejecting the story

➤ Rewrite request

➤ Sale

Danger, Danger!

Time is the most precious commodity in an editor's life. When an editor takes some of it to scribble a sentence or two on your rejection, take it as high praise. Cory has seen novel manuscript submissions that have earlier personalized rejections stapled to the cover with "Gee, thanks. Please don't patronize me," scribbled by the author beneath. This is not a good idea.

Not every editor uses all of these steps, but most use at least two or three. When you get a personalized form rejection, or better yet, a form with a note at the bottom, that's real progress! It means that you've been noticed, that the editor has read a good chunk of your manuscript, and that he thinks that someday you may write something that he'll want to publish. It means that you're better than 90 percent of what has crossed his desk recently. Have a beer and celebrate!

Note the critical difference between a personal note with a reason for rejecting the story and a rewrite request. When an editor sends you a letter that runs, "Thanks for letting me have a look at this. I'm simpatico with the message here, but I just didn't find the plot of this story engaging enough," take that as a very positive sign, and be sure to send that editor another story.

What you *don't* want to do is try to beef up the plot and send it back to that editor. If she hasn't explicitly asked for a rewrite, she doesn't want to see the story again. What her note was meant to do was encourage you and let you know where she thinks your weaknesses as a writer are, so that someday you can write another story that will work in her magazine.

Even if an editor *does* request a rewrite on something you've submitted, you are under no obligation to do so. You may violently disagree with the editor's suggestions, and at the end of the day, it's your manuscript. If you don't like an editor's suggestions, feel free to ignore them and try another market.

Editors Only Remember the Good Stuff

Some writers worry that their stuff isn't good enough to show to an editor. They put away their manuscripts in drawers rather than take a chance that an editor will see their imperfect work and conclude that they will never have anything to offer to the field.

This is an awfully dangerous misconception. Editors need to take a long view when they publish your work. Since most first novels fail to make a gigantic hatful of money for their publishers, when an editor buys a book from you, she's betting that you will someday write another, and another, and another, and that each will be better than the last, and that they will not be too widely spaced. She's betting that you will build a following and gain critical acclaim and that your books will someday fill the publisher's coffers with smooth, sensual U.S. currency.

It's even more speculative on the magazine publishing side of things. An editor who publishes your early stories will not sell a significant number of copies by dint of your name appearing in the table of contents. Editors who publish your early short work are betting that you will make a name for yourself before you leave the world of short fiction for the more lucrative novel market, and that they will be able to plaster that name all over their magazine's cover and boost their sales.

What this means is that even if an editor isn't buying your work, you still want to be putting it under his nose on a regular basis. You want to let an editor know that you're taking this whole thing seriously, that you're writing regularly, and that your writing is steadily improving. You want to proffer sufficient evidence to convince an editor that it's worth his time to keep on opening your manuscripts, because someday you will send him something that will sell a million copies, win awards, and make him some dough.

You don't need to worry about editors reading your stuff and giving up on you in disgust. Editors know better than anyone else that early stories by talented people are frequently unreadable tripe. And they see enough unreadable tripe on a daily basis that the odds of an editor remembering your unpublishable messes are slim to none. Editors only remember the good stuff, the stuff that's improving—and your best bet for getting remembered by an editor is to give them plenty to remember you by.

Infodump

The exception to the rewrite rule is Stanley Schmidt at *Analog* magazine. Though he rarely explicitly requests a rewrite, he is not adverse to seeing rewritten versions of stories that he has taken the time to comment on.

Sale! But Wait, There's a Catch

When your stories and novels are collecting rejection notices, it's easy to fantasize about a day when you open a SASE and find yourself staring at an acceptance letter. Thinking about what happens *after* your work is accepted can seem like hubris: The acceptance letter can become your goal.

Time Dilation

If you thought that time dilation was strictly science fiction, think again. The time it takes you to actually sell your work will seem negligible next to the time it takes before your mom can get a copy at the corner bookstore.

Here's how you might end up selling your first novel: You've waited patiently while the book languished in the slushpile of an editor at a major trade house, only to find the book rejected after 18 agonizing months. Undaunted, you fire the book off to another publisher, and then another. Finally, years later, you get a phone call:

"Is this J. Random Author?"

"Uh, yeah?"

"Hi! This is John Q. Editor at Spunky Books. I've been looking at *The Space Between My Ears,* and I really, really like it."

"Yeah?"

"Yup. I'd like to buy it. How's that strike you?"

"Uh, yeah! Yeah! That's great!"

"Terrific. Why don't you have your agent give me a call and we'll work out the contract?"

"Agent? Oh, sure, my *agent!* I'll do that! Thanks, thanks a *lot!*"

Chances are, this contracting process will take a long time. Months-long negotiations are not unheard of. Sometime during that period, you might get a list of revisions that your new editor would like to see undertaken for *The Space Between My Ears,* and you need to talk over these revisions with your agent, then get them written. By the time you've got your contracts in hand, you're ready to start waiting to hear back on your revisions.

> **Danger, Danger!**
>
> Rejecting a rotten manuscript is easy. Rejecting a good manuscript is a lot harder: Books that are "almost there" will often get passed to multiple editors and assistants for a read before judgment is passed on them. The upshot of this is that the better your manuscript is, the longer you can expect to wait to hear back from a publisher.

This can take months. Months and months and months. During this time, you'll also be waiting to see the *cover flats,* cover copy, and to find out about the schedule date. Any one of these is subject to more delays. In the meantime, your agent will be pimping the *other* books you wrote while you were waiting to hear about *Ears,* and starting even more waiting in motion.

You may be asked to approach writers you admire for blurbs on your book, and you'll wait to hear back from them. You'll wait for bound *galleys* of your book to get sent around to stores, buyers, and reviewers, and you'll wait for the actual publication.

Once the book is published, you'll wait for it to show up in the stores, and you'll wait to hear about the sales figures and the reviews. During this period, you'll be pimping yourself to the local media machine, lining up interviews, signings, and appearances.

If you're prolific enough, the waiting will recede in your consciousness over time. During this waiting process, you'll also be working on your next book, touring with your previous book, and negotiating reprints of the one before that.

Factoid

Cover flats are stiff sheets of glossy card-stock with a preview of the cover art for your book, often used to help publisher's reps pre-sell the book to booksellers. **Galleys** are page proofs of the final book which are distributed to authors, reviewers, and booksellers.

When Good Magazines Vanish

For magazine writers, the waiting is only slightly less onerous. In general, you can expect to hear back about a short story in three months or less—though some editors routinely take up to a year to get back to you.

Having sold a manuscript, you can expect to see your contract in short order, and your check not long after that.

However, the final, crucial stage of selling a story—having it appear in print—is no faster than novel publication. Most magazines are unwilling or unable to let you know what the schedule date is for your story, often because the story is being held for use as "filler" for an underweight issue in the dim future. Some magazines guarantee publication in a fixed period, say two years, but others—notably *Asimov's*—are infamous for refusing such a clause and holding onto stories for long, long periods before publishing them.

And in today's times, seemingly healthy magazines may shut down with the writer last to know. You may think that your manuscript is in good hands, awaiting publication, but the erstwhile editor is actually on a bread line, and your story is sitting in a pile that's waiting to be sorted through by the bankruptcy trustees.

You need to stay on top of your sold pieces, but you don't want to be a nag. If you've sold a story to a magazine but haven't received a contract, payment, or a publication date, it's a good idea to "ping" the editor every month or so, gently reminding him that you're still out there. If you're worried that a magazine may be folding, by all means, withdraw your story and get it in front of another editor as quickly as possible. Life's too short.

Published at Last

The mailman just arrived and left behind a fat envelope from your publisher. Greedily, you tear into it.

It's your book! You've finally made print. This is some deeply good news. Sure, they might've missed a typo or two, and you were never very happy with the decision to stick a Budweiser girl in a space bikini on the cover, but dammit, you're in print, and that's reason to celebrate.

There are a few things to remember here:

Infodump

The late, lamented *Science Fiction Age* magazine was famous for its prompt response times. Editor Scott Edelman usually responded to submissions in two weeks or less, raising the bar for editorial behavior throughout the industry. Gordon Van Gelder at *The Magazine of Fantasy and Science Fiction* seems ready to assume Edelman's mantle as the fastest editor in the biz, with great, writer-friendly response times.

➤ Keep some copies for yourself. SF goes out of print with depressing regularity, and you're going to want to have a copy or two kicking around to show your grandkids.

➤ Order some copies through your publisher. Your publisher will make books available to you at a deep discount, and having copies to hand out is great for personal appearances, friends and family, and the like.

➤ You should have started your publicity rolling before this, but now it's go-time. You've got the product, and it's time to start making some calls. See the next two chapters for more information on publicity.

Most bookstores are happy to have signed stock, so if you find yourself in a store with your book on the shelf, do seek out a clerk and offer to sign the stock.

If you're a real eager beaver, make up some business cards or bookmarks advertising your Web site or other books, and insert these in the books on the page where you've signed.

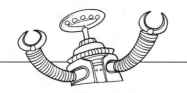

Resale

A fundamental tenet of freelance writing is to never sell something just once. While the payment you receive for a reprint can be quite small relative to the first sale, there are many opportunities for resale that will occur throughout your career.

The Vanishing Publication

The word of the day is *anticlimax*. For years, you've labored to sell a story to the bigs—it took Cory 10 years to make his first pro sale—and then you waited for interminable months for the magazine to hit the rack. Now, four weeks later—poof! it's gone.

That's right: As soon as your issue is supplanted by the next, your story vanishes off the shelf, never to be heard from again. This is why a good freelancer's strategy is to *never sell a piece just once*.

Ideally, your story can find many, many homes over the years, as various adaptations and reprints come into play. It's important to carefully negotiate your contracts so that you retain the rights to reprint your work elsewhere.

Reprints

Your best bets for reprints are:

➤ Online

➤ Anthologies

➤ Other magazines

Web sites like BiblioBytes (www.bb.com) happily "reprint" published work online in html format. While they don't pay upfront for these publications, they do offer writers a split from the revenue the story generates through "banner impressions" (sites like BiblioBytes get paid a small sum by their advertisers every time someone visits a page with a banner ad on it). The advantage of such an online reprint is that is gives you the opportunity to keep your work available to the public while you attempt to market other works, and while you're pitching for body-of-work awards like the Campbell.

Anthologies are tricky to submit to—in general, anthology editors solicit reprints when they're assembling the book. But an author who diligently scans the news sections of *Locus* and *Science Fiction Chronicle* will occasionally happen upon a listing for a new book of, say Exciting Kitchen Appliance Stories, and immediately fire off her long out-of-print *Asimov's* story, "The Fridge That Ate New York," to the editor.

As far as the annual best-of anthologies go (such as Dozois' *Year's Best Science Fiction*, Hartwell's *Year's Best SF*, and Datlow and Windling's *Year's Best Fantasy and Horror*), there's generally not much point in sending stories to the editors, since they widely and exhaustively read the major and semipro markets for likely candidates. The exception is when your story has appeared in a particularly obscure market *and* you know that it's a good fit for the series, based on your reading of previous volumes. *Don't* deluge these already overburdened editors with your manuscripts—you'll just be wasting your money and their time. But *do* send them the occasional story that you think merits a reprint.

A story sold to a Canadian, British, or Australian magazine is often eligible for a reprint in a U.S. magazine (although, following the rules we set out in Chapter 14, "Short-Story Markets," you should be sending your stories to the higher-paying U.S. mags first). Check the magazine's guidelines to see what rights they acquire. If they're only seeking first U.S. rights, you can legitimately send in your Commonwealth-published stories for reprint, though you should mention the publication history in your cover letter.

The Least You Need to Know

➤ Rejection of your work doesn't necessarily mean it isn't good enough, it means it isn't a good enough *fit*. Don't take rejection personally.

➤ Once you're in a waiting mode for a project, start another one.

➤ Only you get to decide when you want to rewrite.

➤ Selling a story isn't the same thing as getting published.

➤ The smart freelancer sells her work over and over.

➤ Always look to resell your work as many times as possible.

Part 4

Marketing and Self-Promotion

If you're writing good material but you'd like to reach more readers, this part can show you how to tap into the power of the media through effective self-marketing techniques.

Who knows, you may even win one of SF's many literary awards. If so, we'll show you how to get the most out of the win. And if the Internet's your thing, you'll find some tips on how to market yourself through the Net, from setting up your own Web site to promoting your work. We'll also talk about using e-mail and newsgroups to build your profile with readers.

Chapter 18

Self-Promotion 101

> **In This Chapter**
>
> ➤ Nailing your promotional strategy
>
> ➤ Synergy: making promotions do double-duty
>
> ➤ Seemliness: promotion without crassness
>
> ➤ Pressing the flesh: promoting yourself in person

In an ideal world, your publisher would bring the full force of its publicity machine to bear on your fledgling career, catapulting you to instant megastardom and forcing your book into Oprah's hands. You'd be attended by flocks of publicists (and the occasional groupie), and the world would hold its breath every time you set pen to paper.

Welcome to reality. Beyond certain *pro forma* exercises—sending out a few review copies, producing some copy in its catalog—your publisher will likely do little to publicize your work, unless you're the kind of brand-name that hardly needs the publicity to begin with.

Good publicity is an essential part of your career. It sells books. It makes money. It builds *careers*. And even the shyest among us can do some self-publicity without peddling our immortal souls or embarrassing our mothers.

Strategy

Bad promotion is worse than no promotion at all. When you undertake a promotional effort, you need to know *why* you're doing it, *what* you're going to do, and *how* you're going to accomplish it. Tie new promotional efforts into existing ones, and carefully vet your promotional ideas to ensure that they'll be as effective as possible. An ounce of preparation is worth a ton of after-the-fact regret.

Cory's long-term goal is to have the wherewithal to write full-time, without having to work a day job to support himself. He knows that there are a lot of ways to accomplish this goal: Inheriting a fortune would do the trick, but that's not on the horizon. A more realistic method is to build a reputation through short-story writing, leverage that reputation to sell a novel, promote that novel well enough to sell a second, then a third, and so on until his backlist is deep enough to provide a modest income.

How long will it take to sell a good whack of short fiction? How long will it take to sell a novel? Will publishers still keep backlists by the time Cory's written enough to have one?

Good strategy copes with these unknowns. Selling short fiction is assisted by training, and the more stories you sell, the easier it is to sell another. Selling a novel out of a slushpile is harder than selling a novel to an editor who knows your work. Backlists as we know them may vanish, but there will be something that steps in and fills the void—readers who are new to a writer they enjoy will always want to read other works by the same writer, so the trick is to ensure that your books are discovered by readers who'll enjoy them.

Thinking strategically about promotion means juggling your short- and long-term goals and ensuring that your materials always communicate your objectives. It means ensuring that you always know *why* you're engaging in any piece of promotion, and where it fits into your goals.

Danger, Danger!

You can spend a small fortune on self-promotion; you can put as much energy into promoting yourself as you do into writing. This is a bad idea. Your first duty is to write and sell your fiction. Promotion serves that goal, not the other way around.

Infodump

When planning a promotional effort, remember that promotion should achieve many goals, promotion should carry clear messages, promotion should be cost- and time-efficient, and promotion should be part of a long-term plan.

Synergy

Part of good strategy is synergy: combining two things to make them more than the sum of their parts. For self-promotion, synergy can be as simple as making sure that your author bio directs readers to your Web site, and that your Web site directs people to your backlist.

Synergy can also be about making the most of your circumstances. If you travel for your day job, approach bookstore owners in the cities you find yourself in, offer to sign their stock, and let them know about your next book. You can bring along a stack of business cards or bookmarks with your Web address on them and insert them into the signed books. You can also list your upcoming publications on the bookmark.

If you're a teacher, produce a classroom reading guide for your book and publish it online; then write a letter to your union newsletter with the address.

If you're a newspaper writer, ask the staff book reviewer which of his counterparts at other papers are likely to be receptive to your books, and see if he'll write a cover letter to accompany the review copies you send them.

The key here is finding ways to make your promotion go as far as it can. Exploit the skills and connections you already have before you try to develop new ones. Capture reader interest with a story and direct it to a novel, then reinforce it with a personal appearance.

Seemliness

No one wants to be the kind of boor who buttonholes strangers and self-aggrandizes at them. No one likes a spammer. The single biggest factor that holds people back from engaging in self-promotion is worry about appearing unseemly.

That's a good instinct! Promotion is all about reaching people—editors, readers, writers—and encouraging them to act in a way that benefits you. It's easy to understand that people don't want to benefit writers who irritate them by imposing on their time and patience.

Seemliness is the critical third leg of strategy. Without seemliness, the most beautiful and well-realized promotional materials end up in the trash.

How do you keep your promotions seemly? It's easier than it sounds. Seemliness merely requires that you use your promotions *appropriately*. If you've published a classroom reading guide, for example, give it to teachers who are looking for such a thing, not bookstore owners! If you've done a *chapbook* of a short story that's up for an award, distribute it as a thank-you to the people who attend your readings at a convention; don't just leave a stack on the literature table.

Seemliness also means *being honest* with your promotions. When you distribute chapbooks at your reading, let people know why you've done it, and tell them about the other good works that are up

Factoid

A **chapbook** is a limited-edition booklet, usually independently produced. Chapbooks are somewhere between pamphlets and mass-market editions.

for the award. Don't get your family and friends to stuff the ballot box. Let bookstore owners who you're pitching a signing to know about the attendance at your other signings, good or bad, and let them know what you intend to do to promote *this* signing.

There's no sin in being proud of your work, and there's no sin in wanting to further your career. Everyone respects a talented craftsperson who is striving to improve his or her lot in life. No one likes self-aggrandizing blowhards. Seemliness means being the former.

Promotion in Person

Not everyone is constitutionally suited to promoting himself in person. There's nothing to be ashamed of if you're the kind of shrinking violet whose tongue goes thick and whose armpits slick up at the thought of promoting yourself face-to-face. Writing is a *solitary* occupation, after all. But if you have the right kind of extroverted personality, there's no substitute for pressing the flesh.

Readings and Signings

Readings and signings are an excellent—and low-cost—means of promoting your work. Be sure to let your publisher and/or distributor's publicity department know when and where you're giving your reading, and see if they can spring loose some free copies of your work to pass around.

Reading in front of an audience is a holy terror for many writers. You can improve your readings through rehearsals, and by remembering to speak *s-l-o-w-l-y*, enunciating each word. No matter how slowly you're speaking, chances are you're talking too fast. Use a tape recorder to practice your reading. If you find that you absolutely, positively can't read in front of a crowd, then don't—better not to give a reading than to just freeze like a deer caught in headlights.

The strategy behind a reading is to attract new readers who will not only buy your book, but will recommend that book to their friends and families. A reading at a bookstore can also turn the staff on to your work, and encourage them to hand-sell your book to customers who ask for a recommendation. Even if you're reading at a library or book fair, you can still approach a bookseller to send down someone with a small table and cash-box to sell copies.

Creating synergy at an appearance is easy. You can promote your readings with announcements on your Web site and to an e-mail list of your fans. If you're

Infodump

Keep your reading selection short—half an hour is just about all that an audience will sit through—and project your voice as you read, speaking in a loud and clear tone. Try to look up from your manuscript often, making eye contact with the audience.

worried about attendance at a reading, spread the labor around by inviting other writers with recent books to read or sign with you. Two writers can often draw in twice the audience, and with three or more you've got a literary festival on your hands!

"As You Know, Bob ..."

You should never read from a book or magazine if you can avoid it. The line lengths, type size, and binding of books and magazines make these difficult to read aloud from. Much better is to print out a copy of the text you want to read. Use wide margins, double or triple spacing, and large (14-point) type. When you practice your readings, keep a pen handy and mark up your reading copy at the spots where you stumble, as a guide for your next read-through. A signed reading copy makes a great freebie for a lucky attendee.

Timing

The time to stage a reading or signing is just after your book comes out. You want to draw readers to your work as early as possible, while the book is on the shelf and the title is getting its push from your publisher. There's no point in wearing yourself out when your book isn't even available. Good timing will sell more books for the bookseller who hosts your event and will give them an impetus to stage another reading.

Venue

If you're lucky, you'll have many options for a reading venue: libraries, both public and university-affiliated; bookstores, book fairs, and restaurants are all good candidates. It's always best to start with the places where you already have a relationship— a place where you spend enough time that they already know you. Politely approach the manager with your proposal and let him know what you're planning to do for the promotion. Putting together a one-page written proposal can be handy as well. Let him know you'll be trying to bring in extra copies from your publisher, and that you'll work to bring in booksellers (if you're not talking to a bookstore manager).

Prepare a list of your needs for the signing: coffee, a bottle of water, a signing table— whatever will make you comfortable. Discuss location and logistics with your host, and come to an agreement in advance on the details. If you have a choice of rooms, pick one that you think will be a little bit smaller than you'll actually need: Reading to 10 people in a venue that only seats 7 is far better than reading to that same group in a banquet hall. For one thing, you won't have to shout to be heard.

Promotion

To promote your signing, start with a list of all the community newspapers and radio and TV stations that run announcements of upcoming events. Put together a concise announcement (for more on press releases, see Chapter 19, "Advanced Self-Promotion"), and mail or fax it in.

Make sure that you post an announcement on your Web site and send a copy to the readers who have previously expressed an interest in your work. You can also post announcements to a Usenet newsgroup or two.

Comportment

Be on time for your reading—in fact, be early! Bring everything you think you'll need: a signing pen, bookmarks, your reading copy (duh!), water, moral support—whatever. Leave time after your reading for questions and answers. Answer questions politely and succinctly, repeating the question before you answer it. Be sensitive to your host's time constraints and call for an end to questions when time gets short. When signing, be friendly and brief. Don't talk someone's head off while those in line behind wait and fume.

Infodump

Get the word out to local bookstores and libraries by producing and distributing a flier with the times, dates, and locations of your book signings, along with your Web address.

Conventions

Chances are there's a regional con within driving distance of where you live at least once a year. Attending this con can be a great way to find the other science fiction writers in your area as well as an opportunity to meet with pros and editors from around the continent.

If the traveling mood takes you and you want to try an out-of-town con, by all means, do. The big one, of course, is the World Science Fiction Convention—whose location is bid on each year by cities around the world—but there are a few other good, writer/business-focused conventions, notably Readercon, World Fantasy, and WisCon.

You know you're doing well if you get invited to be a guest of honor at a convention somewhere. Typically, such an invitation includes round-trip airfare, meals, and your room for the weekend. Remember that the con is run by volunteers on a nonprofit basis. Shortfalls are frequently made up for out-of-pocket, so keep your room-service bills to a minimum.

If you've published a story or two, you can easily get free admission by volunteering to appear on panels. Simply e-mail the convention's programming contact with your credentials and offer your services. You should also include a brief (one paragraph) bio for the program book. Do this a couple months in advance and ask to be sent a list of panel topics to choose from. Don't let your eyes be bigger than your stomach: Pick a reasonable number of panels you think you can make a real contribution to.

You should prepare in advance for your panels by doing a little research and jotting down some ideas for discussion. Once you're on the panel, respect your co-panelists and the audience—don't hog the discussion. If *you* are the moderator, be firm and polite, but don't let any one panelist steal the show.

To get the most out of your time at a convention, be sure to try a little of everything:

Danger, Danger!

Once you've committed to attending a panel, nothing short of a disaster should stop you from being there. There's nothing ruder than standing up your fellow panelists and the audience. If your schedule won't permit you to attend panels at certain times, make sure you give the programming coordinators plenty of notice so that they can revise the schedule or ask someone else to take your place.

➤ Spend some time in the dealer's room, chatting up the booksellers. Offer to sign any stock they've brought along, and pull out your handy-dandy bookmarks to insert in the signed copies.

➤ Visit the Con Suite for a few hours and talk with the readers. Don't sell yourself—or your books!—to them, just participate in the discussion.

➤ Spend some time in the Green Room and at pro-oriented parties getting to know the other writers and editors, but don't intrude on private discussions. This is a great opportunity to find out about upcoming anthologies, vacancies in writer's workshops, and industry gossip.

Being a seemly convention guest boils down to fulfilling your obligation to the con by participating in programming and spending time in the public spaces, being sensitive to the busy-ness and business of booksellers when you approach them, and not intruding on private discussions at parties and in the Green Room.

Reading Groups and Other Appearances

Say what you will about talk show host and entrepreneur Oprah Winfrey, but her televised Book Club segments have sparked a quiet revolution in the marketplace. Across the continent, people have formed book clubs that meet regularly to discuss an agreed-upon work.

For writers, tying into the book club circuit is tricky, since these groups tend to be private and friends-based. The best you can expect is to make your book attractive to book clubs and hope they choose your work.

One way to do this is to produce a *reader's guide* to your book. Many publishers are binding these into books as they're published, but even if your publisher isn't willing to do it, you can make your own and put it online, like the one for "A Lesson Before Dying" at www.randomhouse.com/vintage/read/lesson.

When you do a book launch, reading, or convention appearance, be sure to mention that you've got a reader's guide online, and that you're happy to speak to any book clubs that invite writers to speak.

Tying in with book clubs is a fabulous way to generate good word-of-mouth publicity for your book. Book clubs "hand-sell" books to their friends and families, and are attended by committed readers who really value the written word.

Speaking at a college or high school is another great way to find your audience. The best way to get involved with educational institutions is through personal contacts with faculty members or involved students. Ask them if they know of a creative writing, science, or English teacher who would be receptive to having an author come in as a guest for an hour. Even if you don't have personal contacts with someone at your local institutes of learning, you can "cold call" the department heads and see if they would be interested in bringing you in. Either way, reader's guides are a handy thing to have around when you pitch the idea.

Prepare for a classroom session in advance by discussing the scope of your talk with the teacher. Get a good sense of what the teacher is looking for from you—do they want you to talk about how you turn ideas into stories, or how you sold your book, or where you did your research? Practice your lecture on a patient loved one and refine it until you're delivering a single, clear topic. Make notes for yourself, and bring copies to the class to hand out.

The idea of a classroom session is threefold:

➤ Share some of your knowledge with the class, without boring them.

➤ Interest the students in seeking out more of your work.

➤ Give the students an easy way to find your work.

To that end, you should make your lecture as lively as possible. Use visual aids and take questions. Bring business cards advertising your Web site, chapbooks, and other freebies and pass them around to interested students. If you do it right, you can end up a "house author" for the school, returning year after year to brainwash—er, educate—a generation of readers.

The Least You Need to Know

➤ Good promotion involves strategy: knowing why you're promoting, what you're going to do, and how you're going to do it.

➤ Make your promotional efforts work overtime by tying them into one another.

➤ Keep promotions appropriate: Promote yourself to the people who want to be promoted to, and be honest with your promotions.

➤ Promoting yourself at readings, signings, and conventions is an excellent way to make a lifelong impression on your readers.

Chapter 19

Advanced Self-Promotion

In This Chapter

➤ Promoting yourself in print

➤ Getting your message out to the press

➤ Getting reviewed, getting interviewed: publicity gets personal

➤ Should you hire a PR pro?

In this chapter, we'll be covering instructions for making your own professional materials, putting together an effective media campaign, and comporting yourself in interviews.

We'll cover the finer points of book launches and other publicity, and give you some tips if you want to hire a pro to do it for you.

Printed Matter

This is the age of cheap, easy printing, and you don't need to be a professional designer to produce slick, effective print media on a budget.

Your local copy shop is your best friend. A good relationship with a skilled worker at a Kinko's—or, better yet, the kind of semiprofessional printing house that caters to small businesses—will save you time, money, and regret.

When promoting yourself in print, think *small*. If you can keep your print runs in range of 50 to 100 copies, you'll have the opportunity to learn from your mistakes (you'll make plenty!) and to customize print media for every event.

Cards and Fliers

The easiest forms of printed material to produce are business cards, fliers, bookmarks, and other single-page efforts. As with all promotional efforts, start by defining the *purpose* of the item and how you see it being distributed:

➤ Are you making a business card that you can hand out to people you've met at an event or bookstore managers you've introduced yourself to?

➤ Are you making a bookmark for a signing or reading?

➤ Are you putting together a flier you can leave on a counter at a store, a bulletin board at a community center, or a literature table at a convention?

Visualize each scenario for your item's use, and think about the environment it will be in: pasted into a Rolodex, stuck in a book, or jostling for space on a crowded store counter. Once you've got a picture in your mind, think about …

➤ How you will make your item stand out.

➤ How you will make your item "sticky"—how you'll make sure that your audience will keep it.

➤ How you'll make your item compatible with its surroundings—will it fit on a bulletin board?

Infodump

The self-publisher's bible is Robin Williams's *The Non-Designer's Design Book* (Peachpit Press, 1994). Williams (not the comedian, another Robin Williams) spells out the fundamentals of design in 140 breezy pages with lots of easy-to-follow examples. Run, don't walk, to your local bookstore and devour this title before you try to do anything in print!

The results of this exercise are your functional specifications. You want to make your media as wild and eye-catching as you can, but without sacrificing its clarity or usability.

Some ideas to experiment with:

➤ Odd-sized cards and bookmarks

➤ Incorporating public-domain clip art from clip-art books

➤ Hand-cutting interesting shapes

➤ Colored card stock

➤ *Full-bleed* designs

Once you've laid out your design—using anything from a word processor to a piece of professional desktop publishing software—print one copy and go over it with a fine-tooth comb. Check it carefully for errors, omissions, and human foibles. Show it to friends. Put it aside for a day or two and look at it again. Don't commit to the expense of printing the piece until you're 100 percent sure it's perfect, and even then ask to see one copy before the printer runs the whole job.

Chapbooks and Other Giveaways

Special occasions may call for industrial-strength promotion. You may want to produce a chapbook of a short story for circulation to fans who vote on an upcoming award, or you may want to pull together stickers for a book launch. If your publisher is being recalcitrant about providing you with review copies of your upcoming book, you may want to pay to produce a few dozen of your own.

As with simpler projects, your first step is figuring out *why* you're undertaking the project, *whom* it's for, and *how* they'll use it. Once you've got all that nailed down, *what* you're going to make becomes self-evident.

> **Factoid**
>
> **Full-bleed** designs are those in which the printing extends all the way to the edge of the page. Since most printers require a margin on every edge, full-bleed printing is accomplished by printing on a larger sheet of paper and cropping out the margins with a knife or guillotine.

"As You Know, Bob ..."

There are many tricks you can use to keep costs down for a printing project, but the best is running multiple copies on a single sheet. When designing a printed item, consider how many copies you can fit on a standard 8½ × 11–inch sheet of card stock. Sometimes you can cut your printing bill in half just by shaving a quarter-inch off the width. Remember to add in a half-inch margin all around and leave a minimum of a quarter-inch between each item for cutting. Another advantage of running several cards on the same sheet is that you can create multiple versions of the card without incurring extra cost. For example, you can create four versions of a card, each with a different illustration. The result? A collector's set!

Infodump

The humble rubber stamp can turn *anything* into a piece of promotional material. A small, custom-made stamp can cost as little as $10 to produce. You can use it to stamp your Web address, upcoming book title, or other promotional message onto stickers, pins, clothes, scrap paper, convention badges—anything the ink sticks to! Check your Yellow Pages under "Stamps—Rubber and Plastic."

Infodump

Small colored stickers can be distributed at a convention for use on convention badges. You can rubber-stamp or print a logo or a word from the title of your book on them. These are a great means of drawing people into a reading or launch party.

There are many choices for binding chapbooks, everything from folded, center-stapled pages, to low-cost thermal or spiral binding, all the way up to pricey "perfect" binding like a standard mass-market paperback. Talk the options over with your printer and let your wallet be your guide. Even if you go with center-stapled books, you can still make your project stand out by cropping the pages to nonstandard lengths or widths.

Laying out a book-length project is a daunting task. You need to arrange the type and decorative elements for each page, then ensure that facing pages are laid correctly for the bound edition, watch for paragraphs that break at the ends of pages, and a thousand other bits of arcane printer's art. Your printing house will have its own idiosyncratic expectations of how a book-length job should be delivered; use their advice to keep the setup costs to a minimum.

Book-length projects require even more careful review than single-pagers. Proof the text yourself, then get a friend or two to do the same. Leave yourself as much time to proof the book as you spend designing it.

You're not limited to books as promotional materials. Other options include stickers, T-shirts, baseball hats, iron-on decals, temporary tattoos, magnets, and pins. At the 1993 WorldCon, the editors of *On Spec* magazine distributed cheap plastic novelty glasses with "ON SPECtacle" stickers across the bridge to promote a launch party.

Heat transfers can be run off of standard or color photocopiers—though sometimes you have to go through the additional step of printing to clear acetate so that you can copy a mirror image of your artwork. Once you have the transfers made, you can use a household iron to transfer them onto anything from wood to rice paper to any article of clothing. A trip to your local seconds-and-irregular T-shirt wholesaler can yield a dozen T-shirts for a few dollars apiece.

Press Releases

Getting your message out to the press is easier than it seems. Local newspapers and television and radio stations need local news. Getting a little press coverage often takes nothing more than contacting the producers of your favorite shows and the editors of your favorite papers and letting them know you've got a newsworthy story.

Be sure to coordinate with your publisher on publicity efforts. While the odds are slim that your publisher's PR people will be doing much on your behalf, keeping them abreast of your own efforts is a valuable means of letting them know that you're someone who knows how to capitalize on any publicity that they decide to throw your way.

The press release is the indivisible unit of publicity. As with manuscripts, press releases follow rigidly defined conventions for formatting:

➤ Use plain white 8^1/$_2$ × 11-inch paper.

➤ Use plain black type.

➤ Leave a one-inch margin on all sides.

➤ Double-space your type.

➤ In the top-left corner, type "For Immediate Release."

➤ In the top-right corner, type "For more information contact:" and below, your name, daytime phone number, and e-mail address.

➤ Limit press releases to a single page.

The body of a press release starts with a centered headline. The headline needs to be short, punchy, and newsworthy. "J. Random Author Sells Novel" isn't a great headline—there's no news angle. "Local Writer, J. Random Author, Publishes Seminal Work of Giant-Apes-Enslaving-Mankind Science Fiction" has a good news angle, but runs too long. "Giant Apes Enslave Mankind!" does the job very well.

Your first paragraph is two or three sentences that tell the whole story. These should contain your "hook"—the news angle that makes your story newsworthy. (The fact that you've sold a novel isn't news.) Here's an example: "Giant apes enslave mankind in *Gone Ape!*—an exciting new novel from Smallville-area science fiction writer J. Random Author. Set in the familiar environs of Smallville, *Gone Ape!* is a touching story of love and adventure in a world where genetically modified simians rule with hairy iron fists. Published this month by Arbitrary House books of New York, *Gone Ape!* is Author's first novel, based on his experiences teaching gym at Smallville's own Heinrich Himmler Secondary School."

Your second paragraph should contain a snappy quote and a sketch of your credentials; for example: "'Man, when you teach the kids of Smallville, you don't have to stretch far to write a book about cruel ape-lords,'" quips Author. "'I spent four years writing *Gone Ape!* and it just kept on getting easier.'" Author may be new to novel publishing, but he's hardly unknown. For the past two years, his short stories have displayed remarkable momentum, seeing publication in many of science fiction's best-loved magazines, including *Shameless Stories* and *Eando Binder's Science Fiction Magazine,* and garnering nominations for the prized Wristwatch and Lightbulb awards."

"As You Know, Bob ..."

There are two schools of thought on where your press release's "hook"—the news angle—should go. Some journalists prefer to see a hook in the first sentence, because they don't have the time to hunt for it. Others feel like the hook is their prerogative, and don't want to have it handed to them on a silver platter. Putting an oblique hook in the first two or three sentences is your best bet for pleasing both camps.

Your last paragraph contains your request, your message to the reader: "J. Random Author is available for interviews and will be signing at The Book Nook (121 Main Street) at 7 P.M. on Tuesday, February 29."

Short, simple, and to the point.

Now that you've written and edited your press release to within an inch of its life, where do you send it? How far your press release goes depends on your time and angle. Our previous example is squarely focused on local press, but it could also be of interest to educational reporters on a national basis.

Start by making a list of all the different audiences your news story has: science fiction readers, local librarians, English teachers, engineers, booksellers … the list will be very, very long.

Now, think about where these people get their news. What newspapers, Web sites, magazines, and radio and TV programs do they consume regularly? Write out a list, and make note of which sources overlap one or more audiences. If you can get covered in a venue that reaches several of your audiences at once, you'll get the most value for your efforts.

Now, start calling and e-mailing. The information you're looking for is the name and fax number or e-mail address for a reporter or assignment editor who would be likely to cover your story. The best way to find this information is to actually watch or read the stuff that the outlet you're calling puts out and see if

Infodump

Wire services syndicate stories to a wide variety of subscribing media outlets. Getting a story picked up by the wire is the fastest way to spread the news across the nation. The bigger wire services are Reuter's, Associated Press, and Universal Press Syndicate. Chances are, there's a branch office for each in or near your hometown.

you can identify a likely target. Think laterally here: If you were J. Random Author promoting *Gone Ape!* you might ask to speak to the reporter who covers educational or child-raising issues for his employer. If you can't identify a specific reporter, ask to speak to an assignment editor. Describe your news to that person and ask for the name of a reporter who would be interested.

Don't be surprised if the reporter or editor you speak to is gruff to the point of rudeness. Reporters have jam-packed schedules with hard deadlines and don't generally have the time to shoot the breeze with every yahoo who calls them up.

All you want to accomplish in your first phone call is to confirm the reporter's name and contact info, and ensure that you're speaking to someone who might be interested in covering a story like yours.

Once you've built your list of names, start sending out press releases! Send by fax or e-mail, based on the reporter's stated preference. If you don't have direct access to a fax machine (or fax modem), canvass your friends. If all else fails, most copy shops and postal outlets have pay-by-the-page fax service. Be sure to include a cover sheet with the name of your contact.

The very same day, call the reporter and follow up. Reporters drown in press releases, and they don't hang on to them for days waiting for a follow-up call. Leave a couple hours' grace period, but make sure you place a follow-up call. Ask the reporter if she received the release and if she would be interested in an interview, review copies, or anything else.

The corollary of this is that if you send out a press release with contact info at the top, be sure that you're available at that number for the next few days. There's enough news out there that reporters don't need to chase after hard-to-reach contacts for days—they can just move on to the next story.

As you can see, a press campaign is a lot of work. It gets easier every time you do it, though—you can capitalize on your research as time goes by.

Danger, Danger!

A big media outlet will likely have more than one person who's a good candidate for your story. It's okay to send materials to more than one reporter, provided they cover different material—an education reporter and a book reviewer, for example. *Don't* send your materials to people who cover the same kind of story (like the morning and afternoon news reporters). You're just wasting your time and irritating them.

Interviews and Reviews

Any reporter worth a damn will attempt to flesh out a story with an interview—only the busiest and laziest write articles from press releases.

An interview is a great way to intrigue a wide audience with your work and get them into the stores to buy your books. You need to go into an interview knowing who the audience is and what message you want them to receive. You need what marketers call a "Unique Sales Proposition" (U.S.P.)—that is, a reason to read *your* book instead of someone else's.

Only you can figure out what your U.S.P. is. Why did you write *this* book and not another? What can your book do for someone that another can't? In the case of Karl's novel *Ventus,* his U.S.P. might be that his book presents a future where Internet-style cyberspace has dead-ended and been supplanted by "smart objects" that contain their own intelligence.

Talk over your objectives for the interview with the reporter. Don't try to run the interview, but do let the reporter know what angles you've figured out.

For radio and TV interviews, speak slowly, especially if you're nervous. Try to enunciate every word, pause after every sentence, and let the interviewer finish his questions before you start your answer. On TV, look into the camera when you speak. Feel free to run with your answers, taking interesting sidetracks, but be sensitive to the time constraints of the medium and let the interviewer jump in and wrap things up when time gets short.

Infodump

If you're appearing on TV, avoid densely patterned clothing, especially checks, stripes, and—worst of all—herringbone weaves. These tend to give a strobe effect on camera and look really, really weird.

Print Interviews

In print interviews, you've usually got more time to think about your answer. Don't be afraid to ask the interviewer for clarification if you're not clear about a question.

In all cases, avoid answering with a simple "Yes" or "No." Most reporters are smart enough to ask open-ended questions that demand longer answers, but if you're confronted with a novice who asks you a yes-or-no question, expand on your answer.

Approach reviewers the same way you approach reporters. Identify reviewers who write for the media outlets that you want to appear in and give them a call. Tell them you have a book out and a press package that accompanies it, and ask if they'd be interested in seeing a copy. Forward your materials to them and follow up with a phone call later that day.

As with all press publicity, coordinate with your publisher's publicity people to make sure you aren't duplicating effort and to cadge free review copies of your book to send around.

Reviews

Reviews are a double-edged sword. Everyone loves to get a good review—besides stroking your ego, good reviews sell your book. You can and should clip your good reviews and include them in your press package and book proposals. Sending copies to your agent and editor (and your mom, and your boss, and your high-school English teacher who always said you'd never amount to anything) is a productive course of action. You can even write to the reviewer and thank her for her kind words.

Bad reviews, on the other hand, are horrible. It's hard to say which is worse: a bad review that misses the point or a bad review that gets the point and hates it. Either way, there's no easy way to get over negative ink.

There's also little practical means of addressing a bad review, beyond scratching the reviewer's name off your Christmas card list.

Danger, Danger!

Avoid the appearance of impropriety at all costs when soliciting reviews of your work. Don't send T-shirts, chocolates, or money. Reviewers hate it when people try to bribe them.

Never, ever, ever respond to a bad review. Don't write an irate letter to the editor. Don't tell the reviewer to get stuffed. The very best you can hope for from such a course of action is looking like a whiny baby—at worst, you'll look like a total moron, especially if your letter ends up in print. This includes situations where facts are misstated or lies are told. If things are sufficiently heinous, rest assured that your publisher's attack-lawyers will take care of things. If you're really incensed, you can drop your editor a line and see if he thinks it's worth forwarding to the legal department. Don't *you* get personally involved.

When the person you're criticizing controls the venue you're criticizing in, you can never win. Reviewers always get the last word. As with every frustrating aspect of your writing career, your best recourse is to channel your rage and ire into more writing. Remember, getting ink is the best revenge.

Professional Promotion

Chances are, you're already wearing too many hats: parent, writer, employee, sibling, child. You're overextended and overburdened, and lack the time and inclination to engage in lengthy publicity pushes. And, if you've followed our advice, you're probably well into your next writing project by now.

That's fine. After all, you're a writer, not a PR flack. Maybe it's time to bring in the pros.

Publicists

Professional *publicists* send out press releases, produce promotional materials, and press the flesh for a living. Good publicists are marvels of efficiency and persuasion.

They're not cheap, though. Like any unregulated professional, a publicist will charge whatever he thinks he can get, based on his reputation—from a few hundred dollars a month to thousands a day.

If you're not dependent on the income from your writing and you feel like you've got an angle that a good publicist could exploit, you might consider hiring a publicist with some or all the money from a book sale (there's no point in hiring a publicist for a short-story sale). A few writers—mostly outside of the genre—have had very good results from such a deal, but there's no guarantee that you'll join their ranks. You can research publicists through the Yellow Pages or on the Internet.

An alternative to a publicist is a glib friend who is willing to act as your proxy. Even if you're a sharp self-promoter, some journalists feel that the story is "more real" if it's delivered from someone identifying himself as a publicist. In this kind of homebrew solution, the role of your "publicist" is to place the initial and follow-up calls to reporters, while you handle the production of press releases, research, and interviews.

Factoid

Publicists are professionals who work with the media, influential consumers, and retailers to publicize new products, ideas, and services. They send press releases, handle the media, work their network of personal contacts, and track the competition.

Infodump

Ideas for a launch include readings, performances by local bands or comedians, and door prizes.

Book Launches

This is the most fun part of selling a novel: throwing a party! Finding a venue for a launch involves talking to bookstore, cafe, bar, or restaurant owners about your plans. Let them know that you'll be promoting your launch with press releases, community message board announcements, e-mail, and fliers. Tell them how your other launches have gone, and let them know how many customers you'll be bringing into their place of business.

If you're not launching at a bookstore, invite a chosen bookseller to set up a table from which to sell your books. If you can't interest a bookseller, get some copies from your publisher and have a friend sell them at a slight discount.

Send invitations to local reviewers and journalists using the same techniques you developed when you were sending out press releases.

The Least You Need to Know

➤ You don't need to be a professional designer to produce slick, effective print media on a budget.

➤ Limit press releases to one page and stick to the standard format.

➤ Always include a hook or news angle in your press releases.

➤ Publicists are pricey, but a savvy friend makes a good, free substitute.

Chapter 20

Using the Internet to Promote Yourself

In This Chapter

➤ Manageable marketing schemes

➤ Registering your own domain name

➤ Other Internet tools

➤ Leveraging your e-mail

The Internet is potentially the most important publishing tool since the invention of the printing press. The Net can be intimidating for those of us without the time or aptitude for learning how computers work. Fortunately, you can get a great deal out of Internet marketing and publishing without having to be a computer whiz.

Our brightest prospect in the twenty-first-century publishing melee lies in using the Internet to cultivate a personal network of readers. No matter how impersonal and corporate the publishing industry becomes, it is the readers who buy the book. It is they who ultimately count. If we can build effective bridges to our readership, we can flourish even in the high-pressure, success-oriented publishing climate that is developing.

www.Your-Name-Here.com

It seems like everybody has a Web site these days. Bookstores are cleaning up using online sales, and individual authors have their own sites. A quick browse through

Yahoo!—one of the largest searchable indexes on the Web—reveals dozens of authors' sites, some of them as impressive as corporate portals.

Is there any way you can cash in on this trend? Is it even worth trying? Despite the soaring value of the "dot-com" market, there's no hard data saying how effective online advertising is. And anyway, how is your little site going to be noticed amidst all the towering Amazons and eBays?

Contracting Out

You don't have to know anything about the Internet to get your own Web site. There are hundreds of services that will create a site for you, according to your specifications, for a fee. Check your Yellow Pages under "Internet." You can generally expect to pay upward of $1,500 to create a decent site. Once it's up and running, you'll likely spend another $300 to $400 per year to maintain it.

It's arguably worth the money if you feel you need a presence on the Net but can't design a site to save your life. After all, with a Web site, you get potentially global exposure.

"As You Know, Bob ..."

Karl put up his first Web site in 1993. Over the years he noticed that a disproportionate number of visitors to the site were from Finland. Why Finland? He has no idea, but he's honored and hopes he can get some of his work translated into Finnish to reciprocate.

Rolling Your Own Site

There are hundreds of products out there (many of them free) that can help you create Web pages. In fact, the major word processors such as Microsoft Word or Corel WordPerfect will allow you to save word processing files directly as Web pages.

It's very easy to build your own Web site this way. It's also a lot cheaper than hiring an agency. If you're good with design, you can use an ordinary paint program to create graphics as good as any you'll find on the Net.

You can even find organizations that are willing to give you free Web site space. Both Yahoo! and Geocities, for instance, will give you space to put up your own pages for free. If you're a member of Science Fiction and Fantasy Writers of America (SFWA), you can get a free, pre-built page from them.

Both of us have completely hand-built our own sites. It's fairly time-intensive, but it's creative and fun.

If You (Domain) Name It, They Will Come

How are people going to find your site? You will need to go to Yahoo! and other Internet directories and register your URL—your Web site address—so that people can get to it. Put the URL on your business cards, and (if possible) include it in your bio when you publish short stories or a novel.

The best way to make a Web site accessible, of course, is to name it in such a way that people go straight to it. If your name is Joni Smith, for example, you'll want to have a Web site at www.joni-smith.com.

This is not nearly as expensive or difficult as it might seem. In fact, it's about as easy to get a *domain name* of your own as it is to use a search engine. You can do it all from your browser.

All you have to do is go to www.internic.net and visit one of their listed domain name registrars. Then, simply enter the name of the domain you'd like to register, click a button, and the registrar will tell you if it's already taken. (Don't try to type the name into your browser's Location window to see if the site exists; the name may not be in use but could still be owned by someone, so a negative search in your browser won't mean anything.)

If the domain name (say, my-pen-name.com) is available, you can usually register it on the spot. You'll be billed up to $35 U.S. for the privilege, which you can pay online through a secure credit card transaction or by check when the invoice arrives. It's as easy as that!

What to Put on Your Site

Your Web site is your public face. It's vital that you present yourself as you would like people to see you. Some writers get charged up at the idea of creating a Web site, but once they have it they don't know what to put on it. So they plunk in a little biography and a list of stories they've sold. This "online resumé" isn't going to get many repeat visits from your fans.

Consider what keeps you coming back to a site. News is always good; so are regularly updated links to other interesting sites. Samples of your fiction are even better.

Factoid

A **domain name** is the Internet address you use to visit a Web or address e-mail. Commercial domains are those used for commercial purposes (like promoting a book). Karl registered the domain name kschroeder.com as a base for his Web site. Cory is using craphound.com to promote his fiction and nonfiction sales. We both registered these names ourselves.

Infodump

Having the domain name doesn't mean you have a Web site. You have to attach the name to a particular site. Your next step will be to find an Internet service provider who can give you Web space. Ask them if they will allow you to transfer your domain name to their site. If they can, you're in business. Drop in your Web pages, and you're set!

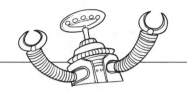

Some authors put previously published short stories on their sites. Karl has done it, but it's potentially dangerous, because it makes you vulnerable to plagiarism. Make sure such stories are copyrighted, if you go this way at all. Better yet, play it safe and just put excerpts on the site.

Here are some ideas for other ways to fill your site:

➤ Links to other Web sites that SF readers would enjoy, such as nanotech or space development.

➤ Commentary on current news items; this has to be updated daily or weekly to be effective.

➤ Anecdotal experiences about the writing industry, for any new writers who might come to your site looking for insights about the writing experience.

> **Danger, Danger!**
>
> Never put a complete, unpublished story on a Web site. Doing this is considered equivalent to publishing it; few SF magazines will consider buying a story that has already been posted to the Web.

➤ Cover or interior art, but only if you can get the rights to it. Never put any art that you don't own the rights to on your site.

➤ News about upcoming events, especially readings, conventions, or book signings where you'll appear.

➤ Personal essays, journals, and observations.

We could go on, but a pattern is emerging: A Web site is a place for fun, interesting, and useful information. As a SF writer, you're one of the best people to provide this kind of material. Consider your site to be a second channel for publication: One that doesn't pay directly, true, but where you can show all your facets to your readers.

Interactive Sites

The best Web sites have some degree of interactivity. This could be as simple as providing an e-mail address where people can reach you. Or it could be more elaborate.

Years ago, Karl added a tiny feedback form at the bottom of every short story and article on his site. People browsing the site were free to fill out the form and tell him what they thought of his work, and how he might improve it. Once the reader filled out the form and clicked the button, Karl's script put his or her comments in a file and sent a copy to him by e-mail. Readers could maintain anonymity when filling out the form, so it wasn't as intimidating as a personal meeting, phone call, or even e-mail.

The feedback form was very simple, but it meant Karl received several e-mails a day from people who had read his stories. Most were overwhelmingly positive (people are inherently nice) so it served as a source of valuable feedback for Karl, and a reminder that he wasn't writing in a vacuum.

Collecting e-mail addresses through a form such as this gives you a way of contacting your audience directly. If you've sold a new story, have planned a book launch or reading, or are going to be attending a particular convention, you can send a message to the list you've compiled. People who've responded positively on your form are most likely to tell their friends, who tell their friends, and so on.

You can do much more elaborate things with a site if you know a little programming, or have a friend who does. There are also free scripts for things like feedback forms that you can download off the Net and set up without having to understand how they work.

Direct Sales

Most of the online bookseller portals have affiliate programs, which allow you to advertise books on your site, and link these to their sites. You can put thumbnails (miniature images) of your novel covers on your site. A reader "clicks through" the thumbnail to end up on the corresponding page on Amazon.com or Barnes & Noble. In other words, people browsing your site can buy your books instantly, without your having to invest in any complicated e-commerce software.

Better yet, as an affiliate, you are usually entitled to a small finder's fee for every click-through that results in a sale. With this in place, you can use your site to aggressively sell your book, then get your usual royalty plus a small (but significant) finder's fee for every sale.

Even if the finder's fee is small, one thing it will provide you with is an indicator of how many people are buying your books from your site. This information can tell you if your site's being wildly successful, or if you should improve it. (Don't even imagine that it will tell you how successful the book itself is.)

The Mighty Usenet

Maybe you don't want to go to all the trouble of creating and maintaining a Web site, but you still want some presence on the Internet. You and the *Usenet* may be a perfect match.

If you can get access to a Web browser, you have access to the Usenet. Netscape comes with a built-in newsreader; Microsoft Internet Explorer uses Outlook (which should automatically be installed on your system if you have Microsoft Internet Explorer).

Even if you don't have a newsreader, you can go to a Web site such as www.deja.com or www.remarq.com and get access to the Usenet directly through your browser.

Factoid

The **Usenet** is the second-oldest collaborative tool on the Internet (after e-mail). Before the World Wide Web came along, the Usenet dominated the Net. Usenet consists of tens of thousands of newsgroups. Newsgroups are like public mailboxes, each one devoted to one particular topic. You can browse anonymously through a newsgroup's messages, or you can post your own messages and replies to messages. Any message you post to a newsgroup becomes visible to anyone who visits that newsgroup.

Infodump

Your Internet service provider should have given you the address of their Usenet news server. The first time you start your newsreader it will ask you for this address. Once you enter it, it will remember for future sessions.

Newsgroups About Science Fiction

The Usenet has a newsgroup for everything. SF and fantasy are well covered. Once you've got a connection to your news server, you should find some or all of the following newsgroups available:

➤ **alt.cyberpunk.** Discussion about all things cyber.

➤ **rec.arts.sf.misc.** Miscellaneous discussion of SF.

➤ **rec.arts.sf.announce.** Announcements (moderated by zorch@uunet.uu.net).

➤ **rec.arts.sf.composition.** Discussion about writing speculative fiction.

➤ **rec.arts.sf.fandom.** Fannish activities, conventions, etc.

➤ **rec.arts.sf.marketplace.** Personal for-sale notices.

➤ **rec.arts.sf.movies.** SF movies that don't have their own groups.

➤ **rec.arts.sf.reviews.** Reviews of SF/fantasy/horror works (moderated).

➤ **rec.arts.sf.science.** Science and theory related to SF.

➤ **rec.arts.sf.starwars.collecting.** Topics relating to *Star Wars* collecting.

➤ **rec.arts.sf.starwars.games.** *Star Wars* games: role-playing games, computer and card games, etc.

228

➤ **rec.arts.sf.starwars.info.** General information about *Star Wars* (moderated).

➤ **rec.arts.sf.starwars.misc.** Miscellaneous topics about *Star Wars*.

➤ **rec.arts.sf.superman.** Discussions about Superman.

➤ **rec.arts.sf.tv.** SF television shows that don't have their own groups.

➤ **rec.arts.sf.tv.babylon5.** Discussion about the *Babylon 5* TV show.

➤ **rec.arts.sf.tv.babylon5.info.** Information about *Babylon 5* (moderated).

➤ **rec.arts.sf.tv.babylon5.moderated.** Moderated discussions of *Babylon 5*.

➤ **rec.arts.sf.tv.quantum-leap.** The TV series *Quantum Leap* and related comics, conventions, etc.

➤ **rec.arts.sf.written.** SF novels, stories, etc.

➤ **rec.arts.sf.written.robert-jordan.** Books by Robert Jordan.

The best way to find out what a given newsgroup is like is to subscribe to it and read several days' worth of messages. Some groups have high traffic, and hundreds of messages per day; others will only have one or two a week.

It's a good idea to "lurk" for a while (read but don't post), until you get an idea of what discussion topics come up so regularly as to be ignored by the majority of users. If you find a topic that interests you, by all means dive in and post a reply to the group.

Netiquette

You don't want to come off as a tyro in the Usenet. Etiquette (or Netiquette, as it's called there) is very important. An example of Netiquette is the general ban on commercial advertising via newsgroup messages. Posting information that's topical to the discussion group is okay, even if it promotes you; but advertising anything even slightly off-topic will get you in hot water with the Usenet crowd. That's known as spamming, and it's a big no-no.

Think of newsgroups as an ongoing, free-for-all talk show set in cyberspace. You can certainly make a name for yourself on the Usenet, but there are only two ways to do it: Be useful, or be a pain in the butt. If you contribute valuable insights to ongoing discussions, you'll get a good reputation. You may get some new readers this way.

Infodump

Subtler forms of advertising are allowed. The best way to advertise on the Usenet is to create a signature file. This file is appended to every message you post to newsgroups. This file (which should be no more than four lines long) can contain info on your latest book, or the URL of your Web site. Anything more detailed than this verges on spamming.

Mailing Lists

E-mail discussion groups have existed for many years. These work by forwarding mail messages from subscribed members to all the other members on a list. Some lists interface with the Usenet, permitting people who only have e-mail a way to post to newsgroups.

Some mailing lists include:

➤ **HIT Imaginative Tech and Science Fiction:** hit@ufrj.bitnet.net

➤ **Quanta Science Fiction and Fantasy:** majordomo@netcom.com

➤ **Rare-SF Discussion of rare Science Fiction and Fantasy:** rare-sf-request@ucsb.edu

➤ **SF-list Science Fiction:** listproc@unicorn.acs.ttu.edu

➤ **SF-Lovers Science Fiction:** sf-lovers-request@rutvm1.rutgers.edu

➤ **STWTTF-L Gender Issues in Science Fiction:** listserv@listserv.net

➤ **UK-SF Science Fiction and Fantasy in the United Kingdom:** listserv@uel.ack.uk

➤ **UK-SF-Books Science Fiction and Fantasy in the United Kingdom:** listserv@uel.ack.uk

You can subscribe to any of these lists by sending an e-mail message to the address given. The first line of your e-mail should be:

Subscribe [list name] [your-e-mail-address]

If all goes well, you'll soon start receiving a flood of e-mail.

Getting Reviewed Online

Many Web sites review SF; some specialize in it. If you want to get your work reviewed, for instance on SFSite (www.sfsite.com), you should read their reviews and find out which reviewer reads your style of fiction. If you can, get in touch with the reviewer directly, and offer to send a copy of your book. There's nothing reviewers like more than a free novel, after all!

You can't *make* anybody review your work. Consider anything you send out to be on spec. If a review does appear, you can't guarantee that it will be favorable, either. Online reviews, like newspaper or magazine reviews, are chancy. But if a well-respected reviewer likes your work, you'll get noticed in the SF community. With luck, that'll translate into sales.

The Least You Need to Know

➤ The best way to promote yourself on the Net is to make personal contact with readers and fans.

➤ Banner ads are for big business; buying banner ads on other people's Web sites will cost you far more than you'll make back.

➤ You can easily create your own Web site or contract out to have it done.

➤ Traditional routes like the Usenet are still at least as effective as Web sites for promoting yourself.

➤ When in doubt, or if you don't have access to a Web browser or newsgroup, use the Internet's most important "killer app": e-mail.

➤ Online reviews of literature are becoming more influential as more people join the Internet community.

Awards

There are dozens of awards of all stripes in science fiction and fantasy: juried, peer, fan, specialty—even rigged, if you believe various conspiracy theorists. A few—the Hugo, the Nebula, the World Fantasy—are recognized inside and outside of the genre, while others cater to obscure audiences.

No genre subject is as fraught with contention as awards. Are the best books and stories represented, or merely the most popular? Or worse still, those written by the most popular writers? There's a saying about academia: They fight so hard because the stakes are so low. This is equally true in genre: While an award carries a modest dollop of prestige, the actual income—either in the form of a cash prize or increased sales—that a winner receives is pretty insignificant.

Nevertheless, many's the writer who aspires to an award—present company included! Whether you think taking home an award is like winning a beauty contest or a Nobel Prize, there's something wonderfully affirming about having a stranger in some form of authority say, "You're number one—the best the genre has to offer."

Blue Ribbons and Chrome Phalluses: The Major Awards

Space restrictions oblige us to stick to the high notes in this section. We'll tackle the major awards, give you some background on them, and let you in on the gossip that surrounds them.

The Hugo

For nearly half a century, the Hugo Award—formally called the World Science Fiction Society's Achievement Award—has been the best-known genre award. It is voted on annually by the attendees of the current World Science Fiction Convention. The received wisdom has it that the Hugo is a fan award, given for the most popular works, as opposed to the author-voted Nebula (coming up in the next section), which is nominally an award for fine writing.

The Hugo Award ceremony has all the trappings of a low-budget Emmy: big-screen TVs, musical fanfares, even tuxedoes and evening gowns. Each year's Hugo statuettes are commissioned by the year's ConCom, and are generally themed to the Con's region. The Hugos at the Orlando WorldCon in 1991, for example, had bases made of mesh from a rocket launch pad; at the Winnipeg, Canada, WorldCon in 1993, the awards were set onto carved maple leaf-shaped bases. The one thing all Hugos have in common is that they're silver rocket ships.

"As You Know, Bob ..."

The Hugo gets its name from Hugo Gernsback (1882–1967), one of the great founding fathers of modern American SF. Gernsback was the founder of *Amazing Stories*, the prototype for all the golden age pulp SF magazines. He is an appropriate figurehead to honor the most popular writing in the field.

While attendance at a WorldCon can run to thousands—most of whom are eligible to nominate and vote—the actual number of nominations and votes cast can be quite low. In 1996, a novelette made it onto the ballot with only 15 nominations!

Of course, this opens up the whole question of politicking: Can shaking hands and kissing babies get your name on a Hugo ballot? Probably. That being said, the writers who take home rocket ships from the WorldCon are talented people who've written kick-ass fiction, despite the poor nominator turnout.

For a writer, having "Hugo Award Winner" or "Hugo Nominee" before your name is a pretty fine laurel. It can open some doors, get you out of the slushpile, and give your publisher a great tag for your book cover. Best of all, it gives the publisher's reps a nice angle to use when pitching your book to the major chain buyers. When it comes time to apply for a grant from your local arts council or university, having a Hugo on your resumé can sure help things along.

The Nebula

The Nebula Award was started in 1965 by Science Fiction and Fantasy Writers of America (SFWA) founder Damon Knight. Originally, the award's purpose was to allow SFWA's members to select meritorious works for an annual best-of anthology, and this anthology exists to this day. In contrast to the Hugo, the Nebula is voted on only by active members of SFWA, and so nominally represents the accolades of your peers, rather than your fans.

Unlike the Hugos, the Nebula nominations are conducted in an open forum, so that every member of SFWA can see just who has recommended whom. This has given rise to a perpetual kerfuffle in which statisticians analyze the recommendation patterns of various members, looking for log-rolling, back-scratching, and out-and-out rigging. Their conclusion? There's *some* odd stuff going on in the Nebula recommendation process, but somehow, the good stuff still wins—most of the time.

The Nebulas are awarded at an annual ceremony that generally rotates between the East and West coasts, and in recent years, it has featured inflammatory keynote addresses and acceptance speeches that have sparked endless recriminations inside SFWA.

"As You Know, Bob ..."

One particularly touchy subject within the Nebula discussion is the award for Best Script. The detractors argue that almost none of the members are screenwriters, so that a Best Script Neb can hardly be considered a "peer" award; and that further, the script-as-written and script-as-shot are often completely different animals, so it's impossible to know if the award is going to the screenwriter or the director. The supporters of the award contend that screens big and small are where the general public encounters SF, and that the members who do write screenplays deserve the same recognition as their brethren.

This came to a head in 1999, when a group of Best Script opposers recommended a pornographic screenplay called *The Uranus Experiment, Part 2,* and managed to get it on the final ballot. The screenplay stands a good chance of winning, which will put SFWA in the awkward position of handing a trophy to a pornographer. Whether the inevitable public relations fiasco leads to the Best Script award being stricken from future ballots remains to be seen.

Winning a Nebula carries the same benefits as winning the Hugo: It gives the sales reps an angle when they're pitching your books to chain buyers, who know that fans look for "Nebula winner" on the cover of the books they're browsing; and it gives you an edge in a grant application and gets you out of the slushpile.

The World Fantasy Award

The World Fantasy Award is an annual *juried* award given to outstanding fantasy published in the previous year. Being juried, it is generally thought to be immune to the kind of jiggery-pokery that haunts the Hugo and Nebula. A volunteer jury reviews works that they find on the stands, that publishers send them, and that others recommend. They deliberate in secret, then present the award at a banquet at the World Fantasy Convention. Nevertheless, rumblings persist— "So-and-so was on the jury, and they *just happened* to pick a book by such-and-such, who *just happens* to be their old collaborator/Clarion classmate/pal/client/editor/girlfriend."

Factoid

A **juried** award is one in which the winner is selected by a jury of knowledgeable individuals, who deliberate in private.

Nevertheless, the World Fantasy Award consistently goes to fabulous works, and the World Fantasy winners are afforded the same respect as Hugo and Neb winners.

Foreigners and Special Interest Groups: Other Awards

There are literally dozens of genre awards. Here are some brief details on each.

Award	Given For	Format	Recent Winners
Analog Readers' Choice Poll	Best stories published in the previous year's *Analog* magazine	Readers' poll	Timothy Zahn, Grey Rollins, Brian Plante
Asimov's Readers' Choice Poll	Best stories published in the previous year's *Asimov's* magazine	Readers' poll	Allen Steel, Bill Johnson, Mike Resnick
Isaac Asimov's Award for Undergraduate Excellence in Science Fiction and Fantasy Writing	Best story submitted by an undergraduate student at an accredited college or university	Juried	David Kirtley

Award	Given For	Format	Recent Winners
Aurora Award	Best works by Canadian writers or writers living in Canada in the previous year	Fan-voted by attendees at Canvention	Robert Charles Wilson, Edo van Belkom
British Fantasy Society Awards	Best fantasy or horror works in the previous year	Fan-voted by attendees at FantasyCon	Stephen King, Stephen Laws
British Science Fiction Association Awards	Best science fiction works in the previous year	Fan-voted by attendees at EasterCon	Christopher Priest, Gwyneth Jones
John W. Campbell Jr. Memorial Award	Best science fiction novel in the previous year	Juried	George Zebrowski
Arthur C. Clarke Award	Best science fiction novel published in the U.K. in the previous year	Juried	Amitav Ghosh
Compton Crook Award	Best novel not previously given an award	Juried	James Stoddard
HOMer Award	Best genre novel published in the previous year	Fan-voted by CompuServe members	Mike Resnick
John W. Campbell Award	Best new writer	Fan-voted along with the Hugos	Nalo Hopkinson
Lambda Literary Award	Excellence in gay and lesbian genre writing in the previous year	Juried	Elizabeth Brownrigg, Clive Barker
Locus Awards	Best works in the previous year	Readers' poll with the largest electorate in SF	Connie Willis, George R. R. Martin, Stephen King
Mythopoeic Awards	Best fantasy book from the the previous year	Juried	Neil Gaiman, Charles Vess
Philip K. Dick Award	Best paperback original in the previous year	Juried	Stepan Chapman

continues

continued

Award	Given For	Format	Recent Winners
Prometheus Award	Best libertarian-themed SF novel in the previous year	Juried	John Varley
Science Fiction Chronicle Award	Best genre works in the previous year	Readers' poll	Bruce Sterling, Gregory Benford
The Skylark	Best contributor to science fiction	Fan-voted by members of the New England Science Fiction Association	Bob Eggleton
Theodore Sturgeon Memorial Award	Best genre short story in the previous year	Juried	Ted Chiang
James Tiptree Jr. Award	Best science fiction or fantasy that explores and expands the roles of women and men	Juried	Raphael Carter

How to Win an Award

Winning an award, like getting famous, has a pretty nebulous meaning. After all, awards are given to people who produce good work—shouldn't winning an award consist of nothing more than producing the best work you can? Yup. However, there are those who, for good or ill, seek to shortcut this process. Coming up you'll find some notes on effective strategies to improve your odds.

How Not to Win an Award

As you can see, there are a lot of awards in the genre, and given how few votes some of them require for a spot in the winner's circle, it's not that hard to take home a prize through a little judicious enlistment of friends and family.

That's a really, really bad idea. Out-and-out vote rigging is antisocial behavior of the first order, and it gets noticed. Making enemies of your fellow writers and your readership is a bad idea at any stage of your career. Besides, it's dishonest.

That isn't to say that all politicking is out. There's nothing wrong with publicizing your work to the people who are voting on an award that you've got your eye on. That's just good self-promotion.

Effective Awards Promotion

The key to effective awards promotion is *appropriateness*. High-pressure tactics such as buttonholing people at conventions or spamming newsgroups or private mailboxes are obnoxious, and worse, they get your message to people who couldn't care less about your fortunes. Not for long, though. Once you start invading their privacy, people quickly decide how they feel about your future: They'd like it to be as bleak as possible.

But good career management doesn't preclude politicking for an award. You just have to be sure that the people who you're approaching are receptive to your message.

So, who are the people you want to target? Your fans—the people who already enjoy your work and the people who are likely to. If someone has sent you an e-mail letting you know how much he liked your stuff, he's a good candidate. Likewise for people who attend your readings at conventions, members of organizations that have invited you to speak, and editors who've bought your work.

Start a special address book of people who you know are interested in your work. If you have a Web site, you can create a form for visitors who want to be included on forthcoming news.

Now that you know who you want to target, you have to decide what you're going to say to them. Again, appropriateness is our watchword. If you're up for an award for a specific story, you can make copies of that story available to your fans, either electronically or in hard copy. There's nothing overly venal about including a cover sheet or blurb about the story's prospects for an upcoming award, along with information on the balloting process.

If you're doing this electronically, you could create a Web page with your story on it and an introduction talking about the award. Tell the award's administrators about the page, and see if they'll create a link to it.

Alternatively, you could send a brief, polite e-mail to your list, letting them know that you're happy to mail them a copy of your story.

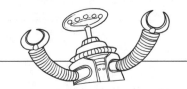

Danger, Danger!

When you send out a bulk e-mail, *don't* just add all the recipients to the CC: (Carbon Copy) field; this will expose the e-mail addresses of each recipient to all other recipients, compromising their privacy and subjecting them to any replies that the message generates. Instead, use BCC: (Blind Carbon Copy), which suppresses the recipient list. Address the message to yourself, so that replies will be directed to you. Be sure to include prominent, easy instructions for people who don't want to receive future mailings.

Going Whole-Hog

More grandiose schemes are good, too. James Van Pelt is a science fiction writer who found himself eligible for the Campbell Award for best new writer. In order to promote himself to the award's audience, he created the definitive Web site with information about the award. He sought out all the other eligible writers he could find and solicited their bios and bibliographies, as well as links to their sites and e-mail addresses. He exhaustively researched the award's history and created informational resources for other researchers. James, a fine writer, ended up a finalist for the Campbell, and he continues to promote the award through his site, even though he is no longer eligible.

Cory undertook a similar, smaller-scale effort for the *Science Fiction Age* Readers' Choice Award. When editor Scott Edelman announced that he would be willing to receive ballots by e-mail for the award, Cory produced an electronic ballot for the prize that would automatically forward the votes to Edelman's mailbox. He arranged for a neutral third-party site to host the page, then contacted the other writers on the ballot to let them know about the existence of the electronic ballot. Then he contacted the managers of several genre news sites and worked with them to link to the electronic ballot. The result? Hundreds of ballots were cast electronically, and Cory tied for best novelette.

Infodump

James Campbell's site is at www.sff.net/campbell-awards, and it's the definitive source of information on up-and-coming genre writers.

Infodump

Robert J. Sawyer, a science fiction writer with a knack for self-promotion, once reproduced an entire, 250-word short story on the back of a business card! (Two hundred and fifty words on a standard-size business card is just 9-point type, no gutters, and *very* tight leading.)

Electronic promotions are an important part of an award strategy, but printed handouts are even more important. The act of giving someone a well-produced handout creates a lasting, memorable impression in their minds, increasing the chance that they'll remember you come balloting time.

The keys here are to produce attractive, desirable materials and to hand them out at appropriate moments. If you're reproducing a short story or a novel excerpt, don't just photocopy the printed pages—take the time to whip up a little, center-stapled chapbook of your story, with a note on the back cover explaining the circumstances of the award. With small runs, you can get creative. Talk to the staff at the copy shop about options for cover stock, die-cuts and crops, binding, and other standout features. Don't get *too* caught up in all of this, though. You don't want to spend an unseemly (and unaffordable) amount on your production. Also, remember to focus on readability: that means black, easy-to-follow type on good-quality, white paper.

Another good paper handout is a business card or business card-size flier. A brief, humorous paragraph with the URL of your Web site and some recent publications is a good example.

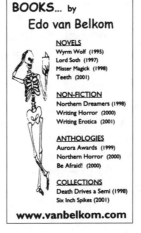

Promotional cards and chapbooks produced by Cory Doctorow and Edo van Belkom.

Your local copy shop can print and crop these cards in runs as small as 10 for very reasonable sums of money, though the per-card cost goes down dramatically at 500.

When handing out your promotional materials, use common sense. A good time to pass around your propaganda is at a reading or signing. They're also a good response to questions like "So, how's the writing going?" Don't break up a party by forcing your stuff on all the guests, though! Also, be sensitive to circumstances: Don't try to give your materials to people who are already overburdened or wearing formal attire without sufficient pocket room.

What Do You Do with an Award, Anyway?

The nominating ballots are in, and damn, you're a finalist! Make no mistake, this is great news. You're in line to win an award, and no matter how obscure the award is, it's recognition in a field where recognition is hard to come by.

Accepting the Award

Now what? In addition to all of your politicking, you're going to need to plan for what you're going to do if you actually *win* the award. First of all, you should get in touch with the award's promoters and find out where the award is being given, and if it's customary for nominees to attend the ceremony. Most awards recognize the financial circumstances of the average writer and are more than willing to let you know if you've won in advance of the award, so that you won't travel across the country only to discover that you've lost. As often as not, the awards are presented at a convention, and the convention's organizers are more than happy to extend free admission to the nominees for an award.

If you do attend an awards ceremony where you stand a chance of winning, you'll need a speech. As we wrote in Chapter 1, "Success at Last!" the shorter your speech, the better. An awards banquet isn't the place to deliver a lengthy polemic on the state of the field, the state of the world, or the state of your finances. Unless you can make your point in a minute or two, just stick to the traditional "I'd like to thank my mama and Elvis" speech.

If you can't attend the awards ceremony and you haven't been told definitively that you've lost, you should plan to have someone accept the award on your behalf. If you're lucky, you've got a friend who will be attending the convention or at least someone who is local to the ceremony and is willing to show up. If not, the award's organizers are usually happy to accept it on your behalf. Send them a brief note letting them know what you want said at the acceptance. In general, an acceptance-by-proxy should be no longer than half the speech you were going to give yourself.

Promoting the Win

You've won the award, and it's safely ensconced on your mantel (or under your pillow). It's time to let the world know about it.

If you've got a project underway that could benefit from some promotion, such as a forthcoming novel or short story, this is the best possible time to promote it. Even if you don't, this is a good time to promote your "brand" as a local genre writer.

Infodump

Even if you don't end up winning, the very fact that you were nominated is still worth promoting. For example, Cory has been nominated for the John Campbell Best New Writer Award, which will be presented at the 2000 WorldCon in Chicago on September 4. He is making as much hay of this as he can, up to and including shameless plugs like this one.

Use the information in Chapter 18, "Self-Promotion 101," to put together a media plan to get the word out of your accomplishment:

➤ Send press releases to your local media outlets.

➤ Put up a banner on your Web site.

➤ Talk to the managers of your local bookstores about doing a signing or personal appearance (don't forget the libraries!).

➤ Research the department heads of the English and Creative Writing programs at your local colleges, universities, and adult-education centers.
Send them a bio and a note asking if you'd like to address their classes and inquiring about writer-in-residence programs.

➤ Check with your local, state, and national art-grants bodies. Is there a grant available that you could use to finance some time off work while you write your next novel? Having an award under your belt gives you a real edge when applying for these.

Remember, winning the award doesn't actually do a whole lot for your career if no one knows about it!

The Least You Need to Know

➤ Science fiction and fantasy are rife with awards.

➤ The Hugo Award is the biggest fan-voted award, the Nebula Award is the biggest writer-voted award, and the World Fantasy Award is the biggest juried award.

➤ Avoid the temptation to rig an award vote, but by all means, *do* politick for an award that you're eligible for.

➤ Restrict your politicking to those situations and individuals that are appropriate.

➤ Don't forget to use an award to publicize your other projects.

Part 5

The Professional Writer

How do you go from selling a few short stories a year to publishing a novel and having your name on the bestseller list? Why are some SF writers able to make a living writing, while the rest of us have to keep our day jobs?

In this part, we look at the economics of writing. You'll learn how to tackle thorny contract issues, find a good agent, and create realistic expectations of income from your sales. We'll take a guided tour of some organizations that can help you.

Last, we'll take a look into the future of publishing, and discover that things are looking up for science fiction and SF writers.

Chapter 22

Agents

> **In This Chapter**
>
> ➤ What an agent does
>
> ➤ How can an agent help you?
>
> ➤ Your agent as a business partner
>
> ➤ Finding your ideal agent

Writers who are working on their first novel tend to spend a lot of time agonizing over the subject of literary agents. It's true that agents are an important part of publishing. A good agent can help speed you on the road to success, while a bad agent can bog you down.

In this chapter we'll look at what agents do and, more important, how an agent might be able to help you in your writing career.

The Agent Defined

The job of the *literary agent* is to sell books. Of course, if you can sell your own book, you won't need an agent, will you?

Guess again. Nowadays literary agents wear many hats, and there's much more to what they do than just selling. You can benefit a lot from having a good agent in your corner even if you've sold your first novel on your own.

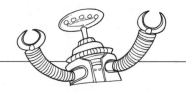

For one thing, an agent can get you a better contract. Most writers are not qualified to negotiate subsidiary rights, or to understand the trade-offs between advances and royalties. This is the bread and butter of a literary agent.

The job of the agent is to know the current state of the industry. Your agent can be your best adviser in deciding which of your ideas for a new novel is most saleable.

These days, agents often serve as first readers, advising their clients on changes that could be made to improve a novel's chance of being bought. Your agent's advice will infringe on your artistic goals, of course; his job is to make the book more saleable, not to be your muse. Your agent is not your boss. You are entirely in charge of your own writing career. An agent may be able to make helpful suggestions, based on his or her experience in the field, but don't look to your agent to make decisions for you.

Money Always Flows Toward You

The critical business rule you must follow as a writer is to ensure that *money always flows toward you*. This means that if you're paying someone to publish your book, you're probably in trouble. If you find yourself paying a reading fee to someone who calls herself an agent, you're *definitely* in trouble.

Your agent's job is to help you make money, not to make money from you.

This is worth emphasizing because the agency business is unlicensed and unregulated. Anybody can set up shop as an agent, and there's a wide range of talent and experience in the profession. You should shop around carefully before choosing an agent. You should also know why you are selecting the agency you choose.

Luckily, there is a professional agency for literary agents, the Association of Author's Representatives (AAR). You should make sure that any agent you approach is, at the very least, a member of the AAR. Your agent should be a member or at least abide by the AAR's Canon of Ethics. The Canon of Ethics is freely available on the AAR Web site (www.aar-online.com).

The Lure: Better Contracts, More Money

When writers first think about getting an agent, it's because they believe an agent can get them a better book contract. This is true; agents are professional contract negotiators. Book contracts are a legal minefield, fraught with promise but also capable of locking you into bad or even disastrous terms.

An agent will rarely accept the boilerplate contract the publisher proposes without some changes. There's lots of flex and give in contract negotiation, but only in certain parts of the contract, and these can be different with different publishers and under different circumstances. It's your agent's job to know about what your publisher really wants out of the contract, and hence what they're willing to give up in your favor. You might be able to find out this information yourself, but that would take time and energy that's better spent writing.

Agents Don't Sell Short Fiction

No matter how famous you become, you'll probably always be the one stuffing your short stories into envelopes and sending them out. Why? The percentages just aren't high enough on short fiction for it to be worth an agent's time selling it.

The better SF markets could net you several hundred dollars for a short-story sale. The 15 or 20 dollars of commission this would net an agent wouldn't pay for his time or office expenses. The only real money for an agent is with the various rights and subrights that go with novel sales.

This is probably a good thing. Selling your own short stories helps keep your finger on the pulse of the market. You wouldn't want to completely retreat into your ivory tower, would you?

Changing Role of the Agent

In today's publishing world, agents have more responsibilities. In the golden age of fiction writing, you as author had two reliable friends: your editor and your agent. You built a relationship with both

Danger, Danger!

Some agents used to charge reading fees to look at a manuscript. This practice is now banned for members of the Association of Author's Representatives (AAR). You should never have to pay an agent a reading fee.

Infodump

The AAR can provide you with a list of member agencies. Write to them at P.O. Box 237201, Ansonia Station, New York, NY 10023. By sending a check or money order for $7 (U.S. funds only), along with a self-addressed, stamped envelope with 55¢ in postage, authors can obtain the Canon of Ethics, a list of member agents, and a brochure on agents and what they can do for you.

over the course of your writing career. The editor guided your artistic growth, and your agent made sure you were solvent.

The consolidation of the publishing industry that happened through the 1980s and 1990s has resulted in leaner, meaner publishing houses. Job security has eroded in publishing, just as it has in practically every other industry. The result is that you can't rely on having one editor who guides you throughout your career. Editors have less and less time to spend on actual editing anyway; they often spend the bulk of their time acquiring new books and coping with publishing-house administrivia. Somewhere in all this bustle, the care and attention your artistic development deserves are being sacrificed.

Enter the agent. You're likely to keep your agent, if he's a good fit for you, for longer than you'll keep your editor. Since nowadays book manuscripts are often rejected without any critique by the publisher, an agent increasingly has to be an author's first reader and artistic guide.

Of course, as always, you are in charge of your own career. But agents today often serve as valuable advisers to fledgling writers.

"As You Know, Bob ..."

Agents make their money on a commission basis; that is, they receive a percentage of your contracted advance. The standard commission on books for North American sales is 15 percent. It used to be 10 percent, but most agencies switched to 15 percent in the 1980s. The standard for overseas contracts is 20 percent. An agent can often get you more than 15 percent above the advance or royalty you could have negotiated yourself, so a good agent pays for herself.

Your Best Ally

Since your agent's income depends on your success, he is your best ally in the publishing industry. Think of it: You have someone on the inside, who knows what's going down and what's looming on the horizon; someone who has your best interests in mind, and who has tied himself to your artistic star.

Your agent has to believe in you; otherwise, why work so hard for you? At times, the fact that you have a friend on the inside will be more important than any particular contract or sales opportunity.

Think of it this way: As an author, your great achievement is your books. An agent's great achievement is the successful career of his client. He cares as much about your success as you care about your books.

Do You Need an Agent?

Much fretting happens when an author finishes his first novel. His writer friends will either ask, "So, who's your agent?" or tell him to send it out on his own.

Do you need an agent? It's tough for beginning writers to answer this one. Let's lay down some guidelines to help make the decision easier.

Honestly Assess Where You Are

If you've published a few short stories, but don't have a novel to shop around yet, then you don't need an agent. It's too soon. You need to build up a bit of a name, and more importantly, get that book finished!

However impatient you are, if you're still in the midst of writing your novel, it's too soon to think about agents. You might be tempted to send out some queries, but the only response you're going to get from any agency is "Sounds great! Send us the whole book so we can assess it." This doesn't save you any time.

Is the book done? Good. More importantly, however, is it the best you can make it? If you compare it to published novels, does it have the same polish? It is critical that you be objective at this point, because you don't want to waste your time or that of a prospective agent.

Infodump

Although an agent's job is to sell novels, don't be afraid to ask your agent's advice if you have a question or two about a magazine or anthology contract that you are signing. Your agent can probably help.

"As You Know, Bob ..."

It's almost impossible for a first-time novelist to sell a novel that's not finished. The pros, who have track records, may be able to land an agent or publisher with an outline and a couple of sample chapters, but if you're not a pro, forget it. The universal requirement is to have a complete work ready.

Does a good contract matter to you? It may be that you only have one novel in you, and this is it. All you care about is getting it published. In that case, an agent may not make much difference to your success. If your book is good it may sell itself, after all.

If, on the other hand, you hope to write and sell more novels, then it's crucial that you manage your contracts. If you are in novel writing for the long haul, then an agent can help you out, and maybe now is the time to approach one.

Is This the Book to Sell?

It's a sad fact that most first novels are not very good. How can you do anything perfectly the first time you do it? It may be that you should tuck your first novel away in a drawer and write a second. But don't guess; you're prejudiced, either in favor or against your own work. If you have peers who regularly read your work, or if you belong to a workshop (see Chapter 5, "Writer's Workshops"), you can bounce your novel off them. If you're still unsure of its quality, it might be worth your time to hire a professional editor to read it for you.

A professional agent can make the same assessment for you, but it's always better to enter negotiations from a position of strength. The better your book is, the more likely you'll land an agent who will enthusiastically get behind it.

You really need to hit the ground running to make it in today's competitive novel market. If your first novel is good but not great, you'll launch your career better if you hold off a year or two, and lead with your second or third novel.

Agents vs. Book Doctors

If you know your book needs work, but aren't sure where to start, an agent may be able to help you. Since your agent is your first reader, he can catch a lot of weaknesses before the book goes to a publisher. Early in your career, however, you might be better served by hiring a professional freelance editor to review the book.

Keep in mind that an agent who is considering a partnership with you also has other work on her desk. If you're new to publishing, you'll be a lower priority to her than established writers. Most agents will read new authors' works and comment on them, but the comments you get may not be in-depth. Also, this is not really an agent's primary task. Every hour your agent spends acting as an editor is an hour she doesn't spend selling or negotiating.

Professional freelance editors (sometimes called book doctors) can be invaluable for beginning novelists. They can also be expensive, meddling, and disastrous. Buyer beware is the rule here; but if you get a reliable reference to a good editor whom you can afford, consider following up on it.

Finding a Good Fit

What kind of writer are you? Are you the aggressive, TV-talkshow kind of self-promoter who scans the industry news looking for opportunities, or are you the contemplative, stay-at-home writer who mows the lawn while thinking about your next chapter? Whatever your style, you should be able to find an agent who's a good match for you.

There are almost as many kinds of agents as there are agencies. Some focus on subsidiary rights like film options; some will encourage you to write Tom Clancy–type technothrillers, or whatever else is currently selling well. Still others will ask you what *you* want, and work only with what you give them.

The obvious answers aren't always the right ones. Let's look at your options.

Corporate Muscle or a Personal Relationship?

Wouldn't it be great if you could land the same agent who sells Stephen King or William Gibson? Surely you'd have it made with such clout on your side.

Maybe. On the other hand, big-name, multiple-bureau agencies are a bit more anonymous. If you've got a hot property, you can bet they'll take good care of you. But if you're an untested quality, or you're into your second or third book and your sales are languishing, don't expect the same attention from them.

Face it: If you're an agent and you have the choice of negotiating the new Dan Simmons novel, or one by a complete newcomer, which one are you going to focus your attention on?

Big agencies often have a number of agents working in them. You could become part of one particular agent's small stable, meaning he'll work harder for you; somebody more senior in the agency will handle the Clancys and Simmonses. Of course, this means you'll probably have a less experienced agent fielding your book.

At the other end of the spectrum are small agencies, some of whom only have one employee (the agent himself). You're sure to get more attention from such an agent, aren't you?

Not necessarily. Some small agencies are almost hobbies for their owners. A small agency may not apply any more enthusiasm or energy to your project than a big anonymous house.

The rule, as always, is buyer beware.

Somewhere in between the anonymous corporations and the one-person hobbyist is your perfect match. There are some very good, responsive, and energetic agents out there who love working with new talent. Before you start sending out query letters, you should try to find out as much as you can about the agencies you're considering:

➤ Get a good comprehensive list of working agents. The AAR can supply you with a large list; we've included a more targeted one in Appendix C, "Agent Listing."

➤ Make sure the agency you're considering has experience selling SF and fantasy. This is important, because you don't want to be some agent's experiment in branching out from Home and Garden books or Westerns.

➤ Find out who represents whom. If authors with works similar to your own are represented by a given agent, maybe you'll find a good fit there.

➤ If you have a chance to meet an author whose agency you're considering, ask him about the agent's style of business. If your prospect is perfect in all other respects but turns out to be brusque on the phone or overly passive when you want career guidance, then you probably won't work well together.

➤ Check the trade publications and reputable Internet sources for warnings about agencies tied to unfair practices, abusive contracts, and the like.

➤ Narrow your list down to those agencies that pass all these tests.

Infodump

The Science Fiction and Fantasy Writers of America (SFWA) maintains an excellent Web page listing agencies, subsidy publishers, book doctors, and vanity anthologies to avoid. Find the page at www.sfwa.org/beware/.

Building a Relationship That Works

Your agent has certain responsibilities toward you. He should be enthusiastic about your work, and if he isn't, he should tell you why. He should actively work to sell your work and provide you evidence that he's doing so. He should be available for discussion, although, of course, he's a busy man and can't be expected to talk all morning.

It should come as no surprise that you as an author have certain obligations toward your agent as well. After all, your agent depends on you for his income. You need to communicate what you're doing. This partnership needs to be built on trust, which means you have to let the agent do his job. If you're going to pick every publisher that your manuscript goes to, and write the cover letters, you might as well sell the book yourself. Give your agent room to maneuver.

This is a business relationship, however chummy it may become. You have to recognize that the priorities of an agent may be parallel to yours, but they are not the same. Don't expect your agent to share your enthusiasm for artistic nuances; be patient with suggestions that may sound overly commercial. You're both speaking from your respective corners, and both your points of view are right.

If things don't work out, exit as gracefully as you can. Many agencies offer a contract to authors that lists what both parties can expect. Such contracts can usually be ended with 60 days' notice. If a handshake is not enough for you, select an agency that offers such a contract.

Acquiring an Agent

So you've narrowed down your choices and are ready to approach them. As with slushpile submissions, you could just pop your book manuscript into a box and mail it, but that's not necessarily going to get you a speedy or positive response. There are better approaches, as you'll see.

Do's and Don'ts of Landing an Agent

Approaching an agent for the first time is a lot like approaching a publisher. Just as you need to sell a publisher on the value of your work, you need to sell an agent on both your work and your future potential.

If you have any short-story sales, awards, good reviews, etc., this is the time to bring them out. Your prospective agent wants to see that you're as serious about the publishing industry as she is. Prove it by presenting your track record.

You can be optimistic, but don't get delusions of grandeur. Rest assured, no agent (or publisher) is going to take seriously a query letter that starts by saying that your book is the best ever written, or will "turn the publishing world on its ear." Unfortunately, they've heard this one before.

Agency Hunt Checklist

Choose your agent carefully. Research your prospects, and by all means, talk to a prospective agent before you hire him to see if you share the same vision of your career. Following are some guidelines for approaching agents; feel free to add to this list any questions that are critical for you.

➤ Query when you have something to sell, not before. This means you should wait until your manuscript is finished and polished.

➤ Your query should consist, at the very least, of a letter introducing yourself and your work, with an included SASE. Hold back none of your credentials; there is no reason to be coy. If you have review clippings, for instance, include copies.

Danger, Danger!

Don't try to butter up the agency. In Chapter 15, "Publishing Your Novel," we discussed the "splashy entrance" approach to selling that never works. The same is true for impressing agents: Don't use fancy gimmicks or ploys to disguise poor credentials. You'll be seen through immediately.

➤ If you have a particular novel project to sell (you should at this point), include an outline with the query. Ask the agent what she thinks of it.

➤ Ask your prospective agent how he manages subsidiary rights, such as movie rights, audio-cassette rights, translations, etc., and what kind of sales expectations are realistic for these rights.

➤ The best time to query is after you've sold a novel on your own. This is the point at which you'll want a good negotiator working on your contract, so it makes eminent good sense to acquire an agent now. Few agents will turn down an offer of this sort.

➤ You can query more than one agency at a time, but only if you're up-front about what you're doing. Tell them it's a multiple query.

The Least You Need to Know

➤ Literary agents can improve your sales and the quality of your contracts. A good agent is well worth the commission.

➤ Agents focus exclusively on novels, screenplays, and other large projects. They do not sell short stories.

➤ You don't need an agent if you don't yet have a completed novel that you wish to sell.

➤ There are many kinds of agents. Shop around carefully before choosing one and talk to a prospective agent before hiring him.

➤ There are good agents and bad agents. At the very least, consult the AAR for a list of reputable firms.

➤ You query an agency the same way you query a publisher: with an introductory letter, outline of your novel, and list of credentials.

Chapter 23

E-Rights, E-Books, and the Future of SF Publishing

> ## In This Chapter
>
> ➤ Electronic books: the future of publishing?
>
> ➤ Unlimited print runs
>
> ➤ The minefield of e-rights
>
> ➤ Should you try online publishing?

Like many other businesses, publishers are coming to grips with the tidal wave of new technology made possible by the Internet. At the same time they're dealing with high paper prices, obsolete business models, and rampant corporate takeovers. Where's it all going?

E-Books

March 14, 2000, marked the moment when the public at large suddenly became aware of the electronic book, or *e-book*. On that day, Stephen King launched his latest novelette, "Riding the Bullet," making it available on the Web as a downloadable e-book. Major newspapers across North America covered the story and the idea of e-books to millions of readers.

What's an E-Book?

There are two parts to an e-book: the reader, which is a physical object that allows you to read the files, and the books themselves, which are computer files.

At the time of this writing, there were only two e-book readers available, but at least seven were scheduled to become available soon. The two original readers are the SoftBook Reader and the Rocket eBook. Owners of Palm organizers or other personal digital assistants (PDAs) can also read e-books if they have the right software.

Although e-book readers are similar technologically to PDAs, they are dedicated reading machines rather than hand-held computers. They are designed to be easy to use and easy on the eyes. They are not quite as easy on the eyes as paper is yet, but new technologies are approaching that should make e-book screens more "paper-like."

Factoid

An **e-book** is the content of a book or novel formatted specifically to be readable on a computer or other electronic device. There are several e-book formats and several types of readers (which allow you to read the files) vying for the market at present.

E-Book Publishers

Nearly all major publishers are now considering or have already launched e-book lines. For some, like Tor Books, e-book rights have been a standard clause of their novel contracts for several years. For others, e-book rights are part of the general electronic rights clause. It's safe to say that in the very near future you won't be able to sell a novel without taking into account the e-book market. If this is the case, it's important you make sure you get properly paid for e-book sales. The most prominent e-book publisher/reseller in 1999 was Rocket eBooks, but many other publishers and hardware manufacturers are starting to eye this potentially huge market. Wary of repeating the Betamax vs. VHS battle of the early 1980s, publishers, in partnership with companies like Microsoft, are hurrying to create a standardized format for e-books.

Chances are that if you sell a novel this year, your contract will contain some clause about e-book sales.

On-Demand Publishing

The previous discussion might make you think that when publishers get together at cocktail parties these days, all they talk about is e-books. You'd be wrong. The biggest topic of conversation in publishing today is *on-demand* printing technology.

On-demand printing may sound like one of those boring in-house topics, about as interesting as offset printer calibration techniques. In fact, on-demand is nothing short of a revolution in printing. While e-books are a new market for traditional print publishers to tap into, on-demand is nothing less than the future of the printed word itself.

The Horrid History of Book Printing

For the past 30 years, authors' backlists (previously published books still in print) have been getting squeezed out of production. The pressure to crank out new best-sellers at the expense of all else has resulted in some of SF's classic works becoming unavailable. Older works are not going to have the same volume of sales that a new book might have. Backlist titles incur all the same warehousing, catalog, logistics, and distribution costs of new titles, however. Viewed from the bottom line, they're just not as good a gamble as new titles.

On-demand printing presents a possible solution to the publishers' dilemma of how to mass-market bestsellers without sacrificing the backlist. This is because on-demand technology lets you print arbitrarily small runs of a book.

Factoid

On-demand technology allows a publisher to print books as they are needed by suppliers: One book, one sale is the ideal of on-demand.

The Miracle of On-Demand

On-demand printing basically just removes the high minimum cost for a print run. Previously, a publisher might have had to commit to printing 10,000 copies of a book even if he knew he could only sell 5,000. Now, the publisher can print in lots of 100 at a time, shipping them in a "just-in-time" way to distributors of booksellers.

Ultimately, bookstores may be able to purchase an inexpensive DocuTech machine capable of producing paperback books of quality comparable to those they receive from distributors. At that point, the Internet could become the distribution channel—straight from the publisher to the bookseller. Every time the bookstore sells a book, another is run off in the back room and put on the shelves; or, if a customer requests a book that isn't on the shelf, he has a cup of coffee while the book is printed for him.

By removing the high barrier to printing small runs, on-demand makes it possible for books to remain "in print" indefinitely. This is great from the point of view of authors, because it means we can potentially receive revenues from our published books until our dying day.

But there's a catch.

Infodump

On-demand publishing may provide more choices to the consumer. It takes no more effort to store the electronic version of a hardcover than it does a paperback book. A publisher could provide either, or a large-print or Braille edition, at the request of the customer.

The Electronic Rights Battle

Unfortunately, electronic rights have always been a gray area in publishing contracts. Throughout the 1970s and 1980s, in fact, many newspapers and magazines sold articles written for them by freelancers to third-party databases. These databases then sold access to the articles to other institutions. The original author of the piece received not a dime for this resale of his or her work. Many writers weren't even aware that their work was being resold; this was in the era before the Internet, remember.

The Internet brought things to a head. Publishers, who had always inserted clauses about "electronic reproduction rights" or "database rights" into contracts, now saw a potential gold mine in keeping these rights. The publishers were a bit quicker off the mark than the writers, and quickly began taking an all-or-nothing approach to these clauses: Give us all electronic rights, or there's no deal.

At first, writers went along with this, because few recognized what selling all electronic or database rights in perpetuity meant.

Redefining "In Print"

The Internet, and now on-demand publishing, have changed the rules of the game. In the past, rights to a literary work reverted back to the author once the work went out of print. This was a clear and legally precise boundary for the exercising of rights by a publisher: Once they'd done their print runs and sold as many copies of a book as they could, the author got the rights back and could, if he chose, sell them again to another publisher.

Reversion of rights is a basic cornerstone of authors' ability to make a living from writing. Once a publisher has lost interest in your work, you should be able to take that work to somebody else who will promote it more enthusiastically. New editions, with new artwork, can attract new customers and repeat business from already-satisfied readers who've loved their old copies of a book to death.

If a publisher keeps no stock, but simply prints new copies on demand from readers, how do we now define "in print"? It turns out that those electronic rights clauses were a Trojan horse. Because the publishers can print up new copies of a book any time they want, the book is never out of print. If you've signed a book with a standard reversion clause, that means that the publisher owns the rights to the book forever.

Factoid

A **reversion** clause specifies when you, as the author of the work, become free to sell it again in the same medium as the current contract. If you're negotiating a hardcover novel sale, the reversion clause puts in legal black-and-white when you can sell those hardcover rights again to another company.

All Rights, Forever

You might say, "Well, that's pretty awful, but I have a good publisher and it's a nice edition of the book." Maybe. But what happens when the publisher loses interest in promoting you? If they let annual sales slip from thousands down to dozens, your revenue from that book dries up. Worse, you can't get it repackaged and resell it. Your work languishes in a kind of limbo, not really dead, but dead as far as attracting new readers is concerned. Effectively, you no longer own your own work. This can become glaringly obvious when you write a new volume in a series and sell it to a new publisher. They won't be able to reprint your older books in the series, because they're still owned by somebody else.

It gets worse. The publisher may be able to print e-book versions of your novel without paying you a dime. They may be able to alter your work, or distribute it on the Web, without your say-so.

Believe it or not, this is the state of the publishing industry right now—including the magazine publishers, who would like to keep your work for their Web sites. Most publishers insist on e-rights clauses nowadays and interpret those clauses as broadly as they can to retain the rights to your work.

So, while on-demand and e-books are the potential saviors of midlist writers, they may also spell our doom. Luckily, the writing community is alert to this danger now, and is fighting back. In fact, we're winning.

David 1, Goliath 0

In terms of actual rights, the publishing industry really doesn't have a leg to stand on. In one celebrated case, the massive Hearst magazine empire told its freelancers that it couldn't drop its claims for e-rights from its contracts, because it was unable to delete individual articles from its database. One brave writer who had sold only plain serial (print) rights took on this Goliath. After a lengthy court battle, Hearst apologized, and—whoops!—suddenly they found they were able to remove her articles from their database after all!

A number of major court cases have been fought by writers, both in Europe and America. Almost without exception, these cases have been won by the writers. In many more cases, writers have found that simply digging in their heels is enough to have unfavorable e-rights clauses dropped or altered. Most publishers, it seems, would rather pay than alienate their authors.

Infodump

One of the most respected literary agents in the field, Richard Curtis, has set up a new company called e-rights.com, specifically to aid authors in negotiating their way through the contractual minefield.

Things are still tough in SF publishing. Recently, however, some savvy agents and authors have begun to negotiate aggressively in favor of more equitable rights.

Electronic Lending Rights Agencies

Many publishers have complained that they can't track individual hits on a Web site, so they can't tell an author precisely how many people have read a particular article or story. For them, sending thousands of checks to all the authors they've ever bought stories from, just because one or two people read those stories online, constitutes a bureaucratic nightmare.

Writers in the U.S. and Canada have responded by setting up electronic lending rights agencies to track use of authors' works and facilitate payment. The Publishing Rights Clearinghouse in the U.S., the Authors' Licensing and Collecting Society in Britain (www.acls.co.uk), and TERLA in Canada take on the onerous task of tracking sales and cutting individual checks for the thousands of authors whose work is used in online form. For the publishers, this means they can pay the agency a lump sum for online rights use and not have to worry about individual cases. For the authors, the agencies represent strong allies in their struggle to ensure that they're fairly paid for their work.

Authors are organizing, and the lending rights agencies allow us to negotiate on an equal footing with big-name publishing houses.

Protecting Yourself

Intimidating though a publishing contract can be, you have nothing to lose by negotiating terms in your own favor. The publisher may dig in their heels, but negotiation is part of the process. No one's going to be insulted that you tried to keep your rights.

Though contract terminology varies, the key things for a writer to watch out for are clauses that slip in Internet and e-book sales in the guise of something else; and sale of rights without a clear reversion clause.

In the first case, you might see an innocuous-looking clause in the contract that gives the publisher "database rights" to your work. Sounds pretty esoteric, so why not give it to them? The problem is that you can call a Web site a kind of database; you can even store stories in a real database application and use a Web site as its "front end." So by giving the publisher database rights, you've actually given them permission to publish your material on the World Wide Web.

Better strike that clause, if you can.

In the second case, say, you've successfully negotiated remuneration for Web sales, e-books, and all other forms of electronic publication. But if the contract still lacks language that defines when your rights revert, you're screwed. After all, in the past, it was obvious when rights reverted: when the book went out of print. Now that a book might never go out of print in electronic form, the old language won't serve any more.

One way to ensure that electronic rights revert to you is to insert a time limit in your contract, if you can. By all means, you can say, "Take all electronic rights for two years. After that, all rights revert to me." That way, the publisher can't use the "but it's still in print" argument on you. "Sorry," you can say. "Time's up."

You can also negotiate minimum sales rates. For instance, if the publisher insists on maintaining electronic rights, you can insert a clause saying that if they make less than a certain number of sales per year of your work, the rights revert. Most publishers won't have a problem with this sort of scheme, because the book will only revert to you when they've ceased making any money from it anyway.

The main thing is to try. You won't always win your e-rights battles, but every time a writer rolls over and blindly accepts a bad clause, it hurts all of us. Collectively, we're winning the e-rights battle. You can do your part, and if you do, you'll definitely profit by it.

Online Publishers: Try or Avoid?

Publishing on the Internet got off to a rocky start. Early attempts at Web publishing lacked a good business model. Without reliable advertising and payment systems, sites like omnimag.com foundered.

Despite these difficulties, online SF magazines have flourished. Most pay either peanuts or nothing at all but they do give you the instant gratification of seeing your name in print—even if it's on the screen and not on paper.

A second wave of online publishers has appeared over the past couple of years. These are well-funded, highly organized operations that use on-demand technology to produce printed books. They usually act somewhat like vanity presses, in that they charge authors a fee to publish them; but the fee can be as low as $100. In return, they offer high royalties—as high as 50 percent.

"As You Know, Bob ..."

Publishers are not all-consuming monsters. They have very specific goals. You'll be able to negotiate from a position of strength if you know what your publisher wants to do with the e-rights to your work. Rather than taking an adversarial approach to contract negotiation, try to work out a reversion scheme that satisfies both you and the publisher.

Danger, Danger!

Online publishing is changing so quickly that everything we say here is in danger of being obsolete before this book hits the stands. You should treat this discussion as a jumping-off point, and watch industry news carefully to learn what's actually happening.

Buck Rogers on the Web

Most online SF magazines are just Web sites. The vast majority are done by enthusiastic fans, and don't pay. They'll gladly take your work and make it available for anyone to read. For writers who are just starting out, such sites provide the fastest route to publication—but you might as well start your own Web site and keep your stories there.

You'll also find pro and semipro magazines sprouting on the Web. The sites for magazines such as *Jackhammer* (www.eggplant-productions.com/jackhammer) and *Neverworlds* (www.neverworlds.com) pay for publication, and generally buy first world serial or worldwide electronic publication rights. Most of these publications can be considered semipro because they pay 1¢ per word or less (often a flat payment, say $15).

For a larger listing of Web-based SF magazines, refer to Appendix D, "Online Resources."

Instant Books

Online book publishers produce novels in electronic format; a few of them also boast some on-demand printing technology. Following are some of the Web-based book publishers operating in early 2000. This list is bound to change rapidly as more companies enter the field.

➤ **e-rights.com.** Founded by literary agent Richard Curtis, e-rights.com has programs for writers who have recovered rights to out-of-print works. The author can have small lots of a book printed—as few as 48 at a time—for sale at signings, readings, or through an Internet portal.

➤ **BiblioBytes.** This publisher was one of the pioneers in the online sales of complete books. They offer a standard contract with a 35 percent royalty for new works. Submissions should be in electronic form.

➤ **iUniverse.** One of the largest Web publishers, iUniverse offers a number of different options for publishing your work. This is a large site with many choices.

➤ **ToExcel.** Now an imprint of iUniverse, ToExcel specializes in making out-of-print works available again. If you've published a novel that has gone out of print, you can get it back into circulation using ToExcel.

Royalty rates ranging from 35 to 50 percent make online book publishing seem very attractive. The truth is that although there's great potential in Web-based book sales, none of the online publishers were profitable as of early 2000. More to the point, sales figures for a book published online tend to be in the hundreds rather than the thousands. Doubtless this will change in the future as the Web matures. Right now, though, your best bet for a wide audience is through the traditional publishing industry.

Pitfalls of Online Publishing

Services like ToExcel suggest a bright future for midlist writers. There is no reason for any book to be out of print anymore. The downside to this availability, of course, is that you might get locked into a situation where only 5 or 10 copies of your book are sold each year, simply because the consumer has no way of telling which of thousands of books on the portal are worth reading. If you choose the online publishing route, be aware that at the moment online reprint services won't give you the advertising and reviewer push afforded to books published the old way. Your work might never accumulate a big enough audience for you to make a living this way.

Danger, Danger!

Most traditional publishers will not consider publishing a book that has already been made available on the Web. Their logic is that the book has effectively been put into the public domain; anyone can print it off, and no one can control how many copies may be floating around there. This means the publisher can't guarantee sales, since there may be free versions of the book available. (There are exceptions: Bruce Sterling released a free electronic text of *The Hacker Crackdown* on the Net, as did Neal Stephenson with *In the Beginning … Was the Command Line.* But at the time both were famous SF writers, with their reputations and sales volume already guaranteed.) The prudent rule at the moment is if you want to sell your novel to a traditional publishing house, don't sell it to an online house first.

As we've mentioned, you must also make sure that you retain control of your work. There must be some mechanism for reversion of the book's publishing rights to you. Otherwise, you may find you've sold your book once and for all, and will never be able to place it with any other publisher!

Be careful not to become over-enthusiastic when considering online publication. Read the fine print—all of it.

Editor? What Editor?

The biggest problem online book publishers face is their lack of a credible editorial process. Many publishers will publish whatever you give them, provided you pay a small fee ($99 for iUniverse) up front. Depending on where you live, this might be less than it costs to courier a large manuscript overnight to New York.

Infodump

Various online knowledge-filtering services are springing up lately. These allow you to find artworks that people with tastes similar to your own have enjoyed. Such services may go a long way toward obviating the need for an online editorial system. Such systems cannot, however, replace the most important function of the editor: finding diamonds in the rough, and working with an author to make him shine.

The great thing about this kind of online publishing is that now, anyone can get published. And the really awful thing about online publishing is that now, anyone can get published.

Any editor who's spent days wading through the slush-pile looking for a saleable manuscript will tell you that it can quickly turn you off reading altogether. Well, with online publishing, we now have a way for all that slush to be published! This means that instead of a professional editor filtering the bad from the good, it's now up to you, the consumer, to do it.

We have editors for the same reason that we have quality control of food products or kids' toys: to spare you the agony of finding a bad item yourself. Faced with having to browse a hundred bad books to find one good one (say, yours), most consumers will quickly give up. This may explain the low sales figures of the existing online publishers.

If and when traditional publishers or editors begin their own online imprints, the publish-the-slush situation should change. Until that happens, your work will be placed side by side with the worst that literature has to offer; that can't be good for your reputation—or sales.

The Merging of Online and Print

Some day, books will be available in both print and online versions. On-demand printing combined with e-book formats permits huge flexibility in how you package a book. If you want your own copy of a novel in hardcover, trade paperback, large-print, or just electronic form, you'll be able to choose freely. Bookstores will be able to stock all books, all the time; nothing will ever be out of print again. Anything that's not on the shelves can be downloaded and printed in the back room, and every time a book gets printed this way, the electronic lending rights agency that monitors sales will ensure that the author and publisher get paid.

In some cases, for instance for books whose rights have reverted, the author will be the publisher. While sales of your backlist may be slower than your new novel's, you'll make a higher royalty.

Editors and publishers will keep their jobs, though. Nobody wants to wade through tons of slush to find a few good gems, and no author exists whose work can't be improved by a good editor. Things will change, but everyone will benefit.

With luck, we'll shortly see a new golden age of SF publishing, brought to us by the shiny new technologies of our twenty-first century.

The Least You Need to Know

➤ Electronic books are already here and will be an important market for you in the future.

➤ Even more important is on-demand publishing, in which books are published only as consumer demand warrants.

➤ You need to protect your electronic rights when negotiating book and short-story sales today.

➤ Authors are winning the electronic rights battle, but you must be aware to be safe.

➤ Online publishing is a flourishing market, but it's not for everybody.

Contracts

Contracts inspire a species of nauseous dread in the general public that is totally un-warranted. A good contract is a joy to behold: It unambiguously sets out the terms under which two parties are conducting some piece of business. It explains what each party expects from the other, and why they expect these things. Good, honest con-tracts include clauses that cover every aspect of the agreement, and *nothing else*. A good short-story contract doesn't have a word in it about theme-park rights, because theme parks *don't license short stories*.

Contracts are only as good as the people who sign them. You don't intend to sue your publisher, and they don't intend to sue you. Ideally, you are amicable parties, attempt-ing to explicitly set out what you expect of each other.

The unfortunate reality, though, is that while editors buy books, publishers' *lawyers* draft the contracts, and they are notorious grabby-gutses, who attempt to nail every possible benefit for their employers. When you get a contract from your publisher, chances are that it contains some pretty offensive clauses, put there specifically to trap the kind of writer who signs whatever the publisher puts in front of them. It's your responsibility to know which clauses are worth objecting to and which ones aren't, and to negotiate your contract in good faith to strike a fair deal for you and your publisher.

What's Copyright?

"Copyright" refers to all the rights to a work. If you've created a work (a novel, a short story, an article), you automatically own all the rights to it until you surrender some or all of those rights.

In other words, the instant you fire up your word processor and hammer out "Once upon a time, a long time ago, in a galaxy far, far away, God said, 'Let there be light,'" you own all the rights to those words. You can sell a novel based on them, a short story, a movie, a foreign translation, a theme-park ride, an action figure, an electronic book, a Web site, a painting, a cartoon, or a game show. You don't need to take any steps to "register" your rights to that work: You automatically *own* it, it's yours.

There's a bit of folk wisdom that says that you should safeguard your rights to a work by sending it to yourself registered mail and leaving the envelope sealed, or file a copy with the U.S. Copyright Office. Neither of these is required to secure your copyright; the mere act of creation does that.

However! If, some day, you find yourself in a courtroom, arguing that your work is *yours,* that you were the original creator of your words, it helps to have a paper trail showing the process of creating the document. Cory likes to keep copies of his early drafts and file the annotated manuscripts his workshop gives back to him after critiquing a story. Not only does this provide some entertaining moments as he reviews how his ability to revise has progressed over the years, it also provides evidence that he actually created the work.

You own all the rights to your work, until such time as you *explicitly* release those rights.

A publishing contract is a formal mechanism for exchanging some of the rights to your work for money or other considerations. A good contract specifies:

➤ The rights being acquired

➤ The amount being paid

➤ The schedule for payment

➤ The schedule for publication

Infodump

In Appendix A, "Model Contracts," we've provided annotated model contracts from the Science Fiction and Fantasy Writers of America. These provide an invaluable benchmark when comparing the contracts you've received from your publisher.

➤ The particulars of the publication

➤ Your responsibilities to the publisher

➤ Your publisher's responsibilities to you

➤ The terms for ending the contract

➤ The penalties for nonperformance

Rights and Payments

As you read earlier, copyright is not monolithic: When you "sell" a story, you actually sell some of the rights to it. You and your publisher need to negotiate which specific rights they wish to acquire and the amounts they will pay for exercising those rights.

Rights

The rights being specified are particular to each deal. However, the cardinal rule is: *You should only sell the rights the publisher plans to use.* If a publisher doesn't have a Web site, why would they want the rights to excerpt your story on the Web? If the publisher doesn't have any overseas editions, why would they want translation rights?

"As You Know, Bob ..."

Damon Knight, author of "A Beginner's Guide to Contracts," from *The Science Fiction and Fantasy Writers of America Handbook* (Fat Puppy Press, 1995) writes: "Book contracts are written by publishers' lawyers, who are not paid to protect the interests of writers. When a contract contains clauses favorable to writers, it is because generations of writers before you have negotiated them and made them standard."

At a bare minimum, any rights above and beyond those immediately being exercised—such as First North American hardcover rights, or First North American Serial (magazine) rights—should be paid for over and above the base rate for the work.

Sums and Royalties

For short stories, payment is usually straightforward: You receive a flat sum for the one-time publication of your story. Sometimes, there will be additional sums paid in exchange for permission to market the story to foreign markets, but more commonly these sums are expressed as a percentage of the publisher's take on a translation sale: They'll pay you *x* percent of their net take on a foreign sale, when and if such a thing occurs.

In the world of novel sales, things are more complex. Almost all novel-publishing deals are based on royalties: a system that pays you a small piece of the publisher's net take on every book sold. The up-front money you get for a book deal is called an "advance," which is shorthand for "advance against royalties." In other words, your publisher is giving you some money against the eventual revenue your book will generate.

Royalties are sometimes based on a sliding scale, depending on the number of copies sold. For a nonfiction book, the authors might receive a 10 percent royalty on the first 50,000 copies sold, a 11 percent royalty on the next 40,000, and a 12 percent royalty on the copies sold thereafter.

But those percentages aren't based on the cover price! Royalties for packaged books like this one are often paid out based on the publisher's *net* price; that is, the whole-sale price that the publisher sells the book to distributors at. This figure is usually 50 percent, so your purchase of this book has put 36¢ into each collaborator's pocket (after splitting with the publisher, the other collaborator, and the agent). In the fiction world, royalties are more commonly based on the full cover price, which would double that to 72¢ per collaborator.

Infodump

While royalties on net price are common in packaged nonfiction, novel royalties are almost always based on the full cover price. These royalties are called "retail" royalties.

When you sell a short story to an anthology, royalties come into play: The editor agrees to pay you a pro-rated share of half of any royalties he earns after the advance has been paid off. This means that you receive a proportional share of the anthology royalties, splitting with the editor, his agent, and your fellow writers. On a $6.99 paperback where your story constitutes 5 percent of the total book, that comes out to a whopping 1.75¢ per copy! Make a reservation, honey, we're going out for dinner! Usually, these clauses specify that you will receive royalty payments once your royalties total $20 or more—this saves everyone the headache of keeping track of fractional pennies.

Earning Out

Your book won't start paying further royalties until the royalties represented by your advance "earn out"; that is, until your publisher has sold enough copies to pay off the advance. Lots of books don't ever earn out, especially first novels. When this happens, you *don't* have to refund the balance of your advance! Be very careful of contracts that try to nail you for unearned advances—a common ploy is to debit unearned advances from your first book from the advances paid on your next. This is unusual, though more common with series and trilogies.

The timing of the payment is very straightforward in the world of short stories: Either the magazine pays you "on acceptance" (usually within 30 days of the signed contracts arriving at the publisher's office); "on publication" (usually within 30 days of the magazine showing up on the stands); or a set period after publication. The better the magazine, the earlier they pay you. Be very, very careful of magazines that pay *after* publication: This often indicates that the publisher is living hand-to-mouth and won't have the money to pay you unless he sells enough copies of the issue with your story in it.

In the book world, the payment of the advance is usually staged; that is, if the manuscript is complete at the time the contract is signed, payment might be half on signing, half on publication. If the contract is signed before the book is completed, payment might be half on signing, half on completion and acceptance of the manuscript. Payment of royalties is based on semiannual reporting periods, so that twice a year, your publisher will send you an accounting of all the books sold and your share thereof.

Danger, Danger!

Books are sold on a "returns system." That means bookstores can return unsold copies for a refund within a certain period. As a result, publishers withhold a "reasonable" percentage of your royalties against the returns. These withholdings are theoretically reconciled once the returns period has expired and the publisher knows exactly how many copies they've sold. In practice, publishers often use returns as a means of clawing back a hefty chunk of your royalties and rely on writers losing track of the accounting.

Administrivia

It's easy to assume that the real meat of a contract is in the rights assigned and payment offered, but it's really the picky details of a contract that differentiate a good contract from a bad one. You need to keep track of reporting, publication date, and corrections.

Timing

The schedule for publication is an important issue to negotiate, though many publishers are leery of being nailed down on hard dates. Both you and your publisher want to see your book or story sell as well as it can; that's why your publisher's in business. Sometimes, a delay in a book's pub date reflects some bit of marketing strategy from the publisher (maybe they've decided to package the novel as a Christmas gift title, and want to push your summer title back to November); sometimes it just means that your publisher has inadvertently scheduled more books than they can actually handle at one time.

The thing you want to avoid is having a book or story sit in inventory at a publisher for years and years before publication. A good contract will specify a period for publication, say, within two years of the contract's date even if it doesn't nail down an exact date. A common loophole in such a clause is that the publication clock doesn't start ticking until the work is "accepted for publication"—in other words, until the publisher is ready to start the clock. For this reason, it's important to not only state the maximum waiting period until publication, but also for approval of the manuscript. That way, if your publisher keeps pushing back the publishing schedule, you (or your agent) can go to them and argue that they're in danger of losing the rights to publish the thing, and that they'd better print it or buy it again.

Corrections

The particulars of the publication are mostly administrivia, like the title, the copyright, and so on. But there are a few that you want to pay close attention to, relating to revision. A good contract will provide you with a set of "galleys" or "proofs" (typeset prototypes for your book or story), far enough ahead of the publication date that you get a chance to review the changes the editor, *copy editor, proofreader,* and *typesetter* have made, and to ensure that you're okay with them. This clause will also specify the time that you have to get your changes back to the editor.

Factoid

Copy editors make sure that the grammar, punctuation, and spelling in your manuscript are all correct, and that sentences read smoothly. **Typesetters** prepare the book for printing, ensuring that hyphenated words are broken up at logical points, that paragraphs aren't "widowed" with their final word on another page, and other typographical niceties. **Proofreaders** work with the typeset pages to make sure that any errors that the copy editor missed or the typesetter introduced are fixed before the book goes to press. These roles are usually filled by skilled professionals with near-psychotic devotion to detail, but it's *your* book they're working on, and you have the final responsibility of ensuring that you agree with all their changes.

Responsibilities

As we wrote in the introduction to this chapter, a good contract is all about spelling out the expectations each party has of the other. Part of every contract should specify which responsibilities you owe your publisher, and which ones they owe you.

What You Owe

Your book contract is a mutual agreement with your publisher. That means that you have certain responsibilities to them. First of all, you have to deliver your manuscript. The publisher will let you know how much of the manuscript they need to see and when. Writers who hit all of their deadlines are writers that editors like to work with—and writers who don't hit deadlines can be more trouble than they're worth. If you think you're going to miss a deadline, *let your editor know as early as possible.* It's one thing to be late, it's another thing entirely to stand your editor up.

The contract will also specify the format that the editor wants to see the book in. Increasingly, editors expect books to be e-mailed or sent on a floppy disk in a common word-processor format. Typewritten manuscripts have to be re-keyed or scanned for publication, which is a costly undertaking.

Liability

You also need to affirm that you own the rights that you're selling to the publisher. Generally, this means that you are the original author, and that you've got permission for any quotations you've used.

Danger, Danger!

Under current copyright law, almost everything you see in print or online is owned by someone. While there is some provision for "fair use" quotation in law, this is a very fuzzy area, and you are on the hook for ensuring that you've gotten the permission of the copyright holders for any quotes you use. This especially applies to song lyrics, which are the jealously guarded treasures of billion-dollar music publishing conglomerates that live to sue insignificant writers into a bloody pulp. Howard Waldrop's magnificent story "Flying Saucer Rock and Roll" phonetically spells out the lyrics to a number of classic doo-wop songs for this reason.

The publisher will also ask you to guarantee that there's nothing libelous in your book—that is, that you haven't told damaging lies about anyone. In practice, this is nearly impossible to ensure, since some people get very touchy about being included in fictionalized accounts, and will sue at the drop of a hat.

Publishers try to offload the responsibility for such lawsuits onto writers with clauses like, "The writer indemnifies the publisher from any damages arising out of a legal claim or action taken to avoid such a claim." What this means is that if some nutcase decides to sue your publisher, you're on the hook, even if the publisher decides to settle the matter out of court with a nice, fat lump sum payment, which can run in the millions. Of course, collecting such a payment from you, the poor author, may very well be impossible, but this is still a very unpleasant situation to be in.

A more writer-friendly version of this is "The writer indemnifies the publisher from any damages arising from a *finally sustained* claim, such damages not to exceed the lesser of the publisher's liability insurance deductible or the author's total royalties from this book." What this version says is that you're only on the hook if the case goes to court and you lose, and you appeal and lose again, and even then only for the amount the publisher has to pay to their insurer as a deductible, or the total amount you've earned from the book.

In practice, publishers have packs of rabid attack-lawyers who will aggressively litigate any claims made against your book, and even if they lose, it's basically impossible for your publisher to get any money out of you other than the sums that they already owe you for royalties. You want to be very careful of any contract that seeks to attach liability to *other* books—publishers sometimes try to nail you for the amounts earned by other titles you have published or will publish with them. Obviously, you want to avoid this.

What They Owe

Your publisher also owes you certain considerations. In addition to payment and publication, your contract should set out the terms for royalty reporting, free author's copies, and notification of and payment for any subsidiary rights that they've exercised—say, if they've sold a film option based on your book. Additionally, you should have the right to audit the publisher's finances to the extent that they relate to your books; as well as the right to take back your book from the publisher if they go bankrupt.

Breaking Up

Nobody likes to think about worst-case scenarios, but when you're signing a contract, you need to consider the possibility that you and your publisher will part ways. Your contract should set out the terms under which either party can walk away from the agreement.

Voluntary Separation

Every good contract has terms setting out how it can be terminated. You may decide that you can't or don't want to write the book; your publisher may decide that they can't or won't publish it. The terms will be different for you and your publisher, but they'll both have two things in common: notice and penalties.

➤ **Notice** is the period that you have to give your publisher when you intend to cancel the contract: 60 days is pretty standard, but if you're an aggressive negotiator, you can get it to 30 days for you and 60 days for the publisher.

➤ **Penalties** are different for each party. If you cancel the contract, your publisher will expect you to refund any advances they've paid to you. If it's the other way around, you're going to want some or all of the money they would have owed you if they hadn't cancelled payout to you. This is called a "kill-fee," and it can run anywhere from 10 to 100 percent.

Reversion

There's another kind of contract termination: the reversion of your rights when your book goes out of print, or when your publisher fails to live up to their end of the bargain. We talked about reversion in the previous chapter. Simply put, when the rights revert to you, you are free to attempt to sell a new edition of your book or story elsewhere. This normally happens once your book goes out of print or the magazine disappears from the stands.

Sneakier magazine contracts try to slip in extensions to the reversion: They say that your rights don't revert for six months or a year from the publication date. There is no practical reason for this, since magazines rarely depend on back-issue sales for any substantial part of their revenue.

For book publishing, "out of print" must be rigorously defined, like so:

> In the event that the Publisher's edition of the Work shall at any time be out of print, the Author or his representative may give notice thereof to the Publisher, and in such event the Publisher shall declare within thirty (30) days in writing whether or not he intends to bring out a new edition of the Work; if he declares his intention to bring out such new edition, then such edition shall be published no later than six (6) months. If the Publisher fails to bring out a new printing of the Work, then this agreement shall automatically terminate and all rights hereunder shall revert to the Author. At any time after two years from the date of first publication, but not before, the Publisher may on three months' notice in writing to the Author or his representative discontinue publication, and in that event this agreement shall terminate and all rights hereunder shall revert to the Author at the expiration of said three (3) month period.

Notice the salient points of this clause: The book is out of print if it's no longer available to bookstores, *and* if the publisher fails to bring out a new edition in a timely fashion.

"In print" and "out of print" are tricky concepts. Bookstore staff know very well that there are titles in publishers' catalogs that are "Out of Stock Indefinitely"—they can place an order for the books, but chances are they'll never see that order filled. Some authors try to get language inserted that says a book is out of print if a bookstore receives two or more consecutive "Out of Stock Indefinitely" messages when ordering it. This is a good test, but it relies on you having access to a friendly bookstore clerk who can get you photocopies of invoices from their distributors.

Danger, Danger!

The most pernicious danger from electronic publishing is the lack of a good definition of "out of print"—and hence the absence of any rights reversions. After all, it costs the publisher nothing to keep a story available online or for download, but if they're not doing anything to promote it, then why shouldn't you be able to find yourself a publisher who will?

In a good contract, a publisher buys the rights to *publish* your book, not keep it around just in case they decide they want to someday bring it back into print. In essence, you're not *selling* your book, you're just renting it out.

A contract may also set out penalties for nonperformance. You may try to insert a clause that charges interest for late delivery of royalty statements. Your publisher may try to insert clauses that reduce your advance if you're late in delivering the book. This is a real give and take: As you'll see in the next section, this is the sort of thing that contract negotiations are built on.

Negotiating Contracts

As we've implied, contracts are not written in stone. Even if a publisher uses a standard, "boilerplate" contract that they offer to all their writers, chances are there's room for some changes if you ask for them. The trick to negotiation is to know what you want changed and why, and to understand that some clauses may indeed be "deal-breakers," which you won't get your publisher to budge on.

Use an Agent!

If you've just sold your first book, *get an agent* to negotiate your contract. Agents are intimately familiar with the current standards for all the major publishers—sometimes, an agent will negotiate three or four consecutive contracts with the same publisher on behalf of various authors, learning through trial-and-error exactly which parts of the contract are negotiable and which parts aren't.

Like other financial professionals (for example, tax accountants and investment counselors), agents should be income-neutral. An agent should be able to sweeten your deal to the point where his commission is covered by the extra money he gets you. Writers who eschew agents because they want to hang on to their 15 percent are penny-wise and pound-foolish.

Another advantage of using an agent for contract negotiations is that it insulates you from any ill will engendered by the negotiation process. You're not the one who has to threaten and cajole your editor: Your agent does it for you. Good cop, bad cop.

Danger, Danger!

You've spent years cultivating a relationship with an editor and you've finally sold her a story, and your heart is full of warm feelings. When the contract arrives, you need to realize that your publisher has a dual personality: The editor is Dr. Jekyll, and the contracts department is Mr. Hyde. Don't let your feelings of trust and camaraderie for the editor blind you to any horrors lurking in your contract.

An editor who balks at negotiating with your agent should raise all kinds of red flags. Negotiating with an agent is a short and painless process for most editors, since agents already know what's what. If your editor doesn't want to talk to your agent, you need to think hard about why not.

But even if an agent *has* negotiated your contract, *you need to read and understand every word in the deal.* Agents aren't perfect, nor do they understand exactly what your priorities are. You're paying your agent 15 percent of your deal to act on your behalf: It's your responsibility to make sure that you've spent your money wisely.

Sucker Contracts

Contracts are not carved in stone. When your publisher mails you a contract, it represents a starting point for a discussion of what each of you expects from the other.

Infodump

The American Society of Journalists and Authors (ASJA) maintains an up-to-date list of standard contracts from a variety of publishers at www.asja.org/php_scp/cwpagenew.htm. They keep track of sneaky new clauses and pass along tips about which publishers keep their good contracts behind the counter until you ask for them.

It's not uncommon for publishers to have two standard contracts: the one they send to new writers in the hopes that they'll just sign, no questions asked; and the real contract that they send to wised-up pros who refuse the first.

If you're holding a contract that bears little resemblance to the model contracts in Appendix A, you may be looking at a sucker contract. Check for the standard red flags:

➤ Contracts that don't adequately elucidate "out of print"

➤ Contracts that ask you to indemnify the publisher from all legal claims, sustained or not

➤ Contracts that don't specify a publication deadline

➤ Contracts that seek to attach liability for un-earned advances or legal claims to other work

➤ Contracts that ask for rights that are unrelated to the publisher's business

If you think you've been dealt a bad hand by your publisher, the easiest fix is for you or your agent to give their contract person a quick call and explain that there're a lot of changes you'd like to make to the contract. Then ask if there might be another version of their standard contract that excludes the offending clauses. That's often all it takes to get the "real" contract.

Infodump

Contracts protect you and your publisher. If a publisher wants to buy something from you without a contract, there's something fishy going on. Politely suggest that you send them a copy of the SFWA model contract shown in Appendix A.

Infodump

Changing a contract is simple: Just make the correction in ink and initial alongside of the change. Have your publisher do the same, and it's legally binding.

Give and Take

Whether you're negotiating your own short story or reviewing the contract your agent has shaken loose, you need to understand that negotiation is a process of give and take.

Know going into negotiations which parts of the contract are negotiable for you and which parts aren't. If you don't want to give up action-figure rights on principle—but aren't really worried about the potential lost revenue they represent—then offer that up to the publisher in exchange for the things that *do* matter to you. Recognize when your publisher is willing to make concessions, and reciprocate.

If there really are deal-breaker clauses in the contract, then stand firm on them, but don't open up by saying, "If clauses one through six b) are not struck, this deal is off." Usually, publishers realize when a clause is unfair and are willing to negotiate around it. If you really can't agree on a deal-breaker, then break the deal—but don't blackmail the publisher. After extended discussion, politely let the publisher know that you absolutely can't proceed unless the clause is changed. If the publisher still won't change it, well, it's time to try to sell the piece somewhere else. That's why they call it a deal-breaker.

Above all, be polite and businesslike. Don't accuse anyone of trying to rip you off, even—*especially*—if they are. Your career is built on professional relationships and reputation, and the last thing you want is a reputation as a jerk who can't be negotiated with.

The Least You Need to Know

➤ You automatically own the copyright to your work as soon as you create it.

➤ Contracts specify which rights are being sold and for how long.

➤ Liability should only be assumed for sustained claims and only up to the publisher's insurance deductible.

➤ Your work reverts to you once it's out of print.

➤ The first contract a publisher offers isn't always the only contract.

➤ Negotiation is a process of give and take, but if the publisher won't budge on something you feel strongly about, walk away from the deal.

Chapter 25

Taxes and the Writer

In This Chapter

➤ Defining your status: hobbyist or sole proprietor?

➤ Profits, losses, and write-offs

➤ The benefits and perils of incorporation

➤ Taxes, the Canadian way

If there's one topic that can get people riled up, it's taxes. Nobody likes to pay them, and few of us can negotiate the maze of forms, regulations, and dependencies every year without getting something wrong. All in all, it's a topic most of us would rather avoid.

But guess what? As a writer, you have certain advantages, because your story sales count as income. Depending on whether you count yourself as a hobbyist, sole proprietor, or a corporation, you can write off a lot of your expenses.

Congratulations! You're Self-Employed

So, you've got your tax forms and you've got your receipts and figures for fiction sales you made last year. How should you fill in the forms to get the maximum return you can?

As individual taxpayers, we're used to thinking in terms of a "maximum return" or "minimum tax paid." This is all very well as a personal target, but depending on how you classify your writing business, minimizing your tax hit may not be such a good idea.

You have several options. You could call yourself a hobbyist (but very few ambitious writers want to do that); you can also consider your writing a business and call yourself a "sole proprietorship." Or you could incorporate. Each of these approaches has different implications for you at tax time.

Infodump

The government has finally joined the twenty-first century. You can now download the tax forms you need by pointing your Web browser to www.irs.ustreas.gov, or by visiting their ftp site at ftp.irs.ustreas.gov. If you want more information sent to you by snail-mail, write to the IRS at Internal Revenue Service, Philadelphia Service Center, P.O. Box 16347, Philadelphia, PA 19114–0447. Ask for IRS publication 334, "Tax Guide for a Small Business." They'll be happy to help out.

Other useful IRS guides include: Pub. 463, "Travel and Entertainment"; Pub. 542, "Corporations"; Pub. 552, "Recordkeeping"; Pub. 587, "Business Use of Your Home"; Pub. 917, "Business Use of a Vehicle"; and Pub. 910, "Guide to Information Publications."

If you're interested in writing as a career, and you see your sales increasing over the next few years, what you call yourself should keep in step with the realities of your career. Why? Well, if you get greedy, call yourself a sole proprietor right from the start and show a hefty loss every year, the auditors are going to pay you a visit at about year five. You may have difficulty convincing the IRS that you're a business for many years after that.

If you focus on keeping your taxes to a minimum by writing off every single possible writerly deduction, you're going to set off all kinds of red flags with your local taxperson. A better strategy is to choose your deductions carefully, writing off enough each year to produce the textbook loss-followed-by-profit curve that most new business experience. If you're on this curve, you're unlikely to be audited except at random, and in the long run you'll be able to write off more, and hence take home more of your earned income.

Following is a set of simple steps to take you from the starting gate to the finish line as a truly self-employed writer.

Starting Out: The Hobbyist

"Hurray!" you say, "I made a whole $50 last year from my first sale to *Annoying Stories*. How's that going to affect my taxes?"

Well, that depends. If you're selling a few short stories a year and you don't expect that sales volume to increase, then for tax purposes you should probably consider your writing to be a hobby. Yes, this probably rankles, but it's a practical matter: As we'll see in a moment, if you treat your writing income as real business income, you'll eventually have to justify yourself by showing profits.

As a hobbyist, you will note your fiction sales in the "Other Income" field on Form 1040. You can make deductions, but only if you can itemize them; these must be entered in Schedule A. There's nothing more to it than that, except that your deductions are not allowed to be more than your income from a hobby. Averaged over a few years, this will probably be the case when you're starting out; your first few sales won't pay much, but you won't have spent huge amounts on postage to make them, either.

Even if you do hope that your writing career will take off, it's probably prudent for you to call yourself a hobbyist for the first couple of years. Once you treat yourself as a business, the government will look for that classic upward-trending pattern in your business income. It's wise to wait until you see those trends happening yourself before considering yourself a business on your tax forms.

An exception to this is if you are experiencing high costs as you write. If your expenses really do outstrip your income, you might take the sole proprietor route. Be aware, though, that you can only do this so long before you'll be asked to prove that your business has some expectation of a profit.

"As You Know, Bob ..."

The idea of writer as hobbyist came out of a 1965 court case, *C. Lamont*, in which a distinction was made between losses incurred by a writer working because of an interest in literature, and one writing for profit. Writing for its own sake, in other words, doesn't count as a business activity.

Sole Proprietorship

Once you've reached a more professional stage, you may want to start treating your writing as a business for tax purposes. The easiest kind of business is a *sole proprietorship*.

How do you know you're at the next stage? Well, say you're starting to sell stories to big markets, and maybe you're even being considered for an award or two. You've got a novel half done and it's looking good. When you total up your time spent in writing-related activities last year, it's at least 500 hours, maybe more. At this point, you might consider yourself to be a sole proprietorship come tax time. You get certain advantages, and there are no forms to fill out or lawyer's fees.

The attraction of treating your fiction sales as business income is that a lot of things count as deductible expenses that otherwise wouldn't. The taxes for this income are calculated differently from your income as hobbyist or employee. Stuff like office expenses, computer costs, paper, and postage all become potential write-offs.

As a sole proprietor, you can also lose money, which is what you'll want to do, at least for the first couple of years. Most fledgling SF writers actually put a lot more time and effort into their craft than they give themselves credit for. Technically, your travel expenses to and from your local writing workshop are deductible, for instance. Even the software you use may have cost you more than you make this year. Taking a loss on your writing is pretty realistic if you're merely selling a few short stories a year.

It's in your best interest to reduce the amount of profit you show when you enter your self-employment income on Form 1040. After all, since your employer isn't deducting Social Security, the government feels that they should deduct it directly, which is why you're taxed at a 50 percent higher rate for self-employment income than you are for regular employment.

Factoid

In a **sole proprietorship,** your business and your other affairs (both personal and occupational) are merged. As a sole proprietor, you own and control the business. From a legal standpoint, your sole proprietorship business and you, as the proprietor, are considered to be one and the same. This is different from the case of corporations, where you and the corporation are separate legal entities.

Schedule C Is Your Friend

You declare any income that's from freelancing or contract work on *Schedule C*. Note that you don't use Schedule C for part-time work; if you're working part-time but still get income and Social Security deducted from your paycheck, you won't be able to declare this income on Schedule C. Happily, there's usually no ambiguity about a writer's status: That meager check you received from *Annoying Stories* isn't going to have Social Security deductions against it (but you'll get hit with "self-employment tax" to make up for it). Your income statements will be on Form 1099, and you'll declare it all in Schedule C.

Factoid

Schedule C is also known as "Profit or Loss from Business." It's where you'll write up your writing income and any expenses incurred in making that income.

Trim Those Profits

There's a wide range of things you can write off against this income. Writers enjoy the advantage of being able to make a case for writing off just about anything they do as a research expense: A trip to Disney World is background for a short story; a CD is inspirational material; a night out at the movies is "keeping abreast of the field." The list is truly amazing—but don't get cocky and try to write off cat food because you wrote a novel about superintelligent felines. Extravagant deductions will just bring the IRS down on you; the last thing anybody wants is an audit.

Still, within reason, you can expect to write off the following expenses:

➤ **Home office costs.** If you reserve one room in your house or apartment as an office, you can reasonably expect to write off that portion of your mortgage or rent. Utilities and telephone costs could be added in here, but you must keep track of them in case you need to justify what you did. In general, it's best to formally designate some part of your abode as an office; having a laptop on the coffee table may not be enough for you to write off your living room and get away with it.

Danger, Danger!

Schedule E is called "Rents and Royalties." This is not, repeat *not*, where you should enter any royalties you've received from fiction sales. Fiction royalties come from a business activity; the kinds of royalties that go into Schedule E are those you'd get from passive sources; for example, owning patent rights. Consult your tax accountant for more information.

➤ **Computer and software costs.** The IRS is well aware that most of us use our computers for both business and personal activities. Normally, you'll only be able to write off the percentage of your computing costs that applies directly to your business activities. Luckily, being a SF writer gives you a few potential advantages here. Let's say you've been writing tie-in fantasy gaming novels. You just *might* be able to get away with counting your *EverQuest* game costs as a business expense. Certainly, if you use a Web site to promote your work, you can write off the costs involved in creating and maintaining it. On the other hand, you might have a hard time justifying *Quake III* as a writing tool.

➤ **Research costs.** For a SF writer, software expenses could conceivably blur into research costs (that *EverQuest* expense). Certainly, books that you buy, magazines you subscribe to, and even some travel expenses could be considered research and therefore written off. Once again, exercise common sense about what you try to write off. If you're writing a book set in Mayan Mexico, your holiday expenses in Cancun may not be very convincing if all the money you spent was at the resort.

➤ **Depreciation.** You can use this deduction for big-ticket items such as your computer equipment, office furniture, and automobile expenses. Travel to and from conventions probably won't be enough for you to count your auto expenses, unless you do a lot of it.

➤ **Office supplies and postage.** This one's pretty easy. Keep track of how much you spend on supplies like paper and envelopes, as well as mailing costs. If you're working aggressively at getting published, these costs can add up very quickly.

If you've done your write-offs aggressively enough, you'll probably find your writing business showing a loss. This is great, for a while.

Profits and Losses

As a new business, your writing isn't expected to make a profit in the first several years. The government expects new businesses to lose money for about three years (something to bear in mind if you have dreams of living off the avails of fiction). So it's okay for your writing income to show a loss for a while, provided you can demonstrate the possibility of making a profit some day. (For us, all that amounts to is saying, "Yeah, I'm working on a novel. Who knows, it might be a blockbuster success!")

The government does not, however, expect any business to run at a loss forever (with the possible exception of Amazon.com). If your writing doesn't show a profit three years out of five, you may get a call from the gentle folks at the IRS. This is why you don't want to call yourself a business at the very start of your writing career. It's just common sense to wait until you really *are* a business before starting to take advantage of the tax breaks businesses get.

Infodump

Wait a minute! Isn't an advance against royalties exempt from being taxed? After all, it's just a loan against the money your publisher hopes to make from your book. If the book tanks, you might have to pay it back (though not if you've negotiated your contract properly; see Chapter 24, "Contracts"). You're still going to get taxed for the advance. If you have to pay it back later, you can ask for a reimbursement on the taxes you paid. Strange, but true.

You are considered to have made a profit if your writing income is greater than your writing expenses. It's not a matter of being able to live off what you write. It's just a matter of whether you have a positive or negative balance in this particular part of your business. That being the case, you can control your profit/loss ratio pretty easily. If you're into your sixth year of writing and are in the habit of writing everything off to show a net loss, you might want to think again. Perhaps you should absorb some of those expenses, and pay a little tax, or the government will come nosing around. Rest assured, they'll find more to take from you than you find for yourself.

Writer, Incorporated

You've sold your novel, and the advance is enough for you to take off several months to write full-time. You use that time to churn out more short stories, sell a couple of magazine articles for big bucks, and start your next novel. This is beginning to look serious.

Now is probably the time to consider *incorporation*. While the major reason most people incorporate is to protect their personal assets, taxes and "employee benefits" are a more important reason for us as writers.

Other professionals incorporate to separate themselves from the liabilities incurred in their business activities. For example, an incorporated real-estate agent may get sued for a sour deal, but the suit's claims will apply to the agent's business assets, not her house, home computer, or personal vehicles.

The implication for writers is that you need to decide which "assets" you own and which ones your corporation owns. If your company buys a computer or car, or if it holds the copyright to your work, then it is an asset that could be attached to any claim against you in a lawsuit.

If you've reached the stage where you're looking at incorporation, you've almost certainly got a good accountant working for you. If not, get one! This is the person you'll need to talk to about the particulars of your case. We won't presume to tell you whether incorporation is right for you or exactly how you should set up your business. However, you should be aware of the potential benefits incorporating could bring you:

Factoid

When you **incorporate,** you create a corporation that is a legal individual separate from yourself. As such, it has its own assets, liabilities, accounts, income, and expenses. It also pays its own taxes, and these are distinct from yours, even if you're the sole member of the corporation.

➤ Depending on your situation, you may be able to deduct the full cost of your own health insurance, life insurance, medical insurance, and other traditional employee benefits.

➤ Corporate income is taxed at a lower rate than your personal income. Also, you'll only be taxed on what you've got left after expenses.

➤ Being your own employee means you can pay yourself at a rate that will keep you in a low tax bracket, while expensing such items as your computer equipment, office space, and auto insurance (if you actually use it in your business). By juggling your expenditures between yourself and your corporation, you can minimize your tax bite.

➤ You can fully expense (and more easily justify) large travel expenditures—for instance, to visit your agent or publisher in New York.

Incorporating will probably cost you a few hundred dollars, but it's worth it if your total income from all freelance and contract sources is starting to match your salaried income.

Danger, Danger!

If you wish to form a named corporation, you need to do a name search to determine if there's already a corporation of that name out there. Increasingly important these days, however, is acquiring a domain name that will represent you on the Internet. When you do a name search, be sure to find out whether the name already exists as a domain on the Net. If so, you might cause confusion in people trying to find your business online.

Canadian Taxes

Canadian tax law isn't that different from the United States. Canada doesn't use the category of hobbyist for nonbusiness activities writers, but the limitations on sole proprietorship are very similar.

Most of the same rules about write-offs apply equally to the United States and Canada. There is one significant difference that you should be aware of, though, if you're a Canadian selling SF in the States. This is, of course, the infamous goods and services tax (GST).

GST to You, Too!

The basic rule is this: The Canadian government can't charge tax on sales in the United States. In fact, it would be counterproductive to do so; the whole purpose of a value-added tax is to encourage exports.

Although it may take some getting used to, Canadian authors should remember that if they're selling in the States or overseas, they are exporters, and their writing is an export industry.

At tax time, be sure to claim back your GST costs on foreign sales, even on such things as postage. And whatever you do, don't pay GST subtracted from foreign advances. That money is rightfully yours.

This does not mean that you can get away with not reporting foreign income, of course. You just have to make sure that it, and the expenses connected with it, are clearly part of an export business.

Getting Your Own GST Number

You're going to need a GST number once your income from freelance sources climbs over $30,000 a year (which can easily happen if you do contract work or computer consulting as well as writing).

The easiest way to get a GST number is simply to phone the ministry or write and ask for one. You can reach them at Goods and Services Tax (GST), Central Excise Region, Revenue Canada, Main Floor, 325 Broadway, Winnipeg, MB R3C 4T4; 1-800-959-5525 toll-free, or 204-983-3918; fax: 204-984-7002.

Types of Canadian Corporations

Canada has both national and provincial corporations. Which is best for you? Well, if you want your corporation to have a name and not just a number, it might be better for you to incorporate provincially. Nearly every conceivable corporation name has been taken on the national level; you'll have better luck with name searches at the provincial level. (Of course, you can always elect to get a numbered corporation, which solves the name-search problem.)

Provincial incorporation is also cheaper than national: $330 for provincial versus $500 for a national corporation.

Being a provincial corporation won't have any effect on your ability to sell your writing in other provinces or countries. So for most Canadian writers, provincial incorporation is the way to go.

Whether a provincial or national corporation, your responsibilities for record-keeping and reporting are the same.

The Least You Need to Know

➤ As a writer, you are potentially a business.

➤ If your income from writing is low, you should simply enter your income in the "Other Income" field on Form 1040.

➤ If your fortunes are rising, you can consider yourself a sole proprietorship at tax time.

➤ Only consider sole proprietorship if you expect your income from writing to continue to increase.

➤ If you are making oodles of cash at writing, consider incorporation.

➤ Canadian writers should not pay GST on sales to the United States or overseas.

Writer's Associations

We SF writers are lucky to have a number of extremely energetic peer organizations. These groups can provide you with market news and aid in finding an agent or publisher, as well as that ever-important set of like-minded people with whom you can share your experiences.

In this chapter we look at the main North American associations for SF and fantasy writers. We'll provide in-depth information about the big ones, such as SFWA, and list other specialized organizations that you may find useful.

Science Fiction and Fantasy Writers of America (SFWA)

SFWA is the oldest organization specifically for SF professionals. It was founded in 1965 by Damon Knight, with an initial membership of 78. At the turn of the millennium, there are over 1,200 members and counting. Membership is available in the United States, Canada, and overseas through local and national chapters.

SFWA started out very simply. Acclaimed author Damon Knight wanted to provide writers with information about abusive contracts and market opportunities. In its first incarnation, SFWA was a streamlined organization, lacking any recognizable bureaucracy. There was no provision in the bylaws for any of the trappings of formal organizations—things such as annual meetings and committees. Nonetheless, such services as the *Bulletin* (a monthly trade magazine) and the *Forum* (a private venue for in-house discussion and squabbling) proved so successful that SFWA has grown over the years until now it employs one full-time staffer, as well as over 150 volunteers. The rules and regulations have grown with the organization, in a nearly constant but fruitful battle of simplicity vs. bureaucratic necessity.

What SFWA Can Do for You

The SFWA grievance committee provides a forum for authors to fight against abusive contracts, plagiarism, misappropriation of royalties, and contract violations. The organization retains a lawyer for the purpose of pursuing any action it deems necessary.

Infodump

Although the organization is formally known as Science Fiction and Fantasy Writers of America, the official acronym is SFWA instead of SFFWA. There was a brief fight over this after the organization changed its name in 1992 from Science Fiction Writers of America. People liked the new name, but preferred the old acronym. So it stuck.

As well as fighting for better contracts, SFWA has taken a more direct hand in its members' well-being, providing both a legal fund and an emergency medical fund for needy members.

In day-to-day matters, most members remain in contact with the organization through its newsletter, the *Bulletin*. Published quarterly, the *Bulletin* is packed with industry news and market opportunities, as well as articles by top-name SF writers on everything from orbital dynamics to contract negotiation. It's rare for a writer to throw out back issues of the *Bulletin;* its articles can remain useful for many years.

There are many more benefits to SFWA membership. For complete information, as well as contact names and a membership application form, visit www.sfwa.org on the World Wide Web, or contact Sharon Lee, Exec. Director, SFWA, Inc., P.O. Box 171, Unity, ME 04988-0171 USA; e-mail: execdir@sfwa.org.

Beware the SFWA Auditor

SFWA has also done what few other literary organization in the U.S. have done: Since 1994 they have conducted random audits of publishers to verify that they are fulfilling their contractual obligations toward SFWA members.

Every SFWA member can throw his or her name into a pool from which one name will be drawn. The chosen author will have his novel's financial history audited to ensure he is getting paid fairly.

The first SFWA audit was held in 1994 for L. Warren Douglas's first novel, *A Plague of Change* (Del Rey, 1992). SFWA chose an independent agency, the Royalty Review Service, to conduct the actual audit. The audit showed that Del Rey was treating Douglas fairly, and owed him no royalties beyond what their own statements showed. Perhaps as usefully, the audit provided a snapshot of publishing practices at the time, something every writer would benefit from understanding.

Joining SFWA

SFWA has three types of membership for individuals: Active, Associate, and Affiliate:

➤ **Active membership** is available to any author who has published one novel or three short stories in a professional market, or has produced a script. Active membership gets you all rights and responsibilities of the organization.

➤ **Associate membership** is available to any author who has made at least one *professional sale.*

➤ **Affiliate membership** is open to any professionals with an interest in SF, such as artists, editors, academics, librarians, etc.

Active and Associate memberships cost U.S.$50 per year. Affiliate memberships cost U.S.$35 per year.

The Horror Writers Association (HWA)

Horror writing has become a prestigious and lucrative business. True, it's in a bit of a slump at the turn of the millennium, but authors like Stephen King, Dean Koontz, and Clive Barker can still top the bestseller lists. The Horror Writers Association was formed to address the specific needs of people working in this tough but rewarding genre.

"As You Know, Bob ..."

Many publishers treat sales information like state secrets. It can be difficult or impossible for an author to get precise numbers about sales, returns, etc. from a publisher; hence the need for a random audit to ensure that no publisher consistently shortchanges its authors.

Factoid

What does SFWA consider a **professional sale?** Short-story sales must be to a market that pays at least 3¢ (U.S.) per word. Novels must have been published by a publisher listed in the Literary Marketplace. Sales to publications that don't qualify are considered small-press sales.

A Grisly History

The HWA formed almost by accident. In an interview with *Publisher's Weekly* in 1984, author Robert R. McCammon talked about his desire to see a national horror writer's association. His call for a new organization elicited a lot of interest in the media, even from such staid institutions as *The New York Times* and *The Washington Post*. Response from authors, some of whom had merely read about McCammon's remarks, was also strong. Fittingly enough, the HWA (or HOWL, as McCammon originally called it) had a strange life of its own even before it had any members.

The strong response galvanized McCammon into action. He enlisted the help of Joe and Karen Lansdale, and together they drafted a formal letter inviting 177 of their closest colleagues to join the new organization. The organization was jolted into life with the combined force of 88 founding members on November 3, 1985, at the World Fantasy Convention in Tucson, Arizona.

"As You Know, Bob ..."

The founding declaration of the HWA was "Be it known that the Horror and Occult Writers League is a non-profit organization of professional writers of fiction and non-fiction pertaining to or inspired by the traditions, legends, development, and history of horror and occult. Its members are together for their mutual benefit in an earnest effort to further a more widespread publicity, promotion, distribution, readership and appreciation of the literature of horror and occult."

Dean Koontz was the first president of the HWA. By the time he finished his term, the organization had grown to 300 members. The HWA has continued to flourish in the ensuing years, with the addition of such things as the yearly Bram Stoker Award for Superior Achievement in the field. The organization has members in the United States, Canada, South America, the Caribbean, Europe, and Australia.

Furthering the Cause of Horror

At the time of the HWA's founding, horror literature was becoming known as a publishing category in its own right. Stephen King was widely considered the saint of this particular crusade, leading the genre out of the pulps and into the land of respectability.

The HWA can take a direct hand in helping you with services that include marketing news, career management tools (available in their Authors' Resources databases), and an extensive network of local offices and Internet resources. They can help you locate critics and reviewers for your work, publicize upcoming book launches, or, if you're just starting out, jumpstart your sales by putting you in touch with key markets and opinion-makers.

Joining the HWA

Unlike SFWA, the HWA has a membership category with no requirements: Anyone can become an affiliate member. Still, to realize the full benefits of the organization, you'll want to become an active member, if possible.

In order to become an active member, you should have sold at least three short stories, articles, or reviews to markets that paid at least three cents a word; sold a novel for an advance of at least $2,000; or sold a screenplay, 10,000-word role-playing project, or a computer game.

Dues for the HWA are $55 for members residing in North America and $65 for members residing elsewhere.

Associate memberships are open to professionals who are not authors, such as editors, artists, packagers, and producers.

For more information about the HWA, including how to apply for membership, write to HWA Membership, P.O. Box 50577, Palo Alto, CA 94303 U.S.A.; or visit their Web site at www.horror.org.

SF Canada

Sometimes referred to as the "Canadian counterpart to SFWA," SF Canada actually has a different purpose from SFWA, and a different history. Where SFWA exists to help an already-existing community of professional SF writers, SF Canada was created with the purpose of creating such a community where none had existed before. It's been wildly successful in this.

Bootstrapping Canadian SF

SF Canada was founded at the now-legendary ConText '89 SF convention in Edmonton, Alberta, on July 2, 1989. ConText was a watershed in the history of Canadian SF. At ConText, a whole generation of writers from across the country discovered one another. Many of us had been toiling alone; it was surprising and empowering to discover that there were actually a lot of SF writers working very hard in Canada, and our needs and experiences were very similar.

At the founding meeting, we debated the usefulness of a Canadian organization, since SFWA already existed and had a Canadian arm. Everyone agreed that our situation was unique in ways that SFWA couldn't address. From that discussion, we developed the following purposes for our fledgling organization:

➤ To foster a sense of community among Canadian writers of speculative fiction

➤ To improve communications between Canadian writers of speculative fiction

➤ To lobby on behalf of writers of speculative fiction

➤ To foster the growth of quality writing in speculative fiction

"As You Know, Bob ..."

Founding member of SF Canada Michael Skeet recalls proposing a national SF writer's association to one of the handful of successful SF writers living in Canada in the mid 1980s. "Great idea," said the writer, "but how would you find any members?" Prior to 1989, Canadian SF writers would have formed a very small club indeed.

It was clear to all of us that the Canadian situation differed drastically from that of the U.S. Demographics, economies of scale, and differing cultures meant that it would be foolish to directly model SWAC (the Speculative Writers' Association of Canada, as it was originally known) on SFWA. Issues such as the paucity of Canadian publications and their low pay rates meant that our membership requirements had to be looser than those of SFWA.

SWAC was formed at a time when a number of new Canadian writers were on the verge of breaking into major American publishing success. The founders of the organization recognized that Canadian SF as a whole was in the process of bootstrapping itself; and although Canadian SF writers had existed all along, a Canadian community of SF writers had not. The question in the back of everyone's mind was how best to nurture the very large amount of talent, much of it still "unprofessional" by SFWA standards, waiting in the wings.

Another consideration was the fact that most Canadians sold (and still sell) primarily to the U.S. SFWA exists to protect the rights of writers selling in the United States; it allows Canadian membership, and it does an effective job of policing the American publishing scene. Therefore, why reinvent the wheel? SWAC was to have a different purpose: as an enabling mechanism for up-and-coming talent. Hence the seemingly fuzzy goals of "fostering a sense of community" and "improving communications."

Member Candas Jane Dorsey argued that the organization should have an anarchistic structure. She suggested organizing SWAC along the lines of an amateur press association, to eliminate the need for fees and to keep work at a minimum. For her pains, Candas was voted president of SWAC, which became an incorporated nonprofit organization, with dues, newsletters, committees, and a national convention, with all the bureaucracy that implies.

Canadian SF Takes Off

The nonprofit organizational structure of SF Canada worked well through almost 10 years and three presidents. During this period, numerous new SF and fantasy writers rose to international prominence from their Canadian roots—writers like Terence Green, Nalo Hopkinson, and Peter Watts. Many of these writers have been enthusiastic SF Canada members since their first sales.

In 1999, SF Canada had to retrench because of a minor embezzlement scandal and the drying up of the large pool of volunteers necessary to run an organization structured this way.

Ironically, as the new millennium begins, SF Canada seems to be reverting to the loose anarchistic structure Candas originally proposed. This is not necessarily a bad thing; arguably, SF Canada achieved all of its goals during the first 10 years of its existence. It provided a rich, nationwide forum for the struggling Canadian SF writing community; it supported writers as they went from beginner to pro, until by 2000 there was a strong and energetic "Canadian invasion" of U.S. SF happening. SF Canada may be directly responsible for stopping the exodus of newly successful writers to the United States. SF Canada was also in on the founding meetings that led to the creation of The Electronic Rights Licensing Agency (TERLA).

Infodump

If you're a Canadian SF writer, SF Canada needs you! Your skills and enthusiasm are the fuel this organization requires to continue to provide valuable services to the Canadian SF community.

At the time of SF Canada's founding, the Internet was an academic tool; e-mail was used only by grad students and dabblers in the computer bulletin-board scene. By 2000, SF Canada had begun to conduct 95 percent of its business online. Cory was the first to suggest creating an e-mail listserver for the use of the members; Karl created it as well as the SF Canada Web site, which continues to run strongly today under the direction of Edward Willett. Since online activity far outstripped mail, phone, and face-to-face media in volume and effectiveness, Karl proposed in 1999 that SF Canada reorganize as an Internet-based service for writers, with special services available to members. As of this writing, this initiative is still being debated.

Joining the Fray

SF Canada is open to Canadians and non-Canadians residing in Canada who are "SF professionals." This means that you've either published two short stories or one novel, or you qualify as an artist, editor, academic, or other professional. The qualification of one novel or two short stories is much less stringent than SFWA's, for the reasons described earlier: SF Canada was created to bootstrap a previously nonexistent Canadian SF writing scene.

At the time of this writing, a basic one-year membership in SF Canada cost $25 (Canadian). There is a debate going on over whether to raise the dues so as to be able to afford more services for the members.

If you wish to apply to become a member of SF Canada, or would like more information, write to SF Canada, 103-4570 Queen Mary Road, Montréal, QC H3W 1W6 Canada. To get a flavor for what SF Canada is like, you can also check out their Web site at www.sfcanada.ca.

Other Organizations

Numerous organizations exist that specialize in one or another area of publishing and the arts. Chances are, you've got interests and issues that won't be covered by one of the big umbrella organizations. The smaller organizations covered in this section may be able to help you with your particular set of unique issues and interests.

The Genre Writer's Association (GWA)

Formerly the Small Press Genre Association, the GWA provides market news, interviews, and articles in its biannual *The Genre Writer's News,* and bimonthly *Horror: The News Magazine of the Horror & Fantasy Field*. GWA is open to U.S., Canadian, and overseas writers. Dues are U.S.$25 per year for North America; U.S.$30 per year for overseas.

You can reach the GWA at Dark Regions Press, P.O. Box 6301, Concord, CA 94524 U.S.A.

Science Fiction Poetry Association (SFPA)

The SFPA is a peers' organization for poetry in the SF, fantasy, and horror fields. They publish a bimonthly newsletter, *Star Lines: Newsletter of the SFPA,* sponsor awards, and the occasional anthology.

You can reach the SFPA at 6075 Bellevue Drive, North Olmstead, OH 44070 U.S.A.

Science Fiction Research Association (SFRA)

The SFRA exists to promote and improve the teaching and study of SF and fantasy. Members include writers, editors, academics, librarians, and teachers.

There are several levels of membership available, depending on your interests. Individual memberships cost $60 for U.S. members, $65 for Canadians, and $70 overseas. Membership benefits include subscription to the *SFRA Review* as well as the journals *Extrapolation* and *Science Fiction Studies*.

You can reach the SFRA at 6354 Brooks Blvd., Mentor, OH 44060 U.S.A.

Reproduction Rights Organizations

One of the best services available to authors is through Reproduction Rights Organizations, or R.R.O.s. An R.R.O. licenses the copying of copyrighted material, and collects and then distributes royalties to authors and publishers of the work copied. For instance, if a university professor uses one of your short stories in a course, and makes a hundred copies, the R.R.O. makes sure you get paid for the use of the story. You don't have to track down uses of your own work; the R.R.O. does that for you. All you have to do is cash the checks they send you. (You should get paid even if you're not a member, but such payments would normally go through your publisher, who will probably take longer to get around to cutting you a check.)

Licensees include most universities and public schools, and some photocopy shops and libraries. Any writer can become a member; the amount you get is calculated on a percentage basis depending on the nature of the work published—whether trade, educational, and so on.

In the United States, the R.R.O. is the Copyright Clearance Center. You can reach them at 222 Rosewood Drive, Danvers, MA 01923; 978-750-8400; www.copyright.com.

In Canada, the R.R.O. is CanCopy. It is made up of individual member authors and publishers, and some writer's organizations like The Writers Union of Canada. You can reach CanCopy at 1 Yonge Street, Suite 1900, Toronto, ON M5E 1E5; 416-868-1620; www.cancopy.com.

Getting the Most Out of Your Membership

Writer's associations are only as effective as their members let them be. Even large organizations like SFWA rely on the efforts of dozens or even hundreds of volunteers. Although participation in daily affairs isn't required by any of the organizations we've listed here, you'll benefit from any help you can lend.

Volunteering is a great way to meet other writers, and it's also a good way to learn more about the publishing industry. Services such as standard contracts, random audits, and market information don't just happen; those members who volunteer to help provide them can't help but learn a lot.

Even if you're not sure your association can help you directly, it's always easy to contact other members. Anyone who's had experiences similar to your own may be of help.

Ultimately, this spirit—of writers helping writers—transcends any particular services an association offers. You have nothing to lose by joining. But you have a whole world of helping hands to gain.

The Least You Need to Know

➤ The SF writing field has many organizations useful to writers.

➤ The oldest and most active SF authors' organization is SFWA.

➤ The Horror Writers Association provides assistance and fraternity to writers of horror and dark fantasy.

➤ SF Canada is an organization for Canadian SF and fantasy writers.

➤ Other groups include the GWA, SFPA, SFRA, and Reproduction Rights Organizations.

➤ To get the most out of your membership, consider becoming a volunteer in the organization. Not only will you be helping out, it will be a great way to meet other writers and learn more about the publishing industry.

Model Contracts

In this appendix you'll find the model contracts proposed by the Science Fiction and Fantasy Writers of America (SFWA), reprinted with permission. For more information, see Chapter 24, "Contracts."

Here are SFWA's notes on the contracts:

These contracts were written under the direction of the SFWA Contracts Committee. The model or sample contracts have been written as a guide to writers in understanding common publishing contracts and to help them negotiate better contracts. They are not intended to be used as boilerplate contracts by publishers, writers, or agents, nor should such use be cited as being SFWA approved. These contracts have been written by writers for writers, and are for educational purposes only. As with any legal document, you should consult a lawyer for exact interpretations of law. Advice herein is not intended as legal advice or the practice of law. Some model or sample contracts are badly in need of revision or updating. As part of its ongoing efforts to educate writers about publishing contracts, the Contracts Committee periodically writes new sample contracts or updates old sample contracts. Address comments or suggestions to the Chair, SFWA Contracts Committee.

Paperbacks

AGREEMENT

made this ____ day of ____, 20__

between ____, whose residence address is _____ (hereinafter called the Author); and ____, whose principal place of business is at _____ (hereinafter called the Publisher);

WITNESSETH:

In consideration of the mutual covenants herein contained, the parties agree as follows:

1. GRANT

The Author grants to the Publisher for a period of five (5) years from the date of first publication the sole and exclusive right to publish and sell an English language paperback edition of the Work throughout the United States, its territories and possessions, and Canada. Upon the expiration of this agreement five (5) years from the date of original publication, the Publisher shall have first option to conclude an agreement with the Author for continued publication rights to the Work on terms to be mutually agreed upon. Should no such agreement be concluded within sixty (60) days of the expiration of this agreement, all rights to the Work shall automatically revert to the Author.

2. REPRESENTATIONS AND WARRANTIES

The Author warrants and represents that this Work is original with him and has not heretofore been published in paperback form, that he is sole author and proprietor of said Work with full power and right to enter into this agreement and to grant the rights hereby conveyed to the Publisher; that said Work contains no matter which is libelous and infringes no right of privacy or copyright; that he has not heretofore and will not hereafter during the term of this agreement enter into any agreement or understanding which would conflict with the rights herein granted the Publisher. If the Author shall breach this warranty, the Publisher shall be entitled to injunctive relief in addition to all other remedies which may be available to it. The Author further agrees that he will hold the publisher, its distributors, and any retailer harmless against any recovery or penalty finally sustained arising out of his breach of this warranty, and in this event he will reimburse the Publisher for all court costs and legal fees incurred. Any out of court settlement of any suit filed jointly against the Author and the Publisher shall be made only by mutual agreement in writing between same.

3. ADVANCE

Subject to the provisions hereof, the Publisher agrees to pay the Author as advance against royalties to be earned at the rate hereinafter set forth the sum of $_____ payable as follows: $_____ on the Author's signing of this agreement; $_____ on acceptance by the Publisher of the Author's completed manuscript of said Work.

4. ROYALTIES

The Publisher will pay the Author royalties based upon net sales as reported by the Publisher's distributors as follows: On copies sold at the full retail price as imprinted on the cover: _____% of said retail price on the first one hundred thousand (100,000) copies sold and _____% thereafter. On all other copies sold at special rates, through book clubs, or as remainders, a percentage of the per copy amount received by the Publisher equal to sixty percent (60%) of the percentage of the per copy amount received by the Author under the minimum royalty rate for regular sales, or five percent (5%) of net proceeds to the Publisher, whichever shall be greater.

5. SUBSIDIARY RIGHTS

The Author and/or his agent shall retain in full the exclusive right to sell or license the Work for publication in whole or in part, in English or in any foreign language, in any way, shape, edition, or form not in conflict with the rights granted to the Publisher under this agreement, and shall further retain the full and exclusive rights to license the Work for use in other media, except that the Publisher shall have the right to license second serial rights subsequent to book publication, and shall retain fifty percent (50%) of the proceeds of such licensing or sale. Upon mutual agreement between the Publisher and the Author, the Publisher may act as the Author's agent in any subsidiary rights manner, in which event the Publisher shall receive ten percent (10%) of the amount paid and the Author shall receive ninety percent (90%). However, the legal rights to make agreements for subsidiary rights, licensing, or sale shall remain with the Author.

6. STATEMENTS AND PAYMENTS

The Publisher shall forward to the Author or his agent royalty statements to be computed as of June 30 and December 31 of each year of this agreement within thirty (30) days following such respective dates along with any payments indicated to be due thereby.

The Author shall have the rights to examine or cause his duly appointed representatives to examine the accounts of the Publisher at any time after written demand by the Author. In the event discrepancies between royalty statements and the Publisher's accounts shall total more than one hundred dollars ($100.00) in the Author's favor under this and any other agreement between the Author and the Publisher, the Publisher shall tender such monies due to the Author within ten (10) days, along with reimbursement in full for any duly verified expenses incurred by the Author as a result of the auditing procedure. Should such discrepancies total less than one hundred dollars ($100.00), in favor of the Author, the Publisher shall tender such money due to the Author within ten (10) days, but shall not be liable for reimbursement of the Author's expenses.

7. MANUSCRIPT AND DELIVERY

The Author agrees to deliver to the Publisher on or before and in final revised form an English language manuscript of approximately _____ words.

If the Author shall fail to deliver said manuscript to the Publisher within the time herein provided, or having delivered same shall otherwise breach this agreement, the Author shall thereupon, on demand, repay to the Publisher all sums advanced to him under this agreement.

If, in the opinion of the Publisher, the manuscript is unacceptable or unsatisfactory to the Publisher, the Publisher may reject it by written notice within thirty (30) days of delivery, in which case any sums previously advanced to the Author under this agreement shall be retained by the Author, this agreement shall be deemed terminated and there shall be no further obligation upon the Publisher to publish said work or to make any further payment hereunder, and all rights granted to the Publisher under this agreement shall revert to the Author.

8. EDITING RIGHTS

No changes, additions, deletions, abridgements, or condensations in the text of the Work or changes of title shall be made by the Publisher, its agents, or employees, without the expressed, itemized, and specific written consent of the Author. Prior to setting of type, final copy-edited version of manuscript shall be submitted to the Author.

9. GALLEYS AND PROOFS

Prior to publication the Publisher upon advance notification shall provide the Author with galley proofs of the Work, which the Author shall correct and return to the Publisher within twenty (20) days of receiving same. The expense of the Author's proof corrections exceeding ten percent (10%) of composition costs shall be charged against the Author's royalties hereunder, except that any such correction resulting from the Publisher's failure to faithfully reproduce the text of the manuscript as delivered by the Author shall in no case be charged against the Author's royalty account. Prior to the printing of the book jacket of the Work, the Publisher shall submit to the Author a proof or other facsimile of the jacket text and design for his approval, which shall not be unreasonably withheld.

10. COPYRIGHT

The Publisher is hereby authorized and mandated to secure copyright to the Work in the same name of the Author, to arrange for sale of said Work in Canada simultaneously with first sale in the United States, and to fulfill all other obligations necessary to protect copyright to the Work under United States law and the International Copyright Convention.

11. PUBLICATION

The Publisher agrees to publish and commence distribution of said Work within twelve (12) months of approval and acceptance of the Author's final manuscript. In the event the Publisher shall fail to publish and distribute the Work by said date, this agreement shall terminate forthwith, and all rights hereunder shall revert to the Author. The Author shall retain any payments made to him under this agreement, without forfeiting his rights to seek further damages from the Publisher. However, this mandated publication date may be extended to any other date, and any number of such extensions may be made, upon mutual agreement between the Publisher and the Author.

12. AUTHOR'S COPIES

On publication the Publisher shall give to the Author twenty-five (25) copies of the published Work, which may not be resold. Any further copies desired by the Author may be purchased at fifty percent (50%) of the retail price.

13. INFRINGEMENT

If during the existence of this agreement the copyright shall be infringed, the Publisher may, at its own expense, take such legal action, in the Author's name if necessary, as may be required to restrain such infringement or to seek damages therefor. The Publisher shall not be liable to the Author for the Publisher's failure to take such legal steps. If the Publisher does not bring such an action, the Author may do so, in his name at his own expense. Money damages recovered for an infringement shall be applied first toward the repayment of the expense of bringing and maintaining the action, and thereafter the balance shall belong to the Author, provided, however, that any money damages recovered on account of a loss of the Publisher's profits shall be divided equally between the Author and the Publisher.

14. BANKRUPTCY AND INSOLVENCY

If a petition in bankruptcy shall be filed by or against the Publisher, or if it shall be judged insolvent by any court, or if a Trustee or a Receiver of any property of the Publisher shall be appointed in any suit or proceeding by or against the Publisher, or if the Publisher shall make an assignment for the benefit of creditors or shall take the benefit of any bankruptcy or insolvency Act, or if the Publisher shall liquidate its business for any cause whatsoever, this agreement shall terminate automatically without notice, and such termination shall be effective as of date of the filing of such petition, adjudication, appointment, assignment or declaration or commencement of reorganization or liquidation proceedings, and all rights granted hereunder shall thereupon revert to the Author.

15. INHERITANCE

This agreement shall be binding upon and inure to the benefit of the heirs, executors, administrators and assigns of the Author, and upon and to the successors and assigns of the Publisher.

X_____   X_____

AUTHOR   Witness for the Author

X_____   X_____

PUBLISHER   Witness for the Publisher

Magazines

The following comments are from Michael Armstrong, Chairman of the SFWA Contracts Committee. We've also included his commentary on each clause of the contract in *italics*.

This is a sample magazine contract for the purchase of original short fiction appearing in a print serial publication. The SFWA Model Anthology Contract should be referred to for suggestions on original short fiction appearing in anthologies. Eventually we will have to write a sample contract for electronic publications like *Omni* or *Tomorrow,* but that's another matter I feel should be treated in a separate article. I use the term "sample" rather than "model" to emphasize that this is a guide for negotiating or producing an author-friendly contract, whether initiated by an author or a publisher. Use of this sample contract by a publisher, whether in whole or in part, does not mean that SFWA or the Contracts Committee endorses that use. However, we are grateful to any publisher who uses this contract as a tool in writing author-friendly contracts.

Publishing has always been a volatile and rapidly changing industry. New technologies for publishing and distributing text material will emerge in the near future. No contract written in 1997 can predict exactly how a contract should read in 2001. Thus, this contract will quickly become outdated. However, the basic premise of this contract will serve you well in any contract you negotiate in the future. That premise? Sell the minimal rights possible, hang on to all other rights, and offer the publisher the opportunity to negotiate separate contracts for any other rights the publisher thinks it might want.

The following offered advice in writing this sample contract: Damon Knight, Raymond Feist, John Stith, Sarah Smith, David Alexander Smith, John Bunnell, Keith DeCandido, Gregory Feeley, Robin Bailey, and James Sarafin.

As with previous SFWA Contracts Committee advisories, the information here is for educational purposes only, and is not intended as a substitute for legal advice from a practicing attorney licensed in your state or province. For legal advice you should consult an attorney.

Contract

This contract is made between PUBLISHER whose address is _____
[PUBLISHER'S ADDRESS], hereinafter referred to as the PUBLISHER, and _____
[AUTHOR'S NAME], whose address is _____ [AUTHOR'S
ADDRESS], hereinafter referred to as the AUTHOR.

The parties agree as follows:

Author's Grant.

1. The Author grants permission to include his/her story entitled "_____,"
a work of approximately _____ words, hereinafter referred to as the Work, in
_____ [MAGAZINE'S TITLE], a serial publication bearing an International Standard Serial Number (ISSN) number.

Because some magazines may define a book edition of a magazine as a serial magazine, the clause "serial publication bearing an International Standard Serial Number" has been added. Because they may pay royalties on copies sold, an original anthology series that is published periodically, such as Orbit, Universe, Starlight, *etc., should be considered an anthology, not a serial publication. Foreign editions of the magazine published in book form should also be considered anthologies.*

Rights Purchased.

1(a). This use of the Work by the Publisher entails the assignment of First North American Serial Rights, for publication in the English language anywhere in North America. It is also understood and agreed that the Publisher may use this Work only in the above-mentioned magazine and that all rights not expressly granted herewithin reside exclusively with the Author, including but not limited to electronic rights.

Because some publishers misuse the purchase of foreign rights and other rights, I suggest negotiating for those rights in a separate contract. Some publishers separate payment for those rights. The author can attach the optional riders at the end as a way of specifying purchase of those rights. This clause offers the publisher the right of first offer on those rights.

Options on Further Rights.

2(a). The Author grants to the Publisher the right of first offer on world anthology rights and first foreign serial rights. The Author also grants to the Publisher the right to make an offer on nonexclusive reprint rights.

2(b). If the Publisher desires to exercise any of these offers, separate agreements must be entered to and signed for each use of further rights.

Payments and Royalties.

3. For the rights granted to the Publisher above in 1(a) the Author will receive a payment in the sum of $_____, which will be paid within thirty (30) days of signing this agreement.

As a general rule, set a time limit for the publisher to respond to signing this contract or sending checks. See the reversion clause for what happens if payment is not made.

Access to Records.

4. In the event of Publisher's failure to make timely payment, the Author may have access in person or the Author's agents or by power of attorney to all financial records of the Publisher upon presentation of a copy of this agreement to the appropriate location of said records.

Author's Warranties and Indemnities.

5. The Author represents and warrants that he/she is the sole author of the Work, that the Work is original, and that no one has reserved the rights granted in this agreement. The Author also represents, to the best of his/her knowledge, that the Work does not contain any libelous material.

This is the Author-friendly, weakened version of a Warranty clause. Many publishers may want to add further language regarding rights of privacy, or an Indemnity clause regarding sustainment of damages in court, etc. Jim Sarafin suggests that the publisher protect the writer through the publisher's own liability insurance. He notes that if a writer wishes to be protected under his or her own liability insurance, the premiums will be more than what you can earn selling the story, so why bother selling the story?

No Competing Publication.

6. The Author agrees not to publish or permit others to publish this Work in any form prior to its publication and appearance in the above-named magazine.

Author's Copies.

7. The Publisher agrees to provide the Author with six complementary copies of the magazine upon publication. The Author agrees to inform the Publisher of his/her current address.

Most publishers usually provide three copies, but we should up the expectations on this. If the publisher balks, insist that they offer you additional copies at cost. You might add a similar clause if you negotiate for the sale of foreign rights. Some publishers have a habit of forgetting to pay for foreign rights, and it is only upon discovering the foreign edition that a writer may discover use of these rights.

Changes in Text or Title.

8. The Publisher will make no major alterations to the Work's text or title without the Author's written approval. The Publisher reserves the right to make minor copy-editing changes to conform the style of the text to its customary form and usage. To ensure that no such changes are made without the Author's approval, the Publisher will furnish the Author with galley proofs or page proofs of the Work in advance of publication. Author agrees to return such proofs with corrections in not more than thirty (30) days from receipt thereof.

This protects you from a publisher or editor rewriting your work under the excuse of tight deadlines. Some publishers may suggest that they cannot guarantee sending the author proofs in a timely manner, in which case you remind them of fax machines and express mail service. David Alexander Smith wondered if 30 days was too long a time for the author to respond. Many publishers ask for 10 days, which is not too unreasonable, unless you happen to be nearing the deadline for a project which pays a lot more. Thirty days also allows you time to return the corrected proofs, particularly if you live overseas or at the end of the road in Romping Bears, Alaska.

Reversion of Rights and Withdrawal of Offer to Publish.

9(a). In the event that the Work is not published within 18 months of signing of this agreement, all rights revert to the Author, and the Author has the right to sell or arrange for publication of the above-named Work in any manner. The Author shall keep any payments made by the Publisher to him/her.

This is what happens if a publisher doesn't publish the work. If you're feeling charitable, you might extend the reversion period to 24 months, but no more. If you can think of a good reason for a publisher to need more than 24 months, and you want to be nice, you can add this line: "With the Author's written consent, or for sufficient cause, the publication period may be extended."

9(b). In the event that a copy of the counter-signed agreement is not returned to the Author within thirty (30) days of signing by the Author, or that payment in 3(a) is not made as specified, the Publisher's offer to purchase the Work shall be considered withdrawn.

This is what happens if the publisher fails to send a check or sign this contract. One notorious publisher (now out of business) used to hold off counter-signing contracts up until the date of publication, sometimes for years. The author would get an offer to buy the work and a contract, would sign the contract, and not have the counter-signed contract in hand. In effect, the writer only had an offer to purchase the work, and the publisher could hold that work in inventory without paying a dime. Without a counter-signed contract, the author may not have a claim against the publisher. Clause 9(b) takes care of this problem.

Copyright.

10. The Publisher agrees to list a proper copyright notice for the Work in the name of the Author on the first page of the printed story, and to take all necessary steps to protect the Author's copyright in the United States, and in the International Copyright Union.

Author's Credit.

11. The Author will be credited on the table of contents page and at the beginning of the story as _____ [AUTHOR'S BY-LINE].

Another publisher has strange ideas about the choice of the author's by-line. You may want to use the by-line "James Tiptree Jr." and not "Alice Sheldon." This is how you do that. The convention in manuscript format is that the name under the title is the by-line you use. Put that name here, even if it's a variation of your legal name.

Venue.

12. This agreement shall be deemed executed under the laws of the state of [PUBLISHER'S STATE OF BUSINESS]. [PUBLISHER'S STATE OF BUSINESS] state law shall be the applicable law of this agreement.

As the party making the offer, the Publisher's state of business is where the contract originates. The laws of that state apply. Usually, but not always, this is New York state.

The parties acknowledge that each party has read and understood this contract before execution.

In witness whereof the parties have executed this contract in duplication originals on this _____ day of _____, 20__.

_____   _____

Author or Author's Agent   Date

If signed by Agent, give Agent's address where payment should be sent.

_____

_____

Author/Agent Social Security or Tax ID Number

_____   _____

Name of Publisher or Publisher's Agent   Date

This is the basic signatory stuff that goes at the bottom of most contracts. One publisher doesn't include a space for the author to sign the contract. Instead, he sends the check, and inserts a clause that says something like "by signing the enclosed check, you acknowledge your acceptance of these terms." If you get a contract like that, strike out the appropriate clause and initial it, and include these lines. Contracts should look like contracts, with lines where both parties sign their name to show they agree to the terms.

Please sign and return all copies. One copy signed by all parties will be returned for your files.

RIDER 1 (OPTIONAL)

First Anthology Rights.

1(a). For the right to first publish the Work in an anthology, whether in North America or Overseas, the Author will receive an additional payment in the sum of $_____ [at least 30% of North American Serial Rights]. This sum shall constitute a payment separate from any royalties earned from use of the story in an anthology. The author shall receive a pro-rata share (defined as a comparison of the page count of the author's story compared to the page count of the anthology as a whole) of 50% of the royalty earnings of the anthology. "Anthology" shall be defined as any collection bearing an International Standard Book Number (ISBN). The anthologist or editor will provide the author with copies of any royalty statements.

If you want to sell First Anthology Rights with First North American Serial Rights, add this rider. If you want to negotiate those rights separately, substitute this rider for paragraph 1(a) above. The fees are speculative here. First Anthology Rights should go for more than reprint rights. I picked the number of 30% out of a hat, but I think that's a minimal number. The reversion clause gives the publisher a limited amount of time to exercise any of these rights.

1(b). The Publisher shall provide the Author with at least three (3) copies of the Work so published.

1(c). In the event that this right is not exercised within 18 months of the publication of the Work in the Magazine, this right shall revert to the Author.

RIDER 2 (OPTIONAL)

Reprint Rights.

1(a). For the nonexclusive right to reprint the Work in an anthology, whether in North America or Overseas, the Author will receive an additional payment in the sum of $_____ [at least 20% of North American Serial Rights].

1(b). The Publisher shall provide the Author with at least three (3) copies of the Work so published.

1(c). In the event that this right is not exercised within 18 months of the publication of the Work in the Magazine, this right shall revert to the Author.

Again, the fee is speculative.

RIDER 3 (OPTIONAL)

Foreign Rights.

1(a). For the right to reprint the Work in a foreign magazine edition of the Magazine, the Author will receive an additional payment in the sum of $_____ [at least 20% of North American Serial Rights] for each appearance in a foreign magazine edition of the Magazine. "Magazine edition" shall be defined as a serial publication bearing an International Standard Serial Number (ISSN).

1(b). The Publisher shall provide the Author with at least three (3) copies of the Work so published.

1(c). In the event that this right is not exercised within 18 months of the publication of the Work in the Magazine, this right shall revert to the Author.

See above. As in paragraph 1, this rider defines "magazine." Some publishers may want to buy the right to publish the Work in all foreign editions of their magazine.

Web

AGREEMENT dated this day of [DATE] in which we, the publisher, [NAME], agree with you, the author, {NAME}, that you grant us the nonexclusive right to publish your work entitled [TITLE] on our World Wide Web site. All other rights to the work belong to you. You guarantee that this work is your own and that you have the right to grant us the use of it. We will print a copyright notice in your name and, if applicable, a publication history along with the work; but if it has not been registered with the Copyright Office and you want it to be, that will be up to you. We will code the work in HTML as needed for Web presentation but will make no changes in text or title without your written permission. You may withdraw permission to publish at any time by giving written notice by street- or e-mail to our Webmaster, who will remove your work from our Web site within one week of receipt of such notice.

_____   _____

Webmaster   Date

_____   _____

Author   Date

Agents

As author-agent contracts don't seem to be a one-size-fits-all item, a few alternative contract clauses are included in this draft, accompanied by comments (shown in *italics*).

PRELIMINARY STATEMENT. This agreement (the "Agreement") dated [date of signing], sets forth the relationship between [author's name here] (the "Author"), also published under the name(s) [pen names here] and [name of literary agency here] (the "Literary Agent").

1. LITERARY AGENT REPRESENTS AUTHOR. For the term of this agreement, the Author hereby retains the Literary Agent:

(a) To represent the Author for the sale of the following works ("Represented Works"), written or to be written by the Author and not covered by a prior unagented sale or prior agency agreement: (1) all full-length fiction, and (2) any other writings that Author and Literary Agent may agree upon.

(b) Subject to the Author's approval, to negotiate sales ("Represented Sales") of (1) Represented Works in the U.S., its territories, and Canada ("Domestic Sales"), (2) Represented Works in nondomestic markets ("Foreign Sales"), and (3) derivative or secondary rights in the Represented Works (such as film, TV, recording, or other dramatic media) anywhere in the world ("Subsidiary Sales").

(c) To receive payments and royalties from all Represented Sales as long as the contracts for such sales remain in force.

Author attests that, during the term of this Contract, the Author will employ no other Literary Agent to represent the Author for the Author's Represented Works. It is acknowledged that some of the Author's backlog may be excluded from this contract because it is covered by a prior agreement with another agency.

Some authors prefer to have separate film agents. Whichever way you go, the decision should be clear to both author and agent.

2. CONTRACTS. Literary Agent shall use best efforts to promote the Author's Represented Works. No proposed Represented Sale shall be binding unless approved by the Author in a signed contract (a "Represented Contract"). Author may, in writing, authorize Literary Agent to sign contracts on his behalf.

Authors might want to provide a limited authorization that lets the agent sign only foreign contracts or sign only contracts the author has verbally approved.

3. AGENT'S COMMISSION. The Literary Agent shall be entitled to a commission ("Agent's Commission") equal to X percent of all Domestic Sales, Y percent of all Subsidiary Sales, and Z percent of all Foreign Sales.

While authors would like these commission rates as low as possible, we recognize that agents would prefer them as high as possible. A number of agents charge 10 percent for domestic sales, 15 percent for subsidiary, and 20 percent for foreign, and obviously these rates play a part in the determination of whether a particular agent is the one to sign with.

4. SUBSIDIARY RIGHTS. Subject to Author's reasonable consent, the Literary Agent shall engage all subsidiary or co-agents which the Literary Agent believes best represent the Author in Foreign Sales.

5. EXPENSES BORNE BY LITERARY AGENT. From the Literary Agent's Commission, the Literary Agent shall pay (a) all subsidiary or split commissions required by foreign or subsidiary agents, and (b) such other costs, listed in the attached Rider, as Literary Agent may incur in promoting or selling the Author's Represented Works. The Literary Agent shall not be reimbursed for such expenses and need not account for them to the Author, except that the Author shall reimburse the Literary Agent for unusual expenses, incurred by the Literary Agent with the Author's prior consent, for the Represented Works.

This phrase is the best case for the author, but it's just another component of the give and take between author and agent, and should be factored into the projected agent commission when comparing two otherwise equal agents. Often, the agents charging higher commission rates are willing to include some expenses in their commission. Just be clear on what you'll be expected to pay for, and if you can, limit additional expenses to those applicable to works actually sold.

6. DISBURSEMENTS. On behalf of the Author, the Literary Agent shall collect all payments due the Author under any Represented Contract ("Author's Payments") and shall, within ten days of the funds clearing, disburse the amount of such Author's Payments to the Author, less any Literary Agent's Commission and less any mutually approved expense charges.

7. STATEMENTS. In January of each year, the Literary Agent shall provide the Author with an annual statement showing all Author's Payments, Agent's Commissions, and other itemized deductions for the previous calendar year.

Not all agencies do this, but it's desirable for the author. The minimum notice consists of an IRS Form 1099 that identifies the total payments and total commissions.

8. NOTICES. The Literary Agent and Author shall promptly send each other copies of (a) any legal notice under any Represented Contract, (b) any important communication from any publisher under any Represented Contract, and any material correspondence.

9. TERM. This contract may be terminated voluntarily for any reason by either party upon thirty days' prior written notice to the other, detailing causes for termination, sent via certified mail, return receipt requested, to the addresses below:

If to Literary Agent, at [Literary Agent's address]; if to Author, at [Author's address] or such other address as either party may designate in writing to the other.

After termination, the Literary Agent shall continue to administer Represented Contracts, which the Literary Agent negotiated while this Contract was in force, and retain Agent's Commission on those Represented Contracts. The Literary Agent may make no further sales of the Represented Works.

10. CONTACTS. Mail sent to the Author in care of the Literary Agent may be opened by the Literary Agent and dealt with, unless it is apparently of a personal nature, in which case the Literary Agent shall forward it to the Author promptly. When the Author is approached directly by any party interested in the Author's Represented Works, the Author shall inform the Literary Agent immediately and refer the party to the Literary Agent.

11. AMENDMENT. This Agreement contains the entire agreement between the parties hereto. It supersedes any prior agreement, and may be amended in writing by mutual consent.

Publisher Listing

By rights this is the part of book that you should refer to the most. Everything we've said about getting into print is academic unless you submit your stories and novels to the publishers listed here.

This list is not exhaustive; you should always look up the most current information that you can find on a market before you submit to it. The publishing industry is volatile, after all. Take this list as your starting point, and then build your own. And whatever you do, keep submitting your work!

Primary Novel Publishers

The following publishers are responsible for the vast majority of SF and fantasy titles published in North America. We've only included publishers that published at least 40 titles in 1999. Note that certain large houses such as Del Rey Books and HarperCollins Publishers will return your manuscript unread unless you use an agent.

Ace Science Fiction and Fantasy

Contact: Editorial Dept.

Ace Science Fiction and Fantasy
The Berkley Publishing Group, Penguin Putnam, Inc.
375 Hudson Street
New York, NY 10014
Telephone: 212-366-2000
Web address: www.penguinputnam.com

Ace accepts agented submissions only. Ace exclusively publishes SF, fantasy, and horror. Recently published titles include *The Night Watch*, by Sean Stewart.

Avon Eos

Contact: Jennifer Brehl, Executive Editor

Avon Books
1350 Avenue of the Americas
New York, NY 10019
Telephone: 212-261-6800
Web address: www.avonbooks.com/eos

Avon Eos isn't currently looking at complete manuscript submissions; however, they will consider query letters. They advise sending a one- to two-page query, with a short writing sample attached.

According to Avon, the Eos book line was created to revitalize SF by using new editorial, packaging, and sales techniques. One of Eos's new initiatives is an "online SF convention" called Eoscon. You can find the most recent Eoscon at www.eoscon3.com.

Recently published titles include *Singer from the Sea,* by Sheri Tepper.

Baen Books

Contact: Toni Weisskopf, Executive Editor

Baen Books
P.O. Box 1403
Riverdale, NY 10471
Telephone: 718-548-3100
Web address: www.baen.com

Send full manuscript or outline and three chapters, along with a self-addressed stamped envelope. Author's guidelines are available if you send them a self-addressed stamped envelope.

Recently published titles include *Change of Command,* by Elizabeth Moon, and *Minds, Machines, and Evolution,* by James P. Hogan.

Baen is a small, independent publisher dedicated to SF and fantasy. Although they're interested in all kinds of SF, their slant is toward traditional storytelling, particularly strong, action-oriented fiction such as space opera. Baen is particularly strong in the area of military SF, publishing such authors as David Drake and Jerry Pournelle.

In fantasy, Baen leans toward modern urban fantasy, but once again is open to anything, as long as it's good. Mercedes Lackey is one fantasy author who has had success with Baen.

Authors who sold their first novels to Baen include Lois McMaster Bujold and Elizabeth Moon.

Bantam Spectra Books

Contact: Anne Groell

Bantam Spectra Books
Bantam Dell Publishing Group
Random House, Inc.
1540 Broadway
New York, NY 10036
Telephone: 212-354-6500
Web address: www.randomhouse.com/books/sciencefiction/

Query or submit a partial manuscript with outline/synopsis. Will only accept simultaneous submissions by agents.

Bantam has recently been acquired by Bertelsmann, which already owns Random House/Ballantine; the combined forces of this publisher put 103 SF books on bookstore shelves in 1999. They publish cyberpunk, hard SF, military and sociological SF, and space opera. Recently published titles include *Vast,* by Linda Nagat,a and *Brightness Reef,* by David Brin.

DAW Books, Inc.

Contact: Peter Stampfel, Submissions Editor

DAW Books
Penguin Putnam, Inc.
375 Hudson Street, 3rd Floor
New York, NY 10014-3658
Telephone: 212-366-2096
Web address: www.dawbooks.com

Query with self-addressed stamped envelope.

DAW Books was founded by Donald Wollheim in 1971 as the first independent publisher dedicated entirely to science fiction and fantasy. Although a small publishing house, DAW has traditionally treated its authors very well, striving to keep backlists in print and nurturing authors' careers in the traditional way. DAW's authors tend to be quite loyal, although DAW does not pay the high advances offered by some other publishers.

DAW publishes both science fiction and fantasy. Recently published titles include *Traitor's Sun,* by Marion Zimmer Bradley, and *Mountain of Black Glass,* by Tad Williams.

Del Rey Books

Contact: Shelly Shapiro

Del Rey Books
201 E. 50th Street
New York, NY 10022-7703
Telephone: 212-572-2677
Web address: www.randomhouse.com/delrey
E-mail: delrey@randomhouse.com

Del Rey only accepts agented submissions.

Del Rey publishes a handful of first novels every year. They focus on big selling names like Anne McCaffrey and Orson Scott Card; however, Del Rey sponsors an on-line writing workshop through their Web site. Authors are invited to post writing samples and participate in the review of others' work.

Recently published Del Rey titles include *Star Wars: Episode I: The Phantom Menace*, by Terry Brooks, and *The Demon Awakes*, by R. A. Salvatore.

Roc Books

Contact: Laura Anne Gilman

Roc Books
Penguin Putnam, Inc.
375 Hudson Street
New York, NY 10014
Telephone: 212-366-2000
Web address: www.penguinputnam.com

Query with synopsis and one or two sample chapters. Roc accepts simultaneous submissions.

Roc benefits from having the muscle of Penguin Putnam behind it, and the company is buying a lot of new authors these days. Be aware, however, that most of their recent new titles have come out as mass-market paperbacks. Such titles have a very short shelf life; by publishing new authors in mass-market form, Roc is hedging their bets. Still, the Roc imprint is strong and well-marketed.

Tor Books

Contact: Patrick Nielsen Hayden, Senior Editor

Tor Books
Tom Doherty Associates, LLC
175 Fifth Avenue
New York, NY 10010
Web address: www.tor.com

Submit a synopsis with three sample chapters. No queries or simultaneous submissions.

Tor Books is by far the biggest publisher of SF and fantasy, having produced 79 new titles in 1999. The most important thing about Tor is that they prefer to publish new titles as hardcovers. Arriving in hardcover format guarantees a book will be reviewed, and also guarantees a longer shelf life. The trade-off here is smaller print runs for first editions.

Tor is a leader in reshaping the way publishing is done. Tor is involved in a number of e-text and print-on-demand ventures, and has long pioneered a model that entails working with a broad range of editors based all over the world, rather than merely in New York.

Recent Tor books include *A Deepness in the Sky,* by Vernor Vinge, and *The Cassini Division,* by Ken MacLeod.

Wizards of the Coast/TSR

Contact: Novel Submissions Editor

TSR, Inc.
P.O. Box 707
Renton, WA 98057-0707
Telephone: 425-226-6500
Web address: www.wizards.com

TSR is a publisher of gaming-related novels. They have a number of imprints, including Forgotten Realms, Dragonlance, Magic, the Gathering, and Planescape. TSR typically publishes on a work-for-hire basis, so while you may submit samples of your work, they usually define their own projects for authors.

Secondary Novel Markets

These markets all published between 1 and 40 SF titles each in 1999. Some are big publishers with a small interest in SF; others are small presses that publish only a couple of books per year, but focus almost entirely on speculative literature. Included are some markets that will publish books outside the mainstream, such as erotica or sociological SF.

Arkham House

Specializes in short-story collections. Submissions by invitation only, but you can query to introduce yourself and your work.

Contact: Editorial Dept.

Arkham House
P.O. Box 536
Sauk City, WI 53583

Atheneum Books for Young Readers

Publishes SF and fantasy aimed at preschool to high-school age kids.

Contact: Marcia Marshall, Executive Editor

Atheneum
Simon & Schuster
1230 Avenue of the Americas
New York, NY 10020
Telephone: 212-698-2715

Carroll & Graf Publishers, Inc.

SF, fantasy, thrillers, suspense. Agented submissions only.

Contact: Keith Carroll

Carroll & Graf Publishers, Inc.
19 W. 21st Street
Suite 601
New York, NY 10010
Telephone: 212-627-8590

Circlet Press

Erotic short SF and fantasy stories.

Contact: Cecilia Tan, Editor

Circlet Press
1770 Massachusetts Avenue
Suite 278
Cambridge, MA 02140
Telephone: 617-864-0492
E-mail: circlet-info@circlet.com

Four Walls Eight Windows

Emphasizes literary quality; publishes hardcover and trade originals.

Contact: Acquisitions Editor

Four Walls Eight Windows
39 W. 14th Street
Room 503
New York, NY 10011
Fax only: 212-206-8799

Gryphon Publications

Publishes science fiction, urban horror, suspense. Buys all rights.

Contact: Gary Lovosi

Gryphon Publications
P.O. Box 209
Brooklyn, NY 11228

Henry Holt & Company, Inc.

A large publishing house; very little of what Holt publishes is SF, but they still managed five new SF hardcover books in 1999.

Contact: Marc Aronson, Senior Editor (young adult)

Henry Holt & Company, Inc.
115 W. 18th Street
New York, NY 10011
Telephone: 212-886-9200

Minstrel Books

An imprint of Simon & Schuster, Minstrel publishes juvenile books for kids between the ages of 8 and 12.

Attn: Manuscript Proposals

Minstrel Books
1230 Avenue of the Americas
New York, NY 10020
Telephone: 212-698-7669
Web address: www.simonsayskids.com

Rising Tide Press

Lesbian SF of all sorts—adventure, erotica, fantasy, horror.

Contact: Lee Boojamra

Rising Tide Press
3831 Oracle Road
Tucson, AZ 85705-3254
Telephone: 520-888-1140
E-mail: rtpress@aol.com

White Wolf Publishing

Gaming-related novels, contemporary fantasy, cyberpunk.

Contact: Ms. Staley Krause

White Wolf Publishing
780 Park North Blvd.
Suite 100
Clarkston, GA 30021

Canadian Publishers

Adventure Book Publishers

Canadian publisher specializing in digital books.

Contact: Acquisitions Editor

Adventure Book Publishers
#712-3545-32 Avenue NE
Calgary, Alberta, T1Y 3M1
Telephone: 403-285-6844
Web address: www.puzzlesbyshar.com/adventurebooks
E-mail: adventure@puzzlesbyshar.com

Edge Science Fiction and Fantasy Publishing

Hardcover and trade paperback originals, all forms of SF and fantasy except juvenile.

Contact: Jessie Tambay

Edge Science Fiction and Fantasy Publishing
P.O. Box 75064
Cambrian PO
Calgary Alberta, T2K 6J8
Telephone: 403-282-5206
Web address: www.edgewebsite.com
E-mail: editor@cadivision.com

Editions Logiques/Logical Publishing

French-Canadian publisher. Publishes SF written in or translated into French.

Contact: Louis-Philippe Hebert

Editions Logiques
P.O. Box 10
Station D, Montreal Quebec, H3K 3B9

Telephone: 514-933-2225
Web address: www.logique.com
E-mail: logique@cam.org

Tesseract Books

Prestigious imprint of The Books Collective; responsible for the yearly *Tesseracts* anthologies of premier Canadian SF.

Contact: The Editors

Tesseract Books
The Books Collective
214-21 10405 Jasper Avenue
Edmonton, Alberta, Canada, T5J 3S2
Telephone: 403-448-0590
Web address: www.bookscollective.com

E-Book Publishers

BiblioBytes

General-interest publisher of books for handheld computers.

Attn: Submissions

BiblioBytes
71 Hauxhurst Avenue
Weehawken, NJ 07087-6803
Telephone: 201-601-0300
Web address: www.bb.com

Bookedup.com

This Internet publisher buys only electronic rights, theoretically permitting authors to sell print rights elsewhere.

Contact: Richard Hurowitz

Bookedup.com
P.O. Box 1539
New York, NY 10021
Web address: www.bookedup.com
E-mail: info@bookedup.com

Electric Works Publishing

SF and fantasy, including short-story collections.

Contact: James R. Bohe

Electric Works Publishing
605 Avenue C.E.
Bismarck, ND 58501
Telephone: 701-255-0356
Web address: www.electricpublishing.com
E-mail: editors@electricpublishing.com

iUniverse.com

Online vanity press with several publishing options.

Contact: www.iuniverse.com

Peanut Press

Publishers of electronic books and short stories for handheld computers.

Contact: info@peanutpress.com

Primary Short–Story Markets

Science fiction has traditionally been a short-story medium. Many of the great classics in the field are short works; short SF stories are made into films at least as often as novels. Until very recently, SF was the only field of literature that maintained a thriving short-story market. This market has begun to seriously constrict in the past several years. One can hope that the rise of Internet publishing will provide new markets for short-story writers; at the moment, the jury is out.

The list of primary SF short-story markets used to be much larger. Following are magazines that are classified as professional markets by SFWA's criterion (they each pay at least 3¢ per word).

Amazing Stories

Amazing Stories is currently a quarterly, having recently been bought by Wizards of the Coast. Editorial and production qualities are high, though its circulation is only about 10,000 per issue. *Amazing Stories* buys science fiction exclusively, and pays 5¢ to 6¢ per word.

Contact: Mr. Kim Mohan, Editor-in-Chief

Amazing Stories/Wizards of the Coast, Inc.
1801 Lind Avenue SW
Renton, WA 98055

Fax only: 425-204-5928
Web address: www.wizards.com
E-mail: amazing@wizards.com

Analog Science Fiction & Fact

Analog Science Fiction & Fact was established in 1930, and is still going strong. It buys science fiction with an emphasis on the science, and pays a competitive 5¢ to 6¢ per word.

Contact: Dr. Stanley Schmidt, Editor

Analog Science Fiction & Fact
Dell Magazine Fiction Group
475 Park Avenue S.
New York, NY 10016
Telephone: 212-698-1313
Web address: www.sfsite.com/analog
E-mail: analogsf@erols.com

Asimov's Science Fiction

Asimov's Science Fiction buys more "character-oriented" SF; the flat scientist or engineer heroes from classic hard SF won't cut it here. *Asimov's* only wants serious and compelling stories, primarily SF but also some fantasy. Published 11 times a year, *Asimov's* pays 6¢ to 8¢ per word.

Contact: Gardner Dozois, Editor

Asimov's Science Fiction
Dell Magazine Fiction Group
475 Park Avenue, 11th Floor
New York, NY 10016
Telephone: 212-686-7188
Web address: www.asimovs.com
E-mail: asimovs@erols.com

The Magazine of Fantasy and Science Fiction

The Magazine of Fantasy and Science Fiction (*F&SF*) celebrated its fiftieth anniversary in 1999. Although it is primarily a fiction market, this magazine also publishes reviews, a science column, cartoons, etc. With a circulation of about 10,000, *F&SF* is struggling right now, but it is still one of the premier markets, and pays 6¢ to 8¢ per word.

Contact: Gordon Van Gelder

The Magazine of Fantasy and Science Fiction
Mercury Press
P.O. Box 1806
Madison Square Station
New York, NY 10159-1806
Telephone: 212-982-2676
Web address: www.sfsite.com/fsf
E-mail: gordonfsf@aol.com

Interzone, *Science Fiction and Fantasy*

The best of British SF, *Interzone* is a monthly with a circulation of about 10,000 that publishes both SF and fantasy. Pays £30/1,000 words.

Contact: David Pringle

Interzone
217 Preston Drove
Brighton, England BN1 6FL
E-mail: interzone@cix.co.uk

Realms of Fantasy

Realms of Fantasy is one of the bestselling magazines, although it is only published bi-monthly. They buy at least 30 fantasy stories per year.

Contact: Shawna McCarthy, Editor

Realms of Fantasy
Sovereign Media Co., Inc.
441 Carlisle Drive
Herndon, VA 22070

Secondary Short-Story Markets

Aboriginal Science Fiction

Aboriginal Science Fiction publishes classic tales of adventure and hard SF.

Contact: Charles C. Ryan

Aboriginal Science Fiction
P.O. Box 2449
Woburn, MA 01888-0849
Web address: www.aboriginalsf.com

Absolute Magnitude

Absolute Magnitude is a quarterly magazine specializing in SF short stories. Emphasis is on adventure and hard SF.

Contact: Warren Lapine, Editor

Absolute Magnitude
P.O. Box 2988
Radford, VA 24143
Web address: www.sfsite.com/dnaweb/home.htm
E-mail: dnapublications@iname.com

Atlantic Monthly

Atlantic Monthly has the highest standards for literary fiction. They're interested in contemporary fiction relevant to mainstream issues. Consider this market only if your work truly speaks to people's current experiences.

Contact: Michael Curtis, Senior Editor

Atlantic Monthly
77 N. Washington Street
Boston, MA 02114

Century

Century is dedicated to highly literary SF. Its publishing schedule is erratic, but this is one magazine everyone in the industry reads.

Contact: Robert K.J. Kilheffer

Century
P.O. Box 150510
Brooklyn, NY 11215-0510
Web address: www.centurymag.com

Bloodsongs

Bloodsongs is a quarterly magazine of horror, covering music, art, and film, and including horror fiction of up to 7,000 words in length.

Contact: David G. Barnett, Fiction Editor

Bloodsongs
1921 Colonial Drive
Orlando, FL 32803
Telephone: (407) 898-5573
Web address: www.bloodsongs.com
E-mail: bloodsongs@implosion.com

Eidolon

Australia's oldest science fiction magazine.

Contact: Jonathon Strahan

Eidolon
P.O. Box 355
North Perth, Western Australia 6006
Web address: www.eidolon.net

Harper's Magazine

Established in 1850, *Harper's Magazine* is one of the most prestigious general-interest magazines in the world. They publish one short story per issue.

Contact: Ann Gollin, Editor's Assistant

Harper's Magazine
666 Broadway, 11th Floor
New York, NY 10012
Telephone: 212-614-6500

The New Yorker

The New Yorker has no strict guidelines; however, as with *Harper's* or the *Atlantic Monthly,* you should carefully study the magazine if you are considering submitting your work. They will consider topical fiction.

Contact: David Remnick

The New Yorker
20 W. 43rd Street
New York, NY 10036-7441
Telephone: 212-536-5400

On Spec

A quarterly, *On Spec* covers the English-Canadian SF market.

Contact: Jena Snyder, Editor

On Spec
The Copper Pig Writers Society
P.O. Box 4727
Edmonton Alberta, T6E 5G6
Web address: www.icomm.ca/onspec

Playboy

Although it only occasionally buys SF, *Playboy* has such a huge circulation and pays so well that it's definitely worth trying.

Contact: Fiction Dept.

Playboy
680 North Lake Shore Drive
Chicago, Illinois 60611
Web address: www.playboy.com

The Third Alternative

This British quarterly has been garnering favorable reviews, and has recently published such SF greats as William Gibson and Michael Moorcock.

Contact: Andy Cox

TTA Press
5 Martins Lane
Witcham, Ely, Cambs CB6 2LB, United Kingdom
Web address: www.tta-press.freewire.co.uk/
E-mail: ttapress@aol.com

TransVersions

A relative newcomer in the Canadian short fiction scene, *TransVersions* has a track record of publishing strong, quirky genre fiction.

Contact: Marcel Gagne or Sally Tomasevic

TransVersions
P.O. Box 52531
1801 Lakeshore Road West
Ontario L5J 4S6, Canada
Web address: www.salmar.com/transversions

Weird Tales

Weird Tales is a quarterly focusing on stories of fantasy-based horror, heroic fantasy, and exotic mood pieces. They are open to the odd and unclassifiable—provided that it has some element of the fantastic.

Contact: Darrell Schweitzer, Editor

Weird Tales
123 Crooked Lane
King of Prussia, PA 19406-2570
Web address: www.sfsite.com/dnaweb/home.htm

SF Trade Magazines

Locus

A hugely informative industry news magazine. Essential reading for any aspiring SF or fantasy writer.

Locus Publications
P.O. Box 13305
Oakland, CA 94661
Telephone: 510-339-9196
Web address: www.locusmag.com
E-mail: locus@locusmag.com

Scavenger's Newsletter

Monthly market newsletter covering SF, fantasy, and horror. Accepts market information from freelancers (that's you).

Scavenger's Newsletter
519 Ellinwood
Osage City, KS 66523-1329
Telephone: 913-528-3538
Web address: www.cza.com/scav/index.html
E-mail: foxscav1@jc.net

Science Fiction Chronicle

Bimonthly, award-winning news magazine about the SF field. Together, *SF Chronicle* and *Locus* provide great coverage of everything that's happening in SF.

Science Fiction Chronicle
P.O. Box 022730
Brooklyn, NY 11202-0056
Web address: www.sfsite.com/sfc/home.htm
E-mail: SF_Chronicle@compuserve.com

Agent Listing

The following literary agents all make a substantial portion of their revenue from selling SF, and are open to being approached by new authors. Note that certain agencies prefer to be contacted by mail and don't provide their phone numbers.

For more information about literary agents, refer to Chapter 22, "Agents."

Name: **James Allen, Literary Agent**
Contact: James Allen
Address: P.O. Box 278, Milford, PA 18337

Agent receives 10 percent commission on domestic sales, 20 percent on film sales, and 20 percent on foreign sales. Specializes in hard and sociological SF, humorous SF, traditional, and high fantasy.

Name: **Blassingame Spectrum Corp.**
Contact: Eleanor Wood or Lucienne Diver
Address: 111 Eighth Avenue, Suite 1501, New York, NY 10011
Telephone: 212-691-7556

Agent receives 10 percent commission on domestic sales. Specializes in military and hard SF, space opera, and dark fantasy.

Name: **Jane Butler, Art and Literary Agent**
Contact: Jane Butler
Address: P.O. Box 33, Matamoras, PA 18336

Agent receives 10 percent commission on domestic sales, 25 percent on foreign sales. Specializes in military and hard SF and dark fantasy.

Name: **Maria Carvainis Agency, Inc.**
Contact: Maria Carvainis
Address: 235 West End Avenue, Suite 15F, New York, NY 10023
Telephone: 212-580-1559

Agent receives 15 percent commission on domestic sales, 20 percent on foreign sales. Offers a binding written contract with a two-year term. Specializes in traditional fantasy.

Name: **Circle of Confusion, Ltd.**
Contact: Rajeev Agarwal
Address: 666 Fifth Avenue, Suite 3031, New York, NY 10103
Telephone: 212-969-0653

Agent receives 10 percent commission. Offers a binding contract requiring 60 days notice for termination. Specializes in all forms of SF and fantasy.

Name: **Frances Collin, Literary Agent**
Contact: Frances Collin
Address: P.O. Box 33, Wayne, PA 19087-0033

Agent receives 15 percent commission on domestic sales, 20 percent commission on foreign sales. Specializes in biological SF and high fantasy.

Name: **Richard Curtis Associates, Inc.**
Contact: Richard Curtis, Laura Tucker, or Amy Victoria Meo
Address: 171 E. 74th Street, New York, NY 10021
Telephone: 212-772-7363

Agent receives 15 percent commission on domestic sales, 20 percent commission on foreign sales. One of the largest and most prestigious agencies in the business. Specializes in hard and military SF, space opera, and high and dark fantasy.

Name: **Graham Literary Agency, Inc.**
Contact: Susan L. Graham
Address: P.O. Box 1051, Alpharetta, GA 30239
Telephone: 770-569-9755

Agent receives 15 percent commission on domestic sales, 20 percent commission on foreign sales. Specializes in cyberpunk, traditional and hard SF, and fantasy.

Name: **Ievleva Literary Agency**
Contact: Julie Ievleva
Address: 7095 Hollywood Blvd., Suite 832, Hollywood, CA 90028
Telephone: 213-993-6048

Agent receives 15 percent commission on sales. Offers a written contract. Specializes in contemporary and traditional fantasy and science fantasy.

Name: **Jabberwocky Literary Agency**
Contact: Joshua Bilmes
Address: P.O. Box 4558, Sunnyside, NY 11104-0558
Telephone: 718-392-5985

Agent receives a 10 percent commission on sales. Offers a written contract, binding for one year. Specializes in all forms of SF and fantasy.

Name: **Virginia Kidd, Literary Agent**
Contact: Virginia Kidd
Address: 538 E. Harford Street, P.O. Box 278, Milford, PA 18337
Telephone: 717-296-6205

Agent receives 10 percent commission on domestic sales, 20 percent commission on foreign sales. Offers a written contract. Specializes in all forms of SF and fantasy.

Name: **Michael Larsen/Elizabeth Pomada, Literary Agents**
Contact: Elizabeth Pomada
Address: 1029 Jones Street, San Francisco, CA 94109
Telephone: 415-673-0939

Agent receives 15 percent commission on domestic sales. Offers a written contract. Specializes in space opera, experimental fiction, and fantasy.

Name: **Donald Maass Literary Agency**
Contact: Donald Maass or Jennifer Jackson
Address: 157 W. 57th Street, Suite 1003, New York, NY 10019
Telephone: 212-757-7755

Agent receives 15 percent commission on domestic sales, 20 percent commission on foreign sales. Specializes in all forms of SF and fantasy.

Name: **Susan Ann Protter, Literary Agent**
Contact: Susan Ann Protter
Address: 110 W. 40th Street, Suite 1408, New York, NY 10018
Telephone: 212-840-0480

Agent receives 15 percent commission on domestic sales, 15 percent on dramatic sales, and 25 percent commission on foreign sales. Specializes in contemporary, hard, and cyberpunk SF, as well as traditional fantasy.

Name: **Scovil Chichak Galen Literary Agency, Inc.**
Contact: Russell Galen
Address: 381 Park Avenue S., Suite 1020, New York, NY 10016
Telephone: 212-679-8686

Agent receives 15 percent commission on domestic sales. Offers a written contract. Specializes in all forms of SF and fantasy.

Name: **Valerie Smith, Literary Agent**
Contact: Valerie Smith
Address: 1746 Rt. 44/55, Modena, NY 12548-5205
Telephone: 914-883-5848

Agent receives 15 percent commission on domestic sales. Offers a written contract. Specializes in all forms of SF and fantasy.

Name: **Toad Hall, Inc.**
Contact: Sharon Jarvis or Anne Pinzow
Address: R.R. 2, Box 16B, Laceyville, PA 18623
Telephone: 717-869-2942

Agent receives 15 percent commission on domestic sales. Offers a written contract. Specializes in mainstream and hard SF, fantasy, and science fantasy.

Name: **The Vines Agency, Inc.**
Contact: Jimmy Vines
Address: 409 E. Sixth Street, No. 4, New York, NY 10009
Telephone: 212-777-5522

Agent receives 15 percent commission on domestic sales, 20 percent on foreign sales. Offers a written contract, binding for one year. Specializes in cyberpunk and hard SF, experimental fiction, contemporary fantasy, and magic realism.

Name: **Writers House**
Contact: Merrilee Heifetz
Address: 21 W. 26th Street, New York, NY 10010
Telephone: 212-685-2400

Agent receives 15 percent commission on domestic sales, 20 percent on foreign sales. Offers a written contract. Specializes in sociological SF, cyberpunk, space opera, and dark and traditional fantasy.

Online Resources

This appendix attempts to catalog some of the genre resources available to you on the Internet. Since its inception, the Internet has hosted numerous science fictional resources of all description, and the volume is quite staggering. The links here are just a tiny sliver of the total.

Due to the dynamic nature of the Internet, it's likely that some of these links will have ceased to function at press time and beyond. A current listing of all links in this appendix is available at www.cigsf.com.

Markets

The Internet's market listings and gossip are the home of the most up-to-date and comprehensive information on the subject, aggregating the comments and insight of hundreds, if not thousands, of individual writers.

Listings

Inkspot Markets
www.inkspot.com/market
Links to many market-list sites.

The Market List
www.marketlist.com
Slightly out-of-date at press time, but with good ancillary information like interviews and advice.

Working List of Speculative Fiction Markets
www.bayarea.net/~stef/sf-markets.txt
Again, slightly out-of-date, but with a wealth of notes.

Tracking

The Blackhole
critters.critique.org/critters/
blackholes/
A fabulous market-tracking site,
where writers pool info on response
times from various book and magazine publishers.

Discussion

sff.writing.response-times
webnews.sff.net/read?cmd=xover&group
=sff.writing.response-times
SFF.net's newsgroup for discussion of response times.

Speculations' Rumor Mill
www.speculations.com/rumormill/
topic201.htm
Speculations magazine online forum for
discussion of response times.

Novels

Most science fiction novel publishers were slow to establish their Internet presence,
and the mergers and acquisitions mania in publishing has given rise to numerous
dead links and unused corners on the publishers' sites.

Majors

Avon Eos
www.avonbooks.com/eos/index.html
Avon Books' site. See the FAQ at
www.avonbooks.com/eos/faq.html for
writer's guidelines.

Baen Books
www.baen.com
Site for Baen Books, including author's
guidelines and info on the state and
mechanics of publishing.

DAW Books
www.dawbooks.com
Site for DAW Books.

Gollancz
www.cassell.co.uk/gollancz/
Mostly a catalog for this U.K.
publisher.

HarperPrism
www.harpercollins.com/imprints/
harper_prism/
Site for HarperPrism: as thin as their
editorial staffing levels.

Penguin Putnam
www.penguinputnam.com/clubppi/
news/ace/index.htm
A site for Penguin's imprints: Ace,
DAW, and Penguin.

Random House
www.randomhouse.com/books/
sciencefiction/
Site for Random House's various science fiction imprints, including
Bantam Spectra and Ballantine Del
Ray.

Simon & Schuster
www.simonsays.com/subs/index.cfm?
areaid=44
Publishers of *Star Trek* fiction through
their Pocket Books imprint.

Tor
www.tor.com
Tor Books' site, the oldest genre publisher site on the Net, with a wealth of information and links.

Voyager Books
www.voyager-books.com
Site for Harper's UK genre fiction arm, with contests and author info.

Warner Aspect
www.twbookmark.com/
sciencefiction/index.html
Contests, chats, and discussion groups.

White Wolf
www.white-wolf.com/fiction/
fiction.html
Gaming-based books and quirky fiction.

Small-Press

Arkham House
www.arkhamhouse.com
Venerable specialty press.

Chaosium
www.chaosium.com
Mostly publishes role-playing games, but also some reprinted horror.

Donald M. Grant
www.grantbooks.com
Speculative fiction press.

Mark V. Zeising
www.bigchair.com/ziesing/
Well-known publisher of the quirky and fun.

Ministry of Whimsy
www.mindspring.com/~toones/
ministry.html
New speculative fiction specialty publisher, with a focus on the literary.

NESFA Press
www.nesfa.org/press
Mostly reprints from the New England Science Fiction Association.

Wildside Press
www.wildsidepress.com/index2.htm
Ground-breaking print-on-demand publisher.

Electronic

Peanut Press
www.peanutpress.com
Publishers of electronic books and short stories for handheld computers.

BiblioBytes
www.bb.com
Advertising-support publisher of speculative fiction.

Crowsnest
www.computercrowsnest.com
Publisher of e-books for the RocketBook.

Magazines and Anthologies

The major magazines also dragged their heels in getting online, but they've finally caught up.

Majors

Amazing Stories
www.wizards.com/amazing

Analog
www.analogsf.com

Asimov's
www.asimovs.com

Interzone
www.sfsite.com/interzone

The Magazine of Fantasy and Science Fiction
www.sfsite.com/fsf

Small-Press

Aboriginal Science Fiction
www.aboriginalsf.com

Absolute Magnitude
www.sfsite.com/dnaweb/AMCurr.htm

Back Brain Recluse
www.bbr-online.com/magazine

Cemetery Dance
www.cemeterydance.com/html/mags.html

Century
www.centurymag.com

Dreams of Decadence
www.sfsite.com/dnaweb/DoDCurr.htm

Glimmer Train
www.glimmertrain.com

On Spec
www.icomm.ca/onspec

Pirate Writings
www.sfsite.com/dnaweb/PWCurr.htm

SFF.net anthology
www.sff.net/books/guidelines.html

Transversions
www.salmar.com/transversions

Weird Tales
www.sfsite.com/dnaweb/WTCurr.htm

Winedark Sea
www.winedark.com

Electronic

Jackhammer
www.eggplant-productions.com/jackhammer

Delos Science Fiction
www.scifi.com/scifi.con/word/fantascienza.com/delos.html

Millennium SF&F
www.jopoppub.com

Another Realm
anotherealm.com

Spaceways Weekly
spaceways.mirror.org

Neverworlds
www.neverworlds.com

Infinity Plus
www.users.zetnet.co.uk/iplus

Electric Wine
www.electricwine.com

Workshopping

There's a wealth of workshopping information online, from guidelines to fee-based workshops advertising to free-for-all workshops with thousands of participants.

Guidelines

The Turkey City Lexicon
www.otherworlds.net/otherworlds.
net/turkey.htm
Classic lexicon on workshopping terms.

Other Worlds Workshopping Rules
www.otherworlds.net/otherworlds.
net/rules.htm
Rules for participating in an online workshop.

Critter Workshopping Rules
www.critters.org/rules.html
Rules for participating in an online workshop.

On Workshops
www.nh.ultranet.com/~jimkelly/
pages/writers.htm
James Patrick Kelly's essay on workshopping.

Fee-Based Workshops

Clarion
www.msu.edu/~lbs/clarion/
select.html
The granddaddy of genre workshops.

Clarion West
www.sff.net/clarionwest/index.htm
Clarion on the West Coast.

Writers' Workshop and Institute
falcon.cc.ukans.edu/~sfcenter/
courses.htm
James Gunn's two-week genre-writing workshop in Kansas.

Odyssey Workshop
www.sff.net/odyssey
A six-week genre workshop in New Hampshire.

Viable Paradise
www.sff.net/paradise
A one-week genre workshop in Massachusetts.

Milford
www.jeapes.ndirect.co.uk/milford
A week-long peer workshop held in the U.K.

Synergy
members.aol.com/estillwell/
workshop.html
Workshop for aspiring *Star Trek* writers.

Online Workshops

Critters
critters.critique.org

Otherworlds
www.otherworlds.net

Del Ray Online Workshop
www.randomhouse.com/delrey/
workshop

Conventions

Nearly every science fiction convention has a Web presence. Use these sites to locate conventions in your area and to contact Convention Committees to volunteer to participate in panels.

Listings

about.com's Convention Listings
fantasy.about.com/arts/fantasy/
msub6.htm

Northeastern Conventions
world.std.com/~sbarsky/mcfi/necons.
html

Northwestern Science Fiction Conventions
www.sfnorthwest.org

Ultimate Science Fiction Guide Conventions
www.magicdragon.com/UltimateSF/
cons.html

Overseas Conventions
www.smof.com/conlist.htm

Australian Science Fiction Conventions
home.vicnet.net.au/~sfoz/cons.htm

Scifispace Conventions
www.scifispace.com/html/science_
fiction_conventions.html

Majors

World Science Fiction Convention
www.worldcon.org

World Fantasy Convention
www.worldfantasy.org

World Horror Convention
worldhorror.org

North American Science Fiction Convention
nasfic.org

Awards

Hugo Award
www.worldcon.org/hugos.html

George Flynn's Statistical Analysis of Hugo Voting
www.nesfa.org/fanzines/
votehist.html

Nebula Award
www.sfwa.org/awards

Michael P. Kube-McDowell's Commentary on the Nebula
www.sff.net/people/K-Mac/
nebula.htm

Sturgeon Award
falcon.cc.ukans.edu/~sfcenter/
sturgeon.htm

Aurora Award
www.sentex.net/~dmullin/aurora

News

From gossip to hard news, the Internet is a bottomless well of science fictional news.

Print Sources

Locus
www.locusmag.com

SF Chronicle
www.sfsite.com/sfc

Online Sources

SF Site
www.sfsite.com

Sci-Fi Weekly
www.scifiweekly.com

SFF World
www.sffworld.com

Discussion Groups

Usenet Newsgroup
rec.arts.sf.written

SFF Books
kalliope.hypermart.net/sffbooks

SFF.Net Newsgroups
www.sff.net/sff/news

Speculations
www.speculations.com

Writers

Some writers have modest home pages, others have full-fledged, professionally designed sites (it helps that a number of SF writers also work with computers for a living). There are also massive bibliographic projects and sites devoted to fans.

Databases

Internet Speculative Fiction Database
www.sfsite.com/isfdb

Ultimate SF Guide
www.magicdragon.com/UltimateSF

Homepage Portals

SFSite Author Links
www.sfsite.com/scribe/scribe01.htm

SWFA Author Links
www.sfwa.org/links

Yahoo! Author Links
dir.yahoo.com/Arts/Humanities/
Literature/Genres/Science_Fiction_
and_Fantasy/Authors

Newhoo! Author Links
www.dmoz.org/Arts/Literature/
Genres/Science_Fiction/Authors

About.com Author Links
fantasy.about.com/arts/fantasy/
msub23.htm

SFCanada Author Links
www.sfcanada.ca/links.htm

Reference

Here are some generally useful sites, useful as references for fact-checking, manuscript formatting, news, and so on.

Portals

SF Site
www.sfsite.com

Scifi.com
www.scifi.com

About.com
fantasy.about.com

Inkspot
www.inkspot.com

SFF.net
www.sff.net

Dueling Modems
www.dm.net

Science Fiction Webring
nav.webring.com/ringworld/ent/
scifi.html

Manuscript Formatting

**Bill Shunn on Proper Manuscript
Format**
www.shunn.net/format.html

**Vonda N. McIntyre on Manuscript
Preparation**
www.sfwa.org/writing/vonda/
vonda0.htm

Agents

Writelinks' Agents Links
www.writelinks.com/resources/links/
agents.htm

Writer Beware: Scams
www.sfwa.org/beware

Writers Associations

Science Fiction Writers of America
www.sfwa.org

Horror Writers Association
www.horror.org

SFCanada
www.sfcanada.ca

Contracts

ASJA Contract Watch
www.asja.org/php_scp/
cwpagenew.htm

SFWA Contracts Page
www.sfwa.org/contracts

SFWA's Writer Beware!
www.sfwa.org/beware

Further Reading

This excellent bibliography of books on writing and publishing science fiction is based on research done by Annette Mocek, a librarian at the Merril Collection of Science Fiction, Speculation and Fantasy, a wonderful public science fiction reference library in Toronto, Canada (www.tpl.toronto.on.ca/merril/home.htm). We gratefully acknowledge the many, many contributions the research staff at the Merril have made to this book.

Portions of this bibliography are © 1999, The Merril Collection.

Titles marked with an asterisk (*) can be ordered from www.cigsf.com.

So, You Want to Be a Writer?

* Bickham, Jack M. *Setting.* Writer's Digest, 1994 (ISBN: 0898799481).

* Bova, Ben. *The Craft of Writing Science Fiction That Sells.* Writer's Digest, 1994 (ISBN: 0898796008).

* Bykofsky, Sheree, and Jennifer Bayes Sandler. *The Complete Idiot's Guide to Getting Published.* Macmillan/Alpha Books, 1998 (ISBN: 002868392).

* Card, Orson Scott. *How to Write Science Fiction and Fantasy.* Writer's Digest, 1990 (ISBN: 0898794161).

* Dibell, Ansen. *Plot.* Writer's Digest, 1989 (ISBN: 0898799465).

* Dozois, Gardner, ed. *Writing Science Fiction and Fantasy.* St. Martin's, 1991 (ISBN: 0312089260).

* Nolan, William F. *How to Write Horror Fiction.* Writer's Digest, 1990 (ISBN: 0898794420).

Reed, Lillian Craig. *Revision*. Writer's Digest, 1989 (ISBN: 0898793505).

Stableford, Brian. *The Way to Write Science Fiction*. Elm Tree, 1989 (ISBN: 0241126630).

* Williamson, J. N., ed. *How to Write Tales of Horror, Fantasy and Science Fiction*. F & W Publications, 1991 (ISBN: 0898794838).

Got Any Ideas?

* Bova, Ben, and Anthony R. Lewis. *Space Travel*. Writer's Digest, 1997 (ISBN: 0898797470).

* Brohaugh, William. *Just Open a Vein*. Writer's Digest, 1987 (ISBN: 0898792940).

* Epel, Naomi. *The Observation Deck: A Tool Kit for Writers*. Chronicle Books, 1998 (ISBN: 0811814815).

* Gillett, Stephen L. *World-Building*. Writer's Digest, 1996 (ISBN: 0898797071).

* Jakubowski, Maxim, and Edward James, eds. *The Profession of Science Fiction: SF Writers on Their Craft and Ideas*. Macmillan, 1992 (ISBN: 953647706).

* Leader, Zachary. *Writer's Block*. Johns Hopkins University Press, 1991 (ISBN: 0801840325).

* Nahin, Paul J. *Time Travel*. Writer's Digest, 1997 (ISBN: 0898797489).

* Ochoa, George, and Jeffrey Osier. *The Writer's Guide to Creating a Science Fiction Universe*. Writer's Digest, 1993 (ISBN: 0898795362).

* Schmidt, Stanley. *Aliens and Alien Societies*. Writer's Digest, 1995 (ISBN: 0898797063).

* Stevens, Serita Deborah, R.N., B.S.N. *Deadly Doses: A Writer's Guide to Poisons*. Writer's Digest, 1990 (ISBN: 0898793718).

* Wilson, Keith D., M.D. *Cause of Death: A Writer's Guide to Death, Murder and Forensic Evidence*. Writer's Digest, 1992 (ISBN: 0898795249).

How Shall I Say It?

* Card, Orson Scott. *Characters and Viewpoint*. Writer's Digest, 1988 (ISBN: 0898799279).

* Knight, Damon. *Creating Short Fiction*. St. Martin's, 1997 (ISBN: 0312150946).

* Kress, Nancy. *Beginnings, Middles and Ends*. Writer's Digest, 1999 (ISBN: 0898799058).

* ——. *Dynamic Characters*. Writer's Digest, 1998 (ISBN: 0898798159).

* Turco, Lewis. *Dialogue: A Socratic Dialogue on the Art of Writing Dialogue in Fiction*. Writer's Digest, 1999 (ISBN: 0898799473).

Who Will Buy It?

Alley, Brian, and Jennifer Cargill. *Librarian in Search of a Publisher: How to Get Published*. Oryx Press, 1986 (ISBN: 0897741501).

* Borcherding, David H. *Science Fiction and Fantasy Writer's Sourcebook*. Writer's Digest, 1996 (ISBN: 0898797624).

Budrys, Algis. *Writing to the Point: A Complete Guide to Selling Fiction*. Unifont, 1994 (ISBN: 1886211000).

Curtis, Richard. *Fool for an Agent*. Pulphouse, 1992 (ISBN: 1561464287).

* Dickerson, Donya. *2000 Guide to Literary Agents*. Writer's Digest, 2000 (ISBN: 0898799368).

* Kuroff, Barbara, ed. *2000 Novel & Short Story Writer's Market*. Writer's Digest, 2000 (ISBN: 0898799341).

Science Fiction Writers of America. *Writing and Selling Science Fiction*. Writer's Digest, 1976 (ISBN: 0911654356).

Keep on Writing!

Bova, Ben. *Notes to a Science Fiction Writer*. Scribner's, 1975 (ISBN: 0395305217).

Gustafson, Jon M. *Science Fiction and Fantasy Writers of America Handbook*. Fat Puppy Press, 1995 (no ISBN).

* Seidman, Michael. *Living the Dream*. Carroll and Graf, 1992 (ISBN: 0881848719).

Trade Rags

Locus
www.locusmag.com
P.O. Box 13305, Oakland, CA 94661
510-339-9198
$27/six issues ($30 Canada and overseas)

Science Fiction Chronicle
www.sfsite.com/sfc/home.htm
P.O. Box 022730, Brooklyn, NY 11202-0056
Fax only: 718-522-3308
$25/year, payable to Andrew Porter
(CDN$50 Canada; see Web site for overseas subscription rates)

Writer's Digest
www.writersdigest.com
P.O. Box 2123, Harlan, IA 51593
1-800-333-0133
$19.96/year ($29.96 Canada and overseas)

New York Review of Science Fiction
Dragon Press
ebbs.english.vt.edu/olp/nyrsf/nyrsf.html
P.O. Box 78, Pleasantville, NY 10570
$32/year ($37 Canada, $40 overseas)

Index